Miss American Pie

Shelley Paranormal Society
Book 1

Daphne Winchester

Dangerprone Press

Copyright © 2024 by Daphne Winchester

All rights reserved.

No portion of this book may be reproduced in any form without written permission from the publisher or author, except as permitted by U.S. copyright law.

To Josh

Who always said, "When you sell a book," like it was never a question.

I love you, baby.

Now buy my book.

PROLOGUE

October 13th, 1970

Nothing on Earth can prepare you to see your own dead face on a random Tuesday morning, even after a little over a year of sleepless nights imagining it. The shock wrings out everything, light, sound, breath, and ends up as vomit in the bottom of an industrial-size biological waste bin in the corner of the morgue. Nobody tells you when your identical twin is murdered; you're the one left with the bill. The burden of carrying on for the both of you.

In the summer of 1969, my sister pulled out of the driveway to catch the moon landing on TV at Teeny Martin's house. Neil and Buzz arrived, but Octavia never did. There were hours and hours, blissful, gorgeous, sun-soaked, bee-buzzing hours when nobody knew she was missing at all, where she was both missing and at Teeny Martin's at the same time.

It wasn't until she failed to return home, and the girls called round looking for her, that we realized that she never made it to Teeny's. The assumption she had stayed home to watch it with me was a reasonable one, and later, Teeny would tell the press that very same thing.

The fury will come later. For now, all I have is the impossibility of it all. How could Octavia be dead? Why hadn't I felt it? Twins are supposed to know when the other one dies.

I hadn't felt it. I hadn't known it.

As a consolation, I'm offered a seat on a cold plastic chair and a meager cup of water. Professor Waller had called me out of Econ to come down to this dismal basement with the buzzing fluorescent lights and confirm that, yes, indeed, my twin sister is the body currently under their sheet. Couldn't they have just taken one glance at her, noted I'm a carbon copy, and confirmed with me that I had a twin sister? Taken their solemn nod of acknowledgment and marked it down: Drawer 3 houses Octavia Fox? Wouldn't that be a more humane approach in such grim circumstances?

Instead, the morgue tech peeled the sterile sheet back with almost ceremonial care, revealing Octavia's once-lustrous platinum hair, now limp and colorless. Her waxy white forehead is smeared with some sediment or sludge. Unable to fight the compulsion, my gaze drops to her vacant sage eyes, clouded over like the placid lake they plucked her from, as she stares at nothing now. Her once vibrant and expressive mouth seems fuller, its once-rosy hue replaced by a haunting gray-blue pallor that would forever imprint itself in my memory, a chilling token of my sister's final repose.

In the year since Octavia had gone missing, my parents managed to plow their Studebaker into the Charles. It had been Christmas Eve. The Staties told me that my dad had lost control of the steering on the icy roads. I almost believed them. They looked similar to my sister after they fished them out of the river and demanded I identify them. Waller had been with me then, as well.

"Lydia."

The interruption shoves me back into my body. "W-what?" my face turns up toward my godfather.

Waller's voice and posh accent are betrayed by the concerned expression etched into his aristocratic features. "I said, 'Are you going to be sick again?'" He hands me a clipboard, and I sign a confirmation that, yes, that was indeed Octavia Fox in the room behind me. Crouching in front of me, his ice-blue eyes search mine for a sign that I won't have a nervous breakdown right here on campus.

I shake my head. Sipping the water, I ponder the body in the next room. "Why does she look like that?"

Waller's brows draw tight together. "Like what, love?"

"She was taken over a year ago. Why does she look... fresh?"

"Fresh?"

Closing my eyes so I'm not forced to meet his own, I take a deep breath. "That body hasn't been dead since last summer, Professor."

He acknowledges with a subtle nod, and our attention turns to the window that peers into the morgue. Crumpling my paper cup, I rise, my legs uncertain beneath me. With deliberate care, I maneuver my way back into the room, the creak of the door echoing the weight of the situation.

"Miss Fox, I don't think it's a good idea for you to be in here," the attendant tells me.

"Move." And to my surprise, he does.

My fingers tremble, but my resolve remains rigid. Determined, I lift the edge of the sheet, revealing Octavia's hands. A dark, sinister bracelet of a bruise encircles her dainty wrist. Shifting to the opposite side, I find the identical mark on her other wrist. After scrutinizing her shredded and pruned feet, my gaze meets Waller's.

"She was kept."

"How do you mean?" He asks, but it's in the manner a professor coaxes a student to expand upon their response.

"Her wrists were bound, and she's recently tore up her feet. My guess would be she escaped without shoes."

DAPHNE WINCHESTER

"You want a job or something?" The voice startles both Waller and me, drawing our attention away. A young man with a palpable air of eagerness about him stands in the doorway. He's a fresher face than the one I encountered during Octavia's disappearance, yet the unmistakable aura of a cop surrounds him. Tall and meticulously groomed, his light brown hair is neatly parted with a touch of pomade. A sparse mustache adorns his upper lip. Clad in the quintessential attire of a small-town detective – a modest suit, a tie stained from various encounters, and a shirt so rigidly starched that merely gazing at it makes my skin prickle with imagined discomfort.

"You hiring?" I realize how it must seem. If I were him, I'd write myself on his list of suspects almost as soon as the words leave my mouth. I'm supposed to be the hysterical college freshman with my twin sister lying on a table in a morgue, her body filling the room with the blooming stench of decay and lake bottom. His assessment of me is subtle, so he's the kid of a cop as well. "Where's Detective Prewitt?"

"Retired. I'm Detective Quinn."

"Right," I mutter. It was just like Prewitt not giving me the heads-up. "Which lake was she pulled from?"

"How do you know it was a lake?" Quinn asks me.

"She doesn't stink of chlorine, and her body isn't torn up enough for a river. We're too far from the ocean for her to be transported here with her hair still wet, so... lake."

Quinn's eyebrows shoot up at my assessment. "Cohaquet."

The revelation cramps me up. Lake Cohaquet is less than five miles from where we live. The proximity hits me like a physical blow, and the room sways like a boat in a stormy sea, forcing me to clutch the table supporting Octavia. Without any intention, my grip tightens on the sheet, desperately trying to steady myself as the world spins out of control momentarily.

I pull the whole thing off her on my way to the floor.

Oh.

Octavia.

None of this is right. It doesn't make sense. I stare up at her from my spot on the floor as Waller tries to get me back on my feet. "What... what is that?" I point to her bloated stomach with dark lines crisscrossing all over it and her much heavier breasts. This isn't my sister's body at all. It looks like... "Why does she look like our mom?"

Detective Quinn hastily covers Octavia back up while Waller attempts to steady me. "Miss Fox," Quinn starts. "I need you to consider any relationships your sister may have had. Anybody that she didn't want your parents to know about. Anybody that she might have even wanted to keep from you."

"You're saying–" my usually perfectly organized brain is spilling out a million different thoughts at once on me, and I try to fixate on the one thing that is on fire right now. "What you're not saying, I mean, is Octavia had a baby."

Professor Waller gets me back out of the room and onto the plastic seat just outside again. It's not better. The only thing different about the hallway is the stench of the morgue is dampened by the sharp tang of the bleach they use on the floor out here. It's cloying and sticks to the back of my throat.

"He's asking me if I know who did this to her?" I ask Waller. Waller, my godfather, my father's best friend, his partner in all things academic, tries his hardest to put every ounce of fatherly love that his childless heart can muster as he squeezes my upper arms in comfort. His blue eyes go all watery with concern as he slides his fingers through my hair.

"Do you?" The gentleness of his voice gags me. I am not something to be managed.

Octavia slamming her diary shut when I enter her room, a blush staining her expression. Octavia whispering on the phone in the hallway when she thinks nobody is home. Octavia doodling hearts all over her French homework notebook. Mon amour. Mon amour. Mon amour.

I shake my head. "No. Octavia didn't have anyone like that."

Quinn is hovering in the doorway again, like some kind of modern Orpheus. "You're both pretty girls," he tells me. "You're sure there wasn't anyone?" His voice is light and soft and hasn't been hardened yet by years of police work.

My lips twist into a sneer. "My sister wasn't like that."

"Miss Fox—"

"My sister has been missing since July 20th, 1969. That's over a year, which means she likely fell pregnant while in captivity, Detective Quinn. As unimaginable as that may be, try your hardest." My bottom lip starts quivering in spite of myself.

"You're in shock. Let's take you upstairs to get you looked at," Waller tells me, but he's looking at Quinn as he says it.

"I'm fine," I tell them both. "I'm fine, just... get off me." Quinn locates a blanket inside the morgue and offers to put it around my shoulders. "You're not seriously about to wrap me in a morgue blanket right now, are you?"

Quinn's glance drops down to the tan blanket in his hands. "I... I think it's for when people go into shock," he stumbles.

"Get it away from me, Agent Smart." Wiping my sweaty palms on my tights, my frustration settles on both of them now. "Here's what you're going to do. You'll search every house within a five-mile radius around Lake Cohaquet. You'll probably be looking for a basement; somewhere somebody can keep a person for an extended period without arousing suspicion. You're probably looking for a single man because no way could someone keep another woman locked in his house for that long without his wife catching on."

The detective's gaze searches my face. "You've been thinking about this for a very long time."

"It's been a long year."

"Can we call anyone for you?" Quinn asks. He's not looking at me, though. He's looking at my shaking hands. He's not good at this and I hate it. I don't want him to become good at it.

"No," is all I can offer.

"Your parents?"

"They're dead." Everyone is dead now. Everyone except Waller and me. He squeezes my hand as if to remind me of that.

"Perhaps a friend? A dorm mate?" Quinn presses.

I live in the Fox House, just on the edge of the Shelley College property line, built by my grandfather, the former dean of Shelley College, left to me by my father, a professor of parapsychology at the college. I don't have a dorm. I don't even really have friends, as I had only started Shelley College a couple of months ago, and most of my friends left to go to UMass or New York City. Even Teeny Martin moved to North Carolina with the captain of our football team. "No. Nobody like that. Well, unless you count old Waller here." Quinn squints at Waller when I mention him. The professor is forty, at the oldest.

Waller squats in front of me and gathers my hands in his. He purses his lips together tight. "Do you… do you feel anything?"

I shake my head.

"Anything at all, Lydia. It could be subtle. She's right here, love, maybe if you just focus." Waller's expression turns pleading. "Empty yourself, like your father taught you. Let all of the light and sound fall away until nothing except you and Octavia are left."

His voice takes on the hypnotic quality he and my father used to use on us during their experiments. They'd separate us into different rooms and guide us to find each other. It's almost instinct now to do what that monotone, cool voice tells me. My lids droop on their own. I am Pavlov's dog.

Nothing. In the dark, where I used to find her, she'd clutch my hands and whisper something in my ear from the other room. Impossible. Magical. Our space. And now? Only black. Acres and acres of darkness where my sister used to be.

And he doesn't understand how immense the silence is, how it stretches on for miles, widening the distance between my sister and me into one neither of us can traverse now. All that remains is a gaping, empty silence. The space where she used to be.

My head stays perfectly still, and I open my eyes. Out of my peripheral, Quinn studies us in fascination.

"I'm just thinking, perhaps the connection can help lead us to her killer," Waller reasons.

Standing up, I lean over where he's still crouched on the floor. "There is no connection, Professor. I'm sorry, but you need to face it. That connection to my sister, who was held captive for a year? It doesn't exist."

"Surely—"

"No. You have to stop. We're not a circus act for you or Dad anymore."

"But—"

"She's gone! Don't you understand that?" My words hang thick and suffocating in the air between Waller and myself. Whipping around to face Quinn, I find him frantically jotting down notes in his tiny notebook. "You know where to locate me?"

"Prewitt has your last address at a house on the Shelley College campus?"

"If you need any more help with your job, you can contact me there," I tell him as I snatch my purse from the nearby seat.

"Miss Fox," he calls out as I approach the elevator. I pause. "I swear I'll do everything I can to find whoever did this to her."

"That's what Prewitt said," I tell him and step inside the lift. My fingers hover over the lobby button. "I'll be in touch, Quinn. I'm not letting this go."

With an unnerving rattle, the elevator slides shut and takes me to the lobby. The air grows thin, suffocating me, and I slam my palm against the stop button in a moment of overwhelming anguish. Crumpling into a heap on the cold metal floor of the elevator, I let the image of my lost sister pull me under. Gasping for air only to sob it out, my grief fills the confined space with a sad, thin, watered-down wail. It slips itself free from my chest but loses all power once unleashed. It spirals from me and drains into the grated floor beneath my hands and knees. The lights flicker above. Time ticks by in hot pumps of my heartbeat, making my head and ears throb.

With trembling limbs, I stand up and smooth down my jumper dress. A lump forms in my throat, tightening its grip around me. Restarting the elevator's journey with a press of the button, it chimes loudly upon reaching its destination before opening its doors. The bustling lobby remains indifferent to my shattered state as I navigate through the crowd with unsteady steps.

Practically running the final feet out the door, I step out squinting into the brightness of the October sun. It's a beautiful, horrible day. The sky is brilliant and blue, and my sister, Octavia, will never be nineteen.

CHAPTER
one

*T*wo *Years Later.*

In the dim-lit embrace of a rundown Victorian home, the flickering dance of light from candles casts shadows on our current assignment, an elderly woman named Mrs. Mildred Lovell. Her over-dramatic groans harmonize with the violent and angry tremors of the covered table beneath her withered hands. Aside from a faint waft of mildew and wax, a certain shabby, dusty charm infuses the rundown Victorian. If I held my breath, I could find a certain synchronicity between her groans and the house's settling creaks.

Her client, a middle-aged mother who sought the services of this "psychic," is caught in the grip of abject terror, her hands restrained firmly by the two individuals flanking her. Her adult son, stationed at one side, blotchy and sweaty, is similarly consumed by fear, his gaze unwaveringly fixed on Mrs. Lovell's spectral performance. On the other side sits the husband, an air of mild exasperation etched across his face, his upper-management voice demanding some decorum from his agitated wife.

Amidst the chaos, my diligent researcher, Evie, repeatedly seeks reassurance from me. I sense the rhythmic bounce of her leg against mine under the concealing veil of the tablecloth. The room echoes with a cacophony of emotions, a peculiar blend of terror, exasperation, and a quiet plea for control in the face of supernatural charlatanism. Evie isn't nervous about the paranormal activity. She's nervous about busting the old lady for her scam.

Wayne is supposed to be behind the camera documenting all of us at the moment, but he's taken to bouncing all over the room as things shudder and jerk. Vases fall off mantles and books drop to the floor in loud thumps that might sound like footsteps to the hysteria-prone.

"Get back on the camera," I demand through gritted teeth. His wild eyes tell me that it's not going to happen. "Wayne! Get back on the camera."

Wayne ignores me. He's been muttering, "Oh god," and "Oh Jesus," in varying combinations for the past five minutes. My patience is worn thin.

The old lady turns the drama up at least three more notches when she starts talking to the woman who hired her in a thick, manly voice. A voice that is clearly her own just dropped a few octaves for effect. She insists that she's the woman's father. Grandfather? It doesn't matter.

We were here to talk to her son, who died at age 6 of polio. Six-year-olds don't speak with such deep voices. Only... I left that part out.

The age bit, I mean.

The old woman has no context. We only told her we were there to communicate with a member of the woman's family. In her flimsy, transparent way, she asked if the family member was male. The woman who hired her opened her mouth, but I was the one who answered with a "yes." And only "yes." I wanted to see where she would run with this.

The wrong way, apparently. Evie squeezes my hand with glee at a particularly tumultuous knock on the table. Which is exactly what all of this was, table-knocking. Grateful to have at least one part of my team concordant with me, my eyes dart to Wayne again. His hands twist and tangle together, and his gaze darts to the door. This is an expression I'm intimately familiar with. My tech guy is about to bolt.

My tech guy is about to bolt right before my big moment.

I hate Wayne. He's only on the team for college credit, and he doesn't even have the remotest interest in any of this. Until it gets scary, and then it's all he cares about. The armpits of his white button-down shirt are damp and transparent, and he's inching towards the drawing-room door when the chandelier above us begins to sway.

Convincing bit, that. I hope they secured it first. The first indication that your medium is a fraud? They insist on the séance being in their own home. Typically, I'd give the medium a chance. After all, my job was to investigate the mortal connection to the afterlife. I should believe in this, long to find evidence, but something stank the moment we stepped in here, and the pocket doors slammed shut on their own like that haunted house ride they had down in Disney World.

I'm barely listening to what the old lady is saying, and she's so far off. The woman across from me, the one who lost her son, is sobbing now, and Wayne uses her distraction to run out of the room. I turn to Evie, who's gone wide-eyed at his escape. The astonishment on her face can't match the fury on my own. *What a coward.*

Evie and I glance at each other, and I nod. It's time.

She removes herself from the séance table and moves to the light switch. The old lady warns her not to break the circle, and I roll my eyes. Evie flicks on the lights at my go-ahead, and I stand up, leaning my weight on my hands to press the table down.

"Alright, enough," I say.

The medium appears flabbergasted. She tries to continue her performance. The table rattles harder beneath my palms. "I said, 'Enough.' You've got it all wrong, and I can see the fishing line on the chandelier now that the lights are on, Mrs. Lovell."

From her expression, I gather the woman who hired Mrs. Lovell must have paid a fair amount for this so-called séance, and now it's all falling apart. The wheels turn in her head, trying to come up with an explanation for what's happening. "I don't understand," she whines.

I release my grip on the table, letting it fall back onto all four legs with a loud thump. The old lady is still trying to spin her story, but I'm not having it. I instruct Evie to finish turning on all the lights in the room. "This is ridiculous," I say, addressing Mrs. Lovell's clients directly. "If you really wanted to connect with your son, you should have gone to his grave and talked to him there. It's about as useful as all this," my hands gesture to the trappings of the séance room. The woman gasps at my words, but I ignore her.

Mrs. Lovell is about to burst into tears as Evie turns on the last lamp in the room. In the sudden brightness, we can all clearly see that there are no spirits in this room. A small exhale escapes from between my clenched teeth. I hate this part almost as much as I hate Wayne, who I'm firing after I expose this fraud. "Do you want me to tell them, or should I, Mrs. Lovell?"

The husband stands up, a glower crisscrossing his already pinched features. "Explain yourself, ma'am."

Mrs. Lovell stands up angrily, knocking over her chair in the process. "This is outrageous! How dare you accuse us of fraud!" she spits out, and Evie smoothly blocks her exit before she can storm out of the room.

When the old woman doesn't say anything more, I provide some answers. "I'm sure her assistant, probably someone unfortunately related to her, is under the floorboards with broom handles to move the table. The lights are easy enough. Even Wayne could have set those up. The fishing line on the bookshelves, mantels, and..." My finger points at the chandelier, still swaying. "Get your money back," I tell him and turn to Mrs. Lovell. "And you close up shop, you're done here." Back to the couple who hired her, "If you'll excuse me, I need to check on my colleague."

"I demand my money back!" the client cries out, and I have to stifle the smirk playing in the corner of my mouth.

Her husband steps up before I can exit and holds his hand out to me. My eyes drop to it and then back up to him, my brow furrowing in consternation. Though shell-shocked, he's no longer fuming. The husband clears his throat. "Thank you for exposing this," he says gratefully.

I eye him warily. "Just doing my job."

He nods in understanding before turning to his wife and taking her hand in his own. "We'll find another way to connect with Freddy," he tells her with a gentleness I'll admit I unfairly didn't anticipate.

Evie nods, telling me she'll take over from here. She'll explain that Mrs. Lovell was someone we'd been suspecting of engaging in fraudulent business practices for some time now—Evie's good with people. Kind. Calm. Not like me.

Once I step out, the crisp October breeze whips my pale hair into my face as I search for Wayne. Gravel crunches softly beneath my feet as I stomp across the circular driveway, leading me away from the weathered Victorian house. Wayne leans nonchalantly against the open door of our department's faded blue van, spilling out yellow light from within.

"What the hell was that?" His face twists in confusion as his gaze sharpens on me. "Answer me, Wayne."

"That shit in there got too intense, man." A faint aroma of cigarettes hangs in the air as Wayne takes a drag—the crisp air hints of autumn leaves and fallen rain. My gaze turns to the Victorian behind me as the sound of Mr. Upper Management reads Mrs. Lovell the riot act.

Worrying my lip between my teeth, I had been considering letting Wayne go for some time now. He wasn't working out. Waller's going to murder me. With a heavy sigh, my voice rasps out around the cigarette smoke. "You're done."

"What? I still have the rest of the semester!" His expression goes from surprise to doubt to anger in less than a heartbeat.

"I said you're done. I can't work with a coward. That, in there?" I point at the building. "That was all smoke and mirrors, and we're looking for real evidence, Wayne. What are you going to do if we find something actually scary? Shit your pants?"

"Don't be like this, Lids. You know we got a good thing going on here." He tries to grab at the belt loops on my trousers to pull me closer.

"No. Don't touch me. You're a shitty tech guy, you're a lousy lay, and I don't understand why you're on this team when we both know you're just going to end up selling Pontiacs at your father's dealership when school is done anyways."

The pout is what throws me off. It makes his mustache turn him into a muskrat, and I have to shove my amusement down. "You know what your problem is, Fox?" Here we go.

"I'm sure there's no stopping you from telling me," I sigh as I pull out the camera case so I can go back in and pack up our gear.

"You think you're better than everyone else."

"Oh no, I've never heard this before," I say with feigned shock. "Please give me your manly opinion about what will straighten me out."

Wayne shakes his head at me like I'm some lost cause. "You're only in charge because Waller's practically your dad."

Leaning into him, I bat my lashes. "Aw, Wayne, if you want Waller all to yourself, you could've just asked," I use the baby voice that usually got him to carry the heavy stuff for me. He shoves me back, but I have what I leaned in for.

The van keys.

"You're such a bitch. I'm going to tell everyone in my department to stay away from you, and you'll never find a tech guy again."

Pulling the camera case strap over my shoulder, I pocket the keys and start back for the house. "Find your own ride home."

"We're two states away!" Wayne calls after me.

"Not my problem," I tell him, stepping back inside where Evie is waiting.

DAPHNE WINCHESTER

"I need a new tech guy," I tell Waller on Monday morning.

"No, you have Wayne," he responds, eyes fixed on the file in front of him.

"I fired Wayne."

Waller sighs, finally looking up at me. "You have to stop sleeping with them, Lydia."

"That's not why I fired Wayne. And yes, you're right; I'll get right on not sleeping with them when you fetch me a new tech guy."

"You can't fire an intern, you know."

"He wasn't working out." I shuffle a stack of manila folders off the only other chair and sit down. "I need someone who is interested in this," I motion at the stacks of folders and envelopes all over his messy office. "Not just a camera guy."

Waller studies me, chin resting on his knuckles. "I'll make you a deal."

"Here it comes," I groan.

"I have someone who recently transferred over to our major. He wasn't an engineering major but has a unique interest in the equipment."

"Sounds okay. Where's the but?"

"You have to take on Sam."

I throw my head back, staring at the ceiling. "Not Sam, man. He's nuts."

Sam Hassan has been part of the parapsychology program longer than I have. He's one of those perpetual students. Evie says it's because he's dodging the war, but I think Sam just likes college. Also, Sam thinks he's psychic. Crystals, dowsing, pendulums, scrying; Sam must have sent away for the whole Jeane Dixon kit. Evie is going to kill me.

As if summoned by my thoughts, Evie knocks on the door frame. "There's a phone call from a Detective Quinn for you."

My gaze catches on Waller, and we share a look. I scoop myself out of the chair, ignoring the scattered envelopes I've displaced, and follow Evie to the main office.

Our department's new digs are in the basement this semester, a shift from our previous above-ground location. Waller's rationale was to minimize distractions, but it feels more like isolation. The walls creak, the mortar groans, and the lights click and buzz incessantly, as if the entire building is alive, breathing like a dragon stirred from slumber. It's the oldest building, nestled in the farthest corner of the campus, with flickering lights that set the perfect stage for our exploration of the paranormal.

"Tell me you have something," I say without greeting into the receiver.

"Hello to you, too, Miss Fox," Quinn replies.

"Well?"

Quinn lets out a soft sigh on the other end. "This isn't about Octavia. This is about something else. I was hoping to run it by you first, but now I think maybe I should have just gone directly to Waller."

"Quinn, are you asking me for help with one of your little cases?"

"This was a bad idea."

"Oh no, it's brilliant. Let's hear it." I lean against the wall and grab a handful of caramel corn Evie left on the counter.

"Lydia, this isn't joke time. This is serious. And it's of a sensitive nature to you."

"You said this wasn't about Tavi," I mumble through a mouthful of popcorn.

"Waller studies twins, right? I think he'll approve this case for you when he hears what it's about, but I wanted to check with you first. If you're not interested, I don't want him to push you into it because of the twin thing."

"Wow, Quinn, you're really selling it," I say.

"I have a case. A recent drowning, nothing particularly suspicious about it. It appears to be an accident—"

"But…" When he doesn't reply, I add, "You wouldn't be calling me if there wasn't a but, Detective Quinn."

"Her sister says she's being haunted by her twin that drowned."

The exhalation leaks out of me slowly, and I can feel the sharp deflation in my chest. "How old?"

"Twelve."

My gaze steadies on the fluorescent lighting above my head. An ache begins to push up against the inside of my temples. "I think," I begin. "I think she doesn't need me. I think she needs a child psychiatrist."

"She's been. To several. They all say the same thing: that she's doing it to herself."

"Doing what to herself?"

"Carving words into her skin."

Before I remember that my fingers are sticky, I rub my forehead in frustration for this child, whoever she is. "What kinds of words?"

"This doesn't go beyond you and me. Do we have an understanding?"

"What kinds of words, Quinn?"

"Whore, bitch, pig, and… killer."

Swallowing around a dry throat, I respond carefully. "They're saying that she wrote those words on herself?"

"Yeah, and my captain wants the case reopened because some stupid doctor suggested she might be harboring a confession."

I can't figure out how to respond, but I must ask. "They want to build a case against her?"

"Yes. And I thought you might want to help prevent that, given your own circumstances. I don't think she drowned her sister."

"Are there any other manifestations of this supposed haunting?"

"The older sister says the girl has been sleepwalking out to the pond almost every night. Their parents have been securing her to the bed. The younger brother says he's seen the drowned twin in their basement twice."

"How old is the younger brother?"

"Nine."

"And the older sister?"

"Twenty-four."

"Twenty-four? Is she from a previous marriage?" That's a significant age gap.

"I don't know. I don't think so."

"So… the nine-year-old is impressionable by his older sisters," I say matter-of-factly as if I have anything to base this on. Tavi and I were the only kids in our small family.

"You're asking a lot of questions. Does this mean you'll take my case?"

My eyes dart to Evie, who's been listening to my side of the conversation. "I have to run it past my team first." Evie will agree immediately. "I lost my tech guy this weekend, so we're short."

"Does it bother you?" He asks me.

"Does what bother me?"

"The case. If it's too much, I can find someone else to help."

"You're talking in code, Quinn. Just spit it out."

He pauses for a couple of breaths. "A drowned twin sister? Who may have been murdered?"

"I'm capable of separating work from my own life." I'm lying. He knows it, I know it, but we both pretend otherwise.

"Okay." I can picture him shaking his head at the phone. "Okay, Lydia. Keep me in the loop on what your team decides."

"I will. Take care, Quinn."

"You too," he says and hangs up.

Evie raises her eyebrows at me expectantly. "C'mon," I tell her, and she follows me down the hall to Waller's office. "You interested in a twin haunting?" I ask from the doorway.

He glances up immediately. There's nothing like dangling a twin case in front of him to receive his undivided attention. "I... yes? Of course I am. You know I am."

"New tech guy, then, and I'll take Sam. But you have to make him rein all that spooky shit in, okay? I'm worried that we'll appear unprofessional."

"Good note," he tells me quietly.

"Who's the guy?" Evie asks. "The new tech guy."

"Charlie Song," a voice says from behind us.

Evie and I whirl around. Charlie Song stands there, tall and lean, with shiny black hair a little too long on top. He's wearing a brown suit, probably his nicest, with a floral shirt underneath. Sticking his hand out, he says, "You must be Lydia Fox."

Glancing him up and down, I disregard his hand. "You're joking," I tell Waller. "He's as green as a frosh."

"He's interested, which... after what I'm assuming will be Wayne's colorful assessment of our department, is more than I can say for any other candidate," Waller finishes, leaning back in his chair.

"I'll be the judge of that," I say, giving Charlie an appraising squint. "Sources?"

"Andrew Green—"

"Green's a novelist. Next." Evie's head shoots back and forth between us, and she taps my ankle with her shoe. This is her signal that I'm being rude. I don't care.

Charlie lifts an eyebrow at me. "Thurstone Hopkins."

"Biographer and dabbler. Next."

"Joseph Gaither Pratt. Margaret Mead. John Edgar Coover." Was he sweating?

"Alright, Song, alright. No need to crack an embolism. We're good," I tell him, finally letting him off the hook. "Bonus points for Mead."

"Naturally," Evie snarks next to me.

I turn back to Charlie. "You're interested in what exactly?"

"Thermographic cameras, EMFs, EVP phenomena, Geiger counters. Something that can measure paranormal activity. I'm hoping to specialize in it." His sincerity is so palpable I have to stifle a laugh.

"We don't have any of that equipment. Most of it's all theoretical anyway."

"There's real science here," Charlie says with a crisp straightening of his spine.

"Yeah, fine, you'll do," I tell him.

Waller claps his hands together loudly, causing us to turn his way. "I'll find a way to bend the budget to procure you a couple of those items, and I can borrow or have made things we can't acquire in the engineering department. It's not going to be top quality, I'm sorry to say."

"Can you get him settled?" I ask my researcher.

Evie drops a corner of her mouth at Charlie with uncertainty. "I'll show you where we keep our equipment and where you can make yourself some kind of office. Since we don't actually have offices down here. And use the coffee machine upstairs. The one down here stinks the whole basement up."

They head down the hall, and I tell Waller. "Call Quinn. He has all the details."

"Lydia?" Waller says as I take my leave. I pause at the door. "Don't fuck this one up. He's actually interested in the field and not your pants."

"We'll see," is all I can promise.

CHAPTER *two*

My desk is a chaotic tangle of papers, books, and discarded chip bags, with two half-empty coffee cups and a faded photo of Octavia and me on a trip to Brighton Beach in 1968 nestled in the midst of the clutter. My eyes scan the overflowing ashtray, and I have no idea where anything is. Sifting through the pile, I search for the report I still need to type up for why we released Wayne from the program early.

In stark contrast, Evie's desk is a model of organization. Every pencil and paperclip has its place, neatly arranged and ready for use. A small but thriving plant sits in the corner, its flowers reaching towards the low ceiling. Evie carefully waters it with a small watering can, her movements precise and deliberate. As she goes about her tasks, she takes occasional sips from her steaming mug, the rich aroma of coffee permeating the air.

For some reason, Evie placed Charlie on the desk facing mine. Gone is the suit; he's wearing a tight t-shirt tucked into some jeans now. Typing up what appears to be an inventory of the equipment room, he taps the desk with his pencil when he's thinking. It's maddening.

The plant watering complete, Evie already has her nose buried back in the tome on Hemlock Hall, the estate owned by our next case. It's only been two days since Quinn called, and Evie is immersed in her research. The scent of old paper, stale coffee, and cigarette smoke hangs in the air, almost oppressive. Underneath it all, I catch a hint of lavender, probably coming from Evie's little plant.

"How can a house have a whole book written about it?" I ask, genuinely curious.

"Yeah, it's not like we didn't have to read House of Seven Gables in English Lit or anything," Evie murmurs absently. "Or Fall of the House of Usher."

"Not all of us did the reading, Ramirez," I grumble. "We haven't even agreed to take on the case yet. We said we'd check into it. What's with all the prep?"

With an exasperated huff at my interruptions, Evie closes the book, adjusts where the bridge of her glasses falls on her nose, and focuses on me. "Since you clearly need attention, what do you know about the Carmichael family?"

"Only from what Quinn said on the phone. The client, William Carmichael, is running for Senate."

Charlie stops typing. "And the oldest daughter is Miss Massachusetts." He raises an eyebrow at us when we both turn and stare at him. "What?"

"And you know that because?" Evie asks.

He has the decency to blush and resumes pecking at the typewriter again.

There's a crash from the stairwell, and Sam bursts through the door, his bushy black hair bouncing with every step. "Where's my little momma?" he bellows.

Like a garage sale Frank Zappa, Sam's paisley shirt is open almost to the waist, showing several long strands of beads hanging around his neck and nestled into some smattering of chest hair. He finds me behind the desk and does this weird, wide-legged cowboy walk in his indecently low bell bottoms, slowly reaching my height in the chair.

"There she is!" he chortles with more enthusiasm than the entire campus possesses.

When it's clear he's about to hug me, I hold a slim palm up to his face. "No."

"Peace, pretty girl," he says, holding up two fingers. "Old Sam just wants to show his appreciation for the spot on the team."

"Old Sam can just say thank you like a normal person," I tell him. "Besides, you were the consolation prize. I needed a techie."

Undeterred, Sam's gaze trails me up and down, and gives me a sideways smile like he won't let me step on his moment under any circumstances. "Miss Ramirez, my bronze goddess, how goes the research?" he says, focusing on Evie now.

"First, never call me that again, and second, why are you coming along? I don't understand it. What is that you actually do besides burn sage in corners and cleanse rooms with your crystal do-hickey?"

"C'mon now, Old Sam didn't mean anything by it. And I thought I'd catalog the number of full spectral manifestations seen around Hemlock Hall in the past hundred years for you."

Evie's eyebrow lifts. Sam spoke her dialect.

"What do you mean?" Charlie interjects.

"We haven't met," Sam informs him. "I'm Samir Hassan, but you can call me Spooky or Sam or Spooky Sam." He shrugs. "I go by any of those."

"Nobody has ever called you Spooky, Sam. Stop trying to make that a thing," I remind him and his lips tilt down into the slightest disappointed frown.

Charlie stands up and extends his hand. "Charlie Song," he says.

Sam bypasses the hand. "We don't shake hands here, man. We're all family." He gathers Charlie up in a bear hug. Sam isn't as tall as Charlie, but he lifts him off the ground in some weird show of pacifist dominance.

"Oh, you're going to—look at that," Charlie says and claps Sam on the back several times to let him go.

"New tech guy." Sam gestures at Charlie like we weren't informed. "He's a keeper. I like his vibe. Peaceful energy." He drops to a cross-legged position on the floor and closes his eyes. "Supposedly, compadres, Hemlock Hall has the ghost of a British captain's wife. She's been seen lurking around the grounds on a couple of dozen occasions. An actual lady in white."

Evie's eyes narrow at this. I'm overcome with the horrifying suspicion that she might not have gotten to that part in her book. Don't ever spoil an ending for Evelyn Ramirez.

Charlie, however, appears elated. He perks up at Sam's report and opens his mouth to ask what I assume will be a thousand questions.

Waller walks in. "I have good news and bad news. Which do you want first?"

Evelyn and I both say 'bad' simultaneously while the boys say 'good.'

"The bad news is this is a very high-profile case, so we need to cover our asses, and we need everyone to act on their utmost professional behavior." He scowls at me when he says this.

"What? Me? What about Lucy in the sky with diamonds over there?" I hook my thumb at Sam.

Evie ignores my comment and pushes past my indignation. "What's the good news then?"

"You have a new team member to keep everything on the regular, and she's also here to add a new dimension into the program."

Two new members to the team, and now he's adding a third. On a high-profile case? "Professor," I start, but he interrupts.

"Her name is Shirley Henderson, and she's coming to us from the film department."

My eyes narrow instantly. "And... what role is she playing then, pray tell?"

"Your documentarist. She's going to film you doing your investigation."

"Why?" Evie and I ask at the same time.

Waller sags against my desk. "Our funding is getting cut off next year."

That had to be a mistake. "What are you talking about? My father created this department. He poured his entire fortune into this department."

"And since your parents' death two and a half years ago, we haven't had a single fundraising event. Where do you think our budget goes, Lydia? We need to think about another form of income for the department unless you're ready to break out your mother's social Rolodex and beg for handouts at galas you won't even attend." Waller is looking at me like this is my fault.

"You're the head of this department, isn't that your job? We're your students," Evie reminds him.

"Well spotted, Evelyn," he snaps at her in his tightly clipped British accent. "I am the head of this department, and I'm raising money by writing articles and books and editing documentaries to present for funding. Like a real science department. Shirley is on your team now, and I expect you to treat her with respect."

"What do I have Charlie for if we have a new camera person?"

"Wow. Thanks," Charlie mutters around the pencil clenched between his teeth, paused mid-type.

"Because she's there to document the team, not the case, which is what Charlie's doing. Honestly, Lydia, I thought you'd be more excited about this."

"Man, the air in here is getting to be kind of a downer. I need to go outside to reset and touch some grass," Sam says as he unfolds himself from the rug.

"More like smoke some grass, you mean," I say because I'm mad at Waller, not Sam, but the rest of my team doesn't know that. He pats the back of my hand on his way up to stand.

"C'mon, Lydia," Evie tries to temper me.

"Fine, we'll have our babysitter, but she can't get in the way, Waller. Make sure she's aware of that."

We meet Shirley the following morning. I'm wondering how much information she's gathered. About me, I mean. After they discovered Octavia on the shore of Lake Cohaquet, I had a small following of journalists looking for an exclusive from the surviving twin sister. The morbidity of the story is what made it so alluring. Still, Quinn kept certain details from the press, which I hate to admit I'm profoundly grateful for.

"You Fox?" she asks me as she hustles up the sidewalk. Her equipment is on a trolley trailing behind her.

"You Henderson?" I ask back. She's tall and lithe like a dancer, wearing a burnt orange suit and matching scarf tied up in her rather buoyant afro. Effortlessly beautiful, in the way that a gross excess of money provides, her clear complexion and bright hazel eyes shove me straight into a suspicious mood. There's no way she's going to take any of this seriously. She should go back to her sorority house and forget about death and politics.

"Alright." She puts her hands up in surrender after assessing me in probably the same manner. "You're the boss-lady. Professor Waller already told me what he expects, and now I will tell you what I expect. In return for your informed consent, I'll treat your team with dignity and respect, but you'll have to trust me. I'm going to ask things that are going to annoy you, things that will force you to share with my audience. If there's anything you don't want to talk about on camera, make me aware ahead of time. I'm trying to make a film here for my final project, and I'm not here as your camera girl, got it?"

This is where it gets tricky. Do I tell her about Octavia? Should I assume she's already familiar with our case? All I know is that it's the one subject that's off-limits to me. "Stick with the case and the case only, and we're super," I tell her. "You have the release forms for the team and the Carmichaels?"

"Right here." She pats the leather briefcase she has on her hip. Shirley has more gear than we expected, and the back of the van will get a lot more crowded with her. Sam and Charlie are already loading it all in while we make introductions. She's tall, and I glance down at her feet expecting platforms, but she's wearing a sensible pair of Keds like she's prepared to be on her feet a lot.

"Have you ever filmed something like this? Every case is different, but we'll need a little space. This one's tricky," Evie asks, her thick brows furrowed with concern.

Shirley tilts her head back like nobody has ever questioned her abilities before now. "Don't worry about me doing my job, and I won't worry about you doing yours."

"Fair enough," I concede and hop in on the passenger side.

"I guess I'm driving?" Charlie asks and glances at the ignition, where the keys are dangling.

"Oh yeah, man," Sam pipes up. "I had to link up with the ancestors this morning to get me to an elevated state of being."

"You fucking lit up? At six o'clock in the morning?" My mood is plummeting faster than I anticipated.

"No, no, nothing like that, mon capitan... a little dose of shrooms. You can dig it, right? I need to vibe with the earth."

"Is he always going to talk like that?" Shirley asks.

"Yes," Evie and I say at the same time.

"You, Brown Sugar, can take the bench with Evie. I'm gonna stretch out back here with the gear and let the wind take me."

Shirley's eyebrows lift at his term of endearment.

My fingers are pressing the spot between my brows. "Sam, stop harassing team members. Curb the pet names. It's gross."

"I can fight my own battles," Shirley informs me.

"And I can lead my own team. Look how capable we are." My biting tone makes Evie wince.

"You have a map?" Charlie asks me. "I don't know where we're going."

"It'll take a couple of hours. It's outside Detective Quinn's jurisdiction, but the town doesn't have an investigative unit, so he's out on loan. He said he'd meet us there at eight. It's about an hour north from Stonehill."

Shirley leans in between Charlie and me from the backseat. "So it's true, then, it's that guy running for Senate?"

"William Carmichael, and he's in with Dick," I reply. "This is going to be a sensitive case. I don't want us getting kicked out on the first day if we have something to work with, and these kids aren't merely looking for attention from their rich daddy."

"It's so sad." Evie's voice lowers like she doesn't want to summon the ghosts. "Gone at twelve."

"Yeah, well, gone at eighteen isn't any better," I tell her as I settle into the squeaky captain chair. My gaze peeks up at them in the rearview, and I can see Evie shaking her head at Shirley.

If I don't want Shirley asking, I shouldn't bring it up. Ever.

That's my new rule.

I don't talk about Octavia; instead, I slip Iron Butterfly into the 8-track and crank up the volume until it drowns out everything else.

CHAPTER *three*

Hemlock Hall proves far more elusive than we anticipated. We have to stop for directions three times before navigating the van up the narrow, winding road that overlooks what I can only describe as a sleepy hamlet, as if I'm a colonial-era novelist. My eyes flick to my watch. We're nearly an hour late.

Quinn leans against his car when we finally arrive at the gate. "Finally," he mouths. It's been over a year since I last saw him. The mustache is gone, making him look younger than when I knew him. His light brown hair is tousled by the brisk wind rustling through the surrounding forest, giving him a rugged charm. His green eyes meet mine as I step out and stretch. The autumn air carries the scent of pine and wood smoke, with the underlying stench of decaying leaves. A smirk tugs at the corner of his mouth when he catches my eye. He's left his suit jacket in the car, wearing only a button-up shirt and tie, with his badge clipped to his conservative black trousers.

"Miss Fox," he greets, "Ran into trouble finding the place?"

"Yes, actually. Who should I file a complaint with?" I reply as I walk over to where he's opening the gate for us.

"Take it up with the Commonwealth of Massachusetts. I don't print the maps." His gaze travels from my feet to my face. "Seriously, though, you look..." he hesitates, searching for the right words. "Good. You look really good."

"You were expecting something else?"

"Two years with no leads can be taxing on most." He studies the dirt beneath us as if he's too ashamed to meet my eyes.

"I'm sure you're doing your best, Quinn. Let's see if we can sort this case out." My smoky voice tries to mimic that lilting quality Evie uses, the one that makes her sound like a princess. It comes across more like I'm offering a teenager a poisoned apple. "I'll ride with you up to the house to make sure we're on the same page."

"Divide and conquer," he replies. "I like it."

I wave the van through and hop into the passenger seat of Quinn's detective car. He starts the engine and before shifting into gear, he glances at me. "I need you not to get upset when you see Emily, Lydia."

Lydia? This must be serious. "Oh?"

"She has blond hair."

"I'm going to freak out over hair?"

"Well, you and Octavia..."

"It's hair, Quinn, don't go looking for drama where there isn't any." But I sit back and nibble on my lip. "But... you could've said."

"I know." He's silent as he follows the van. The road to the house is flanked by ancient beech trees, forming a tunnel of red and gold leaves. Their branches twist and tangle like dancers clasping hands above us.

"This is incredible," I murmur, gazing up at the trees.

Quinn leans forward, taking in the view. Halfway up the drive, he turns to me. "I'm sorry for dragging you into this. I ran out of options."

"You must have if you've called the Scooby-Doo kids." I wince, realizing he might not know who Scooby-Doo is.

"That van looked full. Got some new members?" I know he's fishing about Wayne. The last time I saw Quinn, I was still balling Wayne, and he disapproved.

"Wayne's gone. We got a new tech guy—"

"The Asian kid behind the wheel?"

I roll my eyes. "Yes, that's Charlie. But Waller made me bring our resident psychic and a film student."

"Psychic?"

"To 'ascertain whether this is a legitimate haunting or a ruse to cover up a murder.'" I mimic Waller's voice, adding a touch of Agatha Christie for effect.

Quinn nods. "Good. That's what I'd like to determine as well."

"Then we're on the same page."

He stops the car and meets my gaze. After a moment, he says, "Yes, Miss Fox, I believe we are."

A maid stands on the porch of Hemlock Hall, adjusting her dark bun as she descends the steps to greet us. "You're to use the service entrance around back," she instructs.

Okay, I grew up wealthy, I can't deny that, but I didn't grow up maids and service-entrance wealthy. This is old money—'our family sold cannons to the British' wealthy. As an aside, I've never used a "service" entrance in my life, and I'm not about to start.

"No," I say gently. After all, it's not her fault. "You need to inform Mr. Carmichael that we're going in through the front door. We're here to help, but we aren't *the* help."

The maid studies us for a moment before nodding and retreating inside.

"Damn, I wish I'd gotten that on film." Shirley pulls out her camera, and I grab my Polaroid camera bag from the front seat. "Evie, can you pull out the consent forms from my bag on the bench?" Shirley focuses the lens on me more quickly than I anticipated, and I step back a few feet.

"This is Lydia Fox, the Shelley College Parapsychology Department team lead. Can you introduce your colleagues and tell us a little bit about the case you're working on?"

I stare into the camera for a couple of breaths. This wasn't... this wasn't what I thought it was going to be. My throat gets caught up around swallowing, and a drip of sweat beads down my scalp, even though it's a chilly fall day in Eastern Massachusetts.

Charlie steps in front of me. "Hi, I'm Charlie Song. I'm the tech guy, which means I try to capture any measurable data of a haunting, whether it's sounds, sights, or radiation emitting from the phenomena. This is Evelyn Ramirez, our researcher, historian, and folklore expert. Say, 'Hi,' Evie!"

"Hi, Evie!" Evie replies naturally.

"And this is Samir Hassan, our team medium. He's sensitive to things normies like us can't see, hear, or smell."

Sam steps in front of Charlie. "Burnin' sage center stage," he says, throwing up a peace sign.

He turns to me. *Oh god.* "And this is Lydia Fox. She's no-nonsense, cares deeply about her team and the people we're here to help. Don't let her stern exterior fool you." Charlie gestures vaguely in my direction. I muster a half-smile. He continues, "We're here today to investigate a family haunting following an untimely death. Unfortunately, that's all I can say until we gather more information."

Shirley turns off the camera. "That was great, Charlie. Really great." I catch her brow furrowing at me in confusion.

Charlie surprised me. He's a natural in front of the camera. I eye him with newfound appreciation.

Hemlock Hall is a Queen Anne-style mansion that has grown through various additions like mold on cheese. Before heading inside, I peer through the windows and spot a pale-haired girl peeking out from one of the second-story windows. Lifting my hand to wave, the curtain quickly closes, and she's gone from sight. *Emily.*

The maid returns, ushering us into the grand foyer of the manor. I haven't seen a house this ostentatious since Octavia and I attended the Governor's Ball with our parents back in eleventh grade. Still, there's something oddly familiar about it.

The foyer is adorned with dark wood and a menacing wrought-iron chandelier. The maid leads us through the guest areas to a room with a massive fireplace—so large I could stand inside it without bending over. The furnishings are formal and antique. I give Sam a warning glance, hoping he doesn't do anything unusual. If he notices, he gives no sign, settling quietly in the corner as if blending in with his surroundings.

Evie examines the Tiffany lamps while Shirley adjusts the lighting by the two-story windows framing the room. Quinn stands next to me and whispers, "It's a lot, right?"

"I grew up in one of America's oldest colleges. This feels like home," I respond with more confidence than I actually feel.

Charlie holds up a peculiar Geiger counter. It's not like any I've seen before. My expression must reveal my confusion because he gives a shy shrug and mumbles, "I had to make do with what I could find."

My wool pants itch, and I resist digging my nails into my thighs for relief. The tie-neck on my silk blouse feels suffocating, and the matching vest only adds to the discomfort. I need to sit down. The people I've helped in the past were blue-collar types or con artists, not the sort I'd rub elbows with at one of my mother's famous soirées.

And there it is—the thing Quinn warned me not to fixate on. The similarities between Emily and me. I sit on the edge of a spindly-legged sofa and take a deep breath. Quinn sits next to me and nudges my knee with his own.

As William and Esme Carmichael enter the room, their voices are hushed and tense. Esme's face remains tight and sour, while William's expression shifts into a practiced politician's smile. Evie and I exchange worried glances, sensing the underlying tension. The atmosphere crackles with unspoken anger and resentment, like storm clouds ready to burst.

"Detective Quinn," Carmichael says, moving toward Quinn. The detective rises and pats my shoulder, signaling me to do the same. They shake hands, a brief exchange of pleasantries and apologies.

"This is Lydia Fox from Shelley College. We discussed her work on the phone," Quinn adds, providing context.

I hesitate, unsure whether to extend a handshake or offer a nod. I opt for the latter. "Nice to meet you."

Carmichael tilts his head slightly. "Not one of Court's girls?" he inquires.

"The only one left," I reply, my tone brisk. At my blunt response, Sam's head snaps up from where he's been studying the Persian rug.

"I was truly sorry to hear about your parents. Court and I went to college together," Carmichael says, his voice sincere yet somewhat stiff.

"I didn't know that," I admit.

"And your sister, of course." He clears his throat to get rid of the bad phlegm of my sister's murder. It wasn't parlor talk, after all. Quinn introduces him to the rest of the team, and Carmichael introduces us to his wife, Esme. She merely nods in acknowledgment.

"Oh, but where are my manners?" Carmichael exclaims, his tone shifting to one of forced cheerfulness. "With all this trouble, I've neglected basic courtesy. How rude of me." He turns to the maid. "Marian, could you bring us some iced tea?"

I whirl around in surprise. I hadn't noticed the maid standing there. She disappears behind a door and reemerges almost instantly with a tray of tea and muffins.

We help ourselves, feeling awkward as we try not to disturb the antique furnishings. Standing around with our glasses and napkins-wrapped muffins,

Carmichael claps his hands together. "I should show you all the pond," he announces.

Just like that. "I should show you all the pond." As though his twelve-year-old daughter hadn't drowned there less than two months ago. Charlie and I exchange glances, unsettled by the matter-of-factness of his suggestion.

"Oh man," Sam mutters from his corner, his gaze fixed on the shadowy space near the stairs.

"Come along," Carmichael continues, as if we're merely going on a grand tour of the grounds. "You can bring your refreshments."

We look at each other, unsure, then follow him through a recently remodeled kitchen. We abandon our glasses on the countertops and step through the French doors into the garden. *Who drinks iced tea this early in the morning?* I wolf down my banana nut muffin, having skipped breakfast. The gardens are meticulously maintained, yet there's an overgrown wildness encroaching on the carefully curated space.

"Right here, through Emily and Lily's," Carmichael pauses at the mention of Lily. "Right through the Wonderland court." The topiaries are whimsically shaped—giant green mushrooms and flowers, towering rabbits and caterpillars. We stop at a bridge designed to look like a deck of playing cards. The body of water beneath it is only about fifteen feet wide on this side. The bridge seems more for aesthetic appeal, as the pond stretches far across the property, even butting up against the house. I imagine there's a shared wall between the pond and the basement. A small dock floats in the middle for sunbathers.

"Is this where it—?" I begin gently, my voice wavering with the weight of my own history.

Carmichael nods. Mrs. Carmichael hasn't joined us outside. "The pond is called Alice's Tears."

"That's a lovely name the girls came up with," Evie responds.

Carmichael looks puzzled. "Oh," he says, his shoulders sagging. "You misunderstand. We named the Wonderland court here because the pond was already called Alice's Tears. The garden was designed around that name. It was Lily's idea."

"Interesting," Evie murmurs, scribbling down the note in her folder. The sun filtering through her big glasses makes a dollop of light right in the middle of her notes. "Do you know the origin of the name?"

Carmichael shakes his head. "It's always been called that."

"Well, Alice is an Anglo name, so I doubt it's always been called that," Evie observes absently. I shoot her a warning glance. She notes it but continues scratching in her notebook.

Charlie squats down by the edge. "It doesn't look very deep. Could the girls swim?"

"Of course!" Carmichael replies, irritation peeking through his frayed edges. "But, to answer your question, it's deceptively deep."

"I know this is difficult for you, Mr. Carmichael, and I apologize," I say gently. "In the police report, you mentioned Lily was here alone?"

He scrutinizes me before answering. "Yes."

"Was it common for Lily to be out here alone without her siblings?" Quinn glances at me, signaling that he had planned to ask this, but I've jumped in.

"No. Emily was sick that day. She wanted to watch Lily swim from their room."

"So Emily saw Lily drown? Again, I'm so sorry. I know this is hurtful," I continue, as Evie's pen dances across her notes.

"No, thankfully, she didn't. She fell asleep after Lily had been out here for a while. And it's alright. Detective Quinn prepared me for your questions."

Charlie dipped his hand in the water and shook it off. "It's freezing. This happened in late August?" Carmichael nods. "Is it cold in the summer as well?"

"I'm going to assume your people are not native to New England, Mr. Song," he responds dryly, but I note he remembers Charlie's name. Politician standard.

"*My* people are used to even colder water, Mr. Carmichael," Charlie replies stiffly. "Lake Michigan. Chicago born and raised."

Carmichael raises an eyebrow, dubious. "And here's my eldest daughter, Cecilia."

A stunning woman joins our little group, and now I can see why Charlie knew who she was. She has a dirty blonde shag and the whitest smile I've ever seen. One I've seen on several magazine covers at the checkout stand. A crown of morning sun rays circles her head like an illuminated saint. The pen Charlie clenches between his teeth dangles and then drops into the pond as he gazes up at her.

"Daddy, you didn't tell me we were having guests. My! Look at all of you!" Cecilia exclaims, placing her hands on her hips and surveying each of us with interest.

As my gaze shifts to the house behind her, I spot Emily again, watching us intently. But her focus isn't on me.

No, she's fixated on Cecilia. Just like the rest of us.

CHAPTER four

I slip back from the group at the water's edge, my Polaroid camera slung around my neck. Moving to a vantage point where I can capture the pond from various angles, I also take the opportunity to observe everyone from a distance. There's something revealing about stepping back and taking in the broader picture.

The beech trees that form the natural tunnel along the road have begun creeping up the hill, mingling with the hemlocks that gave this place its name. Wildflowers burst forth in vibrant clusters in the places between the trees where the sun can reach. The isolation here is almost intoxicating—there isn't another house in sight.

Charlie is engaged in animated conversation with Cecilia, repeatedly fussing with his hair. Mr. Carmichael and Evie are deep in discussion about the history of the hill. Evie's breathy laugh comes out easily enough, but her fingers twisting in her dark, wavy hair betray her—Carmichael must be lying to her. There's nothing more frustrating to a historian than obfuscation. Sam is conversing with Quinn, who keeps glancing my way, silently pleading for assistance. And Shirley... Shirley is filming all of it.

She directs her lens toward me, and we lock eyes. I'm positioned at the water's edge, the cattails brushing against my tailored wool suit. With her modern, assertive stance and a look that could cut glass, she scrutinizes me as though trying to decipher my motives.

The morning sun beats down on my pale hair as I lift the Polaroid and snap a photograph of her: the house looming behind her, dipped in shadows, contrasted starkly against the bright orange scarf snugly tied in her college-girl afro. Her sunglasses rest in the neckline of her top as she peers through the camera's viewfinder.

While I wait for the film to develop, Shirley lowers her camera to the ground. I wonder what her impressions are, but I don't know her well enough to ask.

Abandoning the pond for the manor, I meticulously photograph the Wonderland Court, trying to absorb the essence of the place. With a hole-punch from my pocket, I perforate the bottom of the photo and attach it to the growing collection on the carabiner hooked to my belt loop. These photos are crucial—they might reveal details I missed on my first pass.

The manor looms over the court and pond like a silent movie villain creeping up on the damsel in distress. I aim my camera and press the shutter. A curtain on the second floor flutters, hinting at some movement within the shadowed interior. I frown, waiting for the image to develop.

A pale-haired girl, strikingly similar to Octavia, stares down at my lens in the picture. But I must have moved because the image shifts—an identical girl appears behind her, ghostly and translucent. A specter of motion.

"You see her, too, right?" Sam's voice is a whisper from behind me. I wrench my head in his direction, startled.

"What?"

His long, graceful finger points to the ghostly figure on the Polaroid. "The one who drowned."

I raise an eyebrow, still glancing over my shoulder at him. "That's probably because she moved. I have hundreds of photos like this," I explain.

Sam's expression darkens into his 'Spooky Sam' mode. "Then why is the ghost wearing a swimsuit, mon capitan?" He walks away before I can respond.

I squint at the photo, uncertain. Perhaps Sam is seeing what he wants to see. I punch a hole in the corner of the photo and add it to the collection, marking it with my pen—just in case.

Evie catches up with me as we find ourselves alone in the topiary garden. "What do you think?"

"I think this family is concealing a lot of trauma," I say. "Well, except for Mrs. Carmichael. She seems to be the only one in this house who's behaving normally."

Evie nods, her expression thoughtful. "It is curious."

"Curiouser and curiouser, don't you think?" I gesture toward the Alice in Wonderland theme that permeates the garden.

"That's just it," Evie muses. "If Emily is being haunted, by whom? Her sister? This mysterious Alice who supposedly cried enough to fill a pond? Other past residents? Because, historically speaking, most people died at home before the 1920s." She crosses her arms over her chest. "I don't like it, Lydia. This feels different from anything we've encountered before. There's something else going on here."

"Secrets." I nod. "This place is practically bursting at the seams with secrets." Nodding toward where Carmichael is talking to Quinn, I ask, "Do you think he'll let us talk to the girl today?"

A mischievous glint dances in Evie's cranberry-painted lips. "Well, how could we possibly know that Emily is off-limits?"

It's one of the reasons I appreciate Evie. She's scholarly, but she's not afraid to bend the rules. I nod toward the house, and we slip inside.

The French door leading to the kitchen is ajar, allowing us to slip back inside unnoticed. The maid has thankfully vanished. We make our way back to the reception area, which feels more like a showroom than a living space.

"It's strange, isn't it?" Evie comments.

"What is?"

"The absence of photographs. They're affluent, but there isn't even a single professional portrait of their children."

I scan the room, noting the stark absence of personal touches. "Perhaps it's too painful for Mrs. Carmichael," I suggest.

We ascend the stairs with a casual air, prepared to employ our 'we're just clueless college students' expressions if anyone catches us. We're mistaken if we thought the upstairs hallway would be adorned with family photos. The walls are bare, covered only by dark wooden panels that seem to stretch endlessly.

I pause outside a door as a shadow moves across the light seeping from beneath it. Evie and I exchange a silent nod. Hoping the shadow doesn't belong to Esme Carmichael, I gently rap my knuckles on the door's deep mahogany.

The shadow stills.

"Hello? Emily? Can we speak with you for a moment?" I call softly. A gasp escapes from the other side. "We're from Shelley College. We're here to help."

The door creaks open just a crack. "I'm not supposed to talk to strangers," she whispers.

"Oh, we're not strangers," I assure her. "Our fathers were friends."

"How can you help? I don't understand." Her whisper carries a note of trepidation, making me question if I should be whispering too.

We wait in silence for a few moments, and I lean against the wall beside the door. "I'm not one of those doctors, if that's what you're worried about."

"Are you here to help her?" Emily asks.

"Who?" Evie interjects before I can respond.

"Lily."

Evie and I exchange a look. "Yes, that's exactly why we're here," I tell her.

To my surprise, the door opens wider, revealing a chaotic room. Drawings, crayons, and markers are strewn across the floor. Watercolors and jam jars full of water and paintbrushes are scattered on every available surface. The room, painted in soft blue, contains two twin beds: one neatly made, the other a tangled mess with no fitted sheet. A tray on her desk holds a stack of food-crusted china.

The overpowering odor of the room nearly makes me gag. The walls are plastered with her artwork. Evie is already examining the drawings. From her reaction after a quick glance, I can tell she's concerned.

"Sorry for the mess," Emily says with a babyish lilt. Her hair is a tangled, dirty nest, and her face is smudged with art. Is she really twelve? She looks so young, standing there in her filthy pajama bottoms and faded Holly Hobby tank top. Her body is a patchwork of bandages, each one taped to various spots on her skin.

"You should see my place," I offer with a reassuring smile. "My name is Lydia Fox, and this is my colleague, Evelyn Ramirez."

"Call me Evie. Only my mom calls me Evelyn," Evie says, her tone warm but slightly distant.

Emily glances down at the hand I'm extending and wipes her palm on her pajamas before giving me a firm shake. "You said you're from the college?"

Evie nods. "That's right. We investigate paranormal occurrences. Do you know that word? Paranormal?"

"I'm twelve, not five," she replies with a hint of irritation. "They let you study that in college?"

"Can you believe it?" I ask, wrinkling my nose playfully. "It's a gas."

"Okay, so tell us what's happening." Evie's impatience is palpable, and I narrow my eyes at her.

"Can I sit here?" I gesture to Lily's bed.

Emily's brow furrows at my request. "I'm not sure. Let me check first." She turns and cracks open the closet door, whispering something into the darkness within. She returns and says, "Lily says it's okay, but don't put your shoes on the bed."

My eyebrows shoot up in surprise. "Well, how generous of Lily. Please thank her for me." Emily gives me a skeptical look. "Your dad mentioned you were asleep when it happened."

Her mouth twists into a half-frown. "Oh. You want to talk about that."

Evie is still peering at the artwork. "These are very good," she murmurs.

"Only some of those are mine," she tells Evie. "Lily is the real artist."

Evie nods appreciatively.

An awkward silence fills the room as Emily moves to her record player on top of her dresser. "Do you guys like The Doors?" she asks.

We measure each other with a wary look. Emily doesn't want anyone eavesdropping. "Of course," I reply, trying to sound casual. "Jim Morrison is a stone fox, right?"

She slides the album out of its burnt orange and yellow sleeve, places it on the turntable, and sets it spinning. The funky intro of "The Changeling" starts to fill the room. Emily sits across from me on her bed, cross-legged, while Evie settles beside me.

Emily's midnight blue eyes fixate on a spot on the floor as she takes a deep breath. "I was sick. So they went to church, and Lily said she wasn't going without me." Her voice drops to a whisper. "Which was crap," she adds.

Evie tilts her head, intrigued.

"She just didn't want to go to church. I mean, who does? Cece pretends she wants to go and acts all penitent when she's there." She raises an eyebrow. "You know that word? Penitent?" Ignoring my reaction, she continues, "But Cece isn't a good girl." She lowers her voice further. "You know why?"

"Why isn't Cece a good girl, Emily?" I prompt gently.

Emily's eyes dart nervously to the door. "She has lots of boyfriends. Momma says that's dirty."

"Okay, Cece aside, what happened after they left?"

"Lily wanted to swim the second they were out the door." She picks something off the bottom of her bare foot. "It gets hot up here in the summer. Sweltering hot."

"You don't have air conditioning?" Evie asks.

Emily shakes her head. "I told Lily I couldn't go down to the pond, but she said I could keep an eye on her from the window."

"Did you try to stop her?"

"No," she admits. "I didn't care. It's stupid. I should've cared."

I nod in understanding. "Okay, so what happened next?"

"I don't know. I think I fell asleep."

"You think?" Evie latches onto this. "But you're not sure?"

Emily swallows hard. "Dad woke me up asking where Lily was."

"Where?" I ask.

When her gaze remains puzzled, I clarify, "Where did you wake up? Your bed or Lily's?"

She chews her lip and points to the bed I'm sitting on, which has a clearer view of the pond. "Anything unusual about it?"

"My head was at the wrong end."

I stand and turn to inspect the room set-up. Slipping the Polaroid out from around my neck, I place it on the nightstand. The head of the bed is against the impressive picture window in their room. With a knowing glance at Emily, I kick my shoes off and kneel on the pillow to spy on our group out at the pond.

I dramatically fall backward with my eyes closed. My legs are still curled from where I was kneeling, but my head is closer now to the foot of the bed. We lock eyes. "Like this?"

She swallows again and nods almost imperceptibly.

Evie scribbles something in her notebook. I want to discuss this with her but not in front of Emily. I straighten up from Lily's bed and slip back into my shoes. "You've been very helpful, Emily. Do you mind if I take some pictures of all this beautiful art?" I hold out my Polaroid.

"I suppose that would be okay," she replies, and Evie hands me another pack of film.

"Could you be my assistant for a few minutes?" I ask Emily. Her face lights up at the prospect. Have they forgotten about her entirely up here? The Doors are now playing "LA Woman." "I need you to use this marker to note whether it's your art or Lily's on this white part, okay?"

Emily hops off the bed, visibly excited. "I can do that."

I take twenty-nine photos in total. Emily labels each one with an 'Emily' or 'Lily,' or 'Emilily' for the joint works. She hands them to Evie, who punches a hole in each one so I can attach them to my belt loop.

"Emilily," Evie whispers when she sees the first one marked like that. "That's adorable."

"That's what Cece calls us," Emily says matter-of-factly. "It's never Emily or Lily, just Emilily." Her expression turns wistful. "I guess not now, huh? Now it's just Emily."

I pause in attaching the photos to my carabiner. "It will always be Emilily. Nobody can take that from you, boss. Got it?" She nods, her lips pressed together. "Now, I have just one more question."

Emily's gaze flickers to her bandaged arms and then back to me. "You want to see them, right?"

"Only if you want to show them to us."

She considers for a moment, her tongue pressing against the inside of her cheek. "I'll show you if you come back tomorrow. I'll even let you take pictures of them. Everyone always wants to take pictures of them."

"You've let people take pictures of them?" Evie asks gently.

"Daddy, of course, and then Dr. Steiner."

"Is he your pediatrician?" Evie asks.

Emily shakes her head. "No, he's a headshrinker. That's what Cece calls him."

I nod in understanding. Her psychiatrist has taken pictures of the words carved into her skin. "You want us to come back?"

Emily steps back to the closet and cracks it open again, conferring with the unseen presence inside. "Lily says you can help."

"Okay, Emilily, we'll help," I assure her. As she leads me to the door, the closet door slams shut with a resounding bang.

Evie lets out a small yelp. I glance at her and hold my hand out, searching for a draft.

Emily spins around and shouts at the closet door, "I'm sorry!"

We hadn't noticed the album had ended. It now emits a soft *tick-tick-tick* sound as it waits to be flipped.

Tick-tick-tick.

CHAPTER five

Emily's crestfallen expression locks on the closet door. I hate it. She's too young to deal with this on her own. Resolute, I straighten my spine and step towards the closet. Octavia would have scolded me for cracking my neck so unladylike, but right now, I need every ounce of bravado I can muster.

Evie gently pulls Emily back, whispering reassurances.

"Lily? My name is Lydia Fox. I'm here to help. Is that okay? Knock once for yes and twice for no."

Silence. Seconds stretch like hours. I glance back at Emily, seeking her reaction.

KNOCK.

Evie flinches, her professionalism wavering for just a moment as she shields Emily. Heart hammering in my rib cage, I force my face to remain calm. We can't afford to lose our composure in front of Emily.

"Okay," I address the knocker, my voice steady. "Thank you. It would be helpful for me to know, however, what I'm here for." Pressing my palm and cheek against the cool wood, I listen for any hint of breath. The silence is oppressive. "Did you drown on accident?"

KNOCK.

I shudder internally but maintain a composed exterior. No sound follows. Taking a deep breath, I turn back to Evie and Emily.

KNOCK.

Spinning back to the closet, I rip the door open, revealing only dresses, jackets, a pile of shoes, and various dolls and stuffed animals. The mildew hits me like a wall, sharp and acrid. My eyes water as I notice a crumpled piece of cloth, hardened on the outside but blooming with black mold at the center—a nightdress.

"*Why* did you do that?" Emily screeches at me and tries to get between me and the closet. We lock eyes with each other until she backs down and edges away.

"Evie, my camera," I say, extending my hand. She drops it into my hand, and I take a shot of the mildewing garment.

"Emily, that's enough for today. I'll discuss the case with your father, but I need to know if you're comfortable being on camera. We might hook you up to some machines, but...," my gaze meets hers in a serious, grown-up manner, "I promise that if you say stop, we stop, and I will never let them do anything to you that might hurt you. Sometimes, it might be scary or uncomfortable, but I will never let any of our equipment or my team cause you any pain. That's my contract with you. Do you agree?"

Emily's curious gaze lifts from where I hold my hand out to her to shake. "What about Lily?"

Evie steps forward, echoing, "What about Lily?"

"Do you promise not to hurt Lily?"

Evie and I exchange glances. "I promise we won't hurt Lily, but if she's here and doesn't want to be, we'll help her move on. You need to be okay with that."

Emily nods, shaking my hand with a newfound determination. "You have a deal."

Evie and I make our way back to the group, and Shirley shoots me an expression telling me I shouldn't be doing things without her. Honestly, my mind slipped, and I forgot Shirley was even here. It's going to take some getting used to. Sam, meanwhile, surveys the house with a knowing nod.

"Mr. Carmichael, this investigation could take a few days. Can you suggest a place in town where we can set up a base camp? And we're going to need access to your house at odd hours. Hauntings aren't always convenient."

His gaze sweeps over me, assessing. "I'll set it up with Marian to give you access to the Hill. In the meantime, your team can make your base in the carriage house on the property if it appeals. The town is quite far. Although, it might be a tight fit for all of you."

"Oh, I'm not staying," Quinn interjects. "I'll check in with Lydia every couple of days until they're finished. If that's okay."

I'm surprised. I didn't think Quinn would leave me without supervision. "We're going to need to set up some equipment in spaces where activity has been seen. And I will need you to fill out these permission forms since a minor is involved, along with some consent releases for Ms. Henderson to film the family."

"Where's the little dude?" Sam asks, derailing my train of thought.

"What?" I ask.

"There's supposed to be another kid, right? A little brother? I haven't seen him. I need to get square with all the auras in this house before I can stay here, right?"

He raises a point and I turn to our host. "Mr. Carmichael? Where is Peter?"

"Boarding school," Mr. Carmichael answers curtly. Peter is nine. My curiosity must show on my face because Carmichael adds, "Peter has some... behavior issues."

Sam's brow furrows. "What? He just lost his sister. Of course, he has 'behavior issues.'"

I gently take Sam's wrist and steer him behind me. "If we could arrange a meeting with him on a weekend, that would be helpful."

"I'm sure that's impossible, Ms. Fox. He's in boarding school abroad."

Like a tea kettle set to go off, I have to fight the verbal tirade rising in the back of my throat. I try to swallow it down. This little boy lost his sister, and his parents shipped him out of the country.

Charlie steps in, calming the tension. "If he hasn't seen anything since he's been gone, we'll manage. Thank you, Mr. Carmichael, for your hospitality and the use of your carriage house."

Carmichael's gaze turns stern. "Marian will show you the carriage house," he says as a parting word and sneers down at his watch as though we've already wasted enough of his time.

Confusion crawls across Quinn's features. "Didn't you tell me the kid saw Lily in the basement?" I murmur to Quinn in a quiet voice so quiet.

His green eyes search my own for a moment. "Yes," he whispers back. "Yes, I did."

Curiouser and curiouser.

True to his word, the distrustful Marian comes out from where she's been waiting for her cue and tells us to head back down the driveway and follow the path to the left of the gate. She hands me a key. "Boys in one room and girls in the other," she suggests.

"Uh... thanks," I reply as I take the key.

"Ms. Fox," she whispers, "don't leave the carriage house after dark. The grounds aren't safe."

My eyebrow arches, and I lean down to her conspiratorially. "Sort of defeats the purpose of us being here, don't you think?"

Shirley smiles wide at Marian and then side-eyes me after the maid walks away. "What the fuck was that about?"

"If you stick with us, you'll discover not everyone agrees with what we're doing."

She walks next to me as we head back out to the van. Her camera points toward my face. "Why is it that you do this, anyway?"

I don't look at her. All I'll give her is my profile. It's easier for me this way, not looking at my sister in that glass eye of her camera. "We all need some kind of peace of mind, don't we?"

"Peace of mind?"

"That this isn't all there is. That there's something else out there when we slip out of these things," I wave my hands over my body.

"If haunting loved ones is what comes after, I'd prefer the dark," Shirley replies with a certainty I can't get behind.

"I guess we'll all find out in the end."

Shirley adjusts her lens, capturing my profile. "Don't tell me you envy the dead."

"I'm just saying, I think the dead have it easier. They're not the ones left behind."

Charlie is walking in front of us, and he's turned his head as he listens in on our conversation. "But if they're still here, trapped inside this house, isn't that exactly what they are?"

"Are what?" This comes out much sharper than intended.

"The ones left behind," he says with a softness to counter my aggravation. Satisfied she's gotten what she wanted, Shirley lowers the camera.

We pile back into the old Dodge and Quinn follows us down to the carriage house to talk to us without the prying ears of Carmichael. The boys unload the van, and Quinn leans up against the side of it. "Listen, it got a little tense up at the house, and I have a feeling it will only get worse. Right now, he's humoring his wife. When that loses its novelty, he will throw you out if you continue to disrespect him."

"Oh, is that what I was doing, Detective Quinn? Disrespecting him? He sent his youngest child away to, and I'm guessing, Great Britain after the death of one of his sisters. How could he do that?"

"If he has behavior issues, there may be more to it. He's running for Senate. You wouldn't believe the atrocities the Kennedys covered up in their own families."

"Yeah, well, William Carmichael is no Jack Kennedy."

"I know you have your own way of doing things, but this is different. This is old money. Nobody wants to see old money humiliated."

My face screws up with horror. "Have you been to a college campus lately, Quinn?"

He chews his lip in thought and tucks a stray strand of my white-blonde hair that keeps whipping into my face behind my ear. "Okay, Lydia, okay," Quinn tells me. "I'll let you do this your way. But I want you to be careful. I'll do what I can on my end."

"Careful of what? Don't tell me you're scared of ghosts." I'm teasing, but he doesn't smile.

"I'm a cop. I'm scared of people. You need to ask yourself, with grounds that overgrown, why is the carriage house empty?"

My brow crinkles at this, and I peer up at the house behind me. "You'll check into it for me?"

"Already on it," he says and tips an invisible hat at me as he gets into his car. He rolls down his window. "I know I'm 'the man' and all, but please listen to my pig guts when I tell you something doesn't smell right here." The engine roars to life, and he backs down the driveway.

When he's gone, I turn back to the house up on the hill. From this far down, I can only see the third story sticking out as it points an accusing finger toward the sky. The house is an enigma. It doesn't have any sense of decency to adhere to any particular time period, yet it isn't quirky or eclectic—just oppressive and sad.

I make a mental note to talk to the maid. Staff in these sorts of places usually have a much more unique perspective than the occupants.

Closing my eyes, I take in the air. The aroma is green, heavy, and thick, a foul odor catches in spots, like scum on stagnant water. It must be blowing in from the pond, but there's no breeze.

"Two bedrooms and a pullout couch," Evie reports. "I'm not taking the couch. My back issues are bad enough."

"I'll take the couch," I tell her, only half listening. "Evie," I begin, "what year was this place built? It isn't standard New England architecture."

"The original house was built in 1747. But, it's Theseus' ship."

"How so?"

"It's been added to so much, I doubt anything from the 18th century remains."

I nod, satisfied with that answer. "And the Carmichaels are the original owners?"

"No, a British officer named Shippington built it. He was hanged during the Revolutionary War. His wife took her own life on the property shortly after. The Carmichaels took over post-war."

"Good," I tell her.

"What do you mean good?"

"The house has no loyalty to the Carmichaels. It's a perfect spot for a haunting—a ghost trap. Leylines run through it, making it hard for spirits to move on. Dad believed houses on leylines have a loyalty to the family that broke ground."

"Yeah?"

"My dad was obsessed with leylines, and this structure sits square in the middle of a fairly serious intersection. Leylines have a pull to them, making it harder for the spirits of the dead to break that gravity and move on. And Dad believed that houses on leylines harbor a sense of loyalty to the family that broke ground on it."

"But it's Theseus' ship. Multiple groundbreakings."

"But the first was Shippington. The land knows. The leylines know. And if Carmichael was friends with my dad, he knows too."

"So, what's good about it?"

"The house will let Lily go because she's a Carmichael, not a Shippington. We might have a genuine haunting here, Evie."

"And if there are ghosts of Shippingtons here? How do we free them?"

"My guess? We'd have to burn the whole structure to the ground. But we weren't hired for those ghosts. We were hired for Lily, no matchbooks needed."

I head to the van to grab my gear and get a plan together with the rest of the team while Evie stares up at the Hall with a certain grim awe.

Don't go looking for ghosts in a graveyard, Lydia.

Shut up, Octavia.

CHAPTER
six

When I return to the van, Sam is waiting for me, smoking a joint and bobbing his head to a tune only he can hear. What strikes me, though, is that he's unnerved. Sam is usually unflappable from what little I've seen of him over the past couple of years.

"You alright there, Sam?" I ask, concern creeping into my voice.

"Groovy, boss," he croaks, his voice hoarse from the grass. He clears his throat and passes the joint to me. I take a long draw, savoring the momentary calm. "You just... does this feel right to you? Cuz none of this feels right to me, man."

"Bad vibes?" I exhale the smoke and hand the joint back to him.

"More like bogus vibes."

I nod, sharing his unease. The only person who's been even remotely honest with me in this house is the twelve-year-old barricaded in her filthy room.

"The problem with this house isn't the dead, momma." Sam says, extinguishing the joint on the bottom of his sandal before tucking it away.

"It's the living." He glances back at the house on the hill, eyebrows knitted in uncharacteristic seriousness.

It's curious. Sam isn't the serious type. And in the span of a breath, the spell is broken. He shakes it off and bends his knees slightly to meet my gaze. "But hey, we got sweet digs to hole up in, right?"

We turn to survey the carriage house, a cottage straight out of a fairy tale. "It looks like a trap for Hansel and Gretel," I mutter.

"I could lick it and see if it's gingerbread," Sam offers. I shake my head at his heroism.

"Provincial Revivalism," Evie says as I stare at the deeply angled porticos and gables. Sam and I both turn to her in surprise, and she shrugs. "My parents are architects. This style was trendy about fifty years ago."

Sam's gaze locks onto her. "I did not know that about you. Oh my god, man, I just had a supernova thought. We should all get drunk tonight and learn more about each other."

Evie and I exchange amused glances. "That sounds like an awful idea," I begin.

"No, no, no, pretty girl. We're like a brand-new team on the first leg of our hero's journey together. We need to bond. Gel. Cohesitate."

"Cohesitate isn't a word," Evie corrects him.

His eyes brighten. "But you didn't say 'no.'"

"C'mon, man. I got shrooms, I got grass, and I'm sure there's alcohol in there. We put on some groovy tunes and just vibe. It'll make us a stronger team." He's a bushy sheepdog begging for treats.

"Tonight, if we're feelin' it. But no pushing it, Sam."

"Bossssss," he drawls, stalking me like he's about to hug me.

My palm meets his chin. "No. No hugging, or I call this whole thing off."

He places a chaste kiss on the heel of my hand. "I'm going to get you one of these days, and you'll see the healing benefits of hugs, Foxy." He walks into the house with a milk crate full of records, leaving Evie and me in his wake.

"I think he might be on to something," Evie murmurs.

"I'm not hugging."

"That we should, you know, team build."

"When has that ever helped? Wayne and I got to 'know one another.' Look how well that turned out." I grab my small carry-on bag and wait for Evie to gather hers. "Besides, Waller said no more fraternizing with the team, which means I'm doomed to a life of celibacy because the only people I talk to are in the department." And forget about love. Love is for fools who can't anticipate pain.

"I didn't say sleep with Spooky Sam, Lydia. I said talk to your teammates."

The truth was, I was terrible with people. Forming relationships outside of sex was challenging. Sure, Evie and I were close, but I'd never even known her parents were architects until now. My cheeks warm with embarrassment at the realization.

"Okay, fine. I concede. We'll do a team thing tonight—" Evie opens her mouth to shout a triumph before I interrupt her "—while we devise a game plan for the case. And stop calling him Spooky Sam. He'd be far too satisfied if he heard you."

When Evie and I follow Sam inside, Charlie is going through his gear in the cottage's living room. Dark wood beams loom across the ceiling, with dried herbs and flowers dangling from their junctions. The fireplace is already roaring, and a hanger and pot connect to the hearth. Maybe this cottage is older than Evie stated earlier. The kitchen is small and well-loved. It doesn't appear to have been updated since the Great Depression. A round dining table crouches below a carriage wheel chandelier. A steep staircase tucked behind a door in the far corner leads to the two bedrooms and bathroom upstairs. It's a tight fit for five, but we'll manage.

"We'll be sleeping in shifts," I announce. "Two pairs, rotating throughout the night to avoid missing anything important."

Charlie nods, holding up walkie-talkies. "You'll wear one at all times. The battery pack is the red one by the camera equipment. Don't clog up the line with idle chatter; use it only when you need a second pair of eyes on any phenomenon."

Sam raises his hand. "What about me?"

Charlie's eyebrow quirks up. "What about you?"

"What'll I be doing?"

Evie smiles indulgently. "You're part of the team. You'll be doing what we do—monitoring the grounds. But if you vibe anything that we might not be able to, call one of us. Particularly me, if I'm up, I'll need to check notes and document the spaces."

"Speaking of documenting," Shirley says, drawing our attention. "Professor Waller wants me to interview each of you on camera from time to time to monitor how fieldwork affects you. It won't be invasive. I should also interview you directly after paranormal phenomena, and Charlie will set up a heart monitor during those incidents to measure stress."

I shake my head. "You didn't mention this earlier."

"Didn't I?"

"You didn't say anything about shoving us in the spotlight during times of acute anxiety."

"Are we part of the investigation, or are we the investigators?" Evie murmurs.

"And we can interview you if you see something scary? If you freak out?" I cross my arms, challenging Shirley.

"I don't see why not. It's all theoretical at this point anyway," Shirley says, adjusting her scarf. "We have no proof this is a true haunting. This trip might just be a stay at the country's worst bed and breakfast. Why are you all looking for trouble anyway?"

After a moment, Sam speaks up brightly. "No worries, movie lady, it's all groovy. We'll protect you. You're in with the best paranormal team the Shelley has ever had. And that's saying something since Waller and Lydia's dad used to do this back in the early sixties." Shirley whirls around and studies me. I glare at Sam. He walks over and claps his hand on my shoulderblade. "Foxy's a real chip off the old headstone."

"You're Courtland Fox's daughter," Shirley says.

Confused, Charlie's head swivels between Shirley and me. "Someone mind catching me up?"

Evie's eyes search my face for permission, and I give her the tiniest nod. "Lydia's dad was in charge of the whole department. Waller's her godfather."

"Okay, yes, good. I feel so much better. I thought something was going on between Lydia and Waller when I clocked the photo of her on his desk," Charlie breathes out.

Evie grimaces at him. "Don't be disgusting, Charlie. He's twenty years older than her."

"Plenty of profs marry their students," Charlie grumbles.

"That picture isn't Lydia," Sam corrects. He walks up to me and bends his knees to catch my eye. His hand reaches out to take one of mine. "That's Octavia, man. Lydia's twin sister."

"I didn't know Lydia had a twin—" Charlie starts.

"She's dead," I say, pulling my hand out of Sam's grip and brushing past Shirley on my way out the door.

I take a seat on a raised garden bed outside, pulling out my cigarette case with shaking hands. Shirley appears with a lighter, and I lean into the flame, breathing deeply as the paper catches. Exhaling the smoke, I frown up at Shirley.

"I'm sorry," I tell her. "That I didn't say anything."

"You didn't displace forty black families in the projects to study leylines," she says, sitting beside me. "Weren't your fault."

"If it means anything, I told him not to. The cops arrested us at the protest, and he paid them to leave me in jail for the weekend, even though we were underage. Tavi never forgave him for that lesson."

"She get arrested, too?"

"We did most things together." I study my hands, watching them shake at the mere mention of her. "But not like in a weird twin way."

"Most?" It's Shirley's documentary voice. I hate it.

"I didn't go with her to watch the moon landing at a friend's house." I huff out a dry laugh.

"Was that when it happened? When she got…"

"Yes."

"Were you supposed to?" She's so careful, like I'm a wild horse.

"It was never supposed to be Octavia." My gaze drifts to the van in the driveway. "The moon landing coincided with Teeny Martin's annual summer party. She was the cheer team captain. If you didn't go, you wouldn't make the cut."

Shirley doesn't say anything. I think she's holding her breath.

"I needed to be on that team. It was stupid high school drama, but I needed to be a cheerleader." My voice trembles, never having voiced this aloud. "It was on the calendar. It was all I talked about for weeks." I rub my forehead with the thumb of my cigarette hand. "I was so stressed out about it that I broke out. And I don't mean just acne; I mean… cystic pustules all over my face. Nobody was going to let me on the team looking like that."

Shirley places her hand over mine, and I continue. "I was…devastated. Neither Mom or Tavi could calm me down. It was stupid teenage girl theatrics. Tavi told me I didn't need friends like that if they didn't understand, but she didn't understand. She never got it. How could she? She never cared about the high school stuff I cared about. She sat in the chess club all lunch and hung out with the nerds. I begged her to go in my place. It would only be a few hours, and we were good at it."

"Good at it?" Shirley's voice is soft, encouraging me to continue.

"Good at being the other. Oh, I couldn't play chess to save my soul, but I could turn into Octavia, and she could turn into Lydia. All she had to do was go, make an appearance, drink a few drinks, talk to Teeny and the other squad members a bit, and look like a cheerleader. That's all she had to do."

"But she never made it."

"James used to make fun of me for being so shallow when I was so smart."

"Professor Waller?"

I nod. "Octavia put on my cutest mini-dress and my white boots, and I never saw her again until she was on a metal table a year later." I throw the cigarette between my feet, squashing it out and blowing the last bit of smoke. "Don't put this in your documentary."

"It wasn't your fault, Lydia."

"Tell that to Octavia."

Charlie pops his head out the open front door. "Am I interrupting?"

I rub my eyes with the heels of my hands for a moment. "Nope, what do you need?"

"If we're all unpacked, I'd like to return to the house to figure out the best spots to start setting up. I'm thinking of the basement. I'm not comfortable putting up cameras in Emily's room, though. It's up to you."

My eyes close, and I search for an answer. I need to speak to Emily again.

Shirley clears her throat. "I think we should also have a camera on the pond."

"That movie will be nothing but fog, then." We all turn toward the voice. Cecilia is walking down the driveway with an overly large picnic basket. "I brought some stuff to fill your pantry." She pulls a bottle of wine out of the basket. "And, of course, booze. What kind of hostess would I be if I didn't bring some booze?"

Charlie brightens. Hastily getting to my feet, I wipe my palms on my wool trousers. "You didn't have to do that," I tell her.

"Of course I did. But you might want to send someone down to grocery shop in the morning. I have no idea how long you will be staying here."

"Do you think we can head back up to the estate to ask some questions so we can figure out where to set up our equipment?" Charlie is looking at her like she's his favorite teacher.

"I'm not sure how much help we'll all be. I haven't seen anything, and Mother might not be willing to talk to any of you."

I clear my throat. "What about me? No cameras, just a conversation over tea." I sweep my platinum blonde hair off my shoulder. It's styled the way my mother would have wanted it, exuding that truly waspy aura.

Cecilia gives me the once-over. "I'll ask. It'll have to be in her sitting room. She struggles with groups of people."

With a nod, I take the basket from her and hand it to Evie as she steps outside. "Can you take this into the kitchen and pack your notes? We're going on a preliminary excursion."

Evie's eyes never leave Cecilia as she takes the parcel from me. "Yeah, sure, I'll be right back."

Intriguing. "I really wish Peter was here," I tell Cecilia. "He's the one who has had the most confrontations with your entity, from what I understand?"

"Peter isn't well, unfortunately, so whatever he told that cute detective of yours can't be taken literally. Besides, it's Emily that's chatting with Lily regularly." She rolls her eyes as if she doesn't believe her younger sister.

Charlie's face bounces between Cecilia and me as if he's watching a tennis match. "Can we talk to Peter on the phone?" he suggests.

"No." Cecilia's face drops the Miss Massachusetts act. "He wasn't told about this investigation, and that's how it will stay. It'll give him ideas."

"Your decision or your father's?" Shirley asks from behind me. She has the camera over my shoulder and focuses on Cecilia.

"My father's decisions and mine are one and the same," she says firmly. A fake smile cracks across her face, and she doesn't take her eyes off mine.

"I'll grab my gear," Charlie murmurs as he pushes past me to return to the cottage.

Sam and Evie come out and realize they've stepped into some kind of push-pull dynamic between me and the beauty queen.

"Tense," Sam says. He ducks his head in front of mine to catch Cecilia's attention. "Is there any way I can talk to Emily? I don't mean alone, because that's awkward, but with Lydia or Evie there?"

"If she's agreeable to it, I don't see why not." Cecilia takes a step back. Her nose wrinkles at my psychic. It's minuscule and fleeting, but it flutters across her features. When her eyes flicker back to mine, I tighten my gaze to let her know I saw it.

She doesn't like Sam. I tuck that information into my back pocket to use later. Turning slightly to Shirley, I whisper, "I'd like to review this later tonight."

"Mm-hmm." It's clear she'd like to as well.

"You guys ready?" Cecilia asks, breaking the tension.

"Let me grab my Polaroid and my tech guy for a brief chat, and we'll be off."

Holding Charlie's bicep tightly, I drag him back into the guest house. "What the hell, Charlie?"

"What do you mean?"

"She's the client. And she's a truly odd client at that. Get your shit together."

"My shit is together, Lydia." His weight shifts onto one foot, and he crosses his arms over his chest. "Oh, I get it."

"What?" My teeth are clenched at his indifference.

"You think..." He chews his bottom lip in thought. "You think she's the one playing me."

My brow furrows at this. "Explain."

"The New England Princess out there is playing us for idiots. She'll drop her drawbridge if we act like we're being played."

"You're trying to catch her off-guard."

His eyes meet mine. "If she thinks I'm just a dumb camera guy smitten with her, she might let me into her circle of trust." His gaze drops to the floor and back up to me. "You and I? We don't know each other well, but you have your way of cracking clients, which I'm going to assume involves a sledgehammer." Pursing his lips in a way that's almost appealing, he brushes his fingers through my hair, "and I have my way of cracking clients." He opens his fist and shows me the bobby pin he's pulled out without me ever feeling it. "We need to learn to trust each other."

My eyebrows raise, and I have to admit, he just impressed me. "Okay, Charlie, okay. We'll play your game of good cop, bad cop. Don't forget whose side you're on."

He steps back and huffs out a laugh. "Yeah. Don't worry. That would be impossible."

CHAPTER *seven*

The walk back up to Hemlock Hall is quiet and tense. Charlie squints at me and then raises his eyebrows, seemingly suggesting I should apologize to Cecilia. For what, I have no clue. I raise my eyebrows back at him, indicating my confusion. The silent exchange doesn't go unnoticed by Evie, who scowls at both of us. Sam plucks wildflowers along the path, and Shirley fusses with her camera.

Shirley stops suddenly and urges us to go on ahead. I glance up to see what has caught her interest and realize it's us on the little path leading to the sprawling manor on the hill. If she captures it in the melancholy way I'm sure she's planning—with string music accompaniment, of course—it will be a beautiful shot.

Deciding to let Shirley do what she does best, I catch up to Evie.

"I want you to keep watch on whatever is going on between Charlie and Cecilia, but don't interfere."

Evie eyes me quizzically, waiting for me to continue.

"Charlie thinks he has a plan to get into Cecilia's head, but I'm worried he's biting off more than he can chew. I think she might be the predator in this scenario."

"I agree, everyone's a little on edge here. It's creepy," Evie replies.

"They did just lose a child," Sam chimes in. I narrow my gaze at him, frowning at his eavesdropping.

"And they're not acting like it," I counter. Pursing my lips tightly, I want to add that when Octavia went missing, my family, who comes from a similar background as the Carmichaels, was consumed by grief. "Lily's passing seems more like an inconvenience to them."

"Every family handles grief differently," Sam reminds me. The urge to shove him makes me grind my teeth. He holds out the small bouquet he's made for me.

"I know that," I snap, snatching the bouquet from his hand and tossing it to the side of the road. He clutches his heart dramatically.

Evie's gaze darts between the two of us. "It doesn't matter. They're acting incredibly odd, but we've only been here a few hours. Time will reveal whether they're hiding something or not."

"Says the historian."

"Says the historian," she agrees, which rankles me.

Once we're up at the house, Charlie takes charge. Having someone else steer us allows me to do what I do best: observe. He clears his throat, his gaze flitting between Cecilia and me. "Cecilia and I will take the pond. It'll be the hardest spot to set up a camera. Why don't you take Sam and go down to the basement? I'll take Shirley since her input on setting up a camera outside at night could be helpful."

"Actually," Cecilia interjects, "the basement has no power, so it'll be even darker down there."

"And I'd like to pick Cecilia's brain on the history of Alice's Tears," Evie adds.

Charlie scratches his chin. Clearly, he wanted Cecilia to himself, but I needed my own eyes and ears on the situation. "Fine. Lydia, you take Sam and Shirley, and I'll take Evie and Cecilia."

Exactly how I planned it anyway; if the basement is a hotspot, I need Sam's feelers out. We measure each other up. "Great," I tell him.

"Great," he parrots back.

"This way," Cecilia says gently, wrapping her fingers around his wrist and tugging him along. "You can ask Marian where the door to the basement is. If you can't find her, it's tucked behind the front hall staircase."

I nod and glance at Shirley. "I hope you have a good light on that thing."

"I am not an amateur," she replies briskly, and I worry that I might've offended her.

"Sam? Flashlights?" Sam, wearing a suede bag strapped across his paisley shirt, pulls out two heavy-duty ones and hands me one. I check my camera, and we head inside Hemlock Hall.

We find the door without Marian's help. The door sticks, and we have to give it a hearty shove. How had Peter gotten down here if we could barely budge the door? "Shirley, do you want us to go down first, or do you want to go down first?"

She turns her camera light on and presses her eye to the viewfinder. Aiming the camera down the stairwell, she takes a few seconds of footage and then turns the camera on us. "I got what I needed for an empty stairwell. Head on down, and I'll frame you two in the shot."

Sam and I frown at the other since the stairwell isn't nearly wide enough for the pair of us to go down side by side. "I'd like to go first," he offers, but I think he's being a gentleman. You can't even see the bottom from here.

I juggle the offer for a few beats in my head. "It's my team. I'll go."

The stairs are dusty and full of cobwebs. Worse, my light only goes about six feet in front of me. Holding onto the railing, I slip down the first flight and turn to the right for the rest of the way. The basement is deep, taking advantage of the hill the manor sits upon. A damp, mildewy stench permeates the stone walls, and the temperature drops at least five degrees, cooling more with each step I take. It makes me wish I had grabbed my sweater.

"Damn," Shirley mutters behind me. "It's freezing down here."

"Good for winter stores, though."

Sam hasn't said anything. He peers around the cavernous main room. Finally, he breathes out, "I didn't realize there'd be so many hallways down here. The basements I've seen have only been one room or a recreation area with a couple of bedrooms."

"I'm going to assume it's approximately the same size as the manor," I whisper. And then I wonder why I'm whispering. Maybe people just do that when it's dark.

"Well, in any case, this might be a two-trip job." Shirley has pulled off the camera and is looking around. "We don't even know where Peter found his sister. It obviously wasn't here."

Sam and I glance around, and then I peer down at our feet. "No prints."

"No prints," Shirley agrees.

"I'm sure there must be another entrance." Sam closes his eyes, trying to remember what he saw of the estate from the outside. "Storm doors?"

"If there were storm doors outside, why wouldn't Cecilia have shown us those?" Chewing my lip in thought, I turn back to Shirley. "So without Quinn's report, we have no idea where Peter said he saw his sister."

"You have it?"

"I left it up at the house. Like Sam, I thought this was a basement, not a maze."

"It's going to make setting up cameras down here a bitch."

"Sam? You sense anything?" He whirls around on me a little too quickly when I ask him this. Concern shadows his features in the cone of the flashlight. "Maybe." His brow furrows in thought, and he wipes a hand on his pants.

"Something wrong?" I ask him.

"It's just... you ever get that feeling you're bein' watched?"

His words make my eyes dart around the dancing shadows on the centuries-old stone walls. "You feel like we're being watched?"

"Uh-uh, nope. I'm outta here," Shirley tells us.

Frustration strangles me, and I lay a gentle hand on her forearm. "This is what you signed up for, Shirley. Don't be a Wayne."

"What's a Wayne?"

"Wayne's a coward who ditched me in the middle of an investigation," I tell her. "Don't be a Wayne."

"Fuck Wayne," she says.

"Fuck Wayne," I agree.

"Fuck Wayne," Sam chimes in. I turn my light on him. "That guy was bogus."

Huffing out a chuckle, I bite my lip and nod in agreement. "You with us, Shirley?"

"Yeah," she says, but there's hesitation in her voice. "Where to?"

I raise my eyebrows at Sam in question, and he mirrors my expression. "Oh," he exclaims. "You mean me. Right. On it, boss lady."

Letting Sam take the lead, he follows his gut into a hall to the left. It's a long one, with other halls branching off it. I stay behind Shirley so she can follow Sam's lead.

A shuffling noise comes from one of the branching halls, and I turn my flashlight towards the sound. Sam is talking about auras and odors, and I've lost the thread of the conversation. A blur of white catches in my light, and I pull to a stop. They keep going, and I tell myself I'll catch up.

Stepping into the hall, I'm confronted with more walls and glassless windows, almost like horse stalls. I catch the pale figure moving farther ahead. It looks like... hair?

"Octavia?" I whisper. But no. Why would Octavia be here? "Lily?" The figure stops and turns. I can't make out any features, merely the vague outline of something that remembers what it was like to be human-shaped.

But there's something so Octavia-shaped about it. "Tavi, wait," I tell her and race toward the pale blur. Sam's assessment of the basement couldn't be more correct. It was a maze—a terrible, twisting, turning maze, and I hit a dead end.

Slamming to a stop, I peer around the room. There's no door, and it's furnished with only a pallet covered with a straw mattress and a makeshift nightstand. In the corner is a rocking chair, facing the wall. Backing out much slower than I came in, a breeze or an exhaled breath skates across my shoulder. Letting out a startled cry, I bat at the air in the direction it came from. There's nothing. "Tavi?"

The figure moves deeper into the labyrinth. At this point, I have no idea where Sam and Shirley are. All I can do is follow my white rabbit and hope she leads me out or to them. I don't want to be in this basement anymore. Sam was right.

Something else *is* down here. Something is watching me. I want out. I need out.

"Lily?" I chase after it. *Her.* I chase after *her*.

She stops about a hundred feet in front of me. My mouth has gone arid. The light shakes in my hand. "Emily?" I try this time. It makes more sense, doesn't it? Why would I assume what I'm chasing is dead when a perfectly broken little pale-haired girl already lives in the manor? Alive. And angry.

She's so angry.

I remember that anger. It grips your gut like a ravenous hunger, but nothing can satisfy it. "Emily, please stop. This isn't funny."

Where are Sam and Shirley? Have I gotten so far that they can't hear me?

"Come on, Lydia," it whispers. No, *she* whispers.

I can't move. She extends her hand toward me. It's a trick; it must be. She's stayed dozens of feet ahead of me this whole time and won't wait for me to catch up now. Placing one foot in front of the other, I take a step forward. Her stillness makes me raise the camera around my neck.

Without looking through the viewfinder, I lift it to eye level and squeeze the shutter. The sound and flash flood the room with harsh, white light. Grasping the ejecting film between my fingers, I peer in the direction she had been standing, but she's gone now. I tuck the photo into my bag.

"Dammit," I mutter, angrily making my way to where she had been standing. It's another room, similar to the first one we entered—almost cathedral-like, but damp and musty. I sweep the flashlight around the room, hoping to find another staircase.

I'm disappointed, and my light starts flickering. Resting the camera on my chest, I slap the flashlight with my free hand. "No," I whisper. "No, no, no. I'm going to kill Sam."

The intensity of the beam diminishes until it sputters out, leaving me in the dark.

"Shit. Shit, shit, shit," I growl between my grinding teeth. Darkness envelops my vision. It feels like my eyes are closed. I can't make out my hand in front of my face. Do I have batteries? My hand dives into my bag, and I fumble for C batteries. I come up empty.

Think, Lydia.

Letting out a trembling breath, I hear something shuffling behind me. Shifting to the right, I grip the flashlight in my fist like a weapon. A hand snakes into my hair and yanks it. *Hard.*

My fingers fly up to identify what's grabbing me, and I brush against the back of someone's hand. I gasp loudly in surprise and flail the flashlight toward the arm, but find only air. Blind, I swipe the air in front of me, trying to hit whoever is breathing heavily and pulling on me.

Nails rake down the arm of my silk blouse, tearing the material and my skin in the process. Yelping in pain, I drop the flashlight and use my other hand to cover the wound. "Stop!" I scream.

A growl, strange and feral, rumbles five or six feet in front of me, and all the breath leaves my body. I freeze.

It shuffles forward. "No," I moan, and it's upon me.

Whatever it is, it's vaguely human-shaped and it stinks. It smells of piss, shit, and dead animals. I try to push it off me, but it throws me off balance and onto my back. I shriek and try to bat it away from me.

Nails dig into my scalp, face, and neck, and I push and claw back. Teeth from its snarling mouth snap inches from my face, and putrid breath and sour spittle spray my cheeks and mouth. I scream louder and fight back in the dark.

The thing begins to burrow into my gut, ripping through my vest and blouse, tearing at me as if it wants to devour me whole. Trying to shove it off, my hand lands on my Polaroid, and I squeeze the shutter.

Light floods the room, blinding me. It also blinds whatever is attacking me. The thing leaps off me and scurries away. Then, footsteps pound against the dirt floor, heading toward me.

"LYDIA!" Sam screams, his light bouncing around the room.

I can't breathe. I can't scream. I can't cry. A strange noise erupts from my throat, like I'm gagging or choking, and his light lands on me.

"Oh my god," he says when he finds me crumpled on the floor. "What do I do? What do I do?"

Sam sets the light down to cover my shuddering, trembling form. I'm freezing, and the sound of my chattering teeth fills the cavernous empty room.

His fingers explore my wounds, checking for anything that needs immediate attention. When he finds mostly shallow scratches, he pulls my shirt and vest tightly closed. "Okay, pretty girl, okay," he breathes out and helps me sit up. "You're okay. Old Sam's got you. I've got you." His soothing words are accompanied by fingers that brush through my hair, searching for additional damage.

The sound that comes out of me doesn't sound human; it's a high-pitched keening noise that starts as if I'm gasping for air, and then I begin screaming. Not the high-pitched, I'm-in-danger kind of screaming, but an angry, guttural, roaring sound that bursts from deep inside me. Pushing at him only makes him hold me tighter against his chest.

"Fuck, Lydia, stop fighting. It's us," he soothes quietly. "What happened? What did this to you?"

This time, another light, a brighter one, swings into the space, and Shirley is there, pointing the camera down at me.

Sobs erupt from me, and I cling desperately to Sam, crying into his shoulder as if I'm going to die if I let go.

"Don't film this," Sam commands Shirley.

"But—"

"Don't fucking film this, Shirley! You think Lydia wants to see this again?" The vitriol in his voice makes me cling even harder to him. I'm practically in his lap now.

"It's my job to film this, Sam!"

It's difficult for me to follow what they're arguing about. He's dragging his fingers through my hair with one hand and rubbing my back with the other.

"Who did this to her?" Shirley demands.

"I don't know. I didn't see anything when I got here. I heard her screaming, and I heard something in here attacking her, but it was gone by the time I reached the door."

"We've got to find a way out of this."

"You fucking think?" He twists us around so he can glare at her. "Are you kidding me right now? Are you still filming her?"

I'm still in his arms. A calmness settles around me—a false calmness, but I'll take what I can get. "Don't tell Waller." The words come out as a hoarse whisper.

"Lydia," Shirley chides. "I have to."

"He'll pull me out. You can't tell him."

"Ever think he *should* pull you out? Jesus, Lydia, you're covered in blood."

"We can't leave." I pull away from Sam and. "We can't leave that little girl on her own here."

"For all we know, that little girl might have done this to you." Shirley's voice is laced with anger. I don't blame her.

"If Emily did this, she's in worse trouble than we thought. But I don't think it was Emily." I untangle from Sam, and he helps me stand.

"What makes you say that?"

"Because whatever did this has been down here a long time." I keep my top closed by crossing my arms around my middle. "And whatever it was, it didn't have blond hair."

I bend down and pluck the photo I took off the dirt floor. Shirley shines her light down on it. Brown hair blurs over a pale forehead in the too-close shot.

"C'mon, let's get her out of here," Shirley says. "I never want to come down here again."

Sam wraps an arm around my waist and lets me lean on him as we find our way back to the stairwell leading us out.

But I can feel it. Whatever attacked me down here. Its heavy gaze follows us all the way out. And I know, sooner or later, I'll have to come back for it.

CHAPTER *eight*

Emerging from the darkness of the basement is a balm to my soul. Limping out into the foyer, Shirley checks to see if anyone is around, and Sam hustles us out the front door. I'm still clinging to him like he might evaporate in a puff of sweet smoke. It's not a good look, but my knees have only just stopped knocking together. Stretched thin and worn, I need his help just to make it to the front door, and then the sun does the rest.

Taking gulps of fresh air, Shirley and Sam both furrow their brows at me like I might scream again. Exhaling in a long, drawn-out gust, I push Sam away and stand on my own. "Right," I finally say, shaking the aches and terror off me like dead leaves. Shirley frowns as I flap my hands for a minute while I pull myself together. "We need to reconvene in private. Shirley, can you fetch Charlie and Evie? Try to extricate them from Cecilia without being obvious, and, for God's sake, don't tell them what happened in front of her."

Shirley purses her lips. "I think we should find you a doctor."

"I'm fine. I swear it. It's only a few scratches. It was... it was just really scary, but I'm okay now."

Her gaze narrows at me as if she doesn't believe a single word I've said. I'm still trying to figure out if *I* believe it. "Shirley, please?"

Sam hasn't said anything; he chews the inside of his cheek in thought. He's not looking at either of us. It's always a little jarring when he goes quiet like this. "Sam?"

"I'm with you, pretty momma; I just—" he glances down at his feet and then back up at me again. "That was fucking terrifying, Lydia. And I'm a scary cat. Look at me," he says, and when I don't, he grasps both my wrists and makes me face him. "I never want to hear you like that again." He clears his throat. "*Any* of you. I never want to hear any of you sound like that."

I swallow around the lump in my throat and nod. "Help clean me up?"

The shadow of the porte-cochère drapes around him, matching his mood. "Yeah, whatever you want," he tells me, heading down the drive toward the carriage house. Shirley points her camera at him and takes a few seconds of shots of him before she turns it on me.

My hands immediately snap up to cover the worst of the damage. "What the fuck, Shirl?"

"You need to tell Waller," she says simply.

"I will. When it's done, okay? Does that suffice?"

She snaps it off and assesses me. "I'll fetch Charlie and Evie."

"Thank you," I say, turning from her to follow Sam down the hill.

The carriage house is unnervingly quiet, and we leave the top of the Dutch door open to air it out. I'm sitting on the dusty couch while Sam fishes around for first aid supplies. Of course, we have the one in the van, but if we can scavenge some here in the guest house, we should use those instead.

He returns with bandages, Betadine, a washcloth, and a bowl of water. Staring at the water, he asks, "Do you want to clean your chest up yourself?"

My head tilts down to check out the damage. "Yeah, I can do it in the bathroom, I think. Or Evie will do it." I tighten the ripped remains of my blouse and vest together.

With a nod, he starts in on my face and neck. The worst is the one on my arm, though, and I hiss in pain when he dabs the Betadine on it. "Sorry," he mumbles.

"Lydia!" Evie cries out as she runs into the door. "What happened?"

My eyes go blurry with tears when I attempt to recount what went down in the basement. Sam pulls Charlie outside, and they have a quiet conversation, with Charlie repeatedly whirling around to stare at me in astonishment.

"My God, Lydia," Evie whispers high and tight when we're in one of the upstairs bedrooms. "How did you get separated from Sam and Shirley?"

"I don't know, I thought I saw... Lily," I tell her. "But it might have been Emily."

"Did she... was it *her* who did this to you?"

"No, I don't think so," I reassure her. "I think this was someone else." I pull the Polaroid out of my pocket.

Evie stares down at it dubiously. "This isn't much to go by."

"I know." Pulling out my bag, I grab some fresh clothes. I choose a brown turtleneck and rust-colored corduroys. "Help me clean my chest up?" The light slants through the small windows and lands on us on the bed. Dust dances in the sunbeam, and I worry about what's taking Shirley so long. "How bad is it? You know, if I wanted to hide this from the Carmichaels," I ask.

Evie pulls away from me then. "Why? Shouldn't they know?"

"No," I say with more finality than I mean. "I don't want them to know about the attack. They might call this whole thing off."

A loud knock comes from the door, and Evie finishes cleaning up the last of my scratches. I yank the turtleneck on. "Come in," Evie says.

Charlie and Sam stand in the doorway. "Is Shirley back yet?"

"No, but we should talk," Charlie says. "May I?" He gestures to the bed, and I budge over to give him space to sit. My gaze darts to Sam, who won't meet my eyes. "Are you alright?" Charlie asks.

"Yeah. I'm fine. And before you ask, yes, I'm really fine."

"What do you want to do?"

Jumping up off the bed, I cross the room to the dresser and inspect my wounds in the mirror. The ones on my face are shallow enough to cover up with some makeup. "We can't leave, Charlie."

"She doesn't want to tell the Carmichaels about the attack," Evie adds.

"What? Why?" Sam asks, concern coloring both syllables.

"They'll call it off, too much liability. We can't leave Emily here," I regard everyone sincerely. "We have to figure out what's going on here, haunting or not."

Charlie sweeps a hand through his dark hair, mussing it. "Haunting or not? Lydia, our only job is the haunting. If there's nothing here, it's case closed."

"We haven't been here at night," Evie adds.

With a nod, Charlie stands up. "We haven't the time to set up now, so we'll have to wait until tomorrow. Do you think you can sweet-talk Carmichael into signing Waller's contract?"

"Yes. I know how to cozy up to these types. My mother's daughter and all that."

Sam swallows and meets my eyes. He shakes his head and goes back downstairs.

"How is he?" I ask Charlie.

"Sam? He's fucked up, Lydia. He thought you were dying."

"Well, I wasn't," I snort. Crossing my arms over my chest, I fix a stormy frown on Charlie. "Are you with me or not?"

"I think we're stepping into more than a haunting here."

Evie is cleaning up the first aid supplies. "I agree with Charlie," she says under her breath.

"What?" It sounds so demanding that I wince, but I can't back down now. "Speak up, Evie."

"I think this is some rich people bullshit that we shouldn't be wading in."

"You *are* rich people," I remind her.

"You know what I mean!"

"What about Emily?"

All the bluster goes out of Evie, and she sits on the other bed. "Okay, yeah. I'll concede there is a child to think about. But if there's nothing here, no paranormal activity at all, Lydia, you have to promise you'll pull us out."

"I promise."

Charlie glances between the pair of us. "I'm going to grab the EMF reader so we can check the grounds tonight after the sun goes down."

Sam appears in the doorway. "Shirley's back. She's with Cecilia. They've brought food."

"Let me finish changing, and I'll be down in a minute."

Charlie and Sam leave me with Evie, and we both speak simultaneously.

"I'm sorry—"

"I shouldn't have—"

Laughing at how ludicrous we are, Evie pulls me into a gentle hug, being mindful of the scratches. "I'm sorry. This place has me so creeped out. This is different than any case we've been on."

Changing into the pants, I sit on the bed to pull on some brown suede boots. "Ev, do you think you could dig into the Carmichaels' past without being super obvious?"

"I could say I'm going into town on a supply run tomorrow and do some research at the courthouse and library if you'd like."

"Yeah, I think we're missing something." I brush my pale hair and give myself a once-over. The scratches feel worse than they appear. Dabbing some foundation over them, I smear on some lip gloss and turn to Evie. "Can you tell I got attacked by a tiny werewolf in the basement?"

"Beautiful as ever, querida." She adjusts her earrings and smooths her plaid skirt. "Let's go. I believe Sam mentioned a party earlier?"

I groan at the reminder. Maybe it'll snap him out of wherever he was, though.

When I hit the bottom step, Cecilia is putting on The Beach Boys, and Sam rushes over to her. "No way, Miss America, I got this." So, maybe Sam's back.

He slips three albums onto the turntable, and Three Dog Night fills the room. "Can you believe she wanted to put on the Beach Boys?" he asks as Evie and I enter.

"We brought dinner," Shirley tells them. "Well, Marian brought dinner, and Cecilia and I followed her." The small wooden table has meatloaf, mashed potatoes, asparagus, some kind of salad, and an honest-to-goodness pie. Apple, if my nose is anything to go by.

"Wow," I say, turning to Cecilia, "This is so much. Thank you."

"Well, we couldn't have you going hungry on your first night," she tells us. "Charlie says you won't be able to set cameras up tonight?"

"We'll go over a plan and put it into practice tomorrow. You staying for dinner, then?" I ask when she takes a seat at the table. My gaze darts to Charlie standing in the small kitchen, struggling with a wine bottle.

"Of course, I hope you don't mind." Cecilia faces me and waits for my response.

My brows shoot up. "Certainly. It's your house." We weigh each other for a few more beats before Sam presses a glass of wine in my hand.

"Come eat. You promised we'd have team bonding tonight, boss."

Taking a large gulp of the wine, I nod. "I did, didn't I?"

"You guys don't know each other well?" Cecilia asked. "I would've never guessed that."

"Charlie and Shirley are new to the department, and Sam has always been around but not on the team," I explain while I fill my plate.

"We'll need to do my nightly interviews with Waller's questions after dinner, so nobody overdo it on the wine, okay?" We all lift surprised expressions at Shirley. I forgot about the interviews.

"Seriously? We haven't even begun the investigation," Evie asks.

"Seriously. It's part of the new requirements for field work," she informed us. Why hadn't Waller talked to me about this?

"You can use one of the upstairs bedrooms," I tell her.

"That'll work; they're meant to be private." She doesn't acknowledge me as she eats. The tension between us causes Charlie to clear his throat and ask some stupid question I'm not even listening to—something about what we wanted to be when we grew up.

Everyone takes turns. Some of the answers are lengthy and long-winded, and I'm glad because it gives me time to fume about having Shirley as a babysitter. I'm already finishing my dinner, and when the question gets to me, I scowl at him.

"A sister," I tell him, and Evie rolls her eyes at me.

Nobody says anything in response. I've killed the mood.

Confused, Charlie opens his mouth to ask me what I mean, but Evie grabs his hand before the words can even leave his mouth. I excuse myself from the table.

Washing my dish in the sink, I dry it and place it back in the cupboard. I do the same with the flatware when Evie appears at my elbow.

"That wasn't fair," she whispers. "Charlie's trying."

"Well, not all of us are into this to make friends."

She stops washing her plate. "I'm not your friend?"

"You know what I mean."

Her dark eyes hold mine for a moment. "Yeah, I think I do." She finishes the rest of her dishes in silence.

Shirley takes everyone to the bedroom one at a time, and then it's my turn. I primly sit on the edge of the single bed.

"This is dumb," I tell her.

"You've made your feelings perfectly clear," she says as she adjusts the lens. Satisfied, she sits on the other bed and gazes down at her paper. "How are you feeling about the progress of the investigation so far?"

"Indifferent. It hasn't started yet."

"Are there any concerns or fears you haven't shared with the team yet?"

"No." My voice is clipped.

"No?" I can tell I'm frustrating her.

"I've shared my concerns," I say with a shrug.

"How are your interactions with the other team members? Any notable conflicts or concerns?"

"Besides my conflict with you? No. Everyone else has been surprisingly pleasant."

Shirley's stern expression darts up from her notebook. "You're not being fair, Lydia. I came on to do a job."

"To be Waller's spy."

"Moving on," she says. "How have you been coping with the paranormal encounters? Are they affecting your emotional well-being?"

"No. I can't categorize anything so far as a paranormal encounter." My stubbornness infuses every word.

"Fine. Last question. Are there any specific experiences or encounters that have significantly impacted you today?" Shirley is almost smug at this question.

"Are you fucking kidding me? He won't see these until the end of the case, right?"

Shirley nods in agreement.

"Someone or something attacked me in the basement this afternoon, and I don't even know if it was the little girl I'm here to help. I don't think it was. I hope it wasn't. But it has me all kinds of fucked up. Is that a sufficient answer for you?"

"Yes," she sniffs. "Thank you for your *cooperation*."

"I need a stiff fucking drink," I tell her and move off the bed. Stopping at the door, I turn my attention back to her. "You coming, Henderson?"

Shirley follows me down, and the music and drinks are flowing much louder now. Cecilia and Charlie are cozied up on the loveseat, while the fire roars. Evie stands by the door with a glass of amber liquid, looking much more relaxed than when I left her. Hell, the four glasses of wine I had at dinner probably have me in the same state, though I'm too stubborn to admit it. Sam slips a song onto the record player and turns to me with finger guns.

"Hey, you're back." He's drunk. Probably. Hopefully. His big dark eyes light on me, and Shirley shuffles past me to join Evie by the open door after pouring her own drink.

Foghat's long guitar riffs start beating a rhythm into the room, and Sam spins over to me and grabs my fingers in his hands. He starts singing along to "I Just Wanna Make Love To You." It makes me laugh, loud and sharp. He's ridiculous.

Spinning me in his arms so my back presses to his chest, he makes me groove along to Foghat, and I hate to admit that I relax against him a little too easily. Closing my eyes, I let him spin me around the room.

Reaching into his pocket, he pulls out a small baggie and a few tabs of acid. "Open, Foxy," he mumbles roughly in my ear. One of his arms wraps around my waist, pulling me tightly to him. His breath dances across my lips, and I taste the whiskey and sweet smoke I'm starting to associate with him. And God help me—I stick my tongue out, and he places the tab on it, then closes my mouth and rubs his thumb across my lips. His fingers trail down my neck and push my hair off my shoulder. "Good girl," he whispers.

Sam releases me and passes the tabs around, insisting on placing all of them himself, just in case I thought I was special. With the song and spell over, I wander over to the makeshift bar and pour myself some of whatever Sam had been drinking.

Everyone takes the acid, including the beauty queen, so don't blame us later when we decide that skinny-dipping in the freezing pond where her sister drowned is the best idea ever. We're running up the hill, still cognizant enough to grab towels but not clear-minded enough to remember it's autumn in Massachusetts and goddamn cold.

The trees move in time to some music only we can hear this far from the carriage house, and the clouds are fat with rain. The rich earth and cattails beckon us to the water, and they jump in with gusto. We were explorers on a new planet, gardeners of Mars. Charlie and Cecilia splash in first. Cecilia yells that the last one to the floating dock has to howl at the moon.

The moon—had it ever been so big and bright? It's a spotlight, and we're the stars—stars in the sky, with the sky reflected in the pond. Evie and Shirley reach the dock first and tumble together in their underwear. Shirley pushes Evie's hair off her face, and they look beautiful. Sam's in the water, holding his hand and calling to me, and it's all perfect.

He's perfect: his curling black hair dripping with diamonds of water, all lean muscle and tan skin, and that gleaming smile of his. I start to strip and then remember that I can't.

I can't remember why I can't—until I do.

"N-no," I say, shaking my head. "I... I don't like deep water, Sam."

"It's okay, Foxy. It's okay. You don't have to go all the way in," he coaxes. "It's not deep here—just to your ankles. Baby steps, alright?"

The water is dark under the night sky, lapping at the small shore. Flashes of her washing up on a beach invade my mind, and I have to bend over at the waist to rid myself of something I have never actually seen. Just to the ankles, he said. Do I trust him?

My gaze lands on him, and my acid-addled brain decides I do. He won't push me farther than I can handle.

Pulling off the turtleneck strangling me, I rip my corduroys down and hop out of them, right into Sam's firm grip. All I'm wearing is my bralette and bikini briefs. They don't match, and I don't care.

His nose traces the side of my face, and I let him. His arms are wrapped around me, and he buries his face in the space between my neck and shoulder. Meanwhile, my traitorous arms slink around his neck like they have a mind of their own.

"I won't let you go too deep," he whispers. I'm shivering, and it's not entirely from the cold.

"It's dumb," I breathe, my eyes taking in the lack of space between us.

"Is it Octavia?"

I nod.

"It's not dumb." His knuckle dips beneath my chin, tilting my face to his. This is a terrible idea. The other four are already on the dock, as far as the moon in my mind's eye.

This is a *terrible* idea, so why can't I stop thinking about him? It's because Waller forbids it. That's all this is.

Right?

My gaze drops to his lips, and he does the same until neither of us can think of anything but how the other might taste. Then he freezes in my arms. His dreamy, dark eyes widen at something behind me, something on the shore.

"Sam?" I say, twisting around to see what he's staring at.

There's nothing on the shore.

"Sam?" He's shaking, all the color drained from his face. My fingers find his shoulders, and I jostle him. "Sam? You're scaring me."

Without tearing his eyes from the bank, he whispers roughly, "You don't see her?"

Oh *fuck*.

"See who? Sam, who do you see?" He doesn't answer me. "Sam!"

His shock is momentarily suspended—he grips me harder and drags me further into the water. Panic explodes in my chest, and I slap at him to keep him from doing the one thing he promised he wouldn't. "It's her. The girl. Lily."

"She's standing on the shore?"

"She's *screaming* on the shore, Lydia. And she's pointing at us. At all of us." I think he's going to be sick. *A bad trip*, I think. He's having a bad trip.

"Sam! Sam, we've got to get you out of the water. Let's warm you up." My eyes dart to the dock. Charlie is kissing Cecilia. I don't even have time to be annoyed. "Charlie! Shit! Charlie!" He stops what he's doing and spins around. "Sam's having a bad trip! Help me carry him back to the house!"

Pulling Sam toward the bank is a chore. He shakes his head down at me. "I can't. I fucking can't, Lydia. She's right there." I think he's going to cry.

My hands grab his cheeks and force his eyes to meet mine. "This is you, Sam. This is what you do, right? Look at me!" His eyes finally meet mine. I smash my lips against his, it's not romantic or sexy, but it gets him to breathe. "You're my psychic, Sam. Snap out of it!"

And he does. He pulls himself together. If anyone was on the shore, she's gone, and he lets me pull him out of the water. I yank my clothes back on and toss him his.

"Oh God," he says and vomits all over the cattails I found so poetic before.

I rub small circles into his back. "Let it all out."

Charlie and the rest are here now, and we lead Sam, who still hasn't dressed, back to the carriage house to wrap him in blankets and put him in front of the fire.

Running up to the bathroom, I splash cold water on my face. When I come back down, Cecilia is gone, and I'm relieved. It should only be us. I turn to Shirley and Evie.

"Shirley, your camera." She scowls at me suspiciously. "Now."

Whether she trusts me or not, she picks it up and starts rolling. I point her toward Sam, and I take a seat next to him on the floor, our backs leaning against the couch. "Tell me everything you saw."

To his credit, he does. He remembers every last detail, which makes me think it wasn't just the acid. I think he saw her. Annoyance and jealousy possess every inch of me. It doesn't seem fair. Pressing my lips together in a tight line, I take a deep breath and say those exact words on camera. Satisfied that we recorded the event, we all drift off—not to our beds, but huddled as a team on the floor before a dying fire.

The pounding on the front door wakes me in the morning. When I extricate myself from Sam's tight embrace and Evie's head on my lap, I'm greeted by the surliest-looking Waller I've ever seen.

"What the *fuck*, Lydia?"

CHAPTER *nine*

Waller glares at me, and as I attempt to close the front door, he shoves it open forcefully. "It's only been *one* day."

Turning on my bare heel, I try to walk away from him, but the commotion he's making is rousing the rest of the team. Waller grabs me by the shoulder and yanks me back. "Do not walk away from me," he says, his eyes flashing with cold fury.

"Don't touch me," I tell him, jerking away.

"I need you to explain why you told Shirley not to inform me you were attacked, Lydia," he hisses. His appearance suggests he hasn't slept, showered, or shaved.

"Because I knew you'd act overprotective and try to pull me out." I say, side-eyeing the team, particularly Charlie, who watches the confrontation with keen interest.

"You're damned right, I would. I'm going to. You're done. Pack your things. We didn't sign on for this."

Licking my lips, I glance over his shoulder to see Detective Quinn outside, looking exhausted as he leans against his Ford Galaxie 500. Waller must have called Quinn. *Damn.*

"Let me wash my face and use the restroom. When I'm done, I'll explain why I tried to keep Shirley quiet." I turn to Charlie. "Can you make some coffee?" He nods but doesn't take his eyes off Waller.

The professor, however, isn't finished with me and follows me up the stairs. Snatching my wrist, he drags me into one of the bedrooms. "I wasn't done with you, young lady."

"You're not my father, James," I snap back. "Let me go."

"This wasn't part of our deal," he says, his face inches from mine. He's seething. Honestly, I've never seen him this angry.

I glance down; he still hasn't let go of my wrist. "What is your problem?" I dig my nails into his skin, forcing him to release me.

"Because nobody touches what's *mine.*" He grips me by the chin when I try to turn away, pushing me against the door.

"I'm not *yours.*"

A dull knock comes from the other side of the wood behind my head. "What?" Waller growls.

"Lydia? Are you okay?" *Sam.*

"Get rid of him," Waller instructs me.

My heart is pounding so hard that I can feel it in my eardrums. "It's fine, Sam. Just a misunderstanding. I'll be down in a minute." I lift my fingers to Waller's, gently stroking the back of his hand. "I'm okay, James. I'm safe. This isn't like Tavi."

His grip loosens, and he lets out a shaky breath, resting his forehead against mine. "I promised your father—"

"This isn't about my father," I say through gritted teeth, struggling to keep my emotions in check. "Let's not pretend this is about my father."

As if realizing how close he is to me, he pulls away from the door and readjusts his horn-rim glasses. "I'm sorry. Shirley said someone jumped you in the basement and tore your blouse open, and I... I feared the worst. I thought I sent you into something terrible."

Still shaking from his unhinged outburst, I lift my fingers to brush the sleeve of his tweed jacket. "I'm okay."

He appears unconvinced. "Let me see."

"No."

"No?" His eyebrow arches in disbelief.

"It's inappropriate. I'll show you my arm and neck if you let me change in private, but not my chest. They're just some shallow scratches."

With a narrowed gaze, he steps out, and I release a shaky exhale as I sit on the edge of the bed. My hair reeks of pond water, and I'm desperate for a shower. I remove the turtleneck and slip into a light V-neck sleep shirt.

Opening the door, I allow him to inspect my neck and the nasty cut on the inside of my left forearm. "What did this to you?"

"I don't know." I hand him the Polaroid I got of my attacker.

"You don't want to tell Carmichael," Waller surmises, sitting on the bed. I take a seat on the one opposite him.

"He'll pull us off the case if he thinks there's a liability issue looming."

To my surprise, Waller nods in agreement, the fight drained from him. He self-consciously tries to tame his disheveled hair, which sticks up in all directions as if he's been tugging at it all night.

I know I'll have to answer to Detective Quinn as well, but I'm determined to have a damned shower before then. "We need to stay. The little girl—"

"Lily," he interjects.

"No, James. The one still alive, damn it." I focus my gaze on the rug between us. "*Emily*. She's in a bad spot, and I'm worried she might be in danger."

"Any activity?"

"Sam saw Lily out at the pond last night," I tell him, and he gives me a pointed, weary look. "And I *believe* him. But, here's the thing, and you'll hate me for this."

"I'm listening," he says as he removes his glasses and cleans them with a cloth he's pulled from his pocket.

"I think he's more sensitive when he's... compromised."

"Compromised? How so? Drunk?"

"LSD," I clarify, eliminating any further guessing.

"Okay." To his credit, he doesn't sound angry. "LSD has been used in our field for nearly a decade now. That doesn't surprise me. Do you have your medical pack with you?"

"Of course," I reassure him. "But you realize we can't prove anything if Sam requires a certain amount of *elevation* to see beyond the veil, right?" He closes his eyes, taking a deep breath before nodding. "And there's something else. I think Emily is having a twin connection to Lily."

This piques his interest, as I knew it would. "It's because of her age."

I can't help but nod. "I think it's because of her age."

"More activity during puberty," he murmurs.

Closing my eyes, I hum in disdain for a sliver of a moment. "Please don't start with that patriarchal, misogynistic nonsense, James."

"Documented studies aside, I suspected you and Octavia were too old when the incident occurred."

"The *incident*?" I leap to my feet. "The fucking *incident*? Get out. I'm going to take a shower, and then have some coffee and toast. Afterward, I'll talk to Quinn before he rushes into the basement, gun and badge out."

Waller's face darkens as he stands. "Very well," he says, closing the distance between us. He tilts my chin up to force my gaze on him. "But you *will* behave, Lydia. Is that understood?"

"I'm not a child."

"This isn't about you being a child. This is about your severe lack of respect for the rules I lay out for your team. You *will* follow them, or I will pull you out of the field." Before I can argue, he leaves the room, and I collapse onto the bed, burying my face in my trembling hands.

After a quick shower and a meager breakfast, I relay everything I told Waller to Quinn. He seems uninterested in my concern that Carmichael will chase us off his estate. "If you press charges, we can issue a search warrant for the basement."

"And where does that leave Emily? You find whatever is in the basement, and then you leave. What happens to Emily afterward? He won't let us set foot on this property again. There's more going on here, and the basement is just part of it."

The rest of the team sits with us at the breakfast table. Evie glances at Quinn and sighs. "I think she's right. Something isn't adding up here."

Detective Quinn's stern gaze sweeps over all of us. "So, tell me, eggheads, what should I do here? I mean, I'm a cop. Lydia got attacked. What am I supposed to do about that?"

"Hold on to it, and we'll probably just add to it the longer we're here. I have extensive documentation on everything that happened in the basement, and I'll gladly turn that over to you if it comes to prosecution," Shirley says, sipping her coffee. "But I'll tell you right now: None of us are going to be caught alone in that basement again if that's what you're worried about."

Quinn nods.

"And it's likely not going anywhere in the next few days," Charlie adds. "And I'm going to set up some equipment down there today. Hopefully, we'll have an answer for you by tomorrow."

Waller is leaning against the wood paneling assessing how to broach the LSD event with a cop in the room. "I understand you guys took a trip last night." He eyes Quinn carefully.

We shrug at each other. "It was mostly uneventful, except for Sam," I say.

Sam avoids eye contact, staring into his mug. "It wasn't ideal, man."

"We'll discuss it before I leave today," Waller says. "I'm going to the Hall to have Mr. Carmichael sign our standard contract, and then we'll maybe take a turn around the pond, Mr. Hassan."

"Yeah, boss. Whatever you want." My chest aches to hear Sam so... un-Sam-like.

"Charlie, you're with me today," I tell him. "I want to see this rig you've pitched."

"Yeah, but I only have enough equipment for one spot, so we'll need to choose the best location," Charlie says, trying hard not to show his eagerness.

I lock eyes with Waller as I tell Charlie, "But I won't be the one helping you set up in the basement." Waller nods once, a silent reminder to *behave.*

"I'm going to need some petty cash today," Evie says, fiddling with the teardrop turquoise pendant dangling from a long chain around her neck.

"What for?" the professor demands.

"Supplies. We need to eat." She gestures toward the kitchen with a flick of her hand.

"You have a trust fund," he reminds her.

"And this is basically my *job*, but I'm not getting *paid*." Her brows knit together, making it clear she won't tolerate any objections. "Also," she glances at me with a questioning look, seeking permission to share the other reason she's going into town. I nod. "I'm going to investigate the Carmichaels. I will hit the courthouse and the library and gather as much information as possible."

"I'll give you a ride and help out with that," Quinn offers.

It catches me off guard. "Really?"

"Yes, really. I'm not going to abandon you here to do my job for me, Lydia, no matter how little you think of our investigation unit." He winks at me, causing Waller to scowl.

"While you're at the courthouse, make sure you request a copy of the blueprints for Hemlock Hall and an ordinance map of the area. When you return, we need to coax Emily out of her room so Charlie can set up some equipment. You, Sam, and I can then talk to Emily more. I want Sam to rule out a few things."

"You're talking about a poltergeist," Sam says dully.

"Yes, and you know why." His avoidance of me is for the best. I'm mortified over how I acted toward him yesterday. It's best to stay professional about the whole thing.

"If she's started her menses, it could account for some of the activity." Sam doesn't look at me as he says it but winces at the implication. "I'd like it noted that I disagree. It's an outdated notion, not to mention fucking bogus when it comes to women."

Shirley glances up from her camera. "Wait. What?"

Waller clears his throat. "Certain parapsychologists, myself not included, tend to point to the cause of a poltergeist being rooted into female rage if a pubescent female resides in the house. For academic credibility, we have to rule out Emily's age as a factor in the phenomena happening in Hemlock Hall."

The expression on Shirley's face shifts from disbelief to disgust to unadulterated fury. "Uh-uh, no. I know you're not going to blame a twelve-year-old girl who just lost her twin sister."

"No, we're not," I tell her, though I'm glaring at Waller. "It's not my fault that our field is full of old men who are afraid of periods, but that's the reality of it." My gaze now turns to Shirley. "We're going to *disprove* it."

Satisfied with that answer, she returns to filming. Charlie, on the other hand, is practically bouncing in his seat. "We should set up the PDU in the living area."

"PDU?"

"That's the rig you were asking about. I named it myself." He practically beams. "Phantasm Detecting Unit."

"No," I tell him. "We're not calling that."

"What does it do, Charlie?" Evie asks, glancing up from the book spread across her lap.

"Okay, so to avoid wasting film, this device triggers the camera and sound equipment to start recording based on noise, temperature changes, or drafts." Charlie's grin is so broad that I'm unsure whether we're expected to cheer or simply acknowledge his pride.

"How does it work?" Quinn asks, and to his credit, he sounds genuinely interested.

"The camera and tape recorder are hooked up to some photo-electric cells and this noise detector. It also responds to vibrations, an electric bulb, this wire circuit, and my electronic thermometer. If the temperature drops suddenly by five degrees or more, it activates the camera and audio equipment. Oh! And there's a weather vane, so if the breeze shifts direction, the camera and recorder start recording."

Okay, maybe I'm a little impressed. "You have to link all those components together?"

Charlie nods enthusiastically. "It's a mainline from the camera, and I attach wires like branches to the central line."

"It's a SPRIG," Evie says softly.

"SPRIG?" Charlie turns to Evie, puzzled.

"Like a sprig of rosemary, except it's wires. It's a spooky rig—a SPRIG." Evie crosses her arms over her chest as everyone stares at her. "Oh, c'mon, the name was *right* there."

I tongue my back molar for a moment to keep from laughing at Charlie's expression. "Seriously, it's far better than PDU."

"Fine," Charlie concedes.

"Why the living area?" I ask him.

"Honestly? It's the biggest room, and... the PD—the SPRIG—takes up quite a bit of space. I hope to consolidate everything one day, but not today."

I nod. "How about we decide where to set it up after Sam talks to Emily?" Sam doesn't lift his head at the mention of his name. I should talk to him. Even Waller is glancing between Sam and me now. "Personally, and I genuinely mean *personally,* I think it should be set up in the basement."

Nobody responds. Waller's stare is so intense that I feel pinned to my seat. He needs to get over this. Pushing away from where he leans, he clears his throat. "I'm going up to the house to talk to Carmichael."

Quinn rises as well. "Do you want me to come?"

"No, this will be delicate. Having law enforcement present might intimidate him." Waller turns to the rest of us. "It's not easy for a grown man, particularly from a certain generation, to admit that he needs help from an outside source regarding his family's safety. I suspect it will take a significant amount of pride-swallowing for him to admit that he needs us."

I wish he'd let me accompany him right now. Observing how he handles this 'delicate' situation would be beneficial, but I'm sure he'll dismiss it as 'man-talk.'

"Well," Quinn turns to Evie, "you have a list? I guess that means you and I can start our own investigation." Evie nods and gathers her bag of books and notepads.

"Shirley, do you want to join Charlie and me?" I ask her.

"Yeah, let me grab some extra gear," she replies, heading into the sitting room to rummage through some camera cases.

"Take your time. I'm sure Charlie has a full wagon to go through."

"Full van," Charlie corrects me, then heads out the door.

Now it's just Sam and me at the dining table. "Sam—"

"If I'm not needed until later, I think I'd like to lie down for a bit, if you don't mind, pretty momma." He gets up but still avoids my gaze.

"Sam, wait." He pauses in the doorway but doesn't turn around. "Don't you think we should talk?"

"I had a bad trip, that's all. It happens to the best of us," he says, continuing past Shirley on his way upstairs. I swallow. That wasn't what I wanted to discuss.

"Just give him some space," Shirley says. "He's processing some heavy shit."

"Speaking of heavy shit." I spin around to face her. "Do you have anything to say to me?"

"Like what?" Her dark eyes narrow.

"Like the fact that you fucking called Waller when I asked you to fetch Charlie and Evie yesterday? I told you not to."

"You're not my boss, Lydia, though you sure act like it." Shirley places her hands on her hips. "Waller's my boss."

"When we're *here,* I'm your boss. You're either a team player, or a rat."

"You run your team like a dictatorship. You act like you're the ultimate authority on every decision."

"I'm the team leader, so yes." My heart pounds. Does everyone see me like this?

"You want me to be a team player? Then act like we're a damn team and not your fucking underlings," Shirley snaps, picking up her gear bag. "I'll be outside when you're ready to stop acting a fool and actually work on this case."

I check my reflection in the mirror beside the door to make sure I've covered yesterday's scratches. I hate the girl staring back at me. Pushing my pale blond hair away, I see the purple bags under my eyes from lack of sleep. My hands shake, and I blame the caffeine, though I know better. This is all falling apart, and we haven't even begun.

Waller was out of line earlier, and I have no idea why. I was genuinely afraid of my godfather, and he'd never scared me before. That's a problem for later. Right now, we need to set up for tonight, and I need to figure out if a twelve-year-old girl is manifesting her own haunting.

"Get your shit together," I tell the girl in the mirror and head out the door.

CHAPTER ten

We drive the van up to the manor due to the sheer volume of equipment Charlie insists on bringing inside. Standing in front of the large double doors, I hesitate to knock. Waller came here to have Carmichael sign our contract, which grants us unfettered access to the house and any outbuildings that may have experienced paranormal activity.

I need to be the one in charge.

Tilting my chin up and straightening my spine, I open the door and walk in. Marian looks unimpressed. Placing her hands on her ample hips, she frowns at me. "What's the meaning of this?"

"We'll be in and out all day," I say. "You'd better get used to us now."

"You *should* be using the service entrance, then."

"*I'm* not a servant. And we've already had this conversation."

Charlie and Shirley enter behind me, carrying hard cases for the cameras. "I know you wanted to talk to Emily first, but could you help me take some readings in the main entrance and sitting room?" Charlie asks.

This is directed at me, of course, because Shirley's role is merely to shadow us and document our actions. "What do you have in mind?"

"First, let's get a base temperature and radiation reading in these rooms. Then, I want to use the voltmeter to ensure we don't have any faulty connections that could spook us later."

"Dad would've liked you," I tell him.

"You think? He's the reason I came to Shelley." As he unpacks gear, he avoids looking at me.

"He used to say that you eliminate anything that might be misconstrued. That's his number one rule. Check the plumbing, check the power, check the temperature. You're missing one thing, though, Boy Wonder."

Charlie spins around to face me as if caught off guard by a pop quiz. Shirley looks up from the camera's viewfinder. "Geographical maps. What's the soil composition? Is it causing the house to settle and creak?"

My shock must be evident. "How did you know that?"

"Unlike some of you, I do my homework." She holds up a copy of *Leylines and Strata* by Courtland Fox.

"Hey," Charlie interjects, "I have that book too. Maps just aren't my thing."

"Well, you're going to have to make them your thing because not all of our field assignments are as cushy as this," Waller says as he walks in with Mr. and Mrs. Carmichael. "Some of them are out in the woods, in the middle of nowhere."

Charlie visibly shudders. Shirley does as well, I note. *Not fans of the outdoors.*

Waller hands me the signed contract. "They only ask that you avoid the basement as much as possible. It is unfinished and lacks power." He raises his eyebrows to ensure I understand.

"Will do," I say, snatching the paper bundle out of his hands.

"The Carmichaels have a rally in Boston today, so they will be gone overnight. I expect you to do the bulk of the investigation to narrow down what exactly is happening to their daughter tonight."

One night? "But—"

"We understand if this timeframe isn't feasible," Mrs. Carmichael says. It's the first time I've heard her speak. "However, Professor Waller has assured us that you can at least limit your investigation to," she turns to Waller, "hot spots? We would prefer not to have a group of college students roaming our halls all night."

Message received. I look down at my watch. It's 9 AM. We have approximately twenty-four hours to figure out where to focus our attention. Charlie and I exchange looks.

"I'm going to head back to my office, darling," Waller says, brushing a strand of hair behind my ear. "I trust there will be no further *incidents* in my absence." His gaze is stern, despite the gentleness of his voice.

"Yes, *sir*," I reply through a strained smile.

"*Good*. Mr. Song and Ms. Henderson, I wish you luck with your endeavors tonight. Chin up and have lots of coffee. I've been in your unenviable shoes before, and I know how long the nights run." He turns to the clients. "Mr. Carmichael, Mrs. Carmichael," he says by way of farewell and strides out the door.

My breath hitches in my chest when he's finally gone.

"That would be us off as well. Cecilia is here if you need anything, Ms. Fox."

"Thank you, Mr. Carmichael."

They leave, and it's just the three of us now. I drop onto the stiff, formal couch. "I'm going outside to smoke if anyone wants to join me," Shirley says.

"Maybe in a minute," I mumble.

As soon as she's out the door, Charlie kneels in front of me. "Are you alright? Is he always like that? Holy shit, Lydia, nobody should talk to you like that. You get that, right?"

"I don't know what you mean." I know *exactly* what he means.

"I saw how he treated you this morning. We all saw it."

"He worries. After what happened to my sister, he's become a bit… overprotective."

"That wasn't overprotective. That was crossing into abusive territory."

"It's fine, Charlie."

"What happened to your sister? I mean, everyone around here acts like they know, and you make strange offhand comments about it, but nobody will let me ask."

I make a show of studying my hands in my lap before looking up at him. "The summer before our senior year, Octavia went missing. She was kidnapped. It was all over the local news. I'm surprised it didn't make it to Chicago."

"Did you ever find her?"

My tongue digs into my molar before I nod. "A year later. Her body was fished out of Lake Cohaquet, postnatal."

"Post—oh!" His cheeks flush crimson. Pressing his lips together, I watch the blush deepen into something more akin to anger. "Did they catch the son of a bitch who did it?"

"No," I reply simply.

"And that's why you're here. Doing these things. You're trying to contact your sister." He searches my eyes for confirmation.

"That's part of it. The other part is that the department is entangled in my inheritance. I can't access the money they left me until I turn 27. Until then, I'm bound by my executor."

Charlie swallows. I swear if an ounce of pity crosses his face, I will punch it. "Professor Waller."

"Yep," I confirm, rising to my feet. Wiping my hands on my corduroy skirt, I survey the room. "But that doesn't mean I'm not good at this."

"I never thought you weren't. Did you think that I thought that?"

Smoothing the hair that falls over my shoulder, I regard him carefully. "I think everyone thinks that all the time."

"Well, it's ridiculous." We stand there awkwardly.

"What's all this?" Cecilia asks as she emerges from the kitchen.

There's a large grandfather clock, at least twelve feet tall, standing next to the archway. I check the time. *How is it already a quarter to twelve?*

I glance down at my watch and see it's only 9:10. The clock is silent. "You should have that clock checked."

Cecilia shrugs and gives Charlie a wide smile. "Are you going to show me how it all works today, like you promised?"

He gives a peculiar chuckle and pulls an electronic thermometer from his bag. "Sure. We were just about to check the ambient temperature in all the rooms downstairs. Do you want to help?"

Cecilia's gaze flickers over to me. "I'd love to help."

"Lydia, could you grab the Geiger counter and the red notebook? I've set it up, so all you need to do is input your readings into the boxes. I need you to cover the center of the room and the four corners, and record your observations in the notebook. We'll repeat this process tonight before any activity, and then, hopefully, during or after the activity."

"You're the only person I know that *hopes* to see a ghost, Charlie," Cecilia teases him.

"We'll need to do this upstairs as well," I remind him, but he's already off with the beauty queen. Shirley arrives a minute or so after they head to the conservatory.

"Where are those two off to?" Shirley asks.

"I think she's going to use the candlestick on Charlie in the conservatory if you know what I mean."

Shirley fights a smile. "You're all right, Fox. I wasn't sure about you before, but I get it."

"You get what?"

"This bad bitch persona. It's all an act."

My eyebrows lift, and I take a half-step back. "What makes you say that?"

"I grew up in the public eye, but you were thrust into it as a teenager on the worst day of your life. You had to develop some kind of armor."

Public eye? "Oh! I... I had no idea. I didn't realize—"

"Do *not* tell me you just realized my mom is Dottie Henderson." She looks at me incredulously. "Wow. And here I thought you didn't like me because of my family."

"No," I say with a laugh. "It was just you."

Crossing her arms over her chest, she surveys me with a new perspective. "That's... well, I'll be honest. That's actually refreshing."

"Always glad to be of service."

Shirley snorts. "No, you're not. But I'll take it." Taking a step back, she surveys the room. "I don't feel anything. Hell, I haven't felt anything since I got here. Am I faulty or something?"

Frowning, I chew the inside of my lip. "Sometimes it takes a bit. Do you want to be able to sense something?"

"Maybe? I don't know. I'm not sure I believe any of this hocus-pocus."

"Good," I tell her, and I mean it. "It's good to have a skeptic on the team. It keeps us honest."

"You're a skeptic too, though. I see how you look at Sam, trying to figure out whether he's full of shit or not."

"Oh, Sam's definitely full of shit, but I guess you could say I'm agnostic. If Charlie finds me some hard data or I see something that *all* of you see, then I might believe. But until then, this is all speculation and... hope."

"You want there to be something more."

"I need there to be something more."

"How long did you know the camera was on?" Shirley asks.

"The moment you turned it on. You always back up before you film." Taking a deep breath, I rifle through Charlie's bag for the Geiger counter. "Thank you for being aware that I don't like the camera pointed at me. But please try to avoid tricking me in the future."

She nods slowly.

"Now, if you'd like to get some super boring footage of me measuring the radiation levels in the room, you're more than welcome. Just... no more prying questions?"

"Deal."

The rest of the morning passes in a blur of measuring and recording, with Charlie's notebooks filling up as we work. Shirley trails behind us, half-listening and half-absorbed in the chatter between Charlie and me about our progress. Once we finish with all the rooms except the bedrooms and Carmichael's study, we head towards the pond, Cecilia unfortunately in tow.

"It's much harder to get readings outside," Charlie explains to Cecilia. "Also, I'm pretty sure we'll need to station two people here tonight." He pauses, considering. "Do you think Quinn would be willing to stick around to help?"

"I doubt Detective Quinn will be available. He'll have work in the morning, whereas we don't have any pressing schedule," I reply.

Sam approaches us, and I realize we're standing in the very spot where he had his vision the night before. "Hey," he greets us. "Sorry about earlier, amigos. I guess I just fell off."

"You've got nothing to apologize for," Charlie says with an easy smile. He seems relaxed in a way that suggests he didn't grow up in the rigid society that I suspect the rest of us did, Sam included.

"Are you feeling better?" I ask him quietly, trying to keep it between us.

"Yeah, pretty momma, no need to worry about me." He still avoids eye contact. "You still wanted to talk to the kid today, right?"

I nod. "Yes, but we're also trying to figure out what to do about the pond tonight."

Sam glances from the ground to the pond, then turns his back on us to gaze up at the house. "Don't stress about the pond. She'll be where us or her sister is tonight. No need to chase her. I'm pretty sure she'll come to us."

Goosebumps blossom beneath my cardigan sleeves.

"Well, that's one problem solved," Charlie says, relief evident in his voice. "Let's see if you two can coax Emily out of her room so I can set up some equipment and get base readings before sunset."

I check my watch. It's a little after two in the afternoon. I wish Evie were here; she had a knack for dealing with Emily. Clearing my throat, I look over at Cecilia. "We'll need Marian's help to tidy up Emily's room so Charlie can set up. Can you assist with that?"

Cecilia scowls, as though I've asked her to clean her little sister's room herself. "She let you in yesterday?"

"Yes, she did."

The beauty queen huffs at this, and Shirley and I exchange a glance. "Shirley, would you mind helping Sam and me with the interview in the sitting room? Let's keep it subtle—we don't want to overwhelm Emily."

"I can be subtle," Shirley reassures me.

With a determined nod, I head back to the manor. "I'll bring her down to the sitting room. Maybe I can persuade her to take a quick shower," I mutter to myself. I had considered asking Cecilia for help, but I sensed Emily wouldn't respond well to her sister's authority.

Outside Emily's door, I hesitate before knocking, opting instead to listen. Shadows dance beneath the narrow beam of light seeping from under the door, just as they did yesterday. Emily is pacing and muttering.

"No, it's a terrible idea. Yes, I know what happened in the basement. No, you're not listening, she's *nice*. I don't want anything to happen to her." It's like eavesdropping on one side of a phone conversation, but I don't remember seeing a phone in Emily's room yesterday. "What do you *mean* she's right outside?"

Emily's shadow abruptly stills. A second shadow appears in front of her, and I catch my breath. "Emily?" I call through the door. "Is someone else in there with you?"

"*Go,*" she hisses at the other shadow. "No!" she snaps back. "Just give me a minute!" After a few moments of shuffling noises and the muffled sound of a door closing, she unlocks her room. "Come in."

Swallowing hard, I twist the handle and push the door open. "Who were you talking to just now?"

"I wasn't talking to anyone," she replies, though her damp, sweaty hair betrays her unease.

"I heard you speaking to someone in here."

She flops onto her bed with a sigh. "Did you need something?"

"Do you think we could get you out of your room and downstairs so my friend Sam can have a word with you?"

Her gaze darts around her messy room. "I don't know."

"Please? It would really help us—and Lily—if you could come downstairs." She nibbles her lip, clearly torn. "Also, Charlie wants to set up some equipment in here, just in case you experience anything unusual tonight.

Her mouth twists in disgust. "A visit from who? Who do you think is coming into my room at night?"

I take a step back, realizing I've touched a nerve. "Whoa. I'm your friend, remember? I'm just here to help."

Emily closes her eyes, exhaling heavily. "You're really not going to leave until you've done everything you can, are you?"

"Nope."

"Fine," she says with a resigned roll of her eyes. "Let me get dressed."

I don't push the issue of the shower. "Can Marian tidy up in here a bit if she promises not to touch Lily's bed or clothes?"

Emily swallows hard, her eyes glistening with unshed tears. "Only if she promises not to touch Lily's things."

"Okay, I'll make sure she knows. We'll even leave her a note to remind her. But Charlie needs a little space to set up his equipment. That will be alright, won't it? We'll take everything out in the morning, I promise. He also needs to take some readings now to measure the temperature and other things, and then again after dark to check for any changes. It's how we assess paranormal activity. You understand, right?"

"Yeah. I'm not dumb," she replies, heading to her closet. After she dresses, she hands me her hairbrush. "Would you help me with my hair? Lily and I used to brush each other's hair before."

Taking the brush gingerly, I lick my lips and kneel down to her level. "Of course I can. I understand." And I did. Oh, how well I understood.

Sitting on Lily's bed, I brush and braid Emily's hair, recalling the nights when Octavia and I would do the same. We'd always do a double-dutch braid before bed so we'd have matching waves for school in the morning.

"You ready to go meet Sam?"

"Lily told me about him."

I freeze in the doorway. "What did she say about him?"

"She said she scared him last night, but she didn't mean to. Lily thinks he's nice, but he's sad."

Swallowing hard at her words, I nod. "Emily, did we wake you up last night?"

"No, why?"

"We were pretty loud by the pond. I just wanted to apologize in case we disturbed you."

Emily took my hand and pulled me down the hall after placing a sign on her door for Marian and securing it with a puppy sticker. "You guys didn't wake me up, Lydia. Lily told me about it this morning."

He's nice, but he's sad.

Sam?

CHAPTER
eleven

When we return to the sitting room, Sam is waiting for us. He has started a fire in the fireplace and sits on the hassock in front of the couch. Classical music plays softly from the record player, and a couple of candles flicker on the coffee table, casting a warm glow over the room.

It seems we've gone all out for this session. Emily surveys the room. Shirley is in the corner behind a tripod, her camera poised. Charlie's equipment is scattered near the front door, as he hasn't set up the SPRIG yet. He enters, still drying his hands from the bathroom.

"Hey," he greets Emily. She blushes slightly and ducks behind me.

"It's okay. That's Charlie. He'll be setting up equipment in your room to monitor it," I reassure her.

"Hi," Emily murmurs.

"I'm going to take these upstairs and capture some baseline readings for your room. Do you know what those are?" Charlie asks, showing her the instruments.

"Yes. Lydia explained," Emily responds. She steps out from behind me, intrigued by the gadgets.

"This one measures temperature," he says, holding up an electronic thermometer. "This one detects radiation, but don't worry about that; it rarely changes. Okay?" Emily nods. "I'm also going to check for drafts, and this is a voltmeter to make sure there aren't any faulty connections causing your lights to flicker. It also helps me ensure my equipment won't overheat if it's running all night." He glances at me, then back at Emily. "I wanted to check with you before going up while Marian is cleaning your room."

Emily considers for a moment. "You won't mess up the bed on the right?"

Charlie gives me a quick glance before responding. "I promise."

"And you won't move the stuffed animals?"

"Wouldn't dream of it." He offers his hand to seal the promise.

To my surprise, she shakes his hand. "Okay."

Charlie grins. "Okay!" He gathers his gear bag and notebooks and heads for the staircase.

Emily looks at me expectantly. I clear my throat. "The lady behind the camera is Shirley. She's a documentarian, which means she records everything that happens here so other parapsychologists can learn from your case."

Emily nods politely to Shirley, then turns to Sam. "You're Sam."

His eyebrows arch in surprise. "That's me. You can call me Spooky or Spooky Sam. But Sam I am, little lady."

Emily crosses the room and sits on the couch across from him. He tactfully avoids drawing attention to the numerous bandages covering the slurs carved into her skin. Clearing her throat, she looks at Sam with a serious expression. "Lily says she's sorry for scaring you last night."

Sam rubs the back of his neck and glances at me for a moment. I offer a slight shrug.

"Well, that's alright," he says to her. "We're all just getting to know each other, right?" Emily nods. "And sometimes, when we're figuring each other out, we step on toes. Your sister? She just stepped on mine a bit last night. I wasn't expecting that."

"You're funny."

His gaze flickers up to meet mine. "So I've been told." He claps his hands and nods to Shirley, who mimics the motion. "I'm going to talk to you a little about Lily. Not about that day, because I'm not a pig, so what happened that day is your business. And you shouldn't talk to pigs without a grown-up. You picking up what I'm laying down?"

"Yes, sir," she replies, her voice brightening.

I realize I've been staring at him and quickly look away. With a slight shake of my head, I settle into an armchair, giving him space to continue.

He presses on. "So, see these candles? One blue, one yellow?" She nods. "I want you to pick the one you like best and focus on the flame while we chat. Watch the fire dance, and if the flame jumps off the wick, raise one finger for me. Can you do that?"

"I can do that. That's easy."

"Super chill, momma. Easy as pie."

Shirley and I exchange amused glances.

Emily situates herself and fixes her gaze on the yellow candle.

"Alright, I'm going to ask some questions that'll sound lame at first, but bear with me." She nods slightly, signaling her readiness. He begins, "How old are you?"

"Twelve."

"What color is your hair?"

"Blond."

"How old is Lily?"

"Twelve."

"What color is her hair?"

"Blond."

"How many letters are in your name?"

"Five."

"How many letters are in Lily's name?"

"Four."

"How many minutes apart were you born?"

"Twelve."

"Who is older?"

"Lily."

"What's the name of the house you live in?"

"Hemlock Hall."

"What color is the rug in your bedroom?"

"Rose."

"Where does Lily live?"

"In my closet." She raises a finger.

"How old are you?"

"Twelve."

"How old will you be next year?"

"Thirteen."

"How old is Lily?"

"Twelve."

"How old will Lily be next year?"

"Twelve." She raises another finger. Shirley and I exchange glances; her eyes widen as she retreats behind her camera.

"Where were you at midnight last night?"

"In my bed."

"Where was Lily?"

"In my closet."

"What were you doing?"

"Sleeping."

"What was Lily doing?"

"Listening." She raises another finger.

"What was she listening for?"

"Danger."

"Why does she listen for danger?"

"To protect me."

"What did she hear?"

"You." She raises a finger.

"What was I doing?"

"Protecting the fox."

Shirley's eyebrows shoot up in surprise. I swallow hard.

"What did Lily do?"

"She followed you."

"Why?"

"She was curious."

"What did she see?"

"Swimming. Kissing. Danger."

"Where was the danger?"

"In the pond."

"What did Lily do when she found it?"

"I pointed at it and screamed." She raises another finger, her voice louder.

"You weren't at the pond, Emily," Sam says, his voice catching as he uses her name.

"I pointed at it and screamed. You were scared."

My breath hitches in my throat.

"The fox was scared. You were scared. Everyone will be scared!"

Sam claps his hands together and blows out the candles. His fingers tremble as he wipes them on his jeans.

Emily blinks, looking at us. "I thought you were going to ask me some questions."

Sam presses his knuckles to his lips, taking a deep breath. His eyes lock onto mine, silently pleading for me to take over.

"I think we've had enough questions for today, don't you? And I'm starving. Would you like to join the team for dinner since your parents are out for the night?" I suggest.

"It's lasagna night. Do you guys like lasagna? Marian makes the best," Emily responds.

"I love lasagna," Sam says, standing up as Emily leads him into the kitchen to help prepare dinner. I don't miss the lingering look he gives me before disappearing through the archway.

Evie walks into the sitting room. "Hey, everyone," she says. "Oh! Hi, Emily!" Emily waves at her before continuing into the kitchen.

"Long day?" I ask, noticing her bloodshot eyes.

"Like you wouldn't believe," Evie replies, collapsing onto the couch.

"Where's Quinn?"

"He dropped me off and said he needed to follow up on some leads. He'll call the manor if he finds anything interesting."

"Didn't even come in to say goodbye," I mutter.

"Don't tell me you're interested in Detective Hot Pants," Evie teases, unraveling her scarf and raising an eyebrow at me.

"No, I just wanted to run some things by him."

"Mm-hmm," she responds skeptically. "We got food. I unpacked it in the guest house. But I'm too tired to cook."

"It's lasagna night, and we're Senator-free until tomorrow morning."

"Oh, God, say it again," she pleads.

I lean in close and whisper sweetly, "Lasagna, garlic bread, green beans, red wine."

"You're my best friend," she sighs, leaning back in relief.

Shirley snorts. "We gonna tell her about that interview that went so far left-field I can't wrap my head around it?"

My eyes dart to the kitchen, where Emily and Sam had disappeared. Charlie comes downstairs and finds us in the sitting room. "You're back," he nods at Evie. "Did you find anything interesting?"

"Maybe. I have the map you wanted and the blueprints," she says to me. "I also stopped by the Presby church and got some birth records going back to the turn of the century, which might be overdoing it. But I figure if a job's worth doing…"

"Yeah, yeah," I cut her off. "We're about to have dinner, Charlie. Is everything set for Emily's room?"

"Yep. I've got her bed, the window, and the closet door in the shot, just as you suggested," Charlie replies, taking Evie's blueprints and ordnance map and placing them with his SPRIG equipment. "We'll set up the rig here after dinner. By the way, has anyone seen Cece?"

I raise an eyebrow. "Oh, it's 'Cece' now?"

Charlie rolls his eyes.

Speak of the devil, and she appears. "I'm here. Marian told me you're all staying for dinner at the manor."

"I'll bet she did," I mutter, and Evie gently elbows me.

"Are you already done interrogating my little sister?"

"It wasn't an interrogation. The police interrogate; we conduct interviews," Shirley retorts with a sniff.

"Whatever." Cecilia waves her hand dismissively. "So, finished with your interview?"

I nod.

"Are you all going to be in the house all night? Seems a bit excessive if you ask me."

"We didn't," I grumble.

Cecilia smiles, but it doesn't reach her eyes. "Let's go eat, Charlie. You must be starving." She loops her arm around Charlie's and leads him through the archway.

When we reach the dining table, Sam is already seated across from Emily. "Emily was just telling me about their nickname," he says as we sit down. I take the seat next to Sam, with Evie on my right. Cecilia claims the head of the table—I assume it's reserved for her father—with Charlie on her right. Shirley sits next to Charlie.

"Oh yes, Emilily. I actually love it," I respond to Sam's comment.

"Did you and Octavia have one?" Cecilia asks, pouring herself a glass of wine.

I pause with the salad bowl in my hands. "No," I reply. "We weren't nearly as creative." Emily smiles at my comment.

"Too bad. It could've been Lydavia or Octydia." I wonder why Cecilia is trying to provoke me.

"Well," I say, serving myself some salad, "I guess we'll never know, will we?" I pass the bowl to Evie.

The conversation remains tense throughout dinner. Cecilia drinks more than she eats, while the rest of us limit ourselves to one glass of wine before switching to water, mindful of it being a work night. This only seems to irritate our hostess further.

"Charlie, you should set up a camera in my room," Cecilia practically purrs, her voice dripping with insinuation.

To his credit, Charlie keeps his composure, though a faint blush colors his cheeks as he focuses intently on his dinner plate.

"Why?" Emily asks, her innocence cutting through the tension.

"What do you mean, 'why?'" Cecilia sneers, her tone sharp.

"We're not allowed in your room. Why would Lily go in *your* room?"

Cecilia's expression turns haughty. "Because not everything revolves around 'Emilily,' you know. There are more ghosts here than just Lily."

"Have you seen any?" Sam interjects, his curiosity piqued. I glance at his plate; he's carefully removed the beefy bolognese sauce from his lasagna and is eating around it.

"Charlie should come and interview me to find out."

Charlie takes a deep breath, setting his utensils down. "Cecilia, maybe you should lie down after dinner," he suggests calmly.

In a flash of anger, Cecilia throws the remaining wine from her glass into Charlie's face. I start to rise, but Sam gently places a hand on my forearm, keeping me seated. Charlie wipes his face with a napkin, maintaining his composure.

"You've had too much to drink and not enough to eat. We have a long night ahead of us; you should get some rest."

Cecilia stands abruptly, leaning on the table as she glares at us. "One little girl starts slicing herself up and look at you all. So desperate to be special. So desperate to find something that's NOT HERE."

Marian rushes in from the kitchen with a bottle of pills in her hand, her voice low as she speaks to Cecilia. Reluctantly, Cecilia takes two tablets. They argue in hushed tones before Cecilia turns to face us, her voice dripping with sarcasm. "Apparently, I'm off my meds again. Please disregard whatever bullshit I spewed this time. I think I'll take Charlie's advice and head to bed. Try not to destroy my house tonight."

I look over at Sam, noticing his hand still on my wrist, his thumb tracing circles over my pulse point. "You needed to let Charlie handle it," he murmurs.

He's right, of course. I often jump into others' battles without considering whether they want my help. Charlie didn't look at me for assistance, so I should have stayed out of it.

To their credit, Evie and Shirley remain silent for a moment, though their exchanged glances reveal their thoughts. Finally, Shirley breaks the silence. "Well, the theatrics were impressive," she remarks dryly. "And me without my camera."

"I'm sure it's not over," Evie reassures her. "What was that all about? Did you and she have a falling out?" she asks Charlie.

"Not that I'm aware of," Charlie replies, looking perplexed. "That was... I have no idea what that was. Grief, maybe. But I hope she just stays in her room and actually goes to sleep. We have a lot of work to do."

Evie moves to Emily's side, her voice gentle. "I'll help you settle in tonight. How does that sound? It can be hard to sleep with a camera on you. We'll warm up some milk and read a bit to help you relax."

"That's fine," Emily responds. "But we've slept with cameras on us before."

"You have?" I ask, surprised.

"Sure, yeah. Dad took us to Shelley College, and we participated in a sleep study to see if twins wake at the same time in the night."

Waller conducted experiments on the girls before? Why didn't he mention this? Evie glances at me, her expression mirroring my own concerns.

Shirley chimes in, "I'll save the interviews Waller wants for later, in case there's any activity tonight. But I'll have to conduct them before heading back to the carriage house."

I nod, not looking forward to another one of Waller's 'interviews.'

Charlie cuts through the tension. "Let's go set up the SPRIG. Lydia, did you mean what you told Waller? That you'd stay out of the basement?"

"I probably should," I admit. "I don't want to endanger the investigation more than necessary."

"Okay, well, after we set up the rig, I'll have you stay with it while we go down to the basement to set up another camera. We should be fine as long as we stick together."

Sam's eyes meet mine, and we share a silent understanding. "You can't split up," I tell Charlie firmly. "No matter what you think you see, don't split up."

Charlie nods, his expression earnest. "I understand."

The SPRIG takes much longer to set up than anticipated. By the time they finish, Evie has already tucked Emily into bed. It's half past nine. We test the camera and recorder a few times, ensuring they're working correctly and that a cough in the next room won't set them off when we turn our attention to the basement.

When they head down, it's a quarter after ten. With no power, Sam and Charlie haul the small generator inside from the van. They found it in the carriage house's potting shed. Shirley and Evie each carry two large work lights, like the ones used on construction sites, down the stairs, following the boys.

The generator sputters to life, and the noise drifts into the sitting room. I relax slightly in my spot by the SPRIG. Having light will make their job easier. They return for the rest of the gear, including Charlie's measuring instruments, and disappear back into the dark stairwell.

Settling into my quiet job of monitoring the SPRIG, I take the blueprints from Charlie's pile of equipment and carefully unroll them on the coffee table. There are about thirty pages in total, and no matter how many times I flip through the pile, I can't find a blueprint of the basement.

Frustration settles around my shoulders like a heavy shawl, and I sift through the pages again. I can't even find the basement door at the base of the stairs—the same door my entire team disappeared through not twenty minutes ago.

Were these drawn up before the basement was dug? That's ridiculous. A cellar of that size can't be added to a house; it has to be dug before the house is built.

A shriek tears through the house, and my head snaps up from where I'm bent over, frowning at the traitorous blueprints. The team probably can't hear it over the generator. I jump to my feet, torn with uncertainty. Another horrifying scream pierces the air, and I realize it's Emily. Without stopping to inform the others, I dash up the stairs and down the hall. Bursting into Emily's room, it's eerily quiet. The only light comes from the moonlight streaming through the window. I flip the light switch on.

Nothing. I try the switch a few more times, but nothing happens. Racing to her bed, I rip the covers back to find no Emily. I do the same with Lily's bed, crawling on my hands and knees to peer beneath the mattresses, finding both beds empty. Exhaling sharply, I stand and stare at the closet door.

Yanking it open, I find it just as empty. I swipe the hanging clothes left and right before shutting the closet door and stepping back into the hall. I listen intently. Nothing—no breathing, no footsteps, nothing.

A thump comes from inside the closet, and I rush back into the room to open the door again. Emily is lying in the fetal position on the wooden floor of her closet.

"Emily!" I cry out, grabbing a blanket from the foot of her bed to wrap around her before pulling her into my arms. "What happened?"

She's shuddering so hard it's difficult to keep hold of her. Blood coats her face and drips onto the collar of her pajama top. There's movement down the hall, and I scramble back from the closet doorway, hoping it's the team. It is. The hall light flicks on, casting a golden glow that reaches a few feet into the room.

"Help!" My voice barely carries above a sharp whisper, shattering the eerie silence. Evie rushes over and crouches beside us.

"What happened? Oh, Emily! Sweetie, you need to tell us what happened! Where's this blood coming from?" Evie gently pushes Emily's hair back, her hand coming away stained red.

Running my fingers through her hair, I scoot us forward into the light, and we all peer down at Emily's forehead. The word 'tattletale' is scratched into her skin, red, raw, and dribbling with blood.

Emily isn't crying or screaming; she's just trembling. Cecilia appears behind us, her face pale as she looks down at her sister. "Let's get her to the kitchen. We need to clean that up," she says, her voice unnaturally steady.

Sam gently lifts Emily from my arms, cradling her with ease as he carries her out of the dark room. "Hey there, momma, it's okay. You're okay. We're gonna sing a little song while we take you downstairs to clean you up, yeah? I'll bet you know this one, too." He begins softly singing "Puff the Magic Dragon," his voice soothing. Evie and Shirley huddle around him, following Cecilia down the hall.

Charlie and I exchange a worried glance. He flicks the switch, but the room remains shrouded in darkness. Shaking his head, he mutters, "I don't understand. I checked all these outlets today."

"Grab the camera," I instruct him, urgency creeping into my voice.

"I won't even be able to check if we got anything until I process the film tomorrow—or not," he adds in frustration. I look over his shoulder at the camera. The film reel hasn't moved, and there's nothing to develop.

Someone cut the power to Emily's room.

CHAPTER twelve

Charlie grabs the camera, tripod and all, as we head downstairs. My mind buzzes with questions, making it hard to stay quiet. At the base of the stairs, I place my hand on his shoulder, prompting him to stop and turn toward me.

"Why wasn't the camera on battery?" I ask, my gaze narrowing.

"Plugging it in makes it more reliable—or so the theory goes. I checked the room with a voltmeter before plugging it in. The battery only lasts a few hours, and I didn't want to risk waking the subject by changing batteries every three or four hours."

"Emily." My voice comes out sharper than I intended.

"Yeah, Emily," he replies, rubbing the back of his neck sheepishly. "Seriously, though, what the hell was that? Who did that to her?"

My gaze drifts past him as I murmur, "She wasn't there the first time I looked."

"What?" Confusion wrinkles his brow.

"I checked the closet, Charlie. She wasn't there," I insist, nibbling on the cuticle of my thumb. "And then... she was."

"That doesn't make any sense. You must've missed her the first time."

My eyes cut to his. "She wasn't there. I'm telling you."

"Come on, let's go check on her," he says, gently pulling me toward the kitchen.

In the kitchen, Sam, Evie, and Cecilia have Emily perched on the counter, dabbing Betadine on her face. Shirley is in the corner, silently filming everything. I want to tell her to stop, but I know this documentation is crucial.

"How bad is it?" I ask Evie, my voice tight with concern.

"The cuts are mostly shallow, except for a few spots. Hopefully, they won't scar," she replies.

"Has she said anything?" I ask, my voice low but tense.

Sam, holding Emily's hand, shakes his head. "No, nothing," he replies, his brow furrowed with concern.

"I'm going to make her something warm to drink. Cecilia, do you have any hot cocoa?" I turn to her, hoping for some semblance of normalcy.

Cecilia doesn't look at me. "I think Marian keeps some Swiss Miss in the coffee cupboard," she mutters, her eyes fixed on some distant point. She sits at the breakfast table, arms crossed tightly over her chest, legs crossed at the ankles, her expression hardened into a scowl.

I retrieve a glass milk bottle from the refrigerator and pour the milk into a small saucepan, setting it on the stove. As the flame flickers to life beneath the pan, I approach Cecilia, standing in front of her. "What's your problem?" I ask, my voice barely containing my frustration.

"This is typical of her," Cecilia snaps, her voice dripping with disdain. "Making a big deal out of it only encourages her. She wants the attention."

"You think she did that to herself?" I'm trying to remain neutral. I'm trying so hard, I swear, but I want to punch her in her perfect teeth right now.

Cecilia sighs, exasperated. "Clearly, she did this to herself. Unless you're suggesting one of you is responsible."

"None of us would do that to a child, Cecilia. And besides, I was the only one with her; there wouldn't have been enough time. The rest of them were in the basement together."

Cecilia tilts her head, her eyes narrowing. "So, it's just you who's unaccounted for. Got it," she says, her voice cold and accusatory.

I step back, feeling the weight of the team's gaze on us. The milk hisses and foams over the top of the saucepan, snapping me back to the task at hand. I quickly turn off the stove and finish preparing the hot cocoa, my mind racing with a mix of disbelief and anger.

"Bring her into the sitting room in front of the fire. I found some lap blankets in the coat closet while taking readings earlier," I tell them, trying to stay composed. Sam nods and gently lifts Emily off the counter, his movements careful and deliberate. We lay her down on the couch, and Evie wraps a blanket around her, tucking it in tightly. Shirley, ever the documentarian, follows us with her camera, lens focused on Emily.

She hasn't done our night interview session yet. I wonder if she'll remember. Of course, she will; she's just waiting for the right moment.

I squat in front of Emily, holding a steaming mug of cocoa. She stares into the fire, her eyes glassy and distant, oblivious to the room and its occupants. Not wanting to startle her, I gently set the mug down on the coffee table and rub her forearms. They're like ice.

"Hey," I murmur softly, trying to reach her. "You in there, kid?"

Evie kneels beside me and places a comforting hand on my shoulder. "Let me try something," she whispers, nudging me aside gently. Leaning closer to Emily, she starts to sing softly, her voice like a lullaby. *"Don't ya love her madly? Don't ya need her badly?"*

Sam, standing nearby, clears his throat and joins in, his voice blending with hers. *"Don't ya love her ways? Tell me what you say."*

The unexpected serenade sounds surreal, but a small smile breaks across my face. Charlie sidles up, putting an arm around my shoulders, and joins the impromptu chorus. *"Don't ya love her madly?"*

"Wanna be her daddy? Don't ya love her face?" I whisper along with them, my voice barely audible.

"Don't ya love her as she's walkin' out the door?" we all sing in unison, and then fall silent.

Emily blinks, her gaze finally breaking from the fire. A single tear slips down her cheek, followed by another. *"Like she did,"* she chokes out, her voice cracking, *"one... one thousand times before."* Her sobs come in waves, hitting us all harder than we expected. Evie and I envelop her in a tight embrace, her body shuddering against us. Sam rubs comforting circles on my back, while Charlie, overwhelmed, quietly steps away. At some point, Cecilia has also vanished, leaving the room without a word.

"There she is," Evie whispers gently to Emily, rocking her slightly. "You're okay."

Emily's sobs gradually subside into quiet hiccups. I hand her the mug of cocoa, then stand up and stretch, feeling the tension in my muscles. I move over to Shirley, who is still filming. "Did you get that?" I ask her, trying to gauge her reaction.

"Hell, yeah, I got that. That was good stuff," she replies, clearly satisfied with the material. "Hopefully, The Doors don't sue my ass."

"Should I put on a pot of coffee?" I suggest, needing something to do to keep my hands busy.

"Yeah, I could use something. You know it ain't even midnight yet, right?"

Grateful for the distraction, I head to the kitchen, Charlie trailing behind me. "I wanted to talk to you," he says as I begin scooping coffee into the filter.

"Yeah?" I prompt, setting up the coffee pot.

"It's about Cecilia," he continues, his tone uneasy.

Finished with the coffee prep, I lean against the counter and fold my arms. "I'm listening."

"I don't get what's going on with her," he says, his voice tinged with confusion. "But... she was the only one unaccounted for when the incident with Emily happened."

I chew thoughtfully on a piece of leftover garlic bread, considering his words. "She said she went to bed."

"Yeah, she did," he confirms, lowering his head. "But what if she's the one hurting Emily?"

I nibble another piece of bread, mulling it over. "Why would she do that? She seems to hate the attention Emily gets from these incidents."

"You don't think it's paranormal, do you? I mean, Lily wouldn't do this. It doesn't make any sense."

"Here's the timeline: You were all downstairs, setting up in the basement. I heard a scream. I didn't react at first, trying to figure out what it was. When I heard it again, I recognized it was Emily and ran up to her room. She wasn't there. I checked both beds and the closet—nothing. I stepped into the hallway, then heard a thump from the closet. When I opened it again, there she was."

"When did Cecilia show up?"

"I don't know. She didn't come in with you guys? I thought you all came in together," I say, rinsing the crumbs off my hands in the sink.

"I wasn't paying attention," he admits. I study Charlie for a moment; he's a good guy, earnest and kind.

"Hey," I say softly, catching his eye. "You don't need to feel responsible for Cecilia. She's not your burden to carry. You don't owe her anything, and you shouldn't let her manipulate you. She's definitely fooled around with other guys before you, she's a grown woman." I pour myself a cup of coffee, adding sugar and cream. "Let's go check on Emily, see if she's said anything yet."

Charlie grabs his own cup and follows me back to the sitting room. Shirley notes our mugs and slips into the kitchen, likely needing a moment to recharge.

Evie and Emily converse in quiet murmurs, while Sam sinks into a wingback chair by the fire, his shoulders slumped. "Anything?" I ask him, noting the weariness etched into his face.

His eyes lift to meet mine, dulled with exhaustion. "The words on her," he mutters, his voice rough. "What do they say under the bandages?"

I glance at Evie and Emily on the couch, then retrieve my satchel from the hook by the door. Rummaging through it, I pull out a police file and flip through the pages, finding the photos of the wounds. I hand the file to Sam.

His dark eyes become unreadable, like deep, murky waters. He furrows his brow, a hard line forming across his unshaven face. He snatches the file from my hand and flips through the photographs.

Bitch

Whore

Pig

Liar

Sam exhales slowly, snapping the file shut. "Envy," he says, almost to himself.

"What?" I ask, startled by the abrupt conclusion.

"Words are powerful. These are all words that suggest jealousy. Even 'tattletale,'" he explains, handing the folder back to me.

"What's wrong, Sam?" I probe gently.

"I thought we were here to investigate century-old ghosts haunting a fancy estate, not to find a little girl being mutilated," he replies, running a hand through his untamed curls.

I sit on the footstool next to him, absorbing the weight of his words. "This is the job. Most of the time, it sucks," I say, taking a sip of my coffee. I pause, considering how to phrase my next thought. "Happy, balanced people don't linger, Sam. My dad taught me that. Ghosts are born from tragedy; they can't tear themselves away or move on. Ghosts aren't spirits. They're ruins."

Sam's shoulders hunch forward, as if my words physically hit him. I pat his back a few times, knowing that the reality of our work can be hard to accept.

Once you embrace the truth, the job loses any romantic allure. Standing, I leave him to his thoughts and head over to check on Emily.

"Feeling better?" I ask, trying to keep my voice gentle.

Emily nods, her face pale. "I'm sorry I scared you."

"Emily, you have nothing to apologize for," I reassure her, my tone firm but kind. Her fingers drift towards her bandaged forehead, and I catch them gently, lowering her hand to her lap. "Try not to touch it."

"What does it say?" she asks, her voice wavering. "Nobody will tell me."

"Does it matter? It's not true," I reply, trying to deflect.

Her eyes, a mix of fear and determination, lock onto mine. "What does it say?" she presses, voice cracking slightly.

I sigh, conceding. "It says 'tattletale,' but that's not who you are."

She frowns, biting her lip. "Who did I tattle on? I haven't really spoken to anyone but Lily in so many days." Her eyes widen with realization. "Oh, Lily!" She turns to Sam, who is sitting by the fire. "Can you check on Lily?"

Sam's eyes meet mine, and he arches a brow. "I'm not sure that's how this works, little momma."

I stand, suddenly needing clarity. "Excuse me a moment. Evie, can I talk to you in private?"

Evie follows me over to where Shirley is setting up her camera. "What's going on?" Shirley asks, eyes bright with curiosity.

"I thought you might want to film this conversation," I say, feeling a pang of discomfort at the idea but knowing it's necessary. Shirley nods and adjusts her lens.

"I think I know why Sam saw Lily at the pond last night," I begin. Evie nods, prompting me to continue. "I think it was the acid."

Evie exhales deeply, her eyes widening. "I was going to bring that up with you today, but everything got so chaotic."

"So, you agree? The LSD opened his 'third eye,' or whatever Sam would say?"

"Yes, but... Lydia, I don't think he enjoyed the experience," Evie replies, concern shading her voice.

Evie and I exchange a glance, considering Shirley's suggestion. "Sam?" I call out, catching his attention. "Could you join us for a minute?" Sam excuses himself from Emily and walks over, his expression curious.

"What do you know about the LSD studies in our department?" Evie asks, her voice measured.

Sam shrugs, looking a bit puzzled. "Waller's had me use it on undergrads to see if they're more receptive to our Zener cards."

I nod, recalling the details. "You were in charge of the ESP study a couple of years ago, right?"

"Yeah, but Waller pulled our funding. Nobody wanted to come down to the basement to 'trip balls' and guess the card I was holding," he replies with a hint of bitterness.

"And what were your findings?" I probe.

Sam rubs the back of his neck, frowning. "It was hit or miss. Some were more receptive, others weren't. Inconsistent results." He narrows his eyes. "Why? Where are you two going with this?"

Taking a deep breath, I decide to be straightforward. "We think you're more receptive to spirits when you're on acid, Sam."

Sam's eyes widen. "Damn, Foxy, not even a little honey in that medicine, huh?" He starts pacing, processing the information. "You think that's why I saw Lily at the pond."

Evie nods. "It's a sound theory."

"Then why haven't I seen ghosts all the other times I was trippin'?" Sam challenges, crossing his arms defensively.

I tap my lips with my index finger, considering it. "Maybe there weren't any around."

"So, what? You want me to drop acid tonight to check on Lily?" Sam asks, incredulous. He folds his arms tighter, like a shield.

"We'd also have a control subject if that makes you more comfortable. Waller would kill us if we didn't," I add, trying to sound reassuring.

"So, someone else trips with me, and we see who hallucinates the drowned girl? Hard pass," Sam says, shaking his head as he starts to walk away.

Without thinking, I grab his wrist, pulling him back into the foyer. "What are you afraid of, Sam?"

"What do you mean, what am I afraid of?" Sam snaps, his voice rising. "Foxy, I used to tell people I was psychic all the damned time. It's practically what I'm *known* for. What I *am* is observant."

"So, it's all been fake? Is that what you're telling me?" I challenge, feeling a mix of frustration and disappointment. I want to believe in his abilities, especially after last night. "Did you or did you not see a little girl at the pond, standing on the shore and pointing at us?"

Sam hesitates, then finally mutters, "Yes."

"I didn't. I was on the same drugs, Sam. In fact, I copied your drink, so I had the same intake of alcohol. I think you're more open to paranormal activity when you're on acid. That should mean something."

Sam closes his eyes, his long lashes casting shadows on his cheekbones. "Are you asking me to take drugs, boss?"

"Only if you want to and only if you feel safe," I whisper, stepping into his space, our breaths mingling. "What can I do to make you feel safe?" His eyes flutter open, locking onto mine. He lets out a shaky breath and rests his forehead against mine.

"You're killing me, Lydia," he groans, closing his eyes again. At some point, his arm has wrapped around my waist, pulling me close. The heat of his lean muscles seeps into my trembling frame. "I'm not a brave man."

"I'll be brave for you," I promise, my voice barely audible. "I won't let anything happen to you."

"How can you promise that?" His voice cracks with vulnerability. "How can you promise to make the visions disappear if I need them to?"

I lick my lips, inhaling the spicy scent of sandalwood that clings to him. Taking a shaky breath, I step back. "I have sedatives. If it gets to be too much, I have authorization to use one on you."

Sam's lost expression makes me ache. I want to tell him that he's not a science experiment to me, that I don't know what he is, but it's not just him who feels this stupid pull between us. But I can't. I can't involve myself with any members of the team like this, and I have to know where to draw the line.

"Okay, Foxy, okay," he sighs, resigned. "I'll do it for you. For Emily."

"Do you want someone else to drop with you?"

"If someone volunteers, fine, but it's not my first rodeo being the only one fucked up in the room." He tries to smile, but it doesn't reach his eyes. *He's nice, but sad.*

I move closer, cupping his cheek. My hand wraps around his neck, and I pull him down, rubbing my cheek along his jawline. What was meant to be a comforting gesture turns into something more as our lips brush. Panicking, I rise on my toes and kiss his cheek instead, pulling him into a hug. He buries his face into my shoulder, his arms tightening around my waist.

"You're really annoying, but I think you're a good person, Sam. I don't want to mess you up," I murmur, stepping away from his warmth.

Back in the sitting room, I clear my throat. "Emily brought up a valid point. Something terrible happened to her tonight, and we should check on Lily. Sam's agreed to do this, but we need a control subject to accompany him."

Charlie raises his hand hesitantly. "It can't be you, right?" he asks.

"I need to stay clear-headed."

"I'll do it," Evie says, surprising us all. "Oh, who are we kidding? We need Shirley on camera, Charlie to check the gear, and you to boss everyone around. It was always going to be me and Sam."

I nod, looking at Sam. "I have pharmaceutical-grade stuff; it's stronger than the street-grade LSD from last night. Is that okay?"

Sam and Evie exchange knowing expressions and then turn back to me. They both nod in agreement. "Alright, let me pull the consent forms from my pharm bag."

As they settle into the sitting room, I pull out a small brown vial with an eyedropper. Evie, the control freak she is, insists on administering it to herself first.

Sam and I exchange a long look before he closes his eyes and sticks out his tongue. With a practiced motion, I place a single drop in his mouth and brush my thumb along his jawline.

"Here's to a safe trip," I say softly.

Sam's eyes flutter open, studying me for a moment before he leans back against the couch, eyes closing again.

CHAPTER thirteen

Emily approaches Evie and Sam on the couch with a mix of curiosity and shock. "Did you give them drugs?" she asks, properly scandalized.

"Come here," I say, patting the couch cushion next to me, trying to soothe her worries. "You can't tell your parents. I know keeping secrets isn't ideal, but they wouldn't approve if they knew this was sometimes part of our process." I open my medical kit to show her. "See these? They're medical-grade hallucinogenics, and we usually use them in the lab. But this time, we needed them on-site. These other vials are sedatives, in case anyone reacts poorly. A nurse trained me on how to administer them. It's all perfectly safe within a controlled setting, Emily. I promise."

She scrunches her face, skepticism written all over it. "Are you sure this isn't just a hippie thing? Dad says hippies are going to try to overthrow the government with drugs."

Sam, overhearing this, lifts his head with a start. "That..." A genuine laugh escapes him, and the sound is like a warm blanket. "Little momma, we can't even button our shirts right when we're rollin'; how are we gonna take over the White House?" His curls bounce when he shakes his head at her. "What are we going to do with the government anyway? We ain't gonna overthrow the man just to become the man."

Emily tilts her head, considering his words. "I guess. But why do you guys like it so much?"

Choosing my words carefully, I explain, "Some believe it helps you focus on things we can't normally perceive. But it's only for grown-ups. Your brain isn't done cooking yet."

"Perceive? Like ghosts?" she inquires, her curiosity piqued.

"Maybe." Nibbling on the inside of my bottom lip, I carefully try to peel her back from her excitement. "But not for everyone. And we can't make any promises. We have no idea if it happens every time. We all took it last night, and none of us saw anything except Sam."

"So, Sam's special?" She probes. Sam's eyes cut to me for my reaction.

"That's what he claims," I respond, a hint of skepticism in my tone. "But I remain unconvinced."

As the conversation shifts, Emily muses aloud, "Evie is the research girl, and Shirley's the camera lady—"

"Documentarist," Shirley interjects, correcting her.

"And Charlie's the gadget guy, and you're the boss. So what does that make Sam?" Emily continues, trying to understand everyone's role.

"He's the medium," I explain. "Every reputable paranormal team has one—a sensitive, someone attuned to things others aren't. My mother used to say they see the world differently."

"Ohhhh, crazy people," Emily nods sagely. "Weird. Sam doesn't seem crazy."

"Crazy isn't accurate," Evie cuts in, sounding like she's starting to dip below the line. "And it isn't polite. It's an ugly word, kiddo."

Emily's throat bobs as she swallows. She's probably never been told it's an impolite word.

"How are you guys holding up?" Charlie asks them. Since they took the acid, he's checked the temperature around them twice.

"Whoever procured that acid is a sadist, Lydia," Evie murmurs. Her voice fades, her focus drifting into the ether. "It's—" She doesn't complete her thought. Instead, she gazes thoughtfully at the portrait above the fireplace. "Who is that?"

Cecilia is here, always appearing when least expected. "Ambrose Carmichael. My great-grandfather."

"What is he holding?" Evie asks, her movements slow and deliberate as if moving through molasses, she struggles off the sofa and stands before the fire. This prompts me to stand behind her and clutch a handful of her blouse just in case she tilts too far forward. "Jesus, Lydia, do you see what I'm seeing?"

"My grandfather was deeply involved in the spiritualism fad. Don't overinterpret it," Cecilia advises in her casual manner, steering the conversation away.

Charlie joins us now. "What are we looking at here?" Shirley inquires, aiming her camera at Ambrose.

"It's a crook and flail," I mutter. "These were traditionally brandished by pharaohs, but were recently popularized by figures like Crowley and his followers."

Evie's focus sharpens on me. Her pupils are dilated; she sways slightly, caught in the grip of her hallucinations. "I've never seen them depicted in a painted portrait before."

I adjust her crooked glasses and whisper, "How can you be a nerd even when you're high?"

She shrugs me off. "It's a gift."

Sam sits forward on the couch, his elbows resting on his knees. His face is buried in his hands. The weight of the room's atmosphere seems to press down on him. I sit next to him once Charlie guides Evie away from the fire.

"Hey, Foxy," Sam says gruffly. He hasn't looked up at me yet.

"How are you feeling?"

"Flowering, blossoming, decomposing, budding, all of the stages of life all mixed up."

"Yeah, you're feeling it," I say with a huff of a laugh.

"Your voice is like sweet whiskey," he tells me, the adoration dripping like thick honey in his voice.

"So how do we go about this, Sam?" I ask him, struggling to ignore what he says while high. "How do I direct your trip so we can focus on what you dropped in for?"

"This room doesn't breathe, pretty momma. It's holding its breath. I need it to breathe," he explains. His fingers lace with mine, pulling my hand into his lap. "You've got such a blue aura all the time. I like making it swirl with reds and pinks when my skin touches yours." My heart races at his words. "Yeah, like that. Just like that." His thumb brushes my cheek. Leaning in, his lips graze the shell of my ear. "You bloom under me, and I can't get enough of it."

Jesus. My thighs clench and I swallow thickly, clearing my throat as I scoot back from him. "How do I make the room breathe for you?"

His gaze lingers on my lips, but what he says answers my question, proving he's been paying attention to me. "Get me something of Lily's," he whispers, his voice rich and raspy.

"Emily," I call her over. "I need something of Lily's. Can I come with you to your room and get something?"

Sam grips me closer. "Don't leave. Don't leave me. I don't want to be alone in case it happens again."

Surprised by his intensity, I assure him, "Okay. No, I've got you. You're not alone." Shirley abandons the camera and asks Emily to take her upstairs.

"I'm sorry. I'm so sorry. I'm not brave," he tells Charlie and me.

Evie is still muttering about the crook and flail in the painting. "Can I look in his study?" she asks Cecilia, her voice tinged with a desperate curiosity.

"No."

"I promise I won't touch anything," Evie assures her, the plea evident in her tone. "I just need a little peeky at Daddy's study."

"Even if I *could* unlock it, I wouldn't let you in there like this anyway," Cecilia explains.

"Why don't you have any family photos in this house? It's weird. Don't you think it's weird, Lydia?"

"It's weird," Sam agrees. Charlie and I exchange glances.

Charlie stands with Cecilia to ensure Evie's safety from the other woman's mood swings. "Was your grandfather a Thelemite?" Evie inquires, her curiosity sharpening despite her altered state.

"A *what?*" Cecilia asks, as if Evie had used a slur.

Evie points to the number 93, cleverly disguised as smoke from the candle sitting on the small table beside him. "93 is a sacred number to Thelemites." She taps her foot, clearly trying to outthink the LSD. "Have you ever seen a book in Daddy's study called *The Book of the Law?*"

"My father is a judge. I've seen a hundred books in his office like that."

Evie's frustration peaks. "Either you're exceptionally skilled at feigning ignorance, or you truly are ignorant," she accuses our hostess sharply.

"I do not have to put up with this abuse!" Cecilia retorts, turning to Charlie for support. "Say something!"

"Say what? She's high." Charlie responds with a nonchalant shrug.

With her mouth creating a hard line across the bottom of her face, Cecilia spins around and abandons us to the sitting room. The history lesson is over.

"I am so sick of her treating us like the help," I grumble.

"Yeah," Charlie nods slowly, his voice measured. "I'm fairly sure you're the only one on this team who's not used to that."

Confused, I ask, "What do you mean by that?"

Evie lets out a long sigh, followed by a giggle that doesn't quite mask her annoyance. "It's nothing. Just forget it." But it clearly wasn't nothing—I couldn't just let it go.

Shirley's voice cuts through the tension. "We're back, and we've found something," she announces.

"This is Monsieur Mistral," Emily tells Sam, who is desperately trying to focus on her and not look high. "Lily's stuffed lobster. She slept with it every night."

Sam appears appropriately reverent for the object in question, and Emily doesn't hesitate when she places it in his upturned palms. He gets up and paces the room, working the stuffed animal between his hands, almost like he's wringing the life out of it.

A shadow of concern crosses his features, and I match his steps, placing a comforting hand on his shoulder. "Everything okay?"

"Nervous." He stops and whirls on me. "Just nervous." Noticing my worry, he smiles to reassure me he doesn't hold it against me, but then his eyes drift away from mine and shift to something in the corner.

"Is she here?" I ask, spinning away to survey the room, the urgency palpable in my voice.

"She's here," Sam confirms, his voice a strained whisper.

Shirley inches closer, her camera poised for action. "What's she look like, Sam? Describe her."

"She's in a blue swimsuit, dripping onto the carpet. She's pale, almost blue, and she's shivering." He swallows audibly, his discomfort visible.

"What's she doing?" I press, my voice barely above a whisper.

Sam's eyes dart frantically from the corner to me and back again. "She's... just standing there."

"Maybe she's frightened?" I turn to Emily, seeking confirmation. "Did she say Sam scared her last time?

Emily shakes her head, her face draining of color. Charlie intervenes, his voice firm, "Emily, remember to breathe."

"Hey, Lily," Sam calls out tentatively. He gasps suddenly, taking a step back, tugging me with him.

"What? What is it?" I demand, my heart racing.

"She's moving closer."

"You're safe," I assure him quickly. "She can't hurt you."

"How do you know? You ever see a ghost before?" His tongue drags his bottom lip in nervously, and he catches me in his gaze before returning it to what I can't see.

"Sam," I whisper, cupping his face gently, trying to ground him. "She's just a little girl who needs our help. Help her."

He nods, steeling himself, and looks back to where he last saw Lily. "She's talking, but it's like someone's turned the sound off. I can't make out the words." His brow furrows and his eyes follow a path from Lily's position to somewhere in the entry foyer. He takes another sharp breath and pushes me behind him.

"What?" I ask him again.

His body tenses. "There's someone else here."

"Who?" Shirley prompts, her tone anxious.

"I don't know, but he's all fucked up. Burned and shit, he's still smoking, man." I run my thumb across his knuckles, trying to anchor him. He glances down at that and back to my face, desperately searching my eyes for something. "You can't see him?"

Shaking my head, I watch as he refocuses on the spectral presence. Turning back to Lily, he scans the room and pauses, his body rigid. Suddenly, he pulls me toward the corner of the room where Shirley typically films, a spot that offers a full view.

"Another one?"

"A woman. And she's… overwhelmed with sadness. It's crushing, Lydia. I can feel her grief splitting my heart."

Emily pipes up, "That's Alice. She's always sad."

Evie, Charlie, and I exchange startled glances. "There's more than just your sister here?" I manage to ask, my voice tinged with incredulity.

"Oh yeah. There are a few: the smoking man, Alice, and the soldier with only half a head, but I haven't seen him in ages and ages."

"And you didn't think to mention this?" Charlie's voice is tinged with disbelief as his eyes rove the room, seeking invisible threats.

"You guys are ghosthunters. I thought you knew," Emily says matter-of-factly. "Dur."

"First," I start, without tearing my eyes from whatever Sam is looking at, "we're *not* ghosthunters. Second, this is kind of need-to-know information! *Sam* needed to know!"

"You said they can't hurt Sam," she replies simply, missing the severity of the situation.

I glare down at the little girl, and she shrinks behind Evie. "That was before there was a whole platoon of them!"

"They can't hurt him. He can't even hear them. I'll bet I can help, though."

"Emily, wait—" I attempt to stop her before she can overload my medium, but she grabs his hand in hers, and he takes a horrified gasp.

"No, wait, stop," he begs whatever is happening to him. His voice is strangled, a mix of fear and confusion. "They're talking all at once, I can't—"

Emily releases him and peers around the room. She holds hands with nothing, someone, and her face changes. "It's alright, Sam, it's alright," she says. "I told her this would be too much for you. I'm sorry for scaring you."

"Lily?" He asks Emily.

"Obviously. I know your Lydia wanted to communicate with me. Go ahead and ask." Lily inside Emily sounds calm, but her gaze flickers between a couple of other empty spots in the room. Her eyes darting to unseen figures send shivers down my spine. "You might need to hurry, though. Sam's attracted attention."

"Has Emily always been able to do this?" I ask her.

"No, this is... I think it's Sam," Emilily says. Her voice trails off as if she's listening to distant whispers. "Hurry, Lydia, they're coming."

I look around the room wildly. "Lily, was your drowning an accident?"

"No—" she's cut off by something that makes her shriek. Again, Emily's face changes. Older, more regal, more panicked. "My children," she cries out. "Have you seen my children?"

"Alice?" Evie asks.

"Yes," she tells us. "My children, I need to find my children."

"You're Alice Shippington," Evie continues dreamily, oblivious to the chaos around her.

"I don't have time for your impertinence!" Alice rages from behind Emily's eyes. The room seems to grow colder with her anger. "The rebels are on their way, and I need to lock my children in the basement so they don't find them!"

Sam groans and drops to his knees. "I can't. I can't do this anymore, Lydia. Please don't make me. It's going to tear the kid apart!"

Alice is shoved aside, and a sneering, twisted face takes her place. Emily walks limp and stalks toward Sam. "You dare ignore me, boy?" she snarls at him. Her voice turns deep and masculine, unlike the fake medium.

"Lydia, please!" Sam begs me. The rest of the room is gob-struck by the whole situation.

I wrench my hand from his grasp and dive for the medical bag, withdrawing a hypodermic needle and a vial of sedative. As I kneel before him, my hands tremble so violently that filling the needle becomes an almost Herculean task. Finally done, I jab him inelegantly in the thigh and let the needle clatter to the floor as he clasps both my hands in his.

"I'm sorry," he gasps, his voice laced with regret. "I fucked up."

I shake my head, unable to think of what to say. "Will it stop when you're out? For her?"

"I don't know," he tells me honestly. "I hope so." Dropping his forehead to my shoulder, I bear most of his weight on my knees until I lower myself to my heels.

"Sleep now, Sam. You're safe," I murmur, threading my fingers through his hair as I attempt to make sense of the chaos that just unfolded.

"I'm s'posed to keep you safe," he slurs, and all of his weight slumps on me. I catch him as well as I can and slowly lay him on his side on the carpet beneath us. Letting out a shuddering breath, I turn to my charge, who appears to be herself again.

Sam was right.

"Are you okay?" I ask Emily.

She's shaking but nods. Exhaustion colors the skin around her eyes, and Charlie coaxes her to lie on the couch with the lap blanket we brought for her earlier.

"Holy shit," escapes my lips, breaking the silence.

"That's nothing," Shirley whispers back, excitement trembling in her voice. "I captured every second on camera. Every. Single. Second."

This spurs Charlie to action, and he jumps up to check his camera and recorder. He breathes a sigh of relief. "It worked. The SPRIG worked, and we not only got it on the voice recorder and camera, but we also got the instrument readings."

"We got something?" Disbelief tinges my voice as Evie wraps her arms around me. *We actually got something.*

"Freakiest night ever. Waller's gonna lose his mind," she tells me.

"Yeah," I say, but the internal conflict about Waller is bubbling beneath the adrenaline surging through my veins. "I shouldn't have asked that of Sam without more information. I fucked up."

"You didn't. How could we have known? There haven't been any other reports of sightings up here in decades," Evie reassures me.

We all turn to the girl sleeping on the couch. "We should find out if there's anything else she's keeping from us." My glance lands on Evie, sitting next to me on the floor. "Hey, you were on the same dose. Did you see anything?"

"Yeah," she breathes out dreamily in my ear. "Sam and Lydia sittin' in a tree, k-i-s-s-i-n-g..."

"You're high," I tell her as I push her away, but I peer down at Sam's head in my lap. Running my fingers through his hair, I glance back at Evie and frown. "This isn't anything."

"Sure," she says, and we leave it at that, content we have enough material to make even Professor Waller happy.

CHAPTER fourteen

It's half past five when Emily finally rouses. Draped in a blanket, with her fist rubbing sleep from her eyes, she looks years younger than her age.

"Is Sam going to be okay?"

"Yeah, I mean, I think so." I reply, scrutinizing her carefully before deciding she's mature enough for the truth. "This caught us unprepared. And being caught unprepared can be very dangerous for a paranormal team. Do you understand what I'm saying?"

Emily stops and turns to me. "Is it because I didn't tell you about the others?"

"Help me understand. Why didn't you mention the other spirits in the house?"

Tears brim in her eyes, stirring a pang of guilt within me. "I thought you guys knew. I really did, Lydia. I promise."

I sigh. "You want to help, right? You want to be a part of this investigation?"

"Yes. I can help. Sam makes me stronger," she tells me.

"You should have told us you could see the spirits in the house. Are they the ones hurting you? And the word you're looking for is amplifier. Sam merely amplifies what you can do. He doesn't make you stronger. You're still in danger. You shouldn't let them in like that."

Emily blinks owlishly at me. "But I helped. I thought I was helping."

Closing my eyes, I take a deep breath. "I'm in charge of this team. You need to come to me with things like these. You can go to anyone else if you don't trust me or I'm not around. They're groovy, right? They won't judge you, and they won't think you're lying, but, Emily, we need you to be more honest with us." We've reached her door. "Do you understand? I get that this is a heavy conversation so early in the morning, but it's important you understand."

"There's more than just Lily, Alice, and the burned man," she confesses, her voice barely above a whisper.

A shiver runs across me. "How many more?"

"*Lots,*" she says and pushes her door open.

"And I don't know who is doing this to me. They've never hurt me before. Maybe they're mad I let Lily drown?" Sitting down on her bed, her anxious eyes dart up at me.

"You didn't let Lily drown. It wasn't your fault." I think for a minute. "Before you return to bed, tell me where your father's study is?"

Emily's eyebrows furrow. "You don't want to go in there. That's where the burned man lives."

"I won't go in, I promise. I only need to know where it's at."

"It's in the other wing. The first door on the left, but he keeps it locked. Nobody is allowed in. Ever. Not even Mother."

With a solemn nod, I let her climb back into bed, slipping out her door and back into the hallway. Sam is still asleep downstairs, and Charlie is packing up his things. Shirley and I babysat Evie through the rest of her excursion, so she's still out. Cecilia never came back down, and from what I've seen from her comings and goings, she lives in the East Wing with her parents. Emily, Lily, and Peter had their rooms in the West Wing.

I tread softly down the hall to the top of the stairs, where my gaze drifts to the left door across the staircase—Carmichael's study.

As the house rests in quiet, a strange allure pulls me toward the room. Nobody is around, and the handle won't budge when I twist it in my sweaty palm. My heart races as I squat down to peer through the keyhole. From what I can see in the dim morning light, it's a typical study, with shelves full of law books and a leather chair.

With a heavy sigh, I stand and turn to head back downstairs. But curiosity pulls me short, and I wonder which room is Cecilia's. Tiptoeing down the hall to avoid waking her, I struggle to determine which room is which; it's just two walls of identical doors. I'm about to turn back when something catches my eye.

One of the doors has holes around the frame, suggesting it once had a padlock hinge—on the outside of the door, intended to keep someone locked in. Frowning, I bend to peer into the keyhole of this one as well.

The room is feminine, adorned with frothy swaths of ruffles and lace in shades of peach and ivory. The thump of a footstep calls my attention down the hall, and Charlie stands under the soft lighting of a wall sconce, hands on his hips. Quickly moving away from the mysterious room, I grab him by the elbow and we head back downstairs.

"What were you doing?" he asks, his tone peppered with suspicion.

"Snooping," I retort, cocking my head to the side, challenging him. "It's part of the job, Charlie."

"And what did you discover while snooping?" The disdain in his voice is unmistakable.

"I found Carmichael's study and another room that, I think, used to have a padlock on the outside."

Charlie scratches his head at that. "What do you mean 'on the outside'?"

"On the outside, like I said. It's meant to keep someone inside the room."

Evie is stretching from where she and Shirley had fallen asleep together, and she mumbles, "Sleepwalking."

"What?" Charlie and I ask her at the same time.

"Sleepwalking. My parents had to put a latch on my sister's door to keep her from wandering around the house at night. They found her on our balcony one morning—on a balcony in a high-rise—so they locked her in."

Cecilia mentioned that Emily walked in her sleep in Quinn's report. "Is it hereditary?"

"I... have no idea. I suppose it would be." I should fetch her a cup of coffee; I need her awake.

"You're thinking of the police report, where they've found Emily out by the pond a couple of times since Lily's death," Charlie adds.

"Look who actually did his homework," I tease him with an arched eyebrow. "But if Emily is the one who sleepwalks, why doesn't she have a lock outside her door instead of the one in the East Wing?"

"They might have made her switch rooms?" Evie suggests.

"Or Cecilia also sleepwalks." I glance at Charlie, with a questioning look, as if she'd confided in him her life story.

"How would I know something like that? We've been here for two nights; it's not like I married her."

"Did you find his study?" Evie asks, switching gears.

"Yeah, if you take a right at the top of the stairs, it's the first door on the left. But it's locked." I catch a glimpse of Evie puffing up, "There's no key in the keyhole, so you can't do your Nancy Drew thing."

She deflates at the proclamation. "Just once. Just *once* I want to be able to do that. Dang."

Reaching across, I pat her shoulder a couple of times in mock comfort. "We should return to the carriage house before the Carmichaels arrive and try to manage a few hours of sleep."

"How are we going to move Spooky Sam?" Charlie asks.

"Carefully, that sedative is no joke. It's going to be like he got hit with a semi when he wakes up. I do *not* envy him."

We manage to move Sam and all of our gear back down to the carriage house in our van. Unable to get him up the narrow stairs, we tuck him into the couch and throw a thick blanket on him. The rest of us retire in the two rooms upstairs.

Around two in the afternoon, we shuffle out of the bedrooms and down the stairs with insufficient sleep. Charlie and I shared a room, each taking one of the twin beds because, let's face it, we were both exhausted. The aroma of coffee draws me downstairs, and Sam sits at the kitchen table, flipping through Evie's notes.

Shock courses through me. He's up and not moaning in pain. "Uhh, hey," I stammer.

His blinding smile flashes up at Charlie and me. "Good morning," he drawls. "Coffee?"

Narrowing my eyes at him, I ask, "Are you actually okay?"

"So good," he tells us. "Slept like the dead."

"Uh-huh," I mutter and pour myself a mug of coffee. Sitting across from him at the dining table, my mouth twists, struggling to find the right words. "That dose would have knocked anyone else out all day."

"Anyone else," he says and clinks his mug against mine. "Not Old Sam."

"Sam, how *old* are you exactly?" Charlie asks him. "I mean, you keep saying that…"

"26, man. 26. Older and wiser, right?" He winks at me coyly over his cup.

Clearing my throat, I attempt to change the subject. "Any sign of life from the ladies?"

"No, and these notes Evie took last night are wild, momma. Look here, she has the word Thelemites with a question mark after it underlined, like, twenty times."

"What's a Thelemite?" Charlie asks.

"Well, if you were a parapsychology major," I begin, and Charlie levels me with a stare.

"I am a parapsychology major *now*. And I'm starting in the middle of it, so please forgive me if I haven't caught up with you guys yet."

"Nah, man, it's all groovy," Sam gives me a pointed glance as if telling me to play nice. "You ever hear of this cat, Alistair Crowley?"

"Yeah, of course."

"Thelema... it's like his esoteric sex cult." Sam waggles his eyebrows at Charlie. "And *all* that implies."

"That's not exact—"

"*Sex* cult, man," Sam says over my objection.

I cross my arms over my chest. "Fine. Crowley's sex cult."

"Don't pout, pretty momma. You know I'm right."

"What's that have to do with last night?" Charlie asks, like an adult.

Sam pushes the notebook across the table to me, and I give it my attention. Her handwriting is wild and unstructured, capturing the chaos of her thoughts, and it fascinates me. Is my handwriting altered when I'm under the influence?

"It was the crook and flail in the painting. It's bothering her. And she thinks she saw a '93' in the smoke in the art. That's a sacred number to Thelemites."

"Why?" Charlie asks.

"Numerology mumbo-jumbo. It's related to 'do what thou wilt; shall be the whole of the law,' which is their truly disturbing ideology. However, I don't know much beyond what I've just told you. Both Dad and Waller thought Crowley was cracked."

"Thelema is the Greek word for 'will,'" Sam adds. Charlie and I both turn in his direction. "What? You think I've been in school all this time and haven't learned anything?"

"So let's say the guy in the painting followed Crowley. What's the big deal?"

Sam and I glance at each other at Charlie's question. "Well, that would be the question, wouldn't it? Someone running for Senate can't be caught practicing magic; he'd be run out of town with pitchforks." I'm working it out as I say it. "And then there's *The Book of the Law*. Its philosophy advocates for chaos—doing what you want without consequences. That's a dangerous ideology if taken out of context, particularly for a politician."

We all sip our coffee and ponder what it means if anything.

"Oh! Emily feels quite badly about last night, Sam. You should talk to her some time today. I reminded her we all have a responsibility to communicate with each other. Could you reiterate that in the Sammiest way possible? She thinks a great deal of you."

Sam blushes and stares down at his coffee. "It wasn't her fault. I should've said I wouldn't do it until we'd done more research. That was on me."

Nobody says what we're all thinking. I shouldn't have asked him to do it. "Are you truly feeling alright?" I ask him, and he drops his hand, tangling his long, beautiful fingers with mine.

"I'm okay. I'd tell you if I weren't because you'd tear my head off later if you found out."

Pulling my hand out from under his, I regard him in my sternest leader face. "You're damned right I would."

Evie and Shirley finally emerge from the tight stairwell, with the former looking like she's been through the wringer. "Please, I'm begging you so much, tell me there is the strongest coffee in the world in that pot."

"Sam made it, so it's generously hairy," I reply.

Evie flops in the chair next to me and glares at Sam. "Why the hell do you look so chipper this morning?"

"Sleep. Lots and lots of sleep, pretty momma."

"Ugh," she tells him, taking her cup from Shirley. "Are you reading my notes?"

"We were going over what you wrote last night." My cheeks flush because I realize those may have been private. "Sorry. We should have asked first."

"No, it's fine, but I'm a little embarrassed. I was a space cadet last night. Pharmacy-grade LSD is not my friend." She glances at Sam again. "Are you sure you're alright?"

"Like I told Foxy, I'm sound as a pound."

"I hate you," I grumble.

Sam flicks his eyebrow up at me and smirks. "Aww, sunshine, don't be like that," he says as he lifts my chin with his knuckle. "You just need some agua. Lots of it."

"So we're not going to talk about Emily going all *Exorcist* last night?" Shirley jumps in.

"Yeah, I guess we need to." I nod in agreement, but I don't start.

"That kid is an out-of-sight conduit," Sam says. "But the trouble is, I think I somehow amplify her. And..." He glances at me before he continues.

"What?"

"I don't want to sound like Waller here, you dig?"

I lick my lips and meet his gaze. With a slow nod, I say, "Twins. You think Lily's death doubled her power as a conduit, and she wasn't prepared?"

"Now you're getting it." He takes another sip of his coffee. "Those others didn't look at Emily like she was a pile of cocaine until Lily took over."

"So what you're saying is—what are you saying?" Shirley asks. Evie is holding her head miserably, trying to keep up with the conversation.

"I think Lily and Emily were both a bit touched before Lily drowned, but now? They're at double power, and with me there amplifying it, the other spirits want to be heard, and they see Emily as their mouthpiece." Sam sits back but keeps his gaze locked on me.

Charlie nods, taking all of this in. "Okay, so Sam doesn't take any acid for the rest of our investigation. Easy, right?"

"Sam taking acid doesn't make him stronger, Charlie. He's still the same Sam. The acid just lets him see what's already there."

"So we should send Sam away." Shirley's tone is starkly unapologetic at her pronouncement.

My chair scrapes the wood floor as I push it back and stand up. "I need to think about this," I say, my voice thick with frustration as I step outside to dig through the van for a cigarette. Waiting for the dash lighter to heat up, someone steps up behind me.

"Are you going to send me away?"

I don't turn. I wait for the lighter to pop and then light my cigarette. Taking a deep inhale, I finally turn around to face him. He has one hand on the open van door and the other on the side paneling.

Turning my head, I exhale the smoke and study him thoughtfully. "Should I?" I challenge.

Sam clenches his jaw, and I fixate on the muscle playing in and out. "Could you send Lily on when it's time?"

"Could you?"

His gaze narrows at me and then flickers to my lips. He lets out a long breath through his nose and regards me seriously. "Do you think this is a joke to me? A lark? Something to do while I hide from the draft?" My eyebrows lift when he says this. "Yeah, I'm aware of what they say about me."

"Sam—"

"I do. I could've done it last night. But you want to know what happened to her."

Swallowing around anything I could have said in response, I realize I've become fixated on his mouth as well. "I need you to understand something," I begin, forcing my eyes up to meet his. "Whatever you think is going to happen between us... can't. Waller has all but told me if I have anything outside of a professional relationship with anyone on the team, I'm out. I can't be out, Sam. I need this."

He steps closer to me, and we're so close that if I breathe too deep, we'll touch. But I don't back away. His deep brown eyes bore into my own. "And what do you think I want to happen between us, Lydia?" he probes, his voice low.

I have the decency to blush at this. "I thought, I mean, maybe I was reading into this wrong. If I was, I'm sorry."

Shaking his head achingly slow, he lifts his hand to tuck a strand of my white-blonde hair behind my ear. "Whatever happens between us will be your own initiative, not mine. Do you understand me?" He drags the tip of his index finger along my jaw at the question.

I nod.

"Use your words, Lydia." His rough voice does things to me.

"Yes. I understand."

He steps back. "Good. Now, about my leaving. Do you want me to go?" Oh, he definitely knows what he's doing. I shake off the heat pooling between us and stand a little straighter, my chin jutting out in defiance.

"Do you think we can talk to Lily without her jumping into Emily?"

His smile starts as a smirk and spreads until that dimple plays in and out of his cheek. "Why didn't you say so earlier? It's time for a séance, Foxy."

CHAPTER fifteen

Sam leaves me beside the van, my cigarette forgotten. I squeeze my eyes shut in a full-face squint, feeling like an idiot. Why does he always leave me feeling so off-balance? It's like there are two Sams: the goofy, adorable hippie and then this completely other Sam who raises my temperature and makes my heart race. Which is the real Sam?

How could he have been in my department for two years, and I just overlooked him? He's been bugging Waller for at least a year and a half to get put on the field team, and Waller has always denied him. What changed his mind? Why did he suddenly dump Sam on me?

Paranoid. I'm being paranoid. I thought the worst of Shirley, and now I'm doing the same with Sam. This anxiety over Waller's scheming is keeping me from getting my head back in the game. My team needs better from me. How can I expect them to trust me if I don't extend the same trust to them?

Straightening up, I head back inside. Sam describes the séance in animated detail with wildly gesticulating hands, while Shirley appears nonplussed, probably mildly nervous about what will happen. Charlie keeps cutting in, asking Sam if he can take measurements during it or if it will throw off the vibes, while Evie scribbles down everything he says into her notebook like there will be a test on it later.

I've hardly listened to a word he's said. Something about drums and magic mushroom tea, and I'm overwhelmed that they're all here. They're all here, and they want to do right by Emily and Lily. I spent so much time in my own head, thinking I'm the only one with an investment in this, all of this... I was wrong. I'm not the only one who needs to speak for the dead. I never even gave them a chance.

"Did you say drums?" I ask.

Sam whirls around at me as I stand at the door, giving me a lopsided grin. "You in, pretty momma?"

I cock my head. "Séances don't usually include drums."

"They do when you do it my way." His gaze catches mine. "You wanna do it my way?"

Evie spits her coffee back in her mug.

Stifling a smile, I keep my eyes on his.

"C'mon, Lydia, you know you want to," Evie laughs.

"Ly-di-a, Ly-di-a, Ly-di-a," Sam chants and begins stalking toward me like he's going to do that thing. That hug thing.

Charlie and Shirley laugh as Sam pounces on me, wrapping his arms around my thighs and lifting me in the air. "Okay, okay! Put me down! We'll do the séance your way, Sam." He does, but he lets me slide slowly against him until we're face to face.

"That's our girl," he says, landing a kiss in my hair.

"This is going to be a mess," I tell them, but my gaze lands solely on him.

"Here's to a mess," he whispers in my ear.

Entheogenic tea and a drum circle—what the hell kind of séance is this? I glance around at them, all of them. It's our séance. That's what it is.

DAPHNE WINCHESTER

We're back with some supplies after a quick trip to the village a few miles away. Sam is off cleaning impurities or something, which I thought meant a shower, but after seeing him waltz off with a towel and minuscule jean shorts that left little to the imagination, I think it means a dip in that freezing pond.

More power to him. Evie and I are off to the manor to discuss where we are in the case with Emily, our *actual* client. If Carmichael happens by or shows any interest, we'll update him as well.

Apparently, Cecilia was at a ribbon-cutting ceremony and left a sweet but pointedly scathing note for Charlie pinned to the carriage house door while we were in town.

Charlie,

I was hoping you could accompany me to the grand opening of the Medford Mall today, but you weren't here. Are you having a good time? I'll stop by on my way back to the manor to ensure you have everything you need. This disappointment in not being able to find you is surprisingly insufferable. Don't do it again.

Love,

Cece

Evie read it aloud in a pinched voice, perfectly mimicking Cecilia's haughty tones. Sam and Shirley broke into the Simon & Garfunkle song while she performed the snotty sonnet. Charlie furrowed his brow and blushed ferociously.

We left Charlie and Shirley to set up the equipment in the living room. Sam instructed them to move all the furniture out of the way and to find all the soft blankets and pillows they could to construct a giant donut-shaped nest for us.

Evie follows me inside the manor, and we stop to peer up at Ambrose Carmichael, who glares down at us. "I'm telling you. Thelemite."

"When have I ever doubted you?" I ask, gracing Evie with big-eyed sincerity.

"I told you Frank was two-timing you with Sherry Mitchell."

The memory of it makes me rankle. "Fucking Frank. When *else?*"

"When I told you, I thought Mrs. Callahan's palm-reading shop was a front for a dope operation."

"Actually, she was smuggling parrot eggs in from Belize," I correct her.

"Practically the same thing."

"Practically the same thing."

"Ladies," Carmichael's smooth blue-blood voice wafts over us, and we both spin on our heels guiltily.

"Mr. Carmichael," I squeal. I admit it's a squeal, I would be remiss to report it was anything but a squeal. "We were—"

"Just looking for you," Evie pulls out of her ass. "To discuss some urgent matters," she adds quickly.

I'm going between looking at him and side-eyeing her now. "Exactly!" Then I lift my finger at him like I'm about to scold him, and I have no idea why I did that. Carmichael and I both glance down at my offending finger. Realizing my error, I whip my hands around my back to avoid future digit confrontations with our extremely wealthy client. "We weren't informed there were more spirits sighted on the property than were initially reported. Unfortunately, it caught us off-guard last night and placed a team member in danger."

He merely raises his eyebrows at this. "But your colleague is well, I assume. Otherwise, you wouldn't be in my sitting room staring at a portrait of my father?"

"Yes, he is. But all of the information up front would have been helpful."

"Your goal here isn't to investigate the supposed ghosts on my property, Ms. Fox, your goal is to ascertain what is happening to my daughter."

I glance over at Evie for help. "That's the problem, Mr. Carmichael. We believe we have evidence that Emily is a conduit for spirits—a mouthpiece if you will. And with more than Lily here, Emily is vulnerable to all kinds of possessions."

"And how do you propose to rid my daughter of this... affliction?"

"We're actively working on it," I assure him. "Tonight, our medium is conducting a session in the carriage house, which requires our assistance." The less we tell him, the better.

"Can you estimate how much longer this will take? My wife grows impatient with this intrusion."

Blinking at him and trying to figure out how to approach this diplomatically, I swallow and say, "Mr. Carmichael, I appreciate the urgency. However, consider how *intruded upon* your twelve-year-old *daughter* must feel. With all due respect, there are malevolent spirits in this house that would eagerly take possession of Emily if we don't resolve this. I understand we're inconveniencing your wife, but Emily's safety is our priority." I turn to Evie and then back to Carmichael. "If you'll excuse us, we'd like to update Emily on her case. Have a lovely evening."

Evie and I walk up the stairs, and I repeatedly mumble, "Just keep walking," under my breath until we're out of his sight. Then I let out a whoosh of breath.

"What was that all about?" Evie asks me.

"That was his polite way of telling us to wrap this up and butt out of his business before the press gets wind of this. We've only got about three days before he sends Emily to a sanitarium, and she will never see the light of day again."

"Which is where you think Peter is," Evie says. She's sharp, always the first to connect the dots. "I wish we were here on our own. This would be much easier if we weren't tiptoeing around."

"I agree, but there's no way Waller could convince him to give us some space. We're already restricted to too few areas."

"Your dad was friends with this guy?"

"Are you friends with everybody at the college? More like acquaintances, I'd think."

"You're not going to want to hear it, but Lydia, you're aware the Carmichael family is a top donor to the Fox Parapsychology Department, right?"

"Meaning if he doesn't like the way this goes…" I stop us in front of Emily's door, my anxiety palpable. "We have to hurry."

We explain to Emily that we'll be at the carriage house tonight conducting a séance, and she is not to come anywhere near it. "Do you understand why?"

"Because you want to talk to Lily without me," she huffs out, clearly unhappy at not being included.

"It's too dangerous for you to be so close to Sam when we invoke the spirits. That's why."

Evie places a hand on her shoulder. "We don't want you hurt."

"It doesn't hurt, though."

With my hands on my hips, I glare at her. "It doesn't hurt yet, but what if they don't let you back in control? What then?"

"We're just trying to keep you safe," Evie adds.

"Fine," Emily replies.

"Fine?" I lift an eyebrow at her.

"Yes, I understand. I'll stay here."

Relieved but still tense, Evie and I leave and head back to the guest house. When we walk through the door, the sun is slipping over the horizon.

Someone cooked dinner, and it's bubbling away on the stove. I take a deep whiff of it, and my stomach growls. Charlie walks in from the pantry, a dish towel slung over his shoulder, a couple of cans of Vienna sausages in one hand, and Spam in the other. "What's cookin'?" I ask him.

"Oh, I needed some comfort food after last night, and nobody was volunteering to cook, so I made budae-jjigae."

I peer over his shoulder to see into the pot. It's like a mishmash of dried ramen noodles, baked beans, and fermented cabbage simmering in vegetable broth red with chili paste. He opens the cans, drains the sausages, places them in a frying pan, slices the spam, and fries it. Then he pulls out some Kraft cheese slices from the fridge. Unwrapping a few, he dumps those into the pot.

"Charlie..." I start.

"I know, I know. But it's amazing, I swear, and it makes a lot."

"Oh, damn, is that budae-jjigae?" Sam asks him. I turn and raise my brow at him. His hair is wet and piled into a bun on top of his head.

"How did you—" I demand. He laughs at my question and dips a spoon into the stew for a taste before he heads upstairs to change. I frown and turn to Charlie for an explanation.

He shrugs.

After he's finished frying the meat, he puts it in a separate dish and sets it next to the pot of stew. We call everyone to eat, and Shirley pulls some banquet beers from the fridge to accompany our simple meal. I've never heard of this local brew, but it goes well with Charlie's budae-jjigae. Evie puts on some dinner music, and we make a real night of it.

I won't be the one to bring it up, but everything feels easier without Cecilia here.

"Okay," I finally say. "Who is partaking in the séance, and who's out? Only one of us needs to babysit, but my two camera techs will have to fight over it."

"Sam and I talked about it, and I'm sitting this one out because he's letting me take measurements while you guys work in the room," Charlie informs me.

"That means I'm in, and I've never done this before, so I'm not sure what's expected of me." Shirley's nervous voice is mildly contagious.

"I don't think any of us here have any idea of what to expect since this is the Sam Show tonight," I tell her.

"Okay, so I've got some far-out tea. We'll drink it, sit in my circle of love, bang on the old skins, and see who pops by for a visit."

"You can't just call for Lily specifically?" Emily made it perfectly clear that we don't want to call the burned man accidentally.

"I can try, man, but it's up to them who answers the call. You pickin' up my vibe?"

"Yeah," but I hesitate. I don't want to make the same mistake I made last night, going in blind. "Walk me through the process, Sam. We need to be safe."

Sam's arm reaches around my shoulder and rubs his thumb along the back of it. "We'll be safe, pretty momma. Safe as houses."

"The houses we frequent aren't so safe," Evie mutters, her tone laced with dry humor.

"Okay, check this out: the tea will open you up and relax you, but it's not like dropping in, right? I'm hoping if we all daisy chain up, you guys will get to see what I do."

When we're finished eating, Sam lights a joint and passes it around. He seems unperturbed by the day's stress. "What time should we start?" I ask him.

"Let's make it midnight." *Is he making this up as he goes along?* "I'd prefer to do it by the pond to grab Lily's attention better, but Charlie's gear won't be as accurate outside."

"Thanks, man," Charlie replies as he washes his bowl in the sink. "That's really considerate of you."

We clean up and try to relax Shirley. She's never done shrooms, so it's adding to her anxiety, yet Sam's grass is doing the bulk of our work. I walk into the living room where she's melting into a pillow in front of the fire. "You think this is going to work?" she asks me.

Her camera is already set up where she wants it; Charlie only needs to push the record button. "I hope so," I tell her with a sincerity softened by the cannabis haze. "We need to talk to Lily, and even without Emily here to talk to her, I think if we can lure her in, we can get some answers."

"How? How you gonna talk to a ghost who can't talk back?"

My lips curl up into a thoughtful grin. I knock on the coffee table that's been pushed out of the way. "One knock for 'yes,' two knocks for 'no.' It's Ghost Hunter 101."

"You think I should take some of Waller's classes?"

"You think you're going to stick around?"

Shirley's gaze lands on my face and pins me like a butterfly to a corkboard. "That depends on how this all goes down, doesn't it?" I nod because it's the only thing I can think to do. She's right. Something is different about this case, like the whole department is riding on how this unravels.

Charlie joins us and is taking initial base readings now. He's also set up his reel-to-reel with headphones and a large boom mike to capture any ambient sounds in the room.

The music drops as Charlie lifts the needle off the record. "I don't want to be rude, but could everyone sit in absolute silence for about three minutes?" He counts down on his fingers to the time he pushes the record button, and we all stand still as statues.

Sam isn't anywhere to be seen, as he disappeared up the stairs a few minutes earlier to put on his 'holy man garb,' whatever that means. I observe Charlie listening to everything he can: the crackling fire, the wind by the windows, and the almost unnoticeable rattle of the Dutch door. Time passes quickly, and I wonder what it sounds like to him. This world at rest before we unhinge it.

I make a note to ask him later. Maybe I will get a listen for myself. We've never had a competent tech person before. He closes his hand into a fist and hits stop on the recorder. "Thank you," he tells us, returning to messing with his toys after turning the record player back on for us.

Evie is scooping the tea into the pot. I don't usually like mushroom tea, so I lean in to give it a whiff. "Oh!"

"Yeah, right? When we were in town, Sam picked up some spices to go into it. And also this adorable honey bear. Rawr."

Notes of cinnamon, cardamom, ginger, and cloves blossom around the rich, earthy scent of the mushrooms. Leave it to Sam to make psychedelics tasty. "Nice. This'll make it go down easier."

"Shirley freaking out?" Evie has been in the department as long as I have and has a long history with Waller's fondness for psychotropics.

I lean out of the galley kitchen and examine our documentarist. "She'll come around. The dope is helping," I say.

"Good, light up another one. We need her to relax."

In theory, I agree, but too much grass will make Shirley tank out on us too early, so I hesitate to give her any more.

"Whoa," Evie says as we wait for the water to boil. Her elbow jabs me in the arm.

Turning to whatever she's gaping at, Sam is talking to Charlie in front of the fire. He's wearing a white linen galabeya.

Evie narrows her gaze at him. "What?" I ask her.

"Sam's more Wellesley, less Cairo, if you catch my meaning. I wouldn't have expected that."

Wellesley? *Old money.* I don't even realize I'm chewing my bottom lip until Sam catches my gaze. He comes over to check on the tea preparation. "A little theatrical," I snicker at him.

"Just getting comfortable, pretty momma."

"And is it?" I ask in an attempt to continue teasing him but the grass makes it come out more flirtatious than I intend. "Comfortable?"

He grabs one of my hands while the other settles on my waist and spins me around the dining room. We slow-dance to Evie's Elton John album on the record player. Bending his knees a little so he can gaze into my eyes, he sings to me how he thinks it's going to be a long, long time, and I let him sweep me away. Our altered state makes everything easy, the company, the house— it leaves me feeling warm and safe and not so alone.

Lifting his hand from my waist, he tucks my hair behind my ear and does that thing with his thumb again, where he rubs it light on my jaw. His slight smile tells me he's definitely aware he has me on the hook, and it's maddening. Swaying with him for one more song, he leans into my ear and tells me he's nervous.

I nod in agreement, not knowing if it's about the séance or us. It doesn't really matter. "So tell me, Foxy, is it comfortable?"

"It's very soft," I admit.

"It was either this or in the nude." If I had been drinking something, I would've sprayed it all over him. "My father would murder me in my sleep if he knew I was wearing this for my hippie-dippie bullshit."

This makes me break into a grin. He takes the small rebellions that he can get. "I don't think it's hippie-dippie bullshit," I tell him.

Sam leans in and brushes his nose along my temple. "No?"

I shiver. "No."

"Because you used to really bemoan me being in your department, you know?" His smirk is still plastered across his handsome face, so I know he's jesting, but it still twinges a flicker of guilt in my gut.

"I did?"

"It was, like, two days ago."

"Well, if I haven't said it before, I'll say it now. I apologize, Samir Hassan. I was wrong to call it hippie-dippie flower-child tree-hugging bullshit."

His eyebrows raise at my additions, and he lets out an amazing laugh. "I forgive you."

Evie claps. "For the record, I called you worse," she admits.

"Oh, I'm aware. And for the record, I forgive you as well."

"I didn't know shit about you," Shirley mumbles from her pillow.

"Same, man," Charlie shrugs.

I glance up at the clock behind Sam. "You ready to get started?"

"Yeah, man, let's jive with some ghosts."

CHAPTER
sixteen

We pass the pot of tea around, each taking a mug and adding honey or milk before we take our seats on the pillows in front of the fire. It's strange without a séance table, and Sam has intentionally left the lights on for Charlie and Shirley.

"Don't we need the room dark and moody?" Evie asks him as she cleans her glasses with the hem of her peasant blouse.

"Why? You need to be in the mood to speak to the dead?" Sam raises an eyebrow at her. "Spirits don't care if it's lights on or lights out, momma, it's all the same to them."

Sipping the tea carefully to determine whether it'll be palatable, I down the whole thing when the temperature finally allows it, and the others do the same. Charlie wears a half-smile across his face as though he's looking forward to playing babysitter tonight.

After about forty minutes of idle back-and-forth banter, I ease back onto the cushion behind me and listen to Sam explain what will happen while we wait for the mushrooms to kick in.

"Lydia and Evie already know that getting into a relaxed, open state of mind is the key, so everyone needs to be cool. The drum will help. Repetitive noises can dull your mind and enhance the relaxation process. When I feel like we've sunk into where we need to be, I'll ask all of you to take each other's hands. Then, hopefully, someone out there will have their ears on. You dig?"

Flowers start popping up from the shabby rug beneath us, and I want to run my fingers through their soft petals. I glance at Evie, who is giggling and pulling at Shirley's curls in wonder. Needing to tell someone about the garden around us, I turn to Sam, and my words get caught in my throat.

"You feelin' it, Foxy?" he asks me, except his lips never move.

"That's crazy, Sam, do that again." I crawl over to him.

"Do what again?" His voice is in my head, running down my spine, making me clench my thighs.

"How are you doing that?" I groan. "You're talking in my head."

"Yeah, you're feelin' it." He moves his fingers through my hair and chuckles. "I'm not doing anything. This is all you, Lydia."

Lydia. I've never heard my name sound so decadent before. It's like velvet coming from him, and I want to catch it from his lips to run it along his skin.

"You good, guys?" Charlie asks from the outskirts of the circle. His voice is the grounding reality beyond the circle's whimsy. "Nobody having a bad time?"

"We're so good, Charlie," Shirley rasps out, her voice dreamy. "I am a cat in a sunbeam."

"It's the fireplace, but whatever," Charlie murmurs under his breath, a soft chuckle hiding in his words. It's hard to concentrate while Sam's long fingers trace up and down my arms.

"Where have you been?" I pant out to Sam—at least, I think I do. The words are missing from the air, and I wonder if I listen on Charlie's magic headphones later if they will linger or if they'll be lost in my head forever.

"I've been right here," Sam says, his lips whispering against the nape of my neck, sending a cascade of shivers down my spine. Sparks flake off my skin like I'm a wildfire. "But, listen—*look* at me when I tell you this."

Concentrating hard on his words, I sit back on my heels and focus on the dark pools of his eyes. "Okay," I breathe, my voice barely above a whisper, desperate not to let him know I'm free-falling into him.

"Fuck, Lydia, I would do anything for you, *to* you—I'd fucking pluck the rings off Saturn to set upon your gorgeous head, but the first time I'm with you isn't going to be while you're off in a field of stars." He looks pained and aching. I can only nod and push myself back from him.

"Okay," I tell him, my cheeks flushing a vivid shade of pink.

"Okay?" His eyes widen with wonder. He takes my hand and presses it over his chest. "Please," he whispers like a prayer. "Please, please, don't play with me. I'm not sure I could survive it."

I lick my lips and lean back in, closer even than before. "Sam?" My voice is husky from the smoke and tea. "I think it's an impossible ask." His eyes study mine, searching for what I'm saying. "You *are* a field of stars," I whisper into his ear and his pupils blow wide at my words.

He opens his mouth to reply, but I've shut Sam Hassan up for the first time. A small smile spreads across my lips, and I reluctantly let him go.

Scrubbing my face with the heels of my hands, I shake it off and smooth my hair back. Sam adjusts his gown around his groin area, and the temptation to peek tugs at my composure. He hides behind his drum and starts a slow and steady beat.

My once vivid carpet flowers are now just a memory, crushed underfoot—either from my earlier crawling or by the weight of my own heart, trampled under the gravity of the situation with Sam, my unexpected voice of reason. I'd have dragged him up the stairs if he hadn't intervened with that frustrating prudence.

Shirley and Evie have also settled back, their initial psychedelic exploration simmering down into something more manageable. Time stretches, unmarked and surreal, as I lose the ability to decipher the wild digits dancing on the clock face. Eventually, Sam sets the drum aside.

"Okay, link hands to make a circle," he instructs us. "We're going to ask if anyone's got anything to say tonight." His eyes flicker to mine, laden with an unspoken query. He squeezes my hand—a silent check-in. I return the pressure, but my gaze falters, unable to meet his.

I'm so embarrassed. This is the second time I've lost control like this, and my heart races with conflicted emotions. I can't justify keeping him on the team after tonight; it's unprofessional, absurd. He's our resident idiot.

Yet, there's a whisper in my mind— *he's my resident idiot.*

Lost in these turbulent thoughts, I barely register Sam's voice drifting across the room, beckoning any spirit that wishes to communicate. My focus snaps back as my eyes catch something pale fluttering at the window. Lily?

"I think I saw Lily in the window," I tell Sam. Everyone cranes their heads to the paned glass beside the kitchen table.

"Lily? Are you here? Would you speak to us?"

Whatever it is ducks out of view. Sam is still calling out to Lily Elizabeth Carmichael to come and speak with us. Her pale blonde hair pops up in the kitchen window at his words. "She's listening," I urge him. Keep up the pull, keep up the call. It's like fishing: give it some slack, then apply steady pressure—Dad's advice—Ghosthunting 101.

I've just referred to the ghost of a drowned child in fishing terms.

You're turning into Dad.

Shut up, Octavia.

The face disappears from the window over the sink. Trying to predict where it might pop up again, I turn to only one other window. It's the one behind me, next to the front door. Shirley's face goes gray, and I realize she's staring at our visitor over my shoulder.

I can't make a solid observation without breaking the circle, and then I wouldn't be able to make her out at all without Sam acting as a conduit. "Lily, come in," I whisper. Sam side-eyes me. "Please just come in." He squeezes my hand to remind me to let him lead.

The apparition must also vacate that window because Shirley visibly relaxes her shoulders. We're left hanging in a stasis of our own making. Sam runs his thumb over my knuckles. He can sense my growing frustration.

"Got you," Charlie announces. "Temperature dropped three degrees."

"Lily, we're here, you're safe," Sam reassures her.

"Five degrees." Charlie is circling us like a shark now.

"We want to help you. Let us be your voice. Use us to help you rest." The vibrations of Sam's voice resonate through my fingertips and seep into my skin.

"Eight degrees," he says, and I can't help but note the triumph in his voice. I'm shivering now, and we all scoot in a little tighter to gather some body heat. This is the benefit of not having a table between us, and I take in Sam's profile curiously, wondering if that had been his intention. Knowing Sam, he would say it was to break down the barriers between human connection or some hippie bullshit like that.

"It's so cold," Evie complains as her breath gusts out of her in a white cloud.

The door blows open as if in answer, and the power goes out. The only light in the room now is from the fireplace, which casts Sam in eerie shadows, his form reduced to a mere silhouette.

"Shit," Charlie says and scrambles over to the cameras. "Nothing is working, not even my batteries."

Darkness saturates the room and creeps at the edge of our circle. "Sam?" I ask him, my voice quivering with barely contained terror. "Do we have her? Is it Lily? Or someone else?"

He doesn't answer me; he's staring at the archway to the mudroom behind Charlie and his equipment. I follow his line of sight, and I gasp.

A hulking shadow, a brute of a spirit, dominates the entire space. It stomps toward us, slicing through Charlie's equipment, coming right for him. "Charlie, dodge left!" I yell out, and he does—just before the entity would have swept right through him.

"Sam?" I whisper. He doesn't tear his eyes away as the apparition, made of smoke and shadow, halts, teetering on the brink of breaking our link. "What do we do?"

"Peace, momma," he murmurs. "Maybe this spirit wants to talk." But his voice trembles, betraying his fear.

"What?" Charlie asks. "What do you guys see? Is it her? Is it Lily?"

"Not Lily," Shirley replies, and she sounds ready to bolt. I can just make out Sam and Evie's grips holding her fast. "I want out, Lydia. I want to go home. This shit ain't funny."

"It's okay," Evie soothes. "They can't hurt you. They can make a lot of noise, and they can stomp around all they want, but—"

One of the tea mugs flies across the room and shatters against the wall.

"Or fucking hit you with something? Nah, I'm out." Shirley tries to get up.

"Stay in the circle," Sam says in a tone I've never heard before. "Sit down and let us handle it. He's here for a reason, Shirley."

Shirley's face whirls toward me, and I try to reassure her, "You need to trust your team."

"You here to tell us something, man? You need our help?" Sam asks him. "Knock once for 'yes,' two for 'no.'"

A knock thunders against the fireplace mantel, jarring a duck decoy off, causing Evie and Shirley to yelp.

Charlie's eyes widen. The knock must've resonated through the headphones. Puzzled, we exchange a worried glance. The audio is working but not the cameras. I hate that I can't think clearly.

"Okay, okay. We got you." Sam pauses to ponder. "Did you live here before?"

Knock.

"Like, here in this house? Not Hemlock Hall?"

Knock.

"Have you been here a long time?"

Knock.

Knock.

"Have you only recently passed?"

Knock. The sound is heavy and resolute, echoing the first one.

"Did you die of natural causes?"

Knock.

Knock.

Sam turns to me, and I nod, urging him to continue this line of questioning. "Oh, man, were you murdered?"

Knock. So forceful that the mirror next to the front door shatters into a spiderweb of broken glass.

Shirley squeezes her eyes shut. "Fuck, fuck, fuck."

Sam swallows. "Do you need to show us something?"

Knock.

"Okay, man. Okay. We'll follow you." At his urging, we all carefully get to our feet. "We should be fine if we're all still connected. We just won't have the safety of the circle anymore."

"We don't have the *what?*" Shirley exclaims, her voice pitched with alarm.

"What about Lily?" I whisper to Sam.

"We take what's given," he whispers back, his voice a mix of resolve and caution.

He leads us up the stairs to the master bedroom. It's so dark up here that we bump into one another. With Charlie on Shirley's camera bringing up the rear, Sam takes point. His one free hand runs along the walls, guiding us and keeping us from running into things. When we stop in front of the closet, the room is bathed only in moonlight. I bury my face into the back of Sam's shoulder for a semblance of comfort.

"What happens if we break the link? We can't search like this," I ask Sam.

"I'll have to finish it alone, but it's okay, I've got this," he reassures me with a firmness that doesn't quite mask his concern.

The figure points to the closet's ceiling at a hatch. Is it the attic? Sam lets go of me to inspect the creasing around the edges of it. Charlie is the tallest, so he maneuvers around us and pops the hatch open.

Sam hisses in a sharp intake of breath. "What?" I ask him.

"It's him. He's in the crawlspace. He's pointing at something."

"Charlie, give me a boost," I order. He hands the camera off to Shirley and laces his fingers together to lift me through the hatch.

It's merely the top of the cottage, not a proper attic. Someone laid a wood floor for storage, and a single file box sits a few inches out of my reach. "A little higher," I tell him, and he exhales heavily with the effort.

My fingers graze the box and then catch just enough so I can slide it across the dusty floorboards toward me. I pull it out and hand it to Sam while Charlie lowers me back down. Brushing the dust off his shoulders, I smile up at him. "Knew that height would eventually come in handy."

"Great, I'm Lydia Fox's personal stepladder," he quips with a light grumble.

The lights flicker back on, and Sam places the box on one of the room's two beds. Evie pushes him aside. "Documents," she exclaims with relish.

Digging through the box, she starts to chew her lip. "This is full of bills, medical information, personal documents, and bank statements... all for Eugene Pickering."

"Who's Eugene Pickering?" Charlie asks, curiosity piqued.

"I have no idea," I murmur, the mystery deepening. "Could he be the groundskeeper?"

Evie adjusts her glasses and narrows her gaze at a particular document that catches her eye. "Look here, a few weeks before Lily's death, he received a hefty payment—a really substantial one—which might explain his absence."

"How much?" Shirley finally manages to regain her composure and joins the conversation.

"$15,000."

"That's a lot of money for a gardener."

The lights flicker and then die, once again dropping us into darkness. "I think he has something else." Sam stares at the door frame. The spirit is no longer visible to us, but Sam's gaze remains fixed on him. I take his hand in mine, hoping to reestablish the connection, but it doesn't work.

"I'm sorry," I say because I hate that he's alone in this once again.

"It's okay. It's the thought that counts," he reassures me softly. To the others, he says, "Let's keep moving. He's signaling us to follow again."

"This better not be a wild goose chase all night," Shirley complains, her voice tinged with fatigue and frustration.

We follow Sam down the stairs, and my gaze slips to where he hasn't yet let go of my hand. With my free hand, I pull his arm closer, hugging it tight to my body.

The entity guides us out of the carriage house and leads us to a storm door obscured by dense foliage. It takes us several strenuous minutes to clear the brush and open the door to the root cellar.

It's not deep, and if we go down, both Charlie and Sam will have to hunch over. Then there's the matter of no light.

We plunge into the dark void of the root cellar, trailing behind Sam. I collide into his back when he halts abruptly. "What happened?" I inquire.

"I don't know. He disappeared," Sam admits, scanning the shadows. "Like... he walked through a wall and didn't come back." Frustrated, he drops my hand and folds his arms. "Look, man, I don't know what you're saying, and it's pitch black down here."

Evie, flailing her arms above her head, catches my eye. "What are you doing?" I ask.

Hunting for something, she finally exclaims, "Aha!" She tugs on a string, and a dim bulb flickers to life, revealing the confined space. The selective electricity is inconsistent with most of our studies. I make a mental note to inform Waller about this.

Sam glares at the wall where we lost sight of Eugene Pickering. Evie, ever the pragmatist, nudges him aside and whirls to face me. "The walls are just dirt, reinforced but still dirt. Why is one wall brick?"

Charlie's realization dawns with dread. "Oh, no."

Shirley squints, piecing it together.

"Oh, fuck, we've been *sleeping* here," Charlie mutters, horror lacing his tone.

I frown at Charlie and Evie, who seem to have connected the dots. "Shit," Sam curses. "I'll go grab some tools from the shed." He vanishes up the steps, leaving us in the murky glow of the lone bulb.

Moments later, Sam returns wielding two pickaxes, one weathered with age, the other evidently its newer replacement. Still grappling with the developments, I watch bewildered as both he and Charlie begin swinging at the spot where Sam had last seen Pickering.

As dust and debris fly, forcing me to step back from the thick cloud filling the tiny basement, it takes them merely ten minutes to breach the wall. When they do, a foul stench unfurls through the air, assaulting my senses and making me scrub at my nose and tear-filled eyes.

"Oh, God," Shirley gasps, retreating up the stairs with Evie in tow. The sounds of their retching reach me, stirring my own stomach into rebellion.

When the dust settles, the sight that greets us is macabre: the half-decayed corpse of Eugene Pickering, ensconced behind a crudely built wall.

"Gene!" Emily's voice shatters the heavy silence as she descends the stairs in a rush.

Dammit. "That was you in the windows?" I blurt out, realization dawning—the face at the window. Had I been so high that I mistook Emily for Lily?

"I just wanted to watch," Emily sobs. In an instant, Sam is there, scooping her up and spinning her away from the grisly scene. His head brushes against the light bulb, casting erratic shadows around the room.

"Nope, this ain't for you, little momma," he insists, ushering her back upstairs.

"Don't touch him," I warn Charlie, thinking ahead. "We'll need to get Quinn here." But then something catches my eye—a gleam in the swinging light. I inch closer, pressing my sleeve against my nose, and lean in to scrutinize the corpse.

A solid silver letter opener juts from his chest, the initials WAC engraved on its hilt.

Evie steps beside me, her voice tight with panic. "William Ambrose Carmichael." I hadn't realized she'd come back. She faces us, her breathing shallow. "What are we going to do?"

CHAPTER seventeen

"You're sure?" I ask her. The room is as silent as the grave itself.

Evie pushes her glasses back up the bridge of her nose and whirls around to take another peek at the engraving. Turning back to us, she nods. "Yes, I checked his records at city hall yesterday. Those are definitely William Carmichael's initials."

Nothing is as sobering as a decomposing body in the room. The mushroom tea is still tickling at my edges, trying to make me clap my hands over my ears and scream until I no longer have a voice. It would be so easy to tip into it, dip my hand into a pool of hysteria, and lick it off my fingers.

I press my fist to my mouth and swallow down my screams, my bile, and my involuntary *laughter,* and study the dirt floor. Charlie opens his mouth to say something, and I don't remove my hand, merely holding a single finger up to allow me a minute of thought.

This is *my* team. This is *my* case. I turn to Evie and Charlie and say, "Both of you, come with me." They ascend the stairs, their footsteps echoing in the silent house. I linger momentarily, casting a final glance at Eugene Pickering's lifeless form. Gripping the string suspended from the light bulb, I pull it, plunging the room into darkness.

Stepping outside, I inhale a lungful of the clean, crisp air of an early October night. The scent of fallen leaves and damp earth fills my senses, blocking out the putrid stench of the cellar behind me. The moon casts an eerie glow, revealing the outlines of my team as they gather.

With a firm push, I close the heavy doors behind me, the creaking hinges breaking the profound quiet. Swiftly, I replace the disheveled shrubbery, the rustling leaves adding an undertone to the night's hushed symphony.

Their eyes are all over me, waiting to see what I'll do next. My face twists into hard lines and furrowed brows. "Get the kid and follow me," I say, my tone firm and commanding. I am my father. I am Courtland Prescott Fox, and I will not let something like a man nobody missed jam himself in the way of *my* case.

Sam stares at me in confusion as I pass him by without acknowledging him or Emily. "Sam, go change. Evie, put on some tea. Shirley, move the equipment. Charlie, put the sitting room back in order. Emily, you come with me up to the bathroom." Everyone gapes at me for a couple of breaths. "Did I stutter? Move."

Emily and I shove into the small space and put the toilet lid down. "Sit," I order. Emily does as she's told. I grab a washcloth from the towel bar and hold it under running water. She sits through my not-delicate scrubbing of the snot, tears, and vomit off her face. "How long has he been gone?"

Emily blinks at me in confusion for a minute. "Gene?"

"Yes." I don't meet her scared eyes.

"Since..." Her gaze darts down to the towel Sam left on the floor after his shower. "Two days after Lily," she tells me.

I nod. "Wash your face and hands. Meet me downstairs when you're done."

"Lydia?"

Turning to her, my eyebrows raise in question.

"N-nothing." Her voice is hoarse from crying. I head back downstairs.

"Is the tea ready?" Evie nods. "Everybody grab a cup and sit down."

Sam changes into a loose lace-up V-neck shirt with rolled-up sleeves and low-cut jeans with ragged hems. He chews his thumb in thought. "Lydia." His hand reaches for my arm, but I'm too quick for him.

I don't miss the concern etched onto his face, however. It's another thing I don't have time to deal with right now. Pouring myself a cup of Evie's robust tea, I return to the sitting room and stand before the fire. Emily comes down the stairs and takes a seat with the others.

Clearing my throat, I take a sip and let out a sigh. "I need everyone to listen to everything I have to say first, and then you'll have your turn." Most of them scrunch their expressions in disapproval before I'm given the chance to utter another word. Straightening my shoulders, I toss my hair back and fix each of them with a hard stare, leaving Sam for last. "The man in our root cellar has been missing since two days after Lily drowned. He's not going to get any deader. What will die if we call the police and report this right now is our investigation."

A flood of outraged gasps fills the room, and I hold my hand up to keep them from interrupting. My face goes cold and hard like I'd seen my father do a hundred times. "We have a job to do here, and in my experience, the cops will trample all over this, and we're going to lose an opportunity. I'm not asking you to give me a week. I'm asking you to give me *two* days. Two days." Unrest ripples through them. My tone is resolute, unwavering. "Listen to me," I command, trying to regain their attention. "*Listen* to me. Do you think a man like William Carmichael would kill someone with something that has his fucking *initials* engraved on it? And why kill someone *after* you paid them off? None of this makes any sense."

Shirley raises her hand to speak. "I agree; this stinks like a setup. The man has to have enemies; he's a politician. If we can put together a stronger case, we might do this investigation justice. You won't get any argument out of me, but I need to know one thing…"

"Which is?"

"Are you going to tell Waller?"

Narrowing my gaze, I draw my bottom lip across my two front teeth. "No. He'll just call Quinn and pull us all out of here."

Sam is staring down between his bare feet. "Who *are* you?" He asks me. "Because this isn't the Lydia Fox I came to work with. This isn't you. We *have* to call them. We *have* to let that poor man out of the cellar, Lydia. I'm never down with the man, but this is a person we're talking about. A person who died in pain. A person whose life was *stolen* from him." He shakes his dark curls and gazes up at me with imploring eyes. His voice cracks with desperation. "Please, Lydia, please. I'm begging you, don't make this decision. This will tear our team apart. I'm telling you right now. It'll tear us apart."

The way he pleads with me makes me waver because I'm unsure if he's talking about the team right now or us, him and me. My heart stutters for a moment, and I tear my gaze away. "It's only for a couple more days," I say, my voice rough with emotion. "What if we had never found him? He could've stayed in the cellar for *decades*. What difference are two more days going to make?"

He runs his fingers through his hair and scrunches up his face in pain. "You're asking us to stay in a house where a man's body is rotting in the basement." His words cling to my skin like cobwebs.

Swallowing, I nod. "Yes, that's what I'm asking."

"You're asking a fucking *twelve-year-old* to keep a secret that is going to rip her to pieces, Lydia. Fucking think about what you're doing? You can't be asking this of us. You can't. I won't do it." Sam turns his watery gaze on Emily and then back on me. "You're asking too much."

Iron slides down my spine, and I jut my chin at him. "Someone has to see the bigger picture. We can't let our emotions take over," I say.

"That's all we *are*, Lydia! Messy bags of bloody emotions!"

Emily bursts into tears. This will not sway me. I will be the levy the team needs. I will not break. I will remain steadfast and true. A bastion of resolve, even if I have to shut them all the fuck down.

"I don't understand," she sobs, and large, hot tears and snot drip from her chin onto her nightclothes.

"We need to figure out who killed your groundskeeper because I think they might have killed your sister."

Emily pins me down with a complicated, wet expression that could probably match my own. "I *know* that! I'm not stupid!" She roars at me. Tears streaming, she continues, "But how can you just leave him like that? How can you just let him rot in the walls of his own house? You're just as much of a bitch as *Cecilia!*" The words are a slap to the face; I won't lie. Scrambling to her feet, she shoves past me and dashes out into the small front yard.

With one last hurt expression, Sam follows her.

Shirley purses her lips. "That could have gone better. You want me to follow them to make sure they don't call the cops from the big house?"

The most brutal shit to swallow is I know Sam won't let her, and it's so painful. It's agonizing to breathe. My stupid traitorous heart knows beyond the shadow of a doubt Sam will stay loyal even as I shatter everything he believed in me. "I think it'll be alright," I tell Shirley honestly. Her shoulders relax at my reassurance.

"Like I said, I believe in investigative journalism more than I do the cops," she tells me again.

I close my eyes and take a deep inhale. I hate believing that Quinn is incapable of reason, but he has rules to adhere to, and I can't ask him to bend them for me more than he already has.

I turn to Evie. Her fists are clenched tightly in her lap. She's trying to breathe as evenly as she can. "Are you out of your God damned mind, Lydia? I mean, seriously, because I need to know. Do you understand how hard this will fucking blow black on us? We are tampering with a *murder* scene. You are not only putting the reputation of our department at risk, you're putting *Waller* at risk. He could lose his job. We could be expelled. This could come back on our parents. My *parents*, Lydia. This will be a media circus; you and I know it."

She stands up, her eyes aflame with her anger. "I've never seen this side of you. I've never thought you'd be someone who'd risk everything just to steal a little spotlight from those *fucking Catholics* in New York!"

"I'm not—"

"No! Shut up! You had your turn! You have a duty to the dead. Not just to the sister of that little girl bawling her eyes out in the yard, but to the fucking dead man in the basement, too! I respected you! I looked up to you! Sam respected you, too. And what about Sam, huh? He senses them, Lydia, and you want him to, what? Live here with Eugene Pickering until you solve your little Scooby-Doo mystery? I've never been so disgusted with anyone in my entire life!"

Evie gets right in my face and pulls her hand back to slap me. Charlie catches it before she can deliver. "Whoa. *Whoa,*" Charlie tells her. "Ease off, Evie. Ease off."

My eyes flicker up to meet Charlie's, and I beg him to back me up—to support me. His chest heaves as adrenaline surges through the room. He glances at the front door where Sam and Emily fled, to Shirley, to Evie, who furiously rips her hand out of his grasp, and back to me.

"I have questions," he breathes out. After I nod, he launches into them. "You said two days." Again, I move my head to agree with him. "What happens if we haven't solved who killed Lily in two days?"

"We call Quinn."

"And if the disciplinary committee at the college calls us up?"

"I'll tell them it was my call, and I demanded it of all of you to receive your class credits." My voice is back to being solid, confident, on the ground, and steady.

"Give me Quinn's card." He holds his hand out in front of me.

"What?" This I didn't expect.

Sam and Emily are standing at the door, watching Charlie and I. Evie moves to the kitchen, where she glares at me with her arms wrapped tight across her chest.

"They need to trust that I'll go to Quinn if you won't. You have 48 hours to solve this. If it's not solved by then, I call Quinn in."

Everyone's eyes land on me, pinning me in place. I walk over to my purse next to the door, dig into my wallet, and fish out Quinn's business card.

With a deadly serious expression, I place it in Charlie's palm. "48 hours. You have my word."

Charlie peers down at it to confirm it's the correct card and turns to everyone else. "I'll call him. Give her two days. You seriously think they'll reopen Lily's case as a murder if they can nail Carmichael on this one? And can they? Unless his fingerprints are on that letter opener, Carmichael has an alibi. He was at church when Lily drowned. Someone could have stolen that letter opener; the groundskeeper caught him on the property, and the thief stabbed him with it." He takes a deep breath. "Lydia's right. Lily's, and possibly Pickering's, murder will go unsolved unless we figure this out. Hauntings or no."

"I can't do this without you," I tell them. "But I'm not going to lie—it won't be easy. And I'm sorry, Emily. It's an unfair and very grown-up thing to ask of you, but I think there are some things you're still keeping from us—things that can help us solve your sister's drowning."

She frowns at me. "Like what? I've told you everything."

"Why is your nightgown lying in a mildewing lump in your closet? Did you go out to the pond? Did you try to save her?"

Emily turns to Sam first and then back to me. "What?"

"In your closet. Your nightgown is in a ball in the corner, which is why it reeks in there."

Confusion clouds her features, and I realize I'm on the wrong track. "Oh no," I mumble and turn to meet Evie's gaze in the kitchen.

She's still so angry, but she suddenly realizes at the same time that I do. "It's another plant," she says.

"It's another plant," I repeat. Turning back to Emily, I tell her, "I'm sorry. I made a mistake, but I'll explain everything soon. Promise me you will touch nothing in your closet. We're going to need everything intact, okay?"

Emily nods.

Closing my eyes, I step back until my back hits the fireplace mantle. "Well?"

"I trust Charlie," Evie says. "But you're going to have a contract to sign in the morning saying you threatened our college credit if we didn't go along with this. You will sign it," she insists. The finality in her tone leaves no room for refusal. A piece of our friendship is irreversibly chipped; it will never be the same as before, and the broken bit wedges into my heart. I wonder how many chips our relationship will be able to sustain before it no longer holds up on its own.

"You already had me," Shirley says. "I'm never down with calling the Five-0."

Emily bites her fingernails. "Only for two days, right?"

"Just two days," I assure her.

"That's how long Gene lived after Lily. He was nice. He used to sneak me ginger snap cookies."

Charlie glances at me and nods. "I hope you know what you're doing, Lydia."

Our eyes lock as Sam steps through the door.

"This is super fucked up, but I would never ask this of any of you if I didn't think it was the right thing to do," I tell them before trailing Sam outside.

In the open night, bathed in shadows, I find Sam seated in the back of the van. His feet dangle over the gravel driveway, a cigarette clenched between his fingers, his wrist cradled in his hand.

"What do you want, Lydia?" His words cut through the air, each syllable carrying an undertone of pain so palpable that I'm compelled to shut my eyes, attempting to silence the aching roar within my chest.

"Can I sit?" I whisper, my voice barely a thread.

He responds with a casual shrug.

"Sam—"

"Did you come out here to make sure I wouldn't run off to the cops? You got your way, didn't you?" He huffs out a chortle, and it's not that velvety soft laugh I love so much; it's hard and bitter. "I'll bet you always get your way, don't you?"

"What do you mean?"

"Batting your bottomless green eyes at anyone you want something from? I meant what I said: I'd do *anything* for you. Apparently, even sell my soul."

"I think you're being a little dramatic, Sam. It's two days."

"Yeah, sure. Two days." He exhales smoke and makes me wait him out. It's maddening. "You know he led me to his body? How long do you think he'd been vying for our attention until I finally saw him?"

"Who? Pickering?"

Sam still won't meet my eyes. He swallows tight and nods. "I mean, fuck, can you imagine? All these kids take over your house, and if you can do something to make them see you, then you can take them to your body, and they'll fucking *free* you. Can you imagine something like that? And then one day, I take the right dose of acid or 'shrooms, and I see him. And then what do we do? We leave him there. We leave him in that fucking wall, Lydia."

Speechless, a lump lodges in my throat, making each breath a struggle.

He nonchalantly flicks the cigarette into the night and stands. "You did the one thing I asked you not to do, not two hours ago, and you did it. You're breaking my fucking heart."

Sam strides away, leaving me with nothing but a field of stars.

CHAPTER *eighteen*

With the mushrooms still in my system, my brain struggles to keep up with what's real and what's not. Everything huffs and puffs and sighs at me in disappointment. I want to peel out of my skin and leave it behind so I stop looking like her, like Octavia. The carriage house looms at me with its filmy, dead-eyed windows, the front path an accusing finger jabbing me in the sternum.

Wiping my nose from the cold, I take a brave couple of minutes to pull myself together enough to head back into the house to put on a coat and scarf. A need to think, a need to walk, a need to escape this crushing guilt pushes me back inside.

Emily is the only one who acknowledges my return. Donning my coat, I meet her cool gaze. "Ready to go back up to the house?" I inquire.

"I'll take her," Sam tells me.

"No, that's okay. Emily and I have some things to discuss, don't we?" Emily swallows when my calm expression settles on her.

Sam intervenes, positioning himself between us. "I don't think you're in any state—"

"I'm perfectly capable of walking Emily back on my own, Sam." We eye each other warily, uncertain of the amount of space either of us needs or wants.

His brow creases in thought. "You shouldn't be—"

"I'll be perfectly safe—"

"With her alone," we both say at the same time.

Oh. This isn't about my safety. It's about Emily's.

The mushrooms, perhaps, enlarge his eyes, making them deep enough to dive into. He's positively aristocratic; only centuries of bloodlines manifest as ancient and noble as Sam's intense gaze. The thought sends a shiver down the entire length of me. He is time itself, tightly wound into the visage of a man.

"You can hardly stand, Lydia," he tells me under his breath, worry drawing his face tight.

"I need something," I gasp out. "Water? Juice? Something."

"Come with me." His long fingers wrap around my wrist, dragging me into the kitchen. Once we're alone, he bends his knees to inspect my pupils.

"You hate me," I say with a quality akin to panic.

"I don't hate you." Sam turns to get a bottle of orange juice out of the fridge and pours me a large glass.

Snatching it out of his hand, I drink it down greedily. "How do you make this stop? It's too much. Everything feels like…" Finishing the sentence is pointless; there aren't words to describe this. If anyone can commiserate with what I'm talking about, it's Sam.

He blinks, and his long, dark lashes brush the tops of his high cheekbones. "You just need to wait it out. The juice should help, though."

"I don't have time to wait it out. There is a giant fucking pendulum swinging against me right now."

"And you're lucky to have it," he hisses back at me. "You should be grateful you have it."

"Don't hate me." It's pathetic. This isn't me.

"I don't hate you." He repeats it, but his patience strains around the edges.

"You do, like the rest of them. You all hate me." My chest is heaving up and down as I give in to the anxiety that I've done this. I've alienated them all.

"Shit," he grumbles and pulls me against his chest. The glass clutched in my hands is squashed between us. "Calm down. I need to be mad at you for a little while, Lydia. You need to let me. Can't you understand that?"

I nod, my tears dotting the collar of his shirt. Pushing my breath out between my lips a couple of times, I steady myself into him. "Okay," I tell him.

He brings a hand up to brush the hair back from my face. "You're okay."

Stepping back, I set the glass in the sink. "I'm taking Emily back. We have dead sister things to talk about. I won't frighten her, Sam, I promise. She's the reason I'm here."

"Take the walkie talkie. If you're not back in an hour, I'm coming to find you."

Swiping my tongue across my bottom lip, I nibble on it thoughtfully. "I didn't mean to…"

"No. We're not talking about this yet. You have to give me some time to be angry. It's important."

I fill the glass with water and chug it, placing it back in the sink when I'm done. Stepping out of the kitchen, I ask, "Ready, kid?" After tugging on my coat, I hold the walkie up to Charlie, sitting on the couch with Shirley. "Taking this," I tell him, and he gives me a thumbs up.

Emily nods, and we head out onto the moonlit path to the manor. An owl hoots somewhere in the beech trees, and dead leaves dance across the grass. I eye her in my peripheral. Her navy wool coat is buttoned up to her ears over her thin pajamas, and her pale blonde hair, plaited into two parts, trails behind her like the reins of a runaway horse.

I reach out and tug one. She turns her pale gaze, eyes so grave for twelve.

"I had a twin sister, too, you know."

Minutes tick by as we make our way up the path, but Emily hasn't responded. Pressing her lips together, she gazes at the pond to our left as we trudge on. "She's dead, isn't she?"

"Yes," I tell her.

"You're wrong, you know."

I look at her.

"You have a sister. It doesn't matter whether she's here or not. She's still your sister."

My breath puffs out in front of me three times while I ponder what she's said.

"What was her name?" She asks me.

"Octavia."

"Pretty." She scratches her nose while she debates asking me. "How did she—"

"She drowned."

Emily pulls up short. "You're lying. You're trying to bond with me so that I won't tell about Gene."

My eyebrows raise at her assessment. "No," I say, surprise coloring my words, "but excellent instincts, kiddo. You'd do well in my department."

"She drowned?" I nod. "How old were you?"

"Eighteen."

She licks her lips in thought. "You got to have more time with her."

"You're still connected to Lily."

"You're not?"

Shoving my hands in my pockets, I shake my head. "Not once. Can I tell you something?" She glances up at me expectantly. "It's sometimes like I lost an arm or a leg, and I'll go to reach for something or stand up, and I remember it's not there anymore."

"It fucking sucks," Emily says.

My surprised laugh cuts the cold air in front of us. "It does," I tell her once I've recovered. "It really does."

We find ourselves standing at the front door. "Will you come back with me to my room?" she asks, her cheeks flushing with embarrassment.

"Oh. Of course. Anything you need."

"It's not like I'm a baby, but…"

"But something in your closet cut your face up last night, Emily. I'll stay with you until you fall asleep if you want."

She nods, and we head upstairs. Once we're back in her room, I take the time to investigate any changes she might've made. She's wedged her desk chair under the handle of the closet door.

After using the bathroom, she hops into her bed. "Would you check under my bed? I know I'm too old for this."

"You're not too old." Crouching on the rug, I lift her bedskirt and peer into the dark space beneath her mattress. Turning, I do the same for Lily's bed.

"I wish I could be as brave as you someday, Lydia," she whispers, but her gaze darts to the closet.

"Do you want me to check the closet, too?" Her lips are pressed so tightly together that the skin around her mouth pales, and she nods reluctantly. "May I?" I ask and gesture at one of the three flashlights she's collected on her nightstand.

With her approval, I take one and remove the chair. The closet is not big, but deep enough that I can take a couple of steps into it before I meet the back wall. Peering around, I take in the two neat sides of the girls' clothing, almost identical to one another. The memory of wearing matching outfits with Octavia surfaces, and I smile despite the tension. We hated it.

An interesting collection of hats, which I admire for a minute, takes up a great deal of space. Most of them are fancy tea party hats with feathers and costume jewelry. Suddenly, one of the feathers flutters softly, and I furrow my brow at it. It does it again, and I step up to it. Holding my hand up, I wait.

A cool breeze dances across my knuckles, and I inhale sharply. Another one hits me in the same place, and I spin in the closet, searching for the source.

There's no window, no attic entry point, no vent. Where is the cold air coming from? Goosebumps travel up my arms.

Of all the times to need Charlie. "Lydia?" Emily calls from the other room.

Right. The kid. Mustn't scare the kid. I pop back out of her closet and shut the door behind me. "Sorry. I was digging your hat collection. You must have had the fanciest of tea parties."

"We liked making the hats more than we liked the tea parties," she tells me, exhaustion weighing down her words.

"Go to sleep, Emily. You're tired." I sit on Lily's bed and wait until Emily's breathing steadies and evolves into soft snores.

Grabbing the flashlight again, I tiptoe back to the closet and slide inside the inky shadows. Shutting the closet behind me, I flip on the light.

Of course, this now makes me the monster in her closet, and I ponder this without missing the irony. Holding my hand out, I search for the source of the wind again. It turns me in the direction of the back corner, and I push an armful of clothes aside. The back corner of Emily's closet is cracked open, just maybe an eighth of an inch.

My eyes widen. A secret passage. A freaking secret passage. I can't suppress my excitement about this discovery, even though it provides access to a little girl's bedroom. But it's a freaking secret passage!

I glance down at my watch. Sam warned me he would come for me if I weren't back in an hour. I have twenty-five minutes left of that hour. Surely, this passage couldn't go very far, right?

Pushing open the passage, it's a tight squeeze as I move between the manor's walls. The corridor is dusty and strewn with cobwebs, and the light only reaches about six feet. My gaze remains steady on the floorboards beneath me until I find an open trapdoor plunging to the first floor. If closed, the width of the door would take up the entire passage; I could cross it and head further into the second floor. I shine the light down into the hole and opt for the shortcut to the first floor as I step into the pooling shadows beneath me.

Once at the bottom of the stairs, a thin shaft of light pierces the darkness about forty feet ahead of me. When I reach it, I find a tiny hole in the wall. I have to stand on my toes to peek through it, but I find the moonlit sitting room on the other side.

"What in the world?" I whisper and step back from it. Reaching the end of this passage, I turn around and head the other way, trying to discern how to get on the other side of the stairs when the hinge catches in my light beam. "Clever," I groan as I lift the stairs where it hinges and duck behind it to continue down the path.

The Carmichaels took their spying very seriously. Or was this the Shippingtons?

I stop. In front of me is another trap door. This one is firmly closed. Holding the light out on my wrist, I check the time. I still have fifteen minutes or so.

That is, if Sam even remembers. I also promised Waller I wouldn't go back into the basement. Biting the inside of my bottom lip in thought, I weigh my choices. Venturing down the stairs just to check if it leads to anywhere surprising and then coming right back up wouldn't be too bad, would it?

I should probably get someone to come back with me. Going alone is something I would definitely yell at one of my team members for. My fingers dip into the wool of my coat and pull out the radio. I let it drop back down. Rubbing my forehead with the tips of my fingers, I know I'm going to give in to temptation.

Nobody has to know.

And nobody will know where to find your body when you don't come back, Lydia.

Shut up, Octavia.

This is stupid. I'm a grown woman who can make her own choices. Shining the light on the trapdoor latch, I yank it open. It's so heavy that it takes a couple of tries before it creaks open much louder than I anticipated. The sound echoes ominously, reverberating down the shadow-laden passage. Placing it gently to rest against the wall, I pause and listen. Sweeping the flashlight down one side of the passage and then the other, I take a tentative step forward, holding on so I don't tumble down the rickety wood stairs. I descend into the bowels of the manor.

The stairs groan from disuse. All I can hear is my breathing and maybe a... dripping sound? I wouldn't be surprised, especially with the cloying perfume of mildew down here, if the pond butted up against the foundation leaked in places. I stop at the bottom of the stairs and swipe my light around, searching for what use this room might have had.

It's mid-sized for the size of this estate, approximately the size of the entire downstairs of the carriage house. There's even a fireplace in here, along with beds, a table, and shelves with jars of things time stole away.

I scan the ceiling, looking for a light. Disappointed but not surprised, I find nothing. My steps suddenly muffle, and I peer down at the braided rag rug beneath my feet. Continuing my search of the quarters, I find a wardrobe too warped with damp for me to pry open.

The air grows colder, and a sense of foreboding settles over me. Screwing my expression up in thought, I do another quick scan with the light. Surely this wouldn't be servants' quarters? There aren't even any windows. A pull-horse toy sulks in its abandonment at the foot of one of the beds. If children had been down here, they certainly weren't servants' quarters then.

And it strikes me. The four beds are all small, and a shiver skitters across my bones. The sound of debris dislodging echoes ominously, causing me to spin my light toward the fireplace. Dust and crumbling mortar shake free from the chimney and sprinkle onto the empty grate in the firebox.

My heart pounds in my chest. Is it a rat or an opossum nesting in the chimney? Holding my light on the pattering rain of dirt and stone, the atmosphere thickens as a shadow darkens the brick. To my horror, a pale white hand the size of a child's appears from the chimney, wrapping grayish fingers around the lintel. My breath catches. Trying not to make a sound, I slink back toward the stairs. A careless movement causes me to hit a shelf, and a squeak of terror issues from my traitorous throat.

I freeze. The searching hand slithers back up into the dark. A red ball bounces out from underneath one of the beds, rolling across the carpet and coming to rest at the toe of my boot. Terror seizes every nerve in my body, and I turn, the light wildly trying to find purchase on the wooden staircase.

The flashlight stutters as though struggling to remember where it left the stairs. I smack it hard, and it fades, flickers, and dies. And here I am, pressed against the cold open shelving, enveloped in suffocating darkness. My eyes take too long to adjust.

Something brushes across my ankle, and I jerk away. This sudden movement causes me to lose my balance, and I pitch forward and land face-first into the dusty rug, and the flashlight rolls out of my reach.

A child's giggle cuts across the dark, echoing eerily close to the floor. It sounds stifled, like someone trying not to be found, like a merry game. I have to choke on my own screams and feel my way across the floor.

Trying desperately to remember which direction the stairs are in, I drag my knees forward and wave my hands in front of me so I don't run face-first into anything—or anyone. When my fingers finally graze what feels like the lowest riser, I try to remain as quiet as possible, resisting the urge to scrabble up the steps and escape this wretched hole in the ground.

Above me, a silhouette, ominous and looming, moves at the top of the stairs. The peephole only lets in the faintest sliver of light into the passage above. I pause and strain my eyes in the darkness, trying to discern the figure's intentions. Can they see me here at the bottom of the steps? Can it hear my ragged breaths? Holding my breath, I wait for the figure at the top of the stairs to make its next move.

Please move on. Please, just go away.

It takes a shuffling step back, and the brief surge of relief is quickly smothered by dread as the trapdoor comes crashing down with a resounding thud. A latch slams into place, sealing me in this underground tomb.

The realization of my predicament sends a chilling wave through me, solidifying the terror of being isolated in the dark, with no one knowing where I am—except the person who locked me in.

CHAPTER *nineteen*

Scrabbling up the stairs, I bang on the trapdoor over my head. "There's someone down here!" I yell. "I'm down here! Unlock the door!"

I stop and listen. Nothing cuts the air but my heavy breathing. The chuckle of a toddler playing hide and seek breaks the silence. "H-hello?" I whimper.

Whipping my fist out in front of me, I bang the side of it on the door again. A hard enough hit could break the latch; this house is old. Slamming myself up as hard as I can, all I manage is bright shocks of pain radiating down my shoulder. "Please," I cry out. "For God's sake, let me out."

It isn't to anybody in particular. It's sharp, hot fear lancing through me like a fire poker. I don't know where my flashlight went, and I didn't have the opportunity to finish mapping the bunker before the light went out. There must be another way.

But that means crawling back down the stairs. Back down to whatever is waiting in the bunker. Cobwebs brush across my face, and I swipe at them in revulsion. Minutes tick by while I gather the nerve to go back. Carefully, I ease my way down one step at a time, reaching the bottom before I'm ready, making me jump from surprise.

Something smooth and small bumps into my fingers, and I know it's the ball again. I flick it away, as if it were an insect crawling across my skin. The floor beneath is smooth and well-worn but uneven. Reaching out, I find the wall and, inch by inch, get back to my feet.

Keeping my fingers touching the wall, I follow it around the room. Bumping face-first into the shelf shocks me, and I emit a high-pitched gasp. It makes whatever is in here with me laugh in a quiet little huff, but it's cut off as if a hand clapped over whatever made the noise.

The weathered shelf gives me splinters every foot or so. I hiss in pain and reluctantly go back to follow it around, hoping to reconnect with the wall eventually. At least the wall is just stone, with no jagged edges of dried-out wood eager to tear into my skin and steal some moisture. Relief floods through me when my fingers touch the stone again.

Standing against the wall, I try to calm down as I lean into the stone. The hairs on the back of my neck stand at attention. Something is behind me. I don't know how I know, but I can sense it. Taking shallow gasps, I work up the courage to turn and face the absolute blackness behind me.

If I reach out my hands, I'll hit whoever is behind me. My whole body trembles, and I clench my jaw to keep my teeth from chattering. Blood rushes to my head and pounds in my ears. I take my fingers off the wall and take a blind step forward without anything to guide me.

A hand moves through my long, loose hair. "*Boo,*" a child-like voice whispers from behind me.

I shriek and run forward, colliding with the dining table, and pain shoots through my right leg, and stars swim in my eyes from stubbing my toe on the base. "Gah," is all that sputters out of me, but I tear to the right, toward the back of the bunker, where I hadn't yet managed to search.

Walking as fast as I can without sight, I swipe my hands out in front of me until I hit the far end of the bunker. Tracing the stone to the left, all I find are more shelves. Trying my luck going the other way, my hands find wood.

My fingers dance all over the wooden surface, landing on a door handle. I yank with all my might to escape the bunker, but it doesn't budge. "No!" I cry out and slap my palm on the door. "No, please!"

At my second strike, I hit cold metal. Feeling around the grooves, I discover it's a latch. With a cry of relief, I manipulate it open. Years of disuse turn this into a wiggling, teeth-clenching ordeal until it finally comes free, and I'm able to pull it open and...

I'm back in the larger basement. It's just more basement—a labyrinth beneath Minos' palace—and I'm stuck down here with the beast and no twine.

A shambling noise picks at my ears from behind me, coming from the bunker. I search for the doorknob and frantically slam it shut before whatever slithered or crawled its way across the floor reaches the threshold. Letting out a shaky breath, I wipe my dusty, sweaty hands on my trousers and try my luck with following the wall again.

Everything echoes in this part of the basement, so I know I'm in one of the high-ceilinged chambers we encountered before. A musty, heady stench invades this part of the basement, and the distant dripping I heard before is closer. It's the pond, which shares a wall with the cellar. I step into a shallow puddle as if to confirm my thoughts.

It's so cold, and my fingers run numb along the chilly stone, so I switch hands. Whenever I reach another corner, I crash into more webs and furiously bat them away from my face. They stick to my lips and chin, tickling my neck. I need a shower.

The intensity of the dark worms its way into the marrow of my bones. Darkness is such a ridiculous thing, I've always thought. Darkness can't hurt you. How could people be so afraid of something so trivial? Now the fear devours me.

"Ariadne," I whisper hoarsely. I am so surprised to hear my voice that I jump back. "I am Ariadne." Whose heartbeat is that? It's fast and hard and fills my head. It drowns out my gasping, erratic breath, and I have to stop. Pressing my fingers to my chest, I bend at the waist and take great gulps of air. "I have to calm down. I can't let fear..."

How am I supposed to even finish that thought when the whole basement fills with nothing but the sound of my traitorous heart? "STOP!" I yell.

It goes away, but in its place comes a footstep, not a heartbeat, from the far side of the cavernous room. Everything is amplified with adrenaline surging through my veins. Unsure I heard it correctly, I wait, holding my breath, with my fingers feeling for purchase along the wall. I inch to the right.

Another footstep, closer now. With my other hand, I press my palm across my lips. The wall ends, and I discover a doorway to one of the corridors I'm sure I wandered down before, or one like it. I can take my chance down the hall or continue my journey around the room's periphery.

What if whatever attacked me before is stalking me again? I slip down the hall, keeping my fingers trailing into the stall-like rooms I saw before. It's an empty stall and then another, but the third isn't a stall at all; it's another corridor.

I squeeze my eyes shut and swallow around the lump in my throat. All I'm doing is going deeper into the maze. More lost, more lost, more lost.

Someone taps their fingernails slow, so slow, farther down from where I'm standing. I can't guess how far. I squint as hard as I can and bite my lip. Keep going. I have to keep going.

Nobody is there; it's a rat, a mouse, or hell, a raccoon. *I don't even have my damn Polaroid with me this time.* It happens again. The tapping. The tapping. The tapping.

Whoever it is wants to play with me.

"I'm t-trying to *help* you p-people," I stutter out. A long, drawn-out sigh is the only answer I receive. Fuck it. I'm going to take my chances down the hall.

Keeping my palm tight to the wall, I break into a jog, trying to move as swiftly as possible to put enough distance between me and whoever else is down here.

My sleeve catches on a nail, and I rip it free rather than try to disentangle myself. Moving much faster now, I can't possibly predict it coming when I run face-first into another door. Fireworks light up behind my eyes, and I swipe the back of my hand under my nose. It comes back wet.

Gripping the doorknob, I pull as hard as I can. Like many of the doors in this hellhole, it doesn't budge. Breathing hard, worried my shadow will catch up to me soon, I feel around the door until I realize my mistake. My fingers wrap around the handle again, and I push, falling into the room beyond. Scrambling to my feet, I slam the door shut and lean all my weight against it.

The doorknob squeaks as it turns agonizingly slow. I grab it and hold it still while something beyond tries to twist it open. Beneath my head, the door shakes in its frame as whoever I left behind fights me to rip it open.

Keeping the handle in my tight grip, the fingers of my other hand fumble around the frame and find another latch. I pull it shut, and this one slides easily as though it had been used recently. With a shaky sigh, I slide down and sit for a moment, gathering my breath and courage.

I'm in another immense room. It's easy to tell because the air sits differently here, not as stifling. Heaving myself to my feet, I push back the hairs sticking to my sweaty face. The sweat makes the cold worse—or it will in a few minutes once I've settled again.

This isn't the place I'm going to die. I have to find my way out. How stupid would it be to die lost in a house? Wiping my nose again, I straighten up and think. Continuing to follow the wall, I run into a pile of furniture, which veers me off course.

I'm walking around the clusters of tables and side chairs, all covered with cool sheets, when I step on something that drives a white hot agony through the sole of my foot, all the way through my boot. "Aggh!" I cry out and drop to the floor in a crumpled heap. I grip my foot in my hands and rock back and forth.

Trying desperately to focus on anything other than the pain, I pull my pants leg up to unzip the inside of my boot and reach down. A board with what I assume is a nail attached to it is stuck fast to the bottom of my foot.

I have no idea how to remove it from my foot. The way my foot is shoved into the boot, and the angle of the nail makes it so I don't have enough room to pull it off. "Fuck," I gasp out. And I mean it. I'm well and truly fucked. It's hard to think straight; the pain is so searing.

The only thing I can do is try to pry the board away. If I use one of the table legs as leverage, perhaps I can pull it off. It's going to hurt like a bitch. I place the top of my foot on the opposite thigh and pull the wood with both hands. It doesn't move.

Burying my face in my hands, I stifle a shuddering groan. Mustering the strength to do it again, I wiggle it back and forth. I'm attempting to unscrew it out of my foot like a wine cork. I'm so close.

A squawk lights up the room and makes me jump, my hand slipping on the board and driving a thick splinter into my palm. The radio I stashed and forgot in my coat. How could I have forgotten it?

Snatching it from my pocket, I depress the side button. "Hello?" I ask, my voice small and pathetic, peppered with pain.

"Lydia?" a voice asks me. It's broken up and mostly static, but it's real. It has to be real.

"Sam?"

"Where are you?"

I peer around in the darkness, trying to find something to help him find me in this stupid maze. "I'm in the basement."

Static. "What—" Static. "—in the basement?"

"Just find me!" I snarl into it, and then in a smaller voice, whisper, "Please?"

"I'm coming," he tells me.

The quiet overwhelms me. I still have a board stuck to my foot, my nose is bleeding, and I have a huge splinter in my hand. "Don't stop talking to me."

"What do you want me to say?"

"I'm sorry," I tell him. "I messed up tonight."

"Lydia—"

"No, let me say it. It's easier in the dark. I shouldn't have demanded. I should have explained. I should have consulted you guys. I act like this is a one-woman show, and I'm sorry. I'll try to do better." Choking back a sob, I lift my finger off the button so he doesn't have to listen to me.

"Are you hurt?"

"Yes," I sniff and wipe my eyes. "I'm hurt, and I have no flashlight, and I'm... scared." A door slams from somewhere in the room. "Was that you slamming the door?" I bite out around clenched teeth. *Not now.* I can't get away if whatever stalked me in the other room found a way around. Tears sting my eyes, and I force my shirt into my mouth so I don't cry out. It hurts so much.

A light sweeps the floor about thirty feet in front of me. My heart slams into my throat. "Lydia?"

"Sam?" I sob out. And he's there so fast. He's on his knees in front of me, gathering me in his arms. Hot tears flood out of me, and I cry hard and long against him. Pushing me back, he examines my injuries.

"What happened? What are you doing down here? Why are you on the floor? Are you hurt?" He points the flashlight at me and drags it up to my face. "Jesus, Lydia, is that blood?" His strong fingers delicately lift my chin in his hand, and he turns my head this way and that to inspect the damage. "Let me see your hands."

I hold them out and study them under his steady light. He studies the splinters. "The blood is from my nose," I tell him. My cold hands shake so severely that he pulls them to his chest and rubs them against his shirt to warm them. When I finally look up from my fingers, his eyes meet mine. "We have to stop meeting like this," he jokes in such a soft tone that I want to melt into him.

You're here.

"Of course I am. I told you I'd come looking for you if you weren't back in an hour." I hadn't realized I'd said it aloud. He searches my eyes for something. "Lydia, I'll always come for you no matter where we're at. Do you understand?"

I nod numbly. He moves his hand up behind my head and pulls me back against him again. With my forehead resting on his warm chest, my heart finally starts to steady into its usual pace. "Can you walk?"

"I stepped on a nail," I mumble against him. He shines the light on the board next to me.

"Here," he tells me as he hands me his flashlight. Scooping me up with one arm under my knees and the other securely around my waist, he somehow manages to lift me from his crouch.

"Please tell me you know the way out."

"It's behind us." Carrying me to the stairs, he starts up.

"How did you find me?"

He's focusing on the stairs, not looking at me. "Lily. Lily came to me in a panic. She made me follow her."

Lily? "Did you ask her?"

"Did I ask her what?"

"You know what, Sam." He takes a deep breath and says nothing until we reach the door beneath the foyer staircase.

"Can you open that for me?" I grab it, but then he whispers, "Wait." Poking his head out where I've cracked the door open, he checks to make sure nobody is around first, and then he carries me to the front door. Shifting my weight in his arms, we head back to the carriage house.

"Well? You didn't answer me," I remind him as he labors down the path. "Did you ask Lily who drowned her?"

"What were you doing? You promised Waller you wouldn't go into the basement."

Is he mad at me? And then I remember that, yes, of course, he's still mad at me. "Emily asked me to check her room before she went to sleep."

"And?"

"I discovered a secret passage in her closet," I tell him.

Sam stops abruptly, his expression a mix of shock and concern. His hold on me tightens. "Someone has access to her room?"

I nod.

"Should we leave her in the house alone?"

"I don't know what else we can do."

He turns us to look at it, Hemlock Hall looming in the distance. "What did you find? Just more basement?"

"I also found a peephole into the sitting room." His brow furrows with that information. "And then below that is a bunker of some sort. I think someone locked some kids down there, Sam. I don't think they ever made it out.."

"You mean, like live kids?"

"No, I mean, like… Revolutionary War-era kids," I tell him, frowning at his expression. "I'm sorry I scared you."

When we return to the carriage house, everyone seems to have gone to bed, leaving Sam and me alone in the living room. The fire is dying, so Sam puts me down and tends to the flickering firelight before disappearing to fetch the first aid kit. "Maybe I should do the paramedic course if I'm going to stay on this team," he says, half-joking yet serious.

"Wouldn't hurt."

"You didn't answer me before about Lily."

"God, you're persistent. No, I didn't. I had other things on my mind." Together, we work my boot off, and it looks like absolutely nothing compared to the deep ache it's giving me. "Here." He holds out two tablets of aspirin and a glass of water. I take the pills and chug the water. Sam sits next to me on the couch.

"I must look a mess."

He snorts. "You do. You should see your face. Did you run into a wall or something?"

"A door."

After painting my foot with Betadine and wrapping it with gauze, he leaves it on his lap and picks up the damp washcloth beside him. "Hands," he orders.

A hiss escapes my grinding teeth when he yanks the worst of the splinters out without warning. Going to work on the rest of the splinters, it ends up being a quiet couple of minutes as he meticulously removes the rest of the wood from my skin.

He wets his lips in concentration, and I'm so focused on his mouth that I don't even realize he's leaned forward to inspect the damage to my face. The cloth is still warm, and I almost whimper at the relief it brings to the bruising. The rag comes away pink with my blood, and this time it's his hands shaking.

I take it from him, and he swipes one last bit of my bottom lip with his thumb as I scrub the blood from the back of my hands. Satisfied I'm not bleeding from anywhere else, he rests his head in his hand while propping his elbow on the back of the couch.

"I'm still so fucking mad at you," he growls.

"I know." Turning to face him, I mirror his pose and brush a curl behind his ear. He leans into my touch and presses his forehead to mine. "I'm sorry."

Close. He's so close that he draws his nose down the side of mine. "Are you?" His voice is a whisper now, ghosting along my cheeks.

Biting my lip, my gaze drifts from his dark eyes with full, thick lashes down to his elegantly sculpted nose before stopping at his full, plush mouth, which I want to devour. "I am so sorry, Sam. You have to believe me. I can't stand the thought—mmph." My apology is cut off when he firmly grabs the back of my head and fiercely presses his lips against mine.

They move over my own with a longing that steals the breath out of my lungs. I grab his head and pull him against me to show him how much I wish I could take it back. How hurting him felt worse than all of them combined. There aren't words for what I need to say to this stupid man who shouldn't be in my department and is only going to get hurt because I can't seem to get out of my own damned way.

His tongue sweeps along mine, and a little groan escapes my lips. He growls and shifts me to straddle his lap without stopping his lips from dragging out sighs and whimpers from me. Sam tastes like tea and cloves and stars.

He pulls away and rests his forehead against mine, his warm breath caressing my face. His arms wrap around my waist, pulling me tight to him. His fingers trail up to brush my hair out of my face, and I shiver. Our eyes meet as we catch our breath, and I want to stop this—before I break his heart.

But how do you stop a freight train? Because that's what this is. This isn't me fooling around with the guys on campus. This is something else. This is an all-consuming fire.

And it scares me a thousand times worse than anything in that basement.

CHAPTER twenty

Frantic banging on the living room window rouses me from where I'm tangled up with Sam on the couch. We must've fallen asleep at some point. The sun blazes through the windows, and Cecilia gesticulates at me from outside as I clumsily scoot up to poke my head over the side of the couch. I glance down at Sam, who is half on top of me so he doesn't fall off the couch. I'll have to crawl over him to reach the door.

Forgetting that I have a hole in the bottom of my foot, I end up falling back on top of him when I try to stand up. I don't understand how he wakes up so fast, but he gently scoops me back onto the couch and scrubs his eyes with his hands. Cecilia taps again, and he scowls at the window.

"What the hell is she doing here so early?" he asks me.

Trudging up to the door, he flips the lock and then murmurs his complaints about the hour as he trudges up the stairs, presumably to use the restroom. Cecilia sweeps into the door wearing a miniskirt and a turtleneck with a scarf in her hair so long it trails after her like a tail.

"Good morning, Lydia," she says cheerily as if we're friendly neighbors. Are we friendly neighbors now? I can't keep up with her mood swings. "Oh my gosh! Your poor face! What happened to you?"

"I ran into some trouble last night, and the door took its offense out on my face," I tell her as I cautiously stand up from the couch to greet her properly. My foot throbs out an excruciating drumbeat.

"I apologize for the early interruption. I wanted to address some misunderstandings from the night before last," she adds, her tone sincere yet still meticulously poised. "I feel really awful."

"I can make coffee." And from the pounding in my head, I need it. Testing my weight on the toes of my injured foot, I limp into the kitchenette.

"Let me," she counters. "You're injured."

Shaking my head, I stop her. "I'm already on my way, can't slow down the momentum. It's probably good to stretch it a little anyway," I respond, masking my discomfort.

Her eyebrows raise skeptically as if she wants to say something, but she shrugs it off. "It seems like someone got up to some naughty business last night," she says instead as she settles into one of the kitchen chairs.

"What do you mean?" Making the coffee gives me something to focus on.

"Your hangover? Waking up with a certain somebody on the couch?"

I wince. *Sam.* I'm going to have to fix it. It was the adrenaline and the mushrooms, and the way he romantically rescued me. My fingers find my lips still swollen from the amount of desperate kissing we engaged in last night.

"That wasn't anything. Sam patched my foot up after I stepped on a nail last night, and we fell asleep."

"Hmm, quite the adventurous evening," Cecilia says as she eyes the bandage while I hobble around on the tiptoes of my left foot.

With the coffee brewing, I take a seat across from her. "What are you doing here so early, Cecilia?"

"Oh! Well aside from wanting to make it up to you all for being a real terror lately, I have amazing news, but I'll wait until everyone comes down. You think Sam will wake them?"

Flashes of last night hit me like a baseball bat to the face. The body, the argument, the bunker, the basement—I bolt out of my chair and empty my stomach into the sink. Cecilia stands behind me and holds my hair back. "There, there," she coos. "You've had quite the night," she observes with an eerie calmness that seems out of place given the situation. "Get it all out. An exciting night, was it?"

I spit into the sink and fill a glass to rinse my mouth. "Illuminating."

"Well, I hope I can *illuminate* you all some more today!" Her lack of concern doesn't surprise me.

Evie is the next one down, looking as polished as ever. You'd never guess a dead body rotted behind a wall in our cellar. Finishing tying her braid off with an elastic, she darts her gaze from Cecilia to me and back again. I'm uncertain where we stand, and I don't want Cecilia to be aware of any strife in our group dynamic.

"Good morning, you two," she says neutrally. "You're here early, Cecilia." She pours herself a cup of coffee.

"It's nine o'clock," Cecilia tells Evie. "I'd hardly consider that early."

"It is for us," Charlie says as he emerges from the stairwell. "We work the night shift, remember?"

Cecilia crosses over to him and pecks his cheek while folding his hand into both of hers. "I have such a surprise for you, darling."

Shirley comes down, followed by an exhausted-looking Sam. He must have warned everyone upstairs about the state of me because not a single one of them has mentioned my injuries. At least, I hope that's what he did and it isn't because they just don't care.

"Oh, Cecilia," Shirley says, "You look lovely in this light. You don't mind if I take a couple of photos, do you?"

Always working, that one. But Cecilia preens at the request and smiles prettily while Shirley grabs her camera bag. "Not lovely enough to make the cover of *Supreme,* though, right?" Cecilia quips, catching Shirley off-guard.

Cecilia has been doing her homework. Shirley whirls around and assesses her shrewdly. "Now, why would I know about that?" Positioning Cecilia by the window, Shirley tilts her head the way she wants and snaps one, two, three photos of her in rapid succession.

Our beauty queen doesn't smile. The overcast sky streaming in through the glass casts her in gloomy light. "Your mother runs it, doesn't she?"

"Prop your elbow on the sill and lean your face into your hand gently so it doesn't stretch the skin." *Click.* "She does. But why would you want to be on the cover of *Supreme?*" Sam puts down a mug of coffee for Shirley, cream and no sugar, just as she likes it. He avoids my eyes.

We're all watching Cecilia and Shirley interact, but Cecilia never peels her eyes away from the lens. "It would be a first, wouldn't it? I like to be first," she says, finally smiling, but her eyes are on Charlie now.

Shirley takes a picture of that subtle expression shift: "*Supreme* is... not my business. Besides, why would you want to be on the cover of a colored magazine?"

"Like I said," she reminds us, clearing her throat and taking a bite of the apple she's plucked from the basket on the table. "I like to be the first. Any*who*," Cecilia clears her throat and takes us all in. "I'd like to apologize for being so moody lately. My schedule has been in absolute tatters since Daddy started campaigning so hard and my duties as Miss Massachusetts coincide with that. Nevertheless, my behavior has been reprehensible and I have been a poor hostess. After all, our state motto is 'we seek peace.'"

Evie's eyes widen. "Not to nitpick, but isn't it, 'By the *sword,* we seek peace'?"

"'But peace only under liberty,'" I finish quietly and clear my throat. "You said you had a surprise for us?"

"Oh! Yes! You're going to be so pleased with me! Maybe pleased enough that we'll make our amends and I'll be on the cover of the book."

"What book?" Charlie asks her.

"The book about *this,* silly. I know your department doesn't have any money. I mean, good gracious, the state of you all. And that equipment is either homemade or *ancient,* Charlie. And Daddy will no longer be donating to your father's little project, will he? With him being *dead* and all. Isn't that right, Lydia?" I narrow my gaze at her. There she is, out with the claws we've gotten used to. "So... book."

To my annoyance, Sam and Charlie form a wall in front of me. I'd like to think they're protecting me from *her,* but I have to assume it's the other way around.

"Daddy and mother are headed to New York today, so I filched these for you."

Parting my wall of over-protective team members, I find Cecilia holding up a set of keys. "Are those?"

"Who wants to snoop in my father's study?"

A half-hour later, we find ourselves standing in front of William Carmichael's study, on only Miss Massachusetts 1972's word that he was out for the next day or so. Charlie swallows loudly, and I concur wholeheartedly.

"For the record, this is a terrible idea," I whisper to Evie, who appears as if she's standing in front of the gates of the Wonka Chocolate Factory.

"You're just mad because it's Cecilia," she sniffs, "And for the record, don't talk to me. We're not good right now."

I pale at her words. My gaze darts over to Sam who still hasn't looked at me once today. Of course, I realize I'm an idiot to think they might just need to sleep on my decision not to call Quinn. Even after Sam and I...

No, I need to focus. We're getting into the study, but I wish we didn't have to rely on Cecilia to do it. The trust is thin all around when it comes to the beauty queen. She opens the door with the flair of a hostess at a car show.

It's dark inside, and I did not expect anything different. The curtains are drawn on the two small windows, and Cecilia moves across the space to yank them open. Dust flies everywhere at the motion. Built-in bookshelves line the walls and a mahogany desk sits toward the back of the room. A couple of leather wing chairs face toward a fireplace, each accompanied by a small side table and Tiffany lamp.

The desk, however, is another matter. I expected the room to be neat as a pin, but towers of books are stacked all over his desk, reminiscent of Waller's office. Evie is reading some of the titles aloud.

"Hugo Radau's *Pharaohs of the Bondage and the Exodus,* Budge and Maspero's histories of Egypt. What is up with your dad's little obsession?" She murmurs mainly to herself. "Ah! Here we go!" Her face finds mine, her earlier fury forgotten in her petty victory. Crowley's *Book of the Law* is waving at me in her hand, exactly like she said. "I knew it."

"Can I see that?" I ask. She hands it over. Opening it to the front page is a bookplate that reads 'From the Library of Ambrose Carmichael.' "I'm still not sure how this ties into anything." I pass it back to her, I eye up the rest of the texts on the desk. They all have to do with esoteric magick or the lives of the Pharaohs. "Crowley obsessed over this garbage."

"Sam? Your thoughts?" Charlie asks him.

Sam draws his thick eyebrows together. "Why are you asking me?" He glances around and lands on Shirley's camera. "Oh, because I'm Egyptian? Don't ask me, man. I slept through that Crowley class."

Evie taps her index finger on her lips. "What if we're reading into this wrong? What if he's not involved with the Thelemites or the Order of the Golden Dawn? What if instead this was passed down from father to son?"

Charlie is digging through his bag to pull out some gear, and Shirley steps over him to get closer to a photo on the shelf. "Is this you and your dad?" she asks Cecilia. The photo is a black-and-white photo of William Carmichael on the steps of a stately building somewhere. He's holding a baby and making it wave at the camera.

"Oh, yes, that's the Nuremberg Trials. My father was a legal aid. He was very proud. Of course, Mother says we were relegated to a hotel room the entire time, but it's an important part of history and significant to his law career." Cecilia lingers in the doorway as though she's not allowed in.

Evie stares at the image briefly before sitting at Carmichael's desk and flipping through Crowley's book. She's hoping to find annotations from the Carmichael family, but I suspect she'll be disappointed.

Sam, on the other hand, randomly pulls books from the corner shelf. I sidle up beside him and ask, "Are you hunting for secret passages?"

"Do you blame me? After what happened to you last night?" He doesn't look at me; he merely continues his search.

We haven't had the chance to tell the rest of the team yet since the disruption by Cecilia happened before anyone else was up. Charlie is standing behind us. "Shit," he says.

Both of us whirl around at him. "What? What is it?"

"The temperature drops almost eight degrees here in this corner."

I whip my hand to feel where he's holding the thermometer. "Get the EMF reader out."

"Yeah," Charlie agrees and hands me the temperature gauge.

"You don't think it's spirit activity," Sam whispers in my ear so Cecilia can't hear us. "You think it's another passage."

"Just keeping my options open, but I doubt there will be any EMF activity over here," I tell him.

"What's this for?" Shirley asks, holding up a padlock. "It's sitting on his desk."

Cecilia shrugs, and I crinkle my forehead in thought. Crossing the room, I reach out my hand to Shirley for it. She drops it into my palm, and I examine it closely for a few seconds. Then I turn my attention back to Cecilia, who remains steadfastly interested in the floor.

"He locks you in your room."

The rest of the group lifts their heads at my accusation. I leave the room and walk a few feet down the hall, where I open the bedroom door with the latch on it. Her pageant sash hangs in a frame over a delicate desk. It's a beautiful room, full of ivory silk and blush accents—a young woman's room.

Stepping back into the hallway, I slide the padlock into the latch. "Why does he lock you in your room, Cecilia?"

"I sleepwalk," she responds quietly, her voice barely a murmur.

"*You* sleepwalk? You told Quinn that Emily was the one sleepwalking," Charlie says, EMF forgotten in his hands.

"Well, it wouldn't look great if the sitting Miss Massachusetts could be found wandering the pond where her sister recently drowned at all hours of the night."

A buzzing noise erupts from Charlie's reader, and our attention is torn from the embarrassed Cecilia to where Charlie is pointing his instrument—*her room.*

He frowns and takes a step forward. "Maybe you were right, Cee. Maybe I *should've* set up some equipment in your room."

"Charlie, wait!" Cecilia chases after him, and I'm prone to follow, but Sam wraps his fingers around my wrist and yanks me back into the study.

"Sam, what—"

"Find it. There's one here in the corner, and we don't want Cecilia to know we've discovered the servants' passage." His eyes finally meet mine, and I nod.

We both frantically pull on the books in the corner, and my hand lands on a duck decoy that refuses to move aside. Struck, I examine it and find a hidden lever underneath. Pulling it forward instead of to the side, a click sounds, and Sam and I smile at each other triumphantly. Mad at me or not, nothing can compare to finding a secret hallway.

He reaches out and pushes the bookshelf. It opens. I take the lead with him right behind me and follow the corridor as it goes past the two bedrooms (both with peepholes, I might add). Around the corner to the bedroom in the back of the wing, Sam peers through the slanted light, and we can see Charlie, Cecilia, Evie, and Shirley all in Cecilia's room.

Placing his finger to his lips, he points down to a latch indicating a door to her room. My eyes widen, and he pulls me back to the study. We pull the bookcase back into place, and the duck slides back with a satisfying *snick*.

Hurrying back to Cecilia's room, I find them arguing about whether Charlie should be taking measurements. "It's, *damn*, it's gone," Charlie complains. "It was *right* here, strongest I've ever seen."

"But now it's gone, so your equipment is faulty. I'd like you to leave my personal space, please," Cecilia ushers them back to her door.

"A few days ago, you were dying to get him into your room," Shirley chides.

"Yes, well, that was before I knew he was going to hunt for actual ghosts in here. Do I need to remind you that I sleep in this room? I don't need those night horrors. Shoo! Now!" They all quit the room to find Sam and I standing in the hall. Cecilia closes her door and faces the crestfallen Charlie. "I think that's enough excitement for today. Don't you people have footage you need to go through or something?"

She's done with us. Cecilia resets Carmichael's study back to where it should be and locks the door behind us.

"I really would've liked more time in his office," Evie grumbles.

"Yes, well, it went queer, didn't it? And that isn't what I signed up for. I have some errands I need to run before Daddy gets back," Cecilia says with a dismissive wave. "But, I do hope what you got was as illuminating as I promised, and that perhaps I've earned a modicum of forgiveness?" Her big eyes flutter toward Charlie, and we leave him behind to give them a moment alone.

We're out under the porte-cochère when I ask Evie, "What do you know about the Pharaohs and human sacrifice?"

Readjusting her glasses, she shakes her head. "What? What are you on about?"

"Well, we all know about Crowley's interest in power exchanges for wealth and immortality and his obsession with the Pharaohs. Did they participate in human sacrifice?"

"Whoa, no, man, shit, that's crazy. You think he did Lily in to get a Senate seat? That's a stretch even for you, Lydia," Sam says, and I can't miss how affronted he sounds.

"Well, I can't think of any human sacrifice aside from the ritual of sending the pharaoh's family and belongings with him into the underworld, but I guess I can research it. Crowley might have mixed and matched." Evie chews her lip in thought. "There's something else bothering me, though."

"What's that?"

"That photo of her and her dad," Evie mumbles. "Never mind. When we return to the guest house, I need to check on something."

Charlie rejoins us, and he and I glance at each other. "That photo was a perfect find, Shirley," I tell her. "It adds an interesting layer to the documentary, especially with Cecilia's insights about her father."

"What do you mean?" Shirley asks me.

"What she means is Lydia thinks Carmichael did it." Sam lights a joint as he says this. He inhales deeply, and we wait while he holds it and slowly exhales. "She thinks it will add a creepy factor to the true crime footage."

They all stop in their tracks to stare at me. "Okay, but hear me out," I say, detailing the secret passage in Emily's closet that leads to the sitting room and the basement bunker, the passage in Carmichael's study, and the one to Cecilia's room. "The silver lining is, if you need to access that study again, Evie, we've discovered the route."

Evie nods. "I'm not convinced. But I would like to go through *The Book of the Law* again if nothing else." We reach the carriage house, and she takes a swift drag off Sam's doobie. Coughing out the smoke, she rasps out, "Imagine going your whole life thinking that there are no consequences to your actions, no matter how diabolical. And now think about that person in Congress."

Once inside, Evie digs through her bag and pulls out the papers she brought back from her trip with Quinn. "No, see? I was right. The numbers don't add up."

I sit across from her at the dining table and take the paper she hands me. It's Cecilia Rose Carmichael's birth certificate. "What am I looking at here, Eves?"

She taps her fingernail on the year. "That photo of her at the Nuremberg trials. She shouldn't have been born yet. She's 24, right? That's what Quinn told us."

"Okay?"

"That would put her year of birth in 1948," Evie taps the birth certificate again. "So why does her birth certificate say she was born in '44? That would make her 28."

Evie and I mirror the other's expression. "Whoa. What?" Charlie asks and snatches the paper out from under our hands.

I need to step outside when the room erupts into everyone talking at once. Closing my eyes, I take a deep breath. There has to be a pattern, a thread I can follow. I have to find it and fix it.

You can't fix everything, Lydia.

Shut up, Octavia.

CHAPTER
twenty one

Walking back in, I slam the door behind me to gather everyone's attention. "Why are we here?" I ask them. It's not a hypothetical question; I genuinely want to know why they think we're on this case.

"Originally? Or now?" Evie asks.

"Whatever, just why are we here? At this house, what do you think our investigation is? I'm curious." Channeling my father, I straighten my shoulders and cross my arms. Sam holds up his hand, and I roll my eyes. "We're not in class, Sam. Just say what you need to."

"I thought we were here because of Lily's ghost," Shirley interrupts. I scribble Lily's name on an index card from Evie's bag and tape it to the wall.

Charlie nods. "I thought we were here for spectral activity, Lily or not." Pursing my lips together, I add a tick to Shirley's card.

I turn to Evie. "That's what we were doing here originally, but I think it's about the body in the basement now. I think it's about Quinn's investigation."

I tape another index card to the wall after I scribble down 'botched police investigation, a murderer on-premises' with a question mark.

Sam's gaze locks onto mine. The deep woods of his eyes, the shadowed places I haven't fully explored yet, measure me up. He swallows. "For Emily. Emily's in danger."

My brows draw together. Of course, Sam would say for Emily. I write 'Emily' on a card and put it above the other two. With my back to them all, I study the cards. "I'm running out of time." It's hardly more than a whisper. Clearing my throat, I tell them, "We're looking at this all wrong."

"Okay?" Evie sits on the couch and pulls out a notepad and pen. "So, how should we look at it?"

"According to Sam, we have some spirits here who can't rest because their murderer is currently on the premises. We can't do anything to help Alice Shippington or the Burning Man, but we can sure as hell help Lily Carmichael and Eugene Pickering. I didn't come into this department because it was my dad's. I came into this department because whoever kept and raped my sister, whoever fathered my sister's baby, whoever dumped my sister in a lake like she was trash, is still out there."

Nobody says a word.

"I don't talk about Octavia's case—it's true. But, I'm telling you right now, if there's a chance we can save Emily from this piece of shit who drowns little girls and stuffs old men into walls, we're taking it. I understand you're here for the paranormal investigation, but this turned into something outside our non-existent pay grade. We need to start looking at who is capable of this on the property. I count only three adults and the maid here."

"You think Carmichael drowned his daughter in the middle of a Senatorial bid?" Shirley's brow lifts in doubt. "Why?"

"That's what we need to look at," I tell her. "Let's discuss what we've gathered about him."

Evie raises her hand, and I frown. "Fine." she says. "Okay, I think his grandfather was a Thelemite, which suggests he might have been exposed to some unorthodox ideas, but I don't think Carmichael practices them. I can't imagine him donning robes and meeting down at the cigar club with a bunch of cultists without the press catching on."

"Good," I jot down the gist and tape it next to another card I've placed with Carmichael's name on it. "What else have we learned?"

Charlie sighs. "The family is being deceptive about Cecilia's age."

Trying to shove down a smirk, I point to him excitedly. "Yes! That's weird, right? I'm fully aware women like to stay young, but that's just... odd."

"Esme doesn't talk to anyone and hardly ever leaves her room. The only times we've seen her is when she's dragged off to be arm candy," Shirley adds.

"I need to think," I tell them. "Sam, you got any more of that grass?"

He heads upstairs to where our bags are. "I'm going to be outside if anyone needs me. If any of you think of anything, please come find me." I grab a beer from the fridge and my leather satchel by the door and head out front.

The carriage house's garden is lovely with its late-season wild roses and stony path. To the side, by the birdbath, are two Adirondack chairs, and I sit down. Pulling the beer tab off, I open my satchel and pull out Quinn's police file and my ring of Polaroids that I took on the first day. Taking a deep drink, I start flipping through the photos.

Sam comes out and sits next to me, beer in hand. He lights the joint and sinks back into the chair. "Pass me the file," he says, handing me the cigarette.

We smoke and work beside each other, neither of us ready to talk about what happened last night. I'm sure he's still angry with me. Either way, it doesn't matter because he's still helping, and I can't exactly complain about that. In my peripheral vision, he pulls his hair into a loose ponytail so it won't flop into his face while he reads the file on his lap. "Sam?"

"Uh-uh, keep working, pretty lady. Your time is running out."

Swallowing around his words, I keep flipping. I land on the photo of Emily in the window, the one I thought was a double exposure on our first day here, but Sam pointed out that the image behind her was wearing something else—a swimsuit.

I despise this. I loathe all of it. I shouldn't have to be out here trying to figure out who drowned a little girl and why. Because there isn't ever going to be a good enough reason. No 'why' in the world will justify this, and I'm so glad I'm not a cop because I have no idea how Quinn manages so much control or how he manages to suppress so much rage all of the time.

How is he not choking on it?

Keep flipping, Lydia. Focus. I stop when I find the artwork on Emily's wall. She's written an 'E' on the drawings she did and an 'L' on Lily's. It's the 'L's I'm looking for.

Holding Sam's Zippo, I unconsciously flip it open and snap it back closed repeatedly while I work.

Click. Snap. Click. Snap. Click. Snap. Clic—

Sam's head pops up from the file when I stop. I'm staring at...

"What am I looking at here?" I hand him the ring with the photograph.

He frowns and cocks his head. "That's Daddy-o, but who's the lady? That's not Mrs. Carmichael."

"Yeah, okay. And what are they *doing?*"

"Is that Carmichael and the blonde lady gettin' busy in the Wonderland whatchamacallit?" He hands the photos back to me.

"The topiary garden," I murmur. Flipping to the following 'L' picture, I find another one, but she's drawn it as though it's through a peephole. "His office?" Sam hovers over my shoulder.

"You think? But..."

"But what?" I ask him.

"Whatever Lily witnessed wasn't meant for a kid." He points to the hand around the blonde's throat and the other hand disappearing up the woman's skirt. It isn't easy to tell. "It's... unsettling, isn't it?" he remarks.

"Lily put these on their wall for anyone who walked in to find. That means... this was normal for her. This wasn't something unusual." I twist around to glance up at Sam. "She had no idea this wasn't something she should be sharing."

Sam sits back down. "Mistress? Or perhaps someone else in the household?" he speculates, adjusting his approach slightly. "The house seems massively understaffed, so maybe a maid?"

"'The house strikes you as massively understaffed?'" I snort. "Okay, *Wellesley*."

His shoulders slump a little at my tease. "Evie told you?"

"I should have guessed, you slip into your old elocution lessons sometimes."

"You're one to talk." His gaze meets mine but then travels down to my mouth, and my distraction begins anew.

I clear my throat. "So you think we got here as Carmichael was cleaning house, or do you think this woman is still on the property, like…"

Sam winces at the thought of Eugene Pickering rotting down in the cellar, and I'm sorry I brought it up. It almost felt like we were settling back into our new normal until I reminded him of why he's so pissed at me.

"I need to see these drawings in person." Getting up, I go inside to show Evie. It still hurts like hell to place my full weight on my foot.

Shirley takes one glance at them and screws her mouth up in disdain. "Politicians and their scandals—does every candidate get a mistress handed to them? He's not even officially elected yet."

"Let's be fair; it's not like this is why he's not getting your vote," Evie teases her. "I mean, the man wants to set Massachusetts back twenty years. I'm disappointed but not surprised, but his wife…"

"Esme Carmichael," I say. "What do we know about her?"

Evie shrugs. "I couldn't dig up much. As far as I can tell, she comes from some rich stock in Europe but doesn't have an accent. She didn't give much of a statement to Quinn. I think he thought he was being gentlemanly and didn't push."

"Has Sam seen any blonde ghosts besides Lily? Could this lady have ended up like the groundskeeper?" Charlie stares at the four photos I've placed on the table for us to study. One shows the topiary garden, one his office, another in what appears to be the kitchen and the other...

"Is that Peter?" I ask. It's a drawing of the pond and the willow tree. The perspective is high so that it could be an angle from the girls' window. Carmichael and his blonde mistress again, but someone is peeking at them from behind the willow.

"Sam has not seen any blonde ladies besides our boss, Emily, Lily, and your girlfriend since I've been here. Alice Shippington is a brunette, as is Mrs. Carmichael and Marian, the domestic." Sam tells Charlie and peers over my shoulder. "I told you something stank about sending that kid away."

"Peter, you mean?" Shirley asks to clarify for the camera.

"Yeah, man. Peter. If your kid just suffered a loss like that, why send him away? It makes no sense."

"Who wants to come with me up to the big house?" Everyone grabs their stuff. It's definitely because we're all hyperaware of the body in the cellar, and none of us can hardly stand the carriage house anymore. I don't have the heart to tell them that I think there are bodies in the Carmichaels' cellar, as well.

This whole hill is one great festering graveyard.

Shirley walks next to me on the way up to Hemlock Hall. "You truly think he'd hurt his kids because of an affair? Isn't that a little... dramatic? Why not just send them off to boarding school like Peter?"

"I don't know. It depends on how much he needs this Senate seat. We should have Evie check their financials."

"Money sounds like a better excuse than a scandal. The Kennedys survived numerous adultery scandals." Shirley doesn't have her camera on, indicating her nervousness about the professional ramifications of implicating an influential man.

"William Carmichael is no Jack Kennedy," I tell her. "But… you're not totally wrong. He's going for Kennedy's senate seat, after all. I'm not sure Boston could withstand another blow to a Roman Catholic politician."

"Unlike Kennedy, though, he's a Republican," Shirley reminds her. "It's going Republican next month."

"You think?" I pull a face. Living on a college campus can sometimes keep you in a nice bubble.

"The war."

She's right, of course. And I'm getting close to convincing myself that Carmichael isn't a real Roman Catholic either—not with all those books. No, Carmichael was a cultivated pretender. Everything those conspiracy theorists on campus fear the most.

Emily lets us in when I show her what I'm looking for. Marian didn't do much to the room, for which I'm extremely grateful. I don't know if I'd ever forgive myself if something happened to Emily's safe space because we lured her out. As it stands, Octavia's room at our house on campus is an untouched shrine. I don't think I've opened the door once this year.

So… a dusty, untouched shrine.

"Do you think I can borrow these?" I ask, handing her the four Polaroids of the drawings I need. "I promise to treat them like they should be in the Louvre. I'll even wear gloves when handling them."

Emily's eyebrow twitches in consternation. She's trying to decide whether she can believe me or not.

"Do you still have your sister's stuff?" She asks me.

Everyone in the group turns to study me at this question, and my gaze drops to my feet. "Yes. Even her Tommy James poster is still on the wall."

"Okay," Emily says, moving over to their art gallery. Searching for Lily's drawings, she spins around on me. "They're *gone.*"

"What do you mean 'gone?'" Charlie asks, moving closer to the wall. He checks the Polaroids in Emily's hands against the pictures on the wall and back again.

"I mean, see?" Emily exclaims, gesturing toward the wall. "The tape is still here where someone's taken it and put one of my pictures over the empty spot!"

"All of them?" Evie asks Emily, but she's holding me in her frantic gaze. We're thinking the same thing—thank God we took the photos on our first day here.

"I told you!" Emily yells at me. "I told you I couldn't leave my room, and you said it was okay, and it wasn't!" Her voice cracks, and she lets loose a flood of angry tears.

We need to calm her down. Cecilia's car isn't outside, so we're alone with Emily.

"I'm getting her something to drink," Evie says and slips out the door.

"I'll help," Shirley says. Her camera is turned off, and I hope she snapped it off when it became clear Emily was on the verge of a breakdown.

Charlie and Sam step out, too. I take Emily's hands and lead her to sit on her bed. Squatting down in front of her, I try to channel my mother. But I know it's a futile attempt; I'm not my mom.

"Stop crying," I tell her. The abruptness with which she cuts off her tears tells me one of two things: She was either faking the tears, or nobody has ever said that to her.

"W-what?"

"I said, 'Stop crying.' Crying never helped anyone. It's not going to help you or me, but do you know who it *is* helping?"

She wipes her nose on the back of her sleeve. "Who?"

"The person who fucking drowned your sister."

Emily's eyebrows shoot up at my swear word.

"Look at these photos—really *look* at them. What are these, Emily? Who's that woman with your dad? Why the hell would Lily draw something like this?"

Evie appears next to me and hands Emily a glass of water. She takes it and dutifully downs the whole thing, handing it back to Evie. Inhaling deep through her nose, her fingers reach out for the loose photos I'm holding.

After studying them, she glances back at me and shakes her head. "I don't know."

"Really?" My voice is hard and sharp. I cross my arms over my chest and give her a doubtful expression.

"Really. Lily didn't talk a lot. She wasn't like us."

This takes me aback. The reports didn't mention anything that indicated she was anything other than a normal middle-schooler. "What do you mean she wasn't like us?"

"Daddy said she was daydreamy, lost in her head. She played by herself most of the time, and she said there were kids in the basement who were her friends." Her gaze drops down to her bare feet. "I don't go in the basement. We're not supposed to. Besides, it's fucking scary down there." She peeks at me to test if I'll chastise her for using my word.

I don't.

"So tell me about this art," I gently encourage her.

Emily shrugs. "I didn't watch her. Who cares what kids draw? I didn't start the art wall. Lily did. So I added to it whenever I finished one, but I mean," she points at the ring of Polaroids in my hand, "most of them were hers."

Spinning back to the wall, she's right; most of them have *LC* in the corner. "You never wondered what her drawings might mean?"

"No. I mean, would you? We draw kid's stuff. Lily drew what she saw. Like this one," she says, pointing to the one in the corner. "It's a bird falling out of a nest and a squirrel eating it. Eating it. If she discovered something weird or interesting, she drew it."

"And what did you draw?" I ask her.

"Fashion, mostly. Or... here's me marrying Jim Morrison," she says shyly and blushes crimson.

Evie and I glance at each other.

"I don't want to leave you here alone," I tell Emily.

"Why? Everyone else does."

Sam leans into the doorway. "Not today, little mama." I toss him a grateful expression, and he takes Emily's desk chair and braces it against the closet door handle. "Grab your things; you're coming with us. You got a key to this door?"

Emily shakes her head at him. His long fingers reach past me where I'm leaning against the desk, and he pulls off a long piece of transparent tape.

"What are you going to do with that?" She asks him.

We step out into the hall, and Sam pulls the door closed. He adheres the tape from the frame to the door, saying, "If this is broken when we return, we'll know someone's been in here."

Emily stares at Sam like he's hung the moon. It's not much, and it won't tell us who broke in, but the effort doesn't go unnoticed.

"Lily's going to be mad," Emily mumbles as she heads to the staircase.

"About what?" I ask.

"You locked her in the closet."

Trying to find words of reassurance is impossible. Emily deserves more than platitudes. "Perfect. She should be mad," I tell her. "Mad gets more shit done than sad."

CHAPTER twenty two

"Are you sure she never talked to you about this?" I ask Emily again, this time with different wording. We're back at the carriage house, and Emily is eating some leftover stew Charlie reheated on the stove.

"I'm trying to remember, Lydia." Her expression turns sniffy, and she tilts her nose up to mimic Cecilia. "You'd think I'd remember if my sister told me our dad was having an affair."

"Alright, then." With a huff, I dig back into the pile of research we've compiled.

"Hey," Evie says gently, "I have a question for you that has nothing to do with Lily or your dad or any of it."

"Shoot," Emily says, slurping soup off her spoon.

"Why is Alice so upset?"

Sam and I glance at each other. We've all been wondering about the different spirits here, but too much has been happening to investigate Hemlock Hall's deep history.

Emily doesn't even peek up from her bowl; she just continues to eat merrily, telling us, "Oh, Alice locked her kids in the basement to hide them from the colonial soldiers."

It's a strange feeling when all of your blood drains out of your face at once. Dizziness overwhelms me, and I bend in half to put my head between my knees.

"She doesn't remember that part. I think they killed her and had no idea the kids were down there." Licking her spoon, her grave expression fixes on Evie. "I suppose they starved to death."

To her credit, Evie doesn't react the way Emily expects. She maintains eye contact with Emily and leans back in her chair. "Thank you for sharing that," she says calmly.

"Sure," Emily replies, turning to face us. "But how come none of you want to know about the Burning Man?"

Sam sits next to her at the table, his fingers forming a steeple, pressed against his lips. "Now, what do you know about Ambrose Carmichael?" he asks.

Emily's eyes grow two sizes bigger at his question. "How did you know that was Grandpoppa?"

Sam smirks slightly. "I didn't, but I can play games, too. You remind me of my little sister, Amira. Were you planning to drag out your little guessing game for a while?"

A scowl drops across her fair features like a veil. "Dad says bad men killed him because he was getting too powerful."

"How was he becoming too powerful?" Shirley asks eagerly, her curiosity piercing the room's tension.

Emily shrugs. "Dunno. Dad says our blood is magic. It's pure, not like the men who burned Grandpoppa."

I purse my lips. My father, Courtland Fox, was a Captain in the Second World War, and he held a rank in the Office of Strategic Services. He never tolerated Nazis or their vile beliefs. Emily's words about her father echo those dark ideologies, reminding me of my father's heated debates with Waller about twin theory and its dangerous flirtations with the Reich's eugenics programs.

My father was a curious man, and Waller's research fascinated him enough to make him his partner, and eventually, mine and Octavia's godfather. However, the idea of artificially creating twins was where Courtland Fox drew the line.

Evie is frantically trying to get my attention. "I have some papers upstairs I need to show you," she says, her urgency clear.

Nodding, I follow her up the narrow staircase. "What is it?"

"Thelemites," Evie blurts out.

"What about them?"

"They burned Ambrose. It's a horrific death for someone who might have wanted to be buried like a Pharaoh," she explains.

"But Pharaohs were buried with servants, pets, and belongings—anything they'd need in the afterlife," I add.

Both of us cover our mouths in shock. "Eugene Pickering," we whisper in unison.

"He went missing two days after Lily drowned," Evie reminds me. "Remember I suggested that if there was a Thelemite cult around here, Carmichael likely wasn't part of it?"

"So, he's self-taught?"

"More like taught by Emily's Grandpop. I think Ambrose crossed some line with their weird code. I mean, 'do as thou wilt is the whole of the law' might not work in the modern era. They could've expelled him for his audacity."

"But…" I rush down the stairs and yank open Quinn's file, scanning it as quickly as I can. Under my breath, I mutter, "Son of a bitch."

"What? What is it?" Charlie asks, now peering over my shoulder.

"What does that look like to you?" I point to Carmichael's alibi.

"I don't know what I'm supposed to be looking at here, Lydia," he admits. "Help me out here."

"He never followed up with the bishop," I say.

"He never followed up with the— wait, what?" Charlie is still clearly confused.

Evie snatches the folder from my hands. "Son of a bitch," she echoes my original indignation.

"Will someone please explain what's going on? All of this vague talk is doing nothing for my documentary," Shirley shouts.

"By all accounts, Carmichael was at church that morning, but nobody saw him during mass. According to Carmichael, it's because he was meeting with the bishop about his senate run," I explain to them.

"But Quinn didn't follow up with the bishop," Charlie finally understands, his voice tinged with excitement.

"Quinn didn't follow up with the bishop!" I exclaim, slapping my hand on the table, causing everyone to jump.

"This is why this town should have its own detective," Evie grouses.

"Should we follow up with the bishop on our own or call Quinn?" Charlie asks.

If we call Quinn, I'm going to have to tell him about Pickering's body in the basement. Am I really so ready to give up the rest of my forty-eight hours?

"Let's talk to the bishop, and if he tells us what I suspect he'll tell us, then we'll call Quinn."

Sam grabs me by the elbow when I reach for my purse. "You're not a detective," he tells me. "This isn't your job."

"It'll take Quinn too long to drive up here, Sam. We can be done in an hour. You guys are the ones that gave me a time limit."

Pinching the bridge of his nose between his thumb and forefinger, he squeezes his eyes shut. "I don't like it. Something's going to happen. I *feel* it."

"Oh, now you decide you're psychic? You see ghosts, Sam, not the future. Grab your stuff."

"Am I coming, too?" Emily asks.

I give her a once-over. "No, you need a shower; you stink," I say more bluntly than I intended. "You can borrow some jeans and a t-shirt from the plaid bag upstairs." Emily's eyes light up at the prospect of borrowing my clothes. "Nothing but the jeans and t-shirts, you dig?"

"I dig!" She chirps and heads up the stairs.

"Anybody want to stay here and babysit?" I ask, trying to gauge who might be willing to stay behind.

Sam frowns, his concern evident. "I don't know, man. I'm uncomfortable leaving her here alone, but I don't want to be alone in a house with a little girl. It's inappropriate."

"Sometimes you're super old-fashioned," Charlie chides him lightly.

"Well, I'm certainly not staying," Shirley declares as she gathers her camera bag. "I'm not going to miss filming this."

"And I need to double-check something with the records office," Evie says cryptically.

Sam looks at me expectantly, his gaze sharp. Crossing my arms tightly, I retort, "Oh no, you can't seriously expect me to stay behind! This was my idea!"

"Charlie can handle the bishop," Sam suggests calmly.

"Yeah, I can do that," Charlie interjects, adding, "I was even an altar boy."

Frustration mounts within me as I realize Sam expects me to babysit. "I'm not a babysitter, Sam!"

"You want to leave her alone knowing what's in the basement?" Sam's question is pointed, reminding me of the stakes.

"Damn," I mutter under my breath, frustration bubbling.

"Or wait for her to finish showering, then take her with us," Sam offers a compromise.

His suggestion makes sense, annoyingly so. "It's not like she's unaware of Pickering," I argue half-heartedly. Sam raises an eyebrow, his expression one of silent reproach. "Yeah, okay, I see how that sounds."

Pulling my fingers through my hair, I dig in with my nails, a physical manifestation of my frustration.

"Let's wait for her," Sam suggests, gently removing my fingers from my tangled hair.

"Yeah?"

"Yeah." His eyes soften, sparking a momentary desire in me to apologize for last night. But I'm not sorry. Not really. It's just ill-timed, given the potential fallout with Waller. I pull away and seat myself on the couch to wait for Emily.

No, I remind myself sternly. I'm the youngest paranormal lead in the history of my father's department, younger even than Waller when he took charge. Screwing this up because I think Sam might be amazing in the sack would be idiotic.

That's all this tension is.

As I sit brooding on the couch, Emily reappears from upstairs. My clothes hang a bit loose on her, but she's managed by rolling up the hems of the jeans and knotting my Shelley College t-shirt at her waist. My apple-scented shampoo lingers in the air around her, and her resemblance to Octavia is striking, splitting my heart in two.

"You're coming with us," I declare.

"To meet Bishop McCormack? No, thanks." She collapses onto the couch beside me and starts flipping through an Elliott O'Donnell book on ghost cases.

Taking the book out of her hands, I scowl at her. "You're holding everyone up. We all need to go into town, and we can't leave you here alone."

"I'm not a child," she snipes back.

My patience flies out the open front door. "Emily, get in the damned van. You're not safe here alone."

Her eyelashes flutter in Sam's direction. "Sam can stay with me."

Glancing between the two, I have to give it to Sam, he looks entirely bewildered by Emily's apparent endearment towards him. I stand over her, hands on my hips. "Oh no, young lady, don't even think about it. Move your ass. Now."

There's a high chance nobody has spoken to her quite like that before. But then again, considering Cecilia is her older sister, I might have just ventured into familiar territory for her. She screws her mouth up and stomps out the door. "Fine, but I'm staying in the *damned* van."

It's fine. I can handle a pissed-off Emily. What I can't handle is a dead Emily.

Charlie drives, and I sit up front with him. I'm wearing a long wool skirt with a tight turtleneck and the quartz pendant Sam insisted I wear, which I discovered I don't hate. According to him, I need some 'extra protection from some seriously nasty vibes.'

When we arrive at the diocese, the secretary isn't taken aback by Charlie, Shirley with her camera, or me in the slightest. Shirley throws down a filming consent form in front of the woman and waits for her to scribble her signature after asking what the camera is for.

"We're doing a documentary on William Carmichael's senate race," Shirley tells her smoothly.

"That's fine," the secretary chirps, waving her hand. "We all adore Judge Carmichael here. Such a pity what happened at the Hall." We nod, and Charlie talks with Miss Marsh about his Chicago parish while I discreetly scan the surroundings. Miss Marsh informs us the Bishop is momentarily available, needing a moment to freshen up before facing the camera.

Never underestimate the power of fame in America. Shirley is fabulous at playing up the journalism angle, and I lean into letting her do her thing. Charlie and Shirley prepare the sound for the 'interview' while I look out the window at our van down the street. Sam is leaning against it while smoking a cigarette. Moments before we came in, he admitted that Catholic churches weirded him out.

"You want to talk about cults, pretty momma? That's the biggest one out there."

DAPHNE WINCHESTER

My father didn't bring us up religious; too much science. I find the ritualism of it fascinating, the pomp and theater of the church decadent in its narcissism.

Bishop McCormack is a pleasant man. His hairline has long receded, probably prematurely. There is nothing sinister about him at all, no matter what Sam's vibes suggest. He's in his mid-fifties, with glasses perched on the end of his nose. He's wearing a suit with his collar, nothing overly ornate as I had expected.

He lets us into his office and signs Shirley's form. Her smart brown suit with an eggplant-colored silk blouse is impeccably tailored, and she would look at home on 5th Avenue if it weren't for the tennis shoes on her feet. I know she wears them so she can move around with the camera more easily, but it really detracts from her executive fox de rigueur.

Charlie leads the questioning and calls me the 'sound girl.' I let him, but a quiet smirk slips across my lips when he says it, and his cheeks flame up.

"How long have you known Senator Carmichael?" Charlie asks and then feigns correcting himself, "I mean, Judge Carmichael, it feels like he's already voted in, doesn't it?"

"Oh, sure, sure," Bishop McCormack says with an easy, rosy smile. "Bill has been going to this church since before me. I arrived here in '58, and Bill has been a parishioner his entire life."

"His entire life? Did you ever meet his parents or grandparents?"

"His mother died when he was very young, you understand. No, Bill was raised solely by his father, Ambrose Carmichael." He drops his gaze to study his hands on the desk blotter for a few breaths, then takes a long drink from his glass of water. The bishop seems concerned that he might have divulged too much.

"Did you meet Ambrose, then?" Charlie jumps on that. We need these seemingly innocuous questions answered before we delve into the ones we really want to ask.

Quinn is going to have my head.

"Yes sir. It's a terrible thing what happened to that man. Tragic, tragic story." He narrows his eyes. Careful, Charlie. Don't push too hard.

"What did happen to Ambrose Carmichael?"

The bishop clears his throat and stands at his desk. "What kind of documentary did you say this was?"

Shirley flashes him a bright grin. "It's for posterity." Her evasive response seems to disarm him.

"Ambrose Carmichael burned to death in a car accident in 1961."

Shrugging my shoulders to relieve the strain of holding the boom mike, I glance around the room. Several bookcases line the walls filled with knick-knacks and photos of him with various influential people, including one with a Pope. But it's the barrister shelf by the window that catches my eye. If I could take a few steps back, I might be able to see what inside is making my pulse thrum in my ears.

"I'm so sorry, that was insensitive of me," Charlie apologizes. "I had no idea. Thank you for sharing that with us."

"Just ensure that doesn't make your final cut, young lady. It's a difficult memory for Judge Carmichael."

"Oh, I understand," Shirley reassures him.

"It must have been difficult then, knowing you were with him on the day that Lily Carmichael passed." Charlie's nonchalant delivery is astonishingly breathtaking.

McCormack furrows his brow. "How do you mean? I didn't conduct mass that day, so I didn't see him."

"You were meeting with him during mass," Charlie says.

"What are you talking about? I didn't meet with Bill Carmichael until two days later when he came to discuss Lily's funeral arrangements." Sweat beads on his brow, and a droplet slides down his left temple, soaking into his collar.

According to the police report, William Carmichael met with Bishop Gregory McCormack during mass on the day in question.

Shirley wraps her fingers around her lens, slowly twisting it to zoom in on the now red-faced bishop.

"I think you're mistaken, but I don't have a perfect memory these days."

"Funny, you recalled when you arrived in this parish, when Ambrose Carmichael died, and William Carmichael's daughter's name," I say. Nothing could have kept that strangled in my throat.

"Alright," he says in a huff. "You need to leave—all three of you."

Shirley glances at me, indicating that she has what she needs. I nod my head and point to the bookcase. "Can you film some footage of that before we leave?" My attention turns to McCormack. "These gorgeous Egyptian canopic jars," I say, "wouldn't happen to be gifts from William Carmichael, would they?"

"Get out! Right now!" That answers that question. Evie will kiss me full on the mouth for finding that detail.

We head out to the van, where Sam straightens on our approach. "We get what we need?"

"We did," I reply, taking the cigarette from his hand. I take a drag and exhale, "Carmichael's alibi doesn't hold up."

Closing his eyes, he nods with a satisfied smile. "I knew it. I knew there was something fishy about that cat."

"Time to call Quinn then?" Charlie asks me. Shirley has her camera on me, pausing before she stashes it into its case in the back.

I take in the three of them. "It's time to call Quinn."

Chapter twenty three

Evie is *off* when we pick her up. I ask her about it, and she dips and sways around the question as if she's a professional dodgeball player.

"Seriously, what is it?" Honestly, I thought she'd be more excited about calling Quinn.

She nibbles her lip in thought, appearing to contemplate telling me, but then shakes her head resolutely. "It's nothing. I think—I think I just spooked myself. If it turns out to be anything, you'll be the first person I tell. I just have to check all of the boxes first."

"Okay. But couldn't you at least *try* to be more nebulous? For me?" My elbow digs into her ribs.

She gives me a half-smile. *Shit. Whatever it is, it's bad.* Adjusting her glasses with her forefinger, she drops her gaze down to her watch again. "Are you going to call him from Hemlock Hall? Or here in town?"

"I thought here in town, given there are too many peepholes in the Hall," I tell her.

"Stop at the train station. You can use the private phone booths."

"Train station, Charlie." He nods and makes the next left.

Charlie and I go by ourselves. We don't need all of them to hover around me, but nobody trusted me to go alone. *Noted.*

I dial the professor first.

"Waller," he answers.

"I think Carmichael did it," I tell him with no preamble.

"Lydia, William Carmichael didn't drown his daughter." His exasperation grates on me.

"His alibi doesn't check out. And..."

"And what?" He sounds tired.

"We found a body in the basement of the carriage house, the groundskeeper, Eugene Pickering. And pay-off receipts in Pickering's attic." It's so quiet on the other end that I wonder if we've been disconnected. "James?"

"Have you called Detective Quinn?" His voice is strained.

"No, I called you first."

"Who else did you tell?"

"All of us, and Emily."

"The child? You told the *child* about it?"

I swallow around the accusation. "She was spying on us. It wasn't on purpose. Also, we have evidence that Lily knew her father was having an affair."

"What kind of evidence?"

"Polaroids of drawings she did. Emily marked which drawings were hers and which were Lily's."

"Child's drawings? And do you have them?" Okay, his incredulity is starting to piss me off.

"No, they were missing when we went to look for them. Emily was quite upset that someone had taken them."

"And you believed her?"

I blink. "What do you mean?"

"I mean, you believed her when she said Lily drew them, and then you believed her when she said someone stole them out of her room?"

"Why wouldn't I?" The booth feels stifling all of a sudden. I turn and slap my hand on the glass where Charlie is leaning against it. He turns around and gives a questioning shake of his head. With a determined tug, I open the booth and drag him in with me. It's a tight fit. "Professor?"

"I mean, Emily is likely in a state of shock, searching for anything that might explain why her sister drowned."

"You think Emily faked the evidence? That's ludicrous. You weren't there; she was positively distrau—"

"What I'm saying, Lydia, is that you have circumstantial evidence at best. Did you find anything related to the day in question?"

"There was a balled-up nightgown in the corner of Emily's closet, mildewing from being wet. Also, I accidentally found a secret passage in the closet that goes into the wall spaces. They're all over the manor."

"A moldy nightgown? You're not at Hemlock Hall to investigate whether Lily Carmichael was murdered or not. You're there to find evidence that Lily is trying to contact her sister from the fucking afterlife! Stop playing Nancy Drew. Lily is not Octavia."

Charlie's eyes widen as he listens to Waller's tirade with me. "I didn't say—"

"You don't need to. I know what you're doing. We haven't solved Octavia's murder, so you're projecting, love. You're too close to this case. I'm pulling you out."

My hands shake as Charlie takes the receiver from me. "Then how do you explain the body walled into the cellar?" He demands.

"Charlie?"

"Yeah," he says, curt and sharp. "Somebody killed the groundskeeper."

"You said someone paid him off?"

"$15,000 from Carmichael," Charlie tells him. The booth is too confining for me to deal with this mounting anxiety beating at my chest, so I lean into Charlie to listen.

Waller emits a long, drawn-out sigh. "Why would Carmichael kill someone after he paid them off?"

Charlie's gaze meets mine. "We have to tell Quinn about the body, Professor."

"Let me handle it. I'll call Quinn."

Biting my lip, I shake my head. "James," I start.

"No, Lydia, let me take care of it. I shouldn't have sent you on this case. It was ridiculous to send you on one so strikingly similar to your own."

"This is NOT similar. Will you let me speak?" Charlie raises his eyebrows at me. "We found that body last night. It's already been hours and hours. What do we do? What do we tell him? Should we say we found it last night or act like we just found it? Are we going to be in trouble?"

"Lydia, as I said before, let me handle this. We're going to go with the truth."

"What do we say when they ask us why we waited?" Charlie asks him.

"Who made the call that you should wait?"

"Lydia," he says and mouths, "sorry," at me.

"We'll say that I made that call. I'll tell him that Lydia called me to ask what you should do, and I said to wait until you could find more evidence. How did you find the body anyway? You said it was in the wall?"

"Sam followed a ghost," Charlie murmurs because it sounds ridiculous.

"Did he now?" Waller shuffles some papers around on the other end. "We'll need to explore that some more, but today, we're focusing on this body. Did you find any evidence of a cause of death, or did he asphyxiate?"

Standing on my tiptoes because Charlie's so tall, I say, "No, it was definitely the letter opener sticking out of his chest with William Carmichael's initials on it."

"You didn't touch it, did you?"

"I'm not new, James, of course I didn't touch it."

"That sounds...," he coughs and takes a drink of something. "Why would he leave that kind of evidence?" Waller is quiet for a few breaths. "That sounds like a desk item. Who else has access to his study?"

"Probably the maid." Charlie bends as much as he can to help me listen better, then adds, "And, well, we were in his office today without his knowledge."

"How did you get in?"

"Cecilia had a key," Charlie replies.

Frustrated, I snatch the phone out of Charlie's hand. "James, I need you to find out what school Peter is at."

"What?"

"Peter Carmichael. He's supposedly at a boarding school abroad. I want to know which one and if someone at that school has eyeballs on him."

"What are you on about?"

"Quinn's report said Peter saw Lily in the basement, right? That's where I got attacked. It wasn't a ghost, James. That idea is ludicrous."

"You said Sam has been having sightings?"

"Yeah, we all have. But we were *high,* so it's not the most reliable evidence. Are you going to call Quinn in or not?"

"You realize if I call him in, you'll lose access to the property, right? Is Carmichael at the estate right now?"

"No, he's out. I don't think any of the Carmichaels are there right now," Charlie answers.

"I'm coming up. You left the body exactly how you found out it, yes?"

"Yes," we say together.

"Good, leave it. Meanwhile, I'll see what I can dig up on Peter Carmichael. Did he say what country or anything?"

"No, just 'abroad.'"

"Well, that's unhelpful. Maybe you should set Evie to this task?"

"I'd have to leave her in town."

"So leave her in town. She's capable. Let her catch a cab back to Hemlock Hall after she's done. I have a long drive, so I should arrive in a few hours."

She's not going to like that. "What do we do about Emily?"

"Charlie?" Waller says.

"Yeah?"

"How much evidence do you think you have?"

"Well, there's quite a lot but no visual evidence; it's all just our group reacting to someone or something. But I have loads of readings—"

"Where is it?"

"Back at the carriage house, why?"

"Someone needs to stay with Evie. I don't want any of you by yourselves. Charlie, don't leave your evidence unattended. Ever. Do you understand me?"

"Yes, sir," Charlie mumbles.

"Both of you return to the carriage house and wait for me."

"But—" He cuts me off.

"Do what I say, Lydia. After I check your evidence, I'll bring Quinn in."

We hang up and stare at each other in bewilderment for a handful of heartbeats. "Why is he being like this?" Charlie asks me.

"I'm pretty sure it's because Carmichael is our largest donor to the program, and he continued contributing after my dad died."

"He doesn't want to lose funding? He's willing to overlook everything we've found to keep the department?"

I dig my fingers into my temples. "It's complicated because now I'm questioning everything. He always does this."

"Does what?"

"He twists everything around." This phone booth has very little room, and it's getting uncomfortable. Reaching behind me, I pull open the door, and we both stumble out.

"Let's go," he tells me. I can't tell if he's angry or frustrated or both, but Charlie pulls me out of the train station by the elbow.

"You guys were gone for a while," Evie says. "Is Quinn coming?"

Frowning, I shake my head. "Waller wants to see what we have first."

"But won't we be charged for obstruction?"

"He says he'll take care of it," I tell her, and Charlie makes a jack-off motion. Evie and Shirley scowl at him. "That's not all. He wants you to stay in town and find out where the hell Peter Carmichael is."

"What? What do you mean?" Emily asks.

"Em, what school does your brother go to?"

"Canterbury Prep," she says, avoiding my gaze.

"Where?" She shrugs.

"Which country, Emily? Speak up."

"Scotland, geez," she retorts. Turning to Evie, I say, "I'm not leaving you. Do you hear me? Head to the train station and try to reach the school. We'll be here waiting for you."

"Okay," she says.

I hand her the roll of quarters. "Do you think that'll be enough?"

Her gaze drops down to the roll, pondering its sufficiency. "I think so."

"Do you want me to come with you?"

"No, this is my job. I'll be fine. Why don't you guys take Emily for some lunch at that diner across the street? This could take a bit. I think it's after dinner in Scotland."

I nod and impulsively hug her. She discovered something that unsettled her today at the city hall records department, and she's not ready to tell me what. Now I'm asking her to find a kid in Scotland on a pay phone. "We're a team, right?" It's awkward, especially when she doesn't hug me back. I drop my arms.

Evie nods and grabs her bag. "Sure, Lydia."

We head across the street to eat something, and Evie goes to work doing what she does best: smooth-talking strangers into doing favors for us.

Sam glances up at me from his milkshake. "We should have a name."

"What?" I let out a bark of laughter, finding his sudden declaration bizarre.

"I mean, Shelley Parapsychology Department is a mouthful, right? And it sounds... I don't know, man, crusty."

"You want like a... team name?"

"We're going to lose our funding," Charlie interjects, dipping one of his fries in Sam's shake.

"You guys should set up a business then. Start charging folks," Shirley suggests, having been unusually quiet today.

"What do you mean?" I ask her.

"You're doing this as a favor to the police department, right?"

"Yeah."

"Charge the police department. They've got the money," she says as if it were the most obvious solution.

"The government isn't going to pay for a ghost hunt, Shirley," I respond.

"Oh no? You think they don't pay for consultants?"

"Consultants?"

"Consultants," Sam drawls out and gives Charlie a high-five. "That's what we are, man, consultants."

Shirley sighs and sips her soda. "Look, all I'm saying is, if you all are getting paid, you could reinvest that money into the department."

"Huh," Charlie murmurs, nodding thoughtfully. "She might be onto something."

"I could pay you," Emily offers. "You're helping me, too."

"Sweetie, we don't want your allowance."

"What allowance? My inheritance doubled when Lily died," she states bluntly. The table falls into an uncomfortable silence. Emily fidgets, squirming under our intense stare.

"What did you say?" I ask her carefully.

"My inheritance. It got bigger when Lily died."

Charlie and I exchange glances. "Sam, get the bill." I reach into my purse and retrieve twenty dollars from my billfold.

Sam arches an eyebrow at me. "My father owns an *island,* Foxy. I think I can cover a diner bill."

I grab Emily's hand and pull her up from the booth. "What did I say?" She whines.

"Where did Cecilia go today?" I ask her.

"What do you mean?"

"Cecilia. She said she had something to do today, and her car wasn't in the driveway. Where did she go?"

"How should I know?" Emily retorts, snatching her hand out of my grip. "You're acting crazy, Lydia."

"Charlie? Did she mention anything to you?"

He shakes his head and exhales deeply. "We really need to head back to the carriage house."

As we exit the diner, Evie dashes across the street, her dark hair bouncing with each stride. Gasping for air, she manages to say, "He's not there," breathlessly. "He didn't make it to the fall session."

I whirl around to face Emily, grasping her shoulders firmly. "Where is Peter, Emily? And don't lie to us. You said your inheritance *doubled.* Why would it *double* if Lily's inheritance was split between the three remaining kids?"

Emily's face turns pale. "I-I don't know," she stammers. "I swear I don't! It's just what Cece told me!"

Sam, returning from settling the bill, gently smooths Emily's hair. "What's going down, little momma? What's got everyone buggin'?"

"I don't know where Peter is, but Lydia doesn't believe me."

"Is he alive?" I press her, my hands still on her shoulders.

"Why would Peter be dead? I don't understand, and you're scaring me!" Emily's voice cracks with fear.

"Whoa, whoa, nobody's trying to scare you," Sam interjects, positioning himself between Emily and me, his expression stern. "That's enough, Lydia."

Waller's words about Emily manipulating the whole situation wash over me. "Christ, we need to get back," I exclaim. "Charlie, let's move. We need to go now. We're being played for fools. If you have anything to add, Evie, now's the time."

"It's Cecilia," Evie asserts. "I think this is all Cecilia."

CHAPTER
twenty four

We pull up to the guest house as the sun sets, casting a chill that settles around us. The drive back is engulfed in near-perfect silence. This isn't what we signed on for—a bit of paranormal data, maybe a genuine sighting, sure, but this? An out-of-control blue-blood beauty queen? Not in my job description.

"Shit," Charlie murmurs, switching the Dodge's ignition off. We remain seated, none of us making a move. "Who came out last?"

The front door is ajar, open just a couple of inches. "Did someone forget to shut the door?" I ask.

"Nobody forgot," Evie replies firmly. We had only been gone three hours. The silence stretches out, filling the already cramped van as we sit in the driveway.

"Sam," I say, my eyes fixed on the door.

"Yeah, momma?"

"Hand me the tire iron from the back."

"Whoa, what? We don't even know if there's anyone in there."

"And we don't know if there isn't. Hand me the damned iron." I extend my hand expectantly.

Charlie sighs deeply, running his palm down his face. "Shit," he mutters again. "I'll go."

"Not very feminist of you," I retort, opening the van door to step out. "I'll be right back."

"No, uh-uh, it's all or none of us," Shirley interjects, pulling her keys from her bag and wedging them between her knuckles.

While I appreciate the solidarity, I'm the team lead. I don't want anyone getting hurt. "Stay here." Gravel crunches under my feet as I approach the house. The sun dips lower, casting long shadows. What seemed a quaint, magical-looking cottage now looms ominously, its every corner shrouded in gloom.

Holding the tire iron like a bat, I carefully toe the door open and peer inside. The scene is chaotic. "Fuck," I mutter under my breath.

"What is it?" Charlie's voice floats from outside as he climbs out of the van.

I shake my head, signaling for patience. "Give me a minute." Slipping into the shadowy interior of the carriage house, I flip the living room light switch. Only the porch light flickers on, casting a dim glow that's just enough to navigate by. I move deeper into the room and turn on a lamp.

Our bags are dumped all over the living room, and cameras, with their film compartments eviscerated, are strewn about. Whoever was here is gone now. Sniffing the air, I scrunch my nose and peer frantically around the room. "Is that smoke?" I call out the open door.

The sound of hurried footsteps on gravel tells me Charlie is already investigating. "No!" His shout slices through the air, prompting everyone else to spill out of the van.

I rush to the small back garden, where the remnants of a fire smolder on the black grill. "My research," Evie gasps, her voice thick with distress.

"No, no way," Shirley exclaims, panic edging her voice. "They didn't burn our footage, did they? Tell me they didn't!"

Guilt claws at me, echoing Shirley's despair. This mess—this disaster—it's on me. I pushed too hard. "Sam?" I call out as he flings open the cellar door. "Sam, wait!"

By the time I reach him, he's already downstairs. "He's gone," Sam's voice is hollow. "Pickering. He's gone."

"This is bad. This is so bad," Charlie says as he kicks a workhorse in frustration. "We need to call Quinn right now!"

"Waller's on his way." It's a feeble reassurance, but it's all I have at the moment.

"They removed the wall completely?" Evie crouches where the wall had been, sifting through the earth floor as if searching for evidence that it had ever existed. "It doesn't even smell like it did before. How do you think they managed that?" She dusts her hands off and moves toward the door. Everyone draws a sharp breath at her observation.

"You know what they're going to say if we tell anyone," Shirley interjects. "We were all on mushrooms."

"I wasn't," Charlie counters. "Neither was Emily."

"How did they know we found anything?" Sam wonders aloud.

"Do you think she said something?" Evie asks, cleaning her glasses with the hem of her blouse. "The only people aside from us who knew about the evidence was Emily."

"And Waller," Charlie adds. "Waller knew, too."

My brow furrows at the implication. "No, he wouldn't do this to us. The haunting phenomena we captured on film, Emily's possessions, they're too valuable. He would never—"

"You said it yourself: Carmichael was a key donor to the department," Charlie interjects angrily. "This is garbage." He storms up the stairs and back into the house.

Shirley and Evie follow him, leaving Sam and me in the cellar. "I know he's your mentor, Foxy, but could he have spoken to Carmichael just to clear things up, as you would with a friend?"

A scowl carves deeper into my face. "It's my fault," I choke out. "I told Waller. I called him before Quinn. I let him talk me out of calling the cops. It's all my fault." My voice breaks as I struggle to force the words from my throat.

Sam wraps his arms around me, pulling me snug against him. "You did what you thought was right. Nobody is blaming you. Maybe we've got this all mixed up, yeah?" He runs his hand through my hair and rests his chin on top of my head.

I cling to him, burying my face in his chest. "I'm messing this up. I'm messing up everything. The team, Waller, Emily, *you*."

"Don't worry about me," he says in his gruff voice, which I sometimes think he reserves just for me. "You didn't do anything wrong." Sam pauses for a half-second. "Okay, maybe you should have called Quinn as soon as we found the body, but other than that..."

I laugh into his soft shirt. "Yeah, you were right. I was wrong."

"I'm sorry, what was that?"

"I said I was wrong, Sam."

"Oh my, Three Dog Night. Did Lydia Fox just apologize to *me?* The department embarrassment, I think you called me?" He tilts my head to face him and rests his forehead against mine. His long lashes flutter against his cheeks. "We'll figure this out."

I'm unsure what 'this' is that we'll figure out. The case? The fieldwork? Us? A certain vulnerability floods my veins, and I rise onto my toes to kiss him hard on the mouth, as if trying to steal some of that courage. Lingering for a moment, I hum in satisfaction at the feel of his lips. His fingers dig into my hips for a heartbeat. "Waller will be here soon. He'd better be able to straighten all of this out." I pull away from him, immediately cold without his tall, lanky frame warming mine. "All of that evidence, though." My fingers tangle in my hair in frustration.

"Lydia!" Evie yells from inside the house. Sam and I bolt up the stairs to find her at the front door. "Emily's gone."

"What? What do you mean?"

"She's gone. She came in from the van. We went upstairs to check on the box of files Pickering left in the attic. By the way, they're gone, and when we came back down, she wasn't here."

"She couldn't have gone far," I tell Evie. "I'll go check her room up at the house. I need someone to stay here and wait for Waller. And for God's sake, don't touch anything."

"Wait!" Evie says and grabs me by the upper arm. "You need to see this." Pulling me over to the van, she shows a newspaper clipping of Cecilia and her parents at some charity event. It's dated two years ago.

"What am I looking at?"

"Right here, there's a good image of his ring on his left hand." I squint at where she's pointing. "And now, Esme's hand." Okay, another wedding ring. "Now, take a little peek at Cecilia's hand." Cecilia's ring matches her father's. Her mother's ring is the odd one out. "It gets worse." How can it get worse?

She doesn't wait for me to ask; instead, her finger returns to Carmichael's ring. "This is the only one where you can make out the words since he's in the foreground, but since they match, I assume Cecilia's ring says the same. Why didn't it catch my eye in person? It's odd, isn't it? Miss Massachusetts wearing a ring on her left hand?" Tapping the image, she lets me work it out.

"Pura sanguine?"

"They're not Thelemites. They're some offshoot, probably something Ambrose invented. They want to be gods, like the Pharaoh." Evie's face is lit up pink with her exuberance.

"I... Evie..."

"Ambrose Carmichael was married to Esther Carmichael. I couldn't find her maiden name. And guess what? There was *another* Esther Carmichael in the family, but she drowned in that pond when she was twelve years old. She was Ambrose's *sister.*"

I have to sit in the Dodge's open side door. "What you're saying is…"

"I think Ambrose Carmichael married his sister a few years after they faked her death. They could've at least used another first name; it's absolutely distasteful."

"And you're saying these pure blood rings that William and Cecilia wear are what?"

"I don't know, and I don't like it. I don't like how they've lied about her age, I don't like how she doesn't have a beau despite being rich, beautiful, and Miss Massachusetts, and I don't like how Lily Carmichael died the same way Esther Carmichael died. Too much coincidence creates a pattern."

"Okay," I tell her. "I have to find Emily while I mull this over. Should we tell Waller?"

Evie blushes. "I mean, we have to, don't we? We can't sit on this. I'm saying some pretty slanderous things about one of the oldest families in America."

"Waller isn't going to be happy."

"Well, fuck him. He doesn't have to be happy. He merely has to help us do the right thing." My eyebrows shoot up in disbelief; Evie's not the type to talk about a professor like that.

"Keep it safe, Evie. We can't lose more evidence." I spin around and head up the trail toward the house.

"Wait up!" Sam runs to catch up with me. "You shouldn't be wandering off by yourself."

"I'm a big girl, Sam," I tell him.

"So was Pickering," he tosses back. "Big, I mean. Not a girl."

"Fine." The lights are on in the manor, and both cars are under the porte-cochère.

"What did Evie have to show you?"

"That the Carmichaels might be a little weirder than previously thought. And I mean in the worst 'keep it in the family' way."

"No," he mumbles under his breath. "That's… Jesus. We've got to get Emily out of this house."

"Peter, too."

Sam halts abruptly at the mention of Peter. "He's still alive."

"What do you mean?"

"I mean, out of all of the ghosts here, we've seen Lily, Alice Shippington, Eugene Pickering, and Ambrose Carmichael. No little boys."

"What about the kids in the cellar? Could Peter be with them?"

"The cellar!" He grabs me by my upper arms and kisses my forehead. "You're a goddamned genius. I'll be back. I'll meet you at the guest house!"

"Wait! What happened to 'we shouldn't be alone'? You don't have a walkie!" I call out after him.

"This can't wait! Go, find Emily!"

He's gone, leaving me awash in the glow of the porch light. Wiping sweaty palms on my skirt, I open the front door, hoping nobody will be down here.

Thankfully, it's empty, and I move across the foyer to the staircase. Come to think of it, I haven't seen the maid in a couple of days. I hope she's just gotten some days off and isn't in a wall somewhere keeping Pickering company.

My footsteps sound so loud on the hall runner, and even though I'm aware the rest of the family lives in the other wing, my heart hammers in my chest just the same. I knock on Emily's door softly.

"Emily? It's me, Lydia. Open the door," I whisper as loud as I can. My eyes dart up toward the tape we put on her frame to indicate if someone had entered while she was gone.

It's undisturbed. Emily hasn't been back to her room.

"Looking for Emily?" Cecilia's voice makes me jump and whirl around. She's leaning against the wall next to a portrait of an ancestor whose family resemblance is astonishing.

"Oh, hey, Cecilia. You haven't seen her around, have you?" She's a couple of inches taller than me, so I have to look up at her when she crosses the hall to stand next to me. She smirks.

"I thought she was with you guys." Her ash blonde hair is pulled into a chignon except for a few loose pieces, giving her an almost deranged Bette Davis look. "Did you lose her?"

Our eyes lock, hers narrowed to my wide-open ones. "You're really beautiful, you know that?" she purrs. "Did you pageant when you were younger?"

"N-no, my mother said judging a woman on her looks is misogynistic."

Cecilia snorts inelegantly. "We're judged on our looks just walking down the sidewalk." She tucks my hair behind my ear, and I notice her cuticles are filthy.

"Anyways, I should get going. Professor Waller should be here any minute."

"You want me to pass on a message?"

"What?"

"To Emily. If I see her. Do you want me to pass on a message?"

Something feels wrong. There appears to be a bit more of Cecilia that she's attempting to keep boxed in, like she wants to scream or hit me, or something wild is clawing to escape from behind her eyes. "Can you ask her to come to the carriage house when you see her? I need to ask her a few questions about Lily."

A smile curves at a snail's pace along Cecilia's lips. "Sure. I can do that." Her fingers wrap around my wrist as I try to slip past her. "Tell Charlie to come see me," she whispers conspiratorially. "It really gets Daddy's *blood* pumping seeing me with that *chink*."

My eyebrows draw together harshly, and her expression dares me to say anything. "I've known girls like you my entire life, and you're going to end up as empty and desperate as the rest." My gaze drops to the Pura Sanguine ring on her finger. "Nice ring." Cecilia releases me and steps back.

I walk away, willing myself not to turn around to make sure she isn't going to hit me over the head with something. Halfway down the stairs, I hear footsteps coming from the opposite wing. Hastening my steps, I slip out the door before either Carmichael can stop me.

Shivering from the cold, or anger, or fear, or whatever, I practically run back to the guest house. Waller's Mercedes is sitting in the drive behind the van.

He yanks the door open before I can put my hand on the knob and pulls me into his arms. I sob into his neck, releasing all of the pent-up anxiety of the past few hours. Releasing me, he puts both hands on my head and pulls me back so he can make sure I'm unharmed.

"Are you hurt? Where have you been? Look at me. *Look at me,*" he demands. "Lydia." My watery eyes finally meet his. "Are you injured?"

I shake my head in his hands. "I think we messed up." This causes me to break into a fresh bout of tears. "Emily. I can't find Emily." Waller pulls me against him again.

"Where's Sam?" Evie asks me.

Sniffing, I pull away from the professor. "What do you mean? He came back here."

"He came back here, grabbed the whole sack of sandwiches from the fridge, and ran back out. We thought he went to find you," Charlie tells me.

I step back from Waller and wipe my eyes. "James, was this you? Did you call Carmichael and tell him about the evidence we had? Did you confront him on the phone?"

"No," he replies. "You have to believe me. I had no idea this was going on in this house."

My gaze lands on Evie, who, with a nod, tells me she told him about the pure blood thing. "There was a body here. You have to believe us."

"Where's the phone? We need to call Quinn in now," the professor asks. "I wasn't expecting all of our footage to be destroyed."

"The only phone is up at the manor," Shirley tells him.

"You don't understand. I think they've taken Emily." Finally, everyone listens to me and turns their attention to where I stand. "Cecilia was acting bizarre up at the house. Her hands are filthy, her hair is a mess, and I think she's done something to her sister."

"Where would Sam have gone? What were you guys talking about on the walk up to the house?" Evie asks me.

"We were talking about Peter and... the cellar. He's gone down to the basement!"

"There hasn't been enough time for Cecilia to have taken Emily very far," Charlie says, his mouth screwed up into a tight frown. Did he actually like her? "C'mon, let's go. We'll call Quinn while the professor keeps Carmichael busy, and then we'll find Emily and Sam."

I just hope we're not too late.

CHAPTER twenty five

The night air bites and nips at us, chasing us along the path to the manor. Shadows stretch across the weedy path, swallowing the edges in darkness. Everything that is happening right now is because of me and my choices. It was my choice not to call Quinn. It was my choice not to pull the plug after I got attacked in the basement. It was my choice not to leave anybody behind in the carriage house today to ensure nothing happened to our evidence.

But that last choice might have saved someone's life. It's all I have to cling to that I'm not absolutely abhorrent at my job. And Emily, if anything's happened to her, I might raze this place to the ground.

Shit. I'm trying so hard not to think about Sam right now. Please be alright.

The ivy-adorned façade of Hemlock Hall looms over us, gloomy and alone as the moon rises behind it. Waller places a reassuring hand on my shoulder.

"We'll find her," he says, his voice steady as a soldier this time, no threats, no admonishments, no gnashing of teeth, no snarling to keep me under his thumb. He thinks I've learned a particular lesson: I should've listened to him.

All I've learned is I need to make better judgment calls.

"Right," I say. "And you mean 'them.' Sam's missing, as well."

"Yes, well, Sam's a big boy."

"So was Eugene Pickering," Evie murmurs next to me.

My heart pounds hard against my ribcage as we approach the front door. Our footsteps crunching on the gravel driveway beneath us are the only sounds. Not even the crickets or frogs from the pond dare to make a peep tonight.

Standing beneath the porte-cochère, I feel impending doom. When I push it, the door creaks open, not even closed entirely. It reveals only the dimly lit foyer. I'll never forgive myself if uncovering the truth here costs a little girl her life.

My gaze flickers over to Evie, whose expression conveys more of the same.

Waller is stiff and agitated as he takes the lead. I'm still conversing silently with Evie when he snaps his fingers in front of my eyes. My attention turns to him. "Stay with me, Lydia."

I nod, and we move cautiously, our footsteps echoing on the cold marble floor, the air thick with tension. My eyes dart between the spots in the walls that I know are peepholes. The unnerving feeling of being watched sweeps over me, pebbling my skin. Someone or something in the walls is judging our intrusion into the Carmichaels' lives.

I give them the middle finger.

"Okay, listen up," Waller commands. "Our priority is the child, but keep your eyes peeled for any paranormal activity."

"Seriously?" I whisper harshly to him.

"This isn't a ghost hunt anymore, Professor," Charlie reminds him.

"And Sam is a priority as well," I say.

"Fine, yes, Sam as well," Waller concedes. "For someone who didn't even want Sam along, you certainly seem overly concerned about him." When I don't offer an explanation, he continues, "Charlie, Evie, you two take the downstairs. Check the sitting room, the kitchen, the dining room, et cetera. We'll meet back here in 10 minutes. Charlie, I know this doesn't need to be said, but record everything, would you?"

"Yeah, boss," Charlie says to Waller but gives me a reassuring smile as he and Evie head off toward the sitting room.

"Need I remind you of the same, Ms. Henderson?" Waller's gaze drops to the camera in her hand. I hadn't realized she wasn't filming.

"Oh, yeah, sure." She lifts the camera to her shoulder, makes some adjustments, and then nods to us when she's ready to follow. The air grows colder the higher up the staircase we go, and it's not my imagination because Shirley says, "Shit. Did someone leave all the windows open up here?"

The wallpaper creeps with veiny shadows from the trees outside, and the line of portraits of long-gone ancestors appears more sinister than ever. They burn with scorn and indignation. I shove down the thought of how desperately lonely this place must have been for Emily in these last few weeks. My chest grows tight as I struggle to take a breath. I slap a palm over my heart.

"Lydia?" Waller asks, concern etched into his arched brow.

"Fine," I lie. "Just... anxious."

"Stay focused," Shirley chimes in, but she grabs my hand and squeezes it. "You're all right, girl."

"Mm-hmm," I agree. Straightening up, I continue following Waller down the long hall.

The first few doors are empty, unused bedrooms—their abandoned furnishings draped with sheets. I pull us to a stop in front of Emily and Lily's room and check the tape on the door frame. This time, it's been tampered with. Cracking the door open, it's unsettlingly quiet, devoid of any sign of life or Emily's recent presence.

"Nothing here," Waller murmurs, his voice sounding out of place amidst the clutter of little girl treasures. "Let's keep moving."

"Wait," I say and yank open the closet door. The passage is sealed tight. It doesn't budge when I push on it. Somebody latched it from the other side.

"Damn it," I mutter under my breath, frustration mounting as the East Wing yields no clues to Emily's whereabouts. "Where could she be?"

"We'll find her," Waller tells me again, somehow tonight's voice of reason.

A sliver of light spills from the crack under a door at the end of the corridor. We exchange glances, and Waller gives me an encouraging nod before cautiously approaching the door. The hinges emit a faint creaking sound, sending an equally creaky shudder down my spine.

"Stay behind me," Waller whispers as he pushes the door open, revealing a narrow staircase leading to the attic.

We creep up the old wooden steps, which groan under our weight. Again, the air grows colder with each step, which is strange because heat rises.

Waller reaches the landing first, his eyes widening in horror at the sight that awaits him. "No," he huffs out. "Don't come up here," his voice a clear warning, his fist stuffed tight against his mouth.

Undeterred, Shirley shoves past me and races up the remaining stairs, her determination to capture the shot overruling caution. I follow. Waller's warning be damned, if it's Emily, I need to know. My blood pumps hard in anticipation of whatever gruesome scene Waller uncovered.

The dim lightbulb hanging from the ceiling and reflected in the attic's grimy windows reveals a macabre tableau: Esme Carmichael. Her lifeless body hangs from the rafters, her sightless eyes staring blankly into the void. Blood drips from the fingers of her right hand, and a kitchen knife lies abandoned and forgotten beneath her dangling, dainty feet. A mixture of shock, revulsion, and sorrow courses through me, my breath catching in my throat.

Marian, the maid, sits propped in the corner, her throat a wet and gaping wound. A pool of blood saturates the floorboards beneath her—*a servant for the afterlife.*

"Sweet Jesus," Shirley whispers, her eye on the viewfinder. Her free hand covers her mouth in a futile attempt to stifle her horror.

Waller places a protective arm around me and urges me to look away, but I can't tear my gaze from her. *Why? Why would she do this?*

"Emily," I can barely choke out her name. "We need to find her."

Waller nods grimly, his arm still tightly gripping my shoulders. "Agreed, but first, we must tell the others about this. Lydia, we need to call Detective Quinn now."

I can't bear to look any longer, so I stumble backward, out of his overly familiar grip and gasping for air. Panic sets in, urging me down the attic stairs and out of the manor. Each step sounds too loud in my ears. Someone will hear.

"Lydia!" Waller calls after me, his voice weighted down with frustration. But I can't stop, can't think—only run. I need to get away from Esme Carmichael's accusing dead eyes.

"Emily!" I gasp, colliding with someone at the bottom of the stairs. It's only Charlie, who tries to steady me as I struggle to regain my balance and breath. He grips my shoulders tight to keep me on my feet, and the dread in my eyes conveys the gravity of the situation. "Esme. She's—" My voice hitches, and I can't finish the sentence, but the strangled sound I utter speaks volumes.

Waller and Shirley catch up, their faces drawn. A door closes somewhere in the manor, causing us to collectively jump and exchange uneasy glances before turning our attention to the source of the noise.

William Carmichael stands haughtily at the top of the grand staircase, his salt-and-pepper hair disheveled, his piercing eyes narrowing in disappointment as they sweep over us. "You were supposed to find a confession from Pickering," he says coldly, addressing Professor Waller. "He admitted to drowning Lily in those damned documents. But you lot found everything but that."

"Mr. Carmichael, Esme—" Shirley starts, but he cuts her off with a wave.

"Weak. Im*pure*. A *mongrel*," he snaps, seething with anger. I realize he's referring to his wife, who hangs from the attic rafters as we speak. "You've made a hell of a mess of my family's affairs, and now I'm left to clean it up."

"We need to call the police," Charlie tells him. The statement only adds to Carmichael's disdain.

"Esme... she couldn't live with the guilt any longer."

"Guilt? For what?" Shirley asks, her camera not on her eye but by her side while she pretends it's off. The dull hum beside me gives it away; however, I don't think Carmichael can see or hear that far.

"Esme discovered Cecilia killed Pickering after learning he'd drowned Lily." We sit with this confession briefly, trying it on as truth. It's a politician's truth, beautiful up front but nothing in the back—a movie set. The elections were just a couple of weeks away. A scandal like that could have buried the Carmichael family.

"Are you telling me you're all complicit in covering up a murder?" Waller asks with disgust.

"What murder?" Carmichael smoothly replies, arching his brow at us. "James, we all have our roles to play in preserving my family's legacy. Every single Carmichael."

"By hiding the truth?" Evie chimes in, her voice laced with anger. "You call that a legacy?"

A shudder crawls up my spine at this confession. I am reeling at the depths to which they would go to protect their secrets. The dim lighting from the chandelier dangling above us casts twisted shadows across Carmichael's face, and my stomach drops.

"Where is Sam?" My voice shakes with the question.

"Lydia," Waller cautions. There are too many variables and too much risk.

"Where's Emily?" Carmichael counters, his voice a thunderous growl that shakes the foundations.

"So, what? We give you Emily, you give us Sam? Is that it?" Evie shouts up at him.

Carmichael's eyes flash with annoyance, but he sighs, and his gaze dances around the room for a few beats before answering. "Your hippie is fine, for now. The longer you keep my daughter from me, the worse it will get for him, though."

Waller grabs me as I lunge toward the stairs at him. "You son of a bit—"

"ENOUGH!" Carmichael barks, silencing us all. "Give me my daughter, and I'll give you that filthy Egyptian."

"That's rich coming from someone who practically worships Egyptians," Evie snipes at him.

Carmichael cocks his head slowly to the side and measures her with a steady, admonitory gaze. "Don't speak of things you couldn't possibly comprehend."

"Pura sanguine," Evie growls back at him. She's puffed up like a mad cat, and her eyes flitter down to his ring.

Carmichael's lips curl into a sinister smile as the realization crashes over me. "Ah, Lydia," he purrs in a voice laced with venom. "Your team might be more perceptive than I gave you credit for."

The room falls silent as we exchange wary glances, our hearts pounding. It becomes clear that Carmichael will not easily relinquish Sam without Emily.

Evie steps forward, her eyes locked with Carmichael's. "What do you want with Emily? More pura sanguine? You have to know that way lies madness."

"Not for the Pharaoh. The people elevated them—better, brighter. They became gods," he whispers, his tone patronizing as though we're all children, Waller included. "But do you truly understand what it means to possess pure blood?"

The room falls silent, each of us held as captive as Sam. I exchange a glance with Shirley, and it is clear that we are both grappling with the weight of saving Emily from this family before it's too late.

I glance over at Charlie, my eyes pleading for him to come up with anything to turn this situation around. Charlie, always quick on his feet, takes a step forward, his charming smile curving at the corners of his lips.

"Mr. Carmichael," he starts, his voice smooth and persuasive. "Surely there is another way, a more peaceful way, to resolve this conflict. Violence only leads to more grief, and I can see that you are a man of intelligence and reason deep down."

Carmichael's scowl deepens as he scrutinizes Charlie. The room holds its breath, waiting for his response.

"You underestimate the power of blood," Carmichael finally replies, his gaze flickering with uncertainty. "Do you not understand the significance of our lineage? Emily possesses the purest bloodlines, a direct link to the ancient pharaohs themselves."

I take a deep breath, summoning all the courage I can muster. "Carmichael," I speak up, my voice trembling but determined. "You said you want Emily in exchange for Sam. But what guarantee do we have that you'll keep your word? How do we know that once you have both of them, you won't simply kill us?"

"You're always the skeptic, aren't you, Lydia?" he chuckles condescendingly. "You question my intentions when it is your very skepticism that has brought you this far—so much like your father." The air hangs heavy against my skin as if the weight of Carmichael's gaze is pressing down on me. My fingers hold a fierce grip on Charlie's arm. "Wait," Carmichael says, his eyes widening at the implications. "You don't know where Emily is, do you?"

I pause, my heart racing, realizing I may have unintentionally revealed a secret. Charlie squeezes my hand reassuringly, his eyes silently urging me to proceed cautiously.

"We're not going to disclose Emily's whereabouts until we have confirmation that Sam is safe and unharmed," I say, my voice steady despite the fear bubbling within me.

A derisive smile tugs at the corners of Carmichael's lips as he leans back against the newel post at the top of the stairs, folding his arms over his chest. "A bold move," he remarks, his tone filled with amusement. "But do you truly think you can outwit the likes of me?"

He wants me to cower under his scrutinizing gaze, but I won't give him the satisfaction. Evie steps forward once more, her voice dripping with defiance.

"We don't need to outwit you, Carmichael. We just need to buy enough time until we find a way—"

A gut-wrenching, primal scream pierces through the stifling atmosphere of the foyer. A wail that shatters all of my cool.

Sam.

I am done playing with this man. I need to find Sam and I need to find Sam now.

CHAPTER
twenty six

The click makes me stop and drag my gaze to the top of the staircase. The man running for senate is pointing a handgun at us. He is *pointing a handgun* at us. The cold metal gleams menacingly in the dim light. I lunge at the stairs, a growl ripping from my throat, a feral sound that doesn't even register with me. Charlie and Waller pull me back, and Evie gasps. It echoes—the gasp and the struggle between my godfather, Charlie, and me.

"What are you doing?" Charlie whispers sharply in my ear. "Do you not clock the hand cannon?"

"Ah-ah," Carmichael tuts. "Emily. Now."

Waller steps between Carmichael and me. "Bill, listen," he begins.

"Oh, shut it, Waller. You're overreaching. You never had Court's brilliance, you never had the societal ties, and you were never anything but a pathetic underling unworthy of taking his place. Court had vision. He understood the power of this house—the power of the leylines beneath it."

Evie juts her chin out. "You're out of your mind. Do you know that?" She straightens and stands next to Waller, forming a wall between Carmichael and me. Charlie takes the hint and does the same. The three of them pivot ever so slightly.

Shirley lifts her camera and makes a show of turning it on.

"I don't think that will be necessary; it's a waste of battery, Ms. Henderson, since the film is never going to leave this hall," Carmichael sneers.

"Fine. I'll get her," I tell him. "I'll go get Emily. You win. But I want Sam in return." My heart is surely going to pound straight out of my chest, and the horror of Sam's scream lingers in my head. "You promise you won't hurt her?"

Carmichael motions for me to hurry, and I make like I'm heading toward the back of the first floor when I'm really trying to maneuver beneath him on the second-floor landing so I can slip through the basement door tucked behind the stairs. The only light I have on me is Sam's lighter, but it'll have to do. The flickering flame casts eerie shadows on the damp walls, making the space feel even more foreboding. Hopefully, they can keep him busy while I search for our team psychic. There's a whimper in the distance, and it urges me forward. The stairs seem much more than before, like they go on forever until my feet hit the bottom, and I peer around, the flame barely making a dent in the overbearing darkness.

The pool of water nearly reaches my ankles now. When I came down here the night before, it had been merely a puddle. Has it only been a single night since then? Is the pond leaking into the basement?

The air is thick and heavy, and the genuinely repellent aroma of wet trash overwhelms me, making my mouth water with nausea. "Sam?" I whisper as loud as I dare. "Where are you?"

Nothing but the constant dripping echoes somewhere in the distance. The hair on my arms stands on end, and a shiver courses through me. *"Oh, Cecilia, you're breaking my heart,"* I sing as I inch forward, trying not to trip over my own feet. "*You're shakin' my confidence daily,*" my voice wavers, and I try to steady my nerves.

Worry for Sam, worry for the others I left behind with a madman with a gun, threatens to buckle my knees, which feel particularly liquidy right now. "Sam!" It's what I call a holler-whisper, but it's silly because just making your yell into a loud rasp is still yelling.

And I'm still drawing attention to my location.

Shit.

A shadow flits across my limited field of vision. It is slight, something bigger than a wild animal that might have found its way into the cellar but definitely smaller than a person—I mean, smaller than an *adult* person.

Oh no. The realization smacks me hard in the face, the reason Sam came down here. "Peter?" I whisper, "Peter Carmichael? We're here to save you."

Yeah, right. But who's going to save you?

Shut up, Octavia.

A cold flood of doubt fills my insides with trepidation. I hope I didn't just promise a ghost that I could save them. Please don't be dead. Please let this be a punishment gone wrong. A horrible, go-straight-to-jail-for-child-abuse kind of punishment, but still a punishment. Carmichael wouldn't want his heir, the person who will carry on his family name, to die, would he?

Carmichael hasn't said a word about Peter, not after he told us he was away at boarding school. I think back, trying to remember a single photograph of him in the house, and I realize the only photo I've seen of him was in the newspaper clipping.

The basement is a labyrinth of old wine barrels and forgotten relics. The casks line the walls, and one has a hatchet buried in it. The stench of the wine in the water assaults my nose, and on closer inspection, I see that someone's bashed all of the barrels open. Yanking the hatchet proves impossible with one hand, so I balance the lighter on one of the barrels and reach out with two hands to pull the ax handle as hard as possible. When it finally breaks free of the cask, it sends me straight into the puddle.

"No!" I exclaim. My lovely wool skirt immediately sucks up all of the wine and pond water beneath my ass. "Great."

But now I have an ax. Things are improving.

"*Oh, Cecilia,*" someone breathes out in the dark, urging me to continue my song. I hold still, as still as possible, and snatch the lighter off the top of the barrel. Holding the hatchet out before me, I whirl toward the sound.

The darkness swallows us both up, and I curse as I grip the hatchet between my knees and struggle to relight the Zippo. Despite my inept fumbling, it finally flares back to life, and I peer around my perimeter. There's nobody there. That nagging sense of déjà vu is back, and I realize we'd been here, at Hemlock Hall, before. Cecilia pushed Tavi into the pond.

"You tell Papa, and I'll cut your hair off," she hissed at us.

I *had* been here before. Octavia and I were both here with our parents at some department function the Carmichaels allowed on the property. He was one of my father's most prominent benefactors and college chum, so of course, we'd been here before.

But why had I forgotten until now? Cece is a bully, and Tavi knew.

We'd been to many donor houses. My father believed in community-funded education and keeping a part of that community was the educator's responsibility. It's the only way society moves forward. Donations and research, research and donations, have gone hand in hand since the cradle of civilization.

But, in my father's pursuit of that community, had I been down here before?

Cecilia locked Octavia and me down here in the cellar when Tavi threatened to tell on Cece for ruining her Easter dress by shoving her into the pond. Why hadn't I remembered that?

Cecilia was a teenager, much older than us. We wanted to swim, but Cecilia said she couldn't because 'people would see.'

People would see *what?*

"Get off me, man!" A voice calls out beyond the pitiful flame on the Zippo.

"Sam!" I cry out in the dark. "Where are you?"

"Lydia?" His voice cracks with relief.

I kick something in my flight toward him, reach down, and grab it. It's Sam's flashlight. Turning it on, I shine the much wider beam around the vaulted space and discover him on the ground in the corner.

"Sam!" I yell again and hurl myself toward him.

"No, Lydia, look out," he tries to warn me, but it's too late, and I'm smacked in the face with what I'm almost certain was a frying pan. I'm knocked heartily back and find myself on my ass again. Stars color my vision like a cartoon.

"Oh, fuck," I groan.

The hatchet is next to me, and the flashlight is a few feet away. The flashlight illuminates the ax in an arc of yellow light. Before I can grab the weapon, a hand snatches it, so I dive for the flashlight instead.

Squinting through the pain and watery eyes, I mop the trickle of blood that burst out of my nose. Sam is only a few feet away, and I crawl sloppily toward him. He's nursing a knee, and his face is a tapestry of black, red, and grey bruises.

We wrap our arms around each other and pull ourselves into a sitting position, leaning against the wall behind us. "I was so worried about you," I sigh into his hair.

"You and me both," he admits. "Why are you alone?"

"Carmichael, he's gone mad, but we have bigger things to worry about. Whoever hit me took my ax."

"You brought an ax?" I can't tell if his voice is filled with anger, humor, or surprise, but I decide it's probably a mixture of all three.

"I *found* an ax, thank you very much. I needed *something*, Sam." I shine the light on his battered face.

"Looks bad, right?"

"I've seen worse," I tell him.

Sam snorts. "Yeah, I believe you." He presses his forehead to mine. "It feels like I was down here forever waiting for someone to notice I hadn't returned."

"We're not having that conversation right now. We have to find another way out. The foyer is no good. Carmichael thinks I've gone to fetch Emily for him since he thinks we took her, and he has a gun."

Sam groans out a chuckle. "Carmichael has a *what*?"

"Seriously, Sam, eyes forward." I shine the light in his pupils. "I think you have a concussion."

"I think you have a concussion, too." He takes the flashlight out of my hands. "Oh shit," he says when he illuminates me.

"What? What is it?"

"I don't know if you have a concussion, pretty momma, but you definitely have a broken nose."

"Shit," I say and cup my palm over my nose. It was a petty time to be concerned about my looks when our lives are in balance, but there it is.

"Anyway, I'm not getting out of here without a stretcher." He shows me his knee. It strains against his jeans in a swollen, battered mess. "You're going to have to find help."

"Who did this to you? Did you get a good look? Was it… was it Peter? Is he dead?"

"A ghost didn't do this to me. Pretty sure that kid didn't do this to me. Oh! I found the kid! He was locked behind one of those doors with the latches." He waves in a general direction that I don't care about. "He's a little feral, but I gave him a couple of sandwiches. Wouldn't come into my light, but he wolfed down the food. That's when Pan-happy started hitting me."

"You found Peter? Sam, that's… that's amazing," I sweep the room with the light. "Where did he go? Who hit you?"

"No idea where little man fucked off to. Between the open door and my attack, his ass probably got spooked. I *thought* it was Carmichael who jumped me," he huffs a dark laugh. "We need to save these kids from these people, Lydia. They had Peter locked up down here. Tell me that's your primary concern."

His gaze levels on mine, measuring me up. I take a deep breath. "I want to say they're my priority, but I can't lie; my priority is the team. I have to make sure the team is okay first."

"Spoken like a leader, but I need the kids out before me. You have to prioritize them first. Please listen to this cricket on your shoulder this time?"

Swallowing, I consider it. "Okay, you're right. But I'm not leaving you in this cellar with someone that now has a hatchet, and let's face it… we both know it's Cecilia. Give me some alternatives here."

"Unless you've got some crutches tucked into that tight turtleneck you're wearing, I don't think I can follow you."

"We need to find a phone." Tapping my finger on my bruised lips, I think hard about this basement and the entrances that I'm aware of. The faint sound of dripping water punctuates the silence, adding to the oppressive atmosphere. "Okay, I think I know another way out, and it sucks."

"Tell me where we're going doesn't have any ghosts, Foxy."

My eyes narrow on him. "Why?"

"Because whoever beat the shit outta me, pig-style, also dosed my ass. I'm rolling right now."

"Why? Why would she do that?"

"I suspect it's to cover up my murder, but maybe that's just the paranoia talking. I mean, the police aren't going to think too hard on a dead hippie with his system full of LSD, am I right?"

"Shit. What about the rest of us?"

"Not to worry you, but I'm fairly certain they're about to pin a murder-suicide on Old Sam."

Swallowing his assessment, I kneel in front of him. He's right. That's precisely what the Carmichaels are planning. Leaning in, I kiss him hard on the lips.

"What was that for?"

"I hate to say it, but you are *brilliant* when you're high. We've got to get us and the kids out of here before Carmichael can shut us up."

"And your way? You didn't answer me?"

Pursing my lips together, I scan the room and land on a push broom nearby. I unscrew the handle and hand it to Sam.

"My way?" I hesitate. "My way includes three Colonial kids who've been shut in a bunker for 200 years."

"Yeah, that's what I thought," Sam sighs and glares at my outstretched hand. "Your way is gonna suck."

CHAPTER
twenty seven

Holding my hand out to him, Sam frowns, uncertain whether I can counter his weight to help him up. "C'mon," I hurry him, bouncing my hand in expectation.

He accepts it and lifts himself experimentally on his one good leg. Biting his upper lip to keep from crying out, my brow furrows. "I'm fine," he huffs out. "Really."

"Where did you find me the other night? I'm fairly sure I didn't make it far from the bunker."

Sam takes the flashlight and shines it around. "Hang on," he tells me. "I'm pretty sure she got the acid from your script bag. It's... kind of kicking my ass right now. But you look glowy or whatever. Like an angel."

"My face is smashed in. I hardly think I look like an angel."

"But, you know, man, your hair is all lit up like a halo. You shine." A goofy grin spreads across his handsome face, and I scowl at him.

"Get it together. I'm glowing because you have a flashlight in my face." I snatch it from his hands and give him a shoulder to lean on.

Nodding, he says, "Yeah, that makes more sense. Over here, I think I found you over here. I think that's your blood."

His blood. My blood. This basement is sick with it, making the house seem to stir around us. At the very least, we're free of the puddle and back on dry ground. However, after a quick peek behind us, the water inches forward even on our current higher ground. The leak is getting worse.

The idea of someone still watching us crawls along my skin, and I want to think it's Peter, but until I'm sure, we need to keep moving.

"Stick close, Peter, we'll get you out," I call out to the darkness behind us. He must be so terribly afraid. "So, Cecilia killed Pickering," I whisper to Sam as we wobble awkwardly to the spot where he said he found me.

"Cecilia? You're sure?"

"Well, no, but it's what Carmichael said. And Esme and the maid are dead." If Sam is surprised, he makes no indication of it.

"Then my 'he's going to kill us all' conspiracy was on the right track." He stops and drops his forehead to my shoulder, wincing with the pain. Muscling through it, he lifts his head back up and continues his train of thought. "I love being right."

"C'mon," I reply.

Back at the spot where he found me with my foot impaled, the door I locked behind me is easier to find. Blood splatter stains the concrete, making the bruised wound on the ball of my foot throb painfully in my sensible pump.

"Yeah, this is the way," I tell him. Despite its size, this basement feels even more vast with the distinct lack of lighting. "With all their money, you'd think Carmichael wouldn't cheap out on basement lights."

With a frown pulling at his lips, Sam points the light at a switch on the wall. "There is lighting down here. It's shut off for some reason." We both have our suspicions about why someone would cut the lights.

"Why do you think Peter is down here?"

"Same reason we're running for our lives; he knows too much. I've been thinking about something." I glance at him expectantly. "You and Evie keep talking about this pureblood thing. That meant something completely different to the Ancient Egyptians. I'm sorry I haven't been overly forthcoming in that department. It's not like we're born with the knowledge of our ancestors. I don't expect you to have an instinctual knowledge of Vikings."

"Why do you think I come from Vikings?"

He twirls my pale hair around his finger. "Well, if you're not, you're damned scary without the Viking blood. I just assumed. You're not short, and you're very blonde. I mean, so blonde, man, I ain't never met a chick with hair like yours."

"Shut up."

"Fuck, please tell me we're close."

"There's a possibility we can hit two birds with one stone while in there."

"What do you mean?"

The door is in sight now, and it's still latched shut. "Well, since you're tripping and we *did* come here on a job, maybe we can do that while escaping."

"Has anyone ever told you that your work ethic is annoying?"

"Waller, every week." Stopping before the door, I slide the latch back and place my hand on the handle. "Last time I was in here, I could sense them but couldn't see them. But I was also on mushrooms, so..." But that wasn't entirely true, was it? There was the hand in the fireplace.

"You still don't believe me?" His disappointment hangs in the air between us, even without the light shining on his face.

"It's hard. Every time we've experienced some kind of phenomenon, we've been on hallucinogenics, Sam. It's daunting evidence, right?"

"I didn't ask if you believed in the evidence. I asked if you believed in me because, until the night at the pond, the most I ever saw were shadows, and I still believed in those."

I halt us before we enter the bunker, turning to shine the light between us. "Emily."

"What about her?"

"She's your conduit. I hypothesize that you'll return to seeing only shadows when we're off her property."

"And you theorize that she's only my conduit because Lily makes her stronger. You think that if we help Lily cross over by solving her murder, Emily won't be as sensitive?"

I lean Sam against the wall and pull on the door. The jamb is sticky with age, and the seal is tight. It finally wrestles free from the frame, and I swing back with it, one leg in the air. Regaining my balance, I continue, "Right now, I want you to focus on Alice. We need to lure Alice into the bunker, and then I think we'll be four fewer ghosts here at Hemlock Hall."

"You're still working. There's a politician upstairs with a gun and a clear reason to murder all of us to protect his legacy, but you're still trying to reach the other side. Why? Please help me understand."

"Because—because of Octavia, okay? If we can help Lily and Alice, we can help Octavia."

"You think Octavia is the key to finding her killer."

"Well, there are only two people in the whole world who know what happened to Octavia, and one of them is dead. So unless you have other ideas." My voice echoes throughout the basement, betraying my agitation.

Sam yanks me into his arms. "You are more than a parapsychologist, Lydia; you are an amazing detective. If anyone can figure out what happened to your sister, it's you. I believe in you."

At first, I resist, then slump bonelessly into his chest. "I'm not sure if what we've been seeing is real. I'm sorry. I'm just not."

"Listen to you. You're not sure, but you still want to help Alice Shippington find her kids."

I pull away from him, realizing he had more weight on me than he probably realized. How am I going to help him up the stairs? Not only that but how am I going to rescue everyone upstairs from this mess?

Quinn, find a phone and call Quinn. Hang tight until he gets here. He is over an hour away. We could all be dead by the time he gets here.

I say none of this to Sam, however. I am not the right person to be in charge here. Technically, Waller is in charge, but he's not done much fieldwork, so I'm unsure if he realizes he's *it* right now.

Waller *is* scarily overprotective of me, however, and *that* I can use.

The air inside the bunker is stale and choked with dust. Before we enter, I shine the light inside and pull one of the tidy dining chairs out from the small kitchen table to take the weight off Sam's knee.

The sweat sliding off his brow and his waxy complexion are sure indicators that he's in much worse pain than he's letting on. My idea to have him pull himself up the stairs backward and on his ass was quickly dwindling. Quinn will need to call an ambulance up here, at least one for Sam, and I'm crossing my fingers that'll be all.

Where could Cecilia have stashed Emily? Or was Emily hiding? Was it she who bolted the secret door in her closet?

Shaking the intrusive thoughts away, I focus on Sam. The worse pain he's in, the higher the chances of a bad trip. I learned that from my father's work on hallucinogenic enhancers. But this isn't the basement of our department, and I'm not zapping Sam with small doses of electricity. I'm fairly certain his knee is dislocated.

He leans on me gratefully when I return to the door jamb and hustle him inside. We ease him into the chair (after I test its weight capacity), and he heaves a long, drawn-out breath. His groan is swallowed up in the stillness of the room.

Unlike the rest of the basement, the ceiling is low here, like this was the original cellar of the house that added more and more over the past two centuries. The Carmichaels aren't likely to be oblivious to this bunker; I found it in my own roundabout way easily enough.

Alice Shippington has never found her children, so I've got to assume their bodies were never removed from this place. That's why she can't find them. The house's blueprints changed so much over the years, so she's probably lost them—or she *forgot*. A shiver runs through me at the thought.

"I'd offer you something to drink, but I'm fairly certain this room is pre-plumbing."

"This place is crazy, man. It's like when we were little, we went on those field trips to colonial war-era sites where they've preserved everything." He glances around and swipes his hand across the graying wood of the dining table. His face screws up with disdain upon inspecting his fingers. "Except, you know, dirtier."

"There he is," I say.

"There *who* is?"

"Wellesley. Evie said you were from there, but I didn't believe her."

"Well, we can't all grow up on venerated college campuses. Some of us come from the wrong side of town."

I snort. "Right. The *wrong* side of town."

He places a hand over mine. "Why do you think I've separated myself from all of it?"

"But have you?" I ask, moving away to search the room. With someone else here and the light, it feels much less scary. "You've been at Shelley for how long now? Have you, though? Have you actually separated yourself from the uptown crowd, I mean?"

"Touché," he says, but winces.

"It's bad, isn't it?"

"I think that would've been evident when I told you I needed a stretcher." My eyebrows shoot up at him. Sam's never snapped at me before. Never snapped at anyone on the team, so far as I could tell. "I'm sorry," he says at my expression.

"Don't be. I deserved it. I push. I push and push and take it too far sometimes. I should be the one who's sorry." Pulling out a seat next to him, I sit down. "How's the acid?"

"Making this room a little more *Addams Family* than I would specifically like."

"Shadows?"

"Fucking *shadows*, man. You get it."

I raise my hand to cup his cheek, and he warmly leans into it. A red ball rolls out from under one of the bunk beds and hits my shoe.

Wetting my lips, I hesitate to glance at it. This time, the light remains steady—there are no flickering shenanigans. When I lift my gaze to him, Sam is staring at me. My eyes never leave his as I kick the ball back toward the bed. Seconds tick by until it hits my foot again. We both let out a breath.

"Do you think you can do this?"

"Do I have a choice?" He asks, but there's a wobble in his voice.

"If I open the hatch up the stairs, could you call Alice down here?"

He takes the flashlight and scans the room, landing on the candleholder on the fireplace mantel. "You still have my lighter?" I nod. "A real pickpocket you are." He tilts his head toward the candles. "Bring those over here, and I'll work out what I can do."

The chair screeches across the wood floor as I move to do as he asks.

"You should take the LSD study out of the lab, you know. Nothing like this ever happens on campus."

As I grab the candle for him, I ask, "Professor Hassan, are you suggesting we take students to locations with paranormal activity and give them a dose there?"

"It wouldn't be the worst idea. And I would've had some kind of heads-up."

I hand him the candle and the lighter. He lights it, and after a few flickers of flame, the stench has us breathing through our mouths. "Ugh. What is that?"

"Animal fat. It actually reminds me a little of the outdoor markets in Alexandria."

"It stinks like ass," I tell him.

"That's what I said," he replies with a smirk. "Okay, let me work. You open the hatch, and I'll try to call Alice down here."

A long creak emits from the door we just came through before I can move. Swallowing, I turn the flashlight toward the noise. Standing in the doorway is Peter Carmichael. His forearm presses against his eyes, and he holds his other hand out in defense.

He's filthy and bone-thin, his skin stretched tight over his fragile frame. His clothes hang off him in tatters, stained with grime and sweat. Shivering and breathing erratically, he takes a step back when the light hits him, his eyes wide with fear and confusion. If I had seen him on my own, in the dark, I would've assumed he was one of the ghosts that haunted this space. His unkempt hair sticks to his forehead, matted and tangled. I'm afraid he's going to bolt.

"It's okay! It's okay," I soothe. "We're not going to hurt you."

Peter's eyes dart around the room, searching for an escape, but his legs seem to wobble under his own weight. I step forward slowly, keeping my voice calm and gentle. "You're safe now. We're here to help you."

He swallows hard, his throat bobbing visibly. The harsh light from the flashlight casts deep shadows on his gaunt face, highlighting every hollow and ridge. Sam shifts slightly in his chair, trying not to scare Peter further.

"Peter," I say softly, "we've been looking for you. We want to get you out of here." His eyes lock onto mine, and I can see the flicker of hope mixed with the overwhelming fear.

I take another cautious step toward him, the musty smell of the basement mingling with the acrid scent of fear in the air. "Can you tell us what happened? How did you end up down here?"

His lips part, but no sound comes out. He's trembling, his breath coming in short, ragged gasps. I extend my hand slowly, palm up, a gesture of trust. "It's okay, Peter. You're safe with us."

Sam brushes my arm with his fingertips to nudge me to move from where I've instinctively blocked him from danger. I step aside. "C'mon, Little Man, I need your help," he tells Peter. "And you want to get out of here, right?"

Peter nods hesitantly and takes a step forward. I try to think of the nicest way to say this, but it comes out of me as, "I'm aware everything is scary right now, but we have to hurry, okay?"

"Caleb," he whispers, his voice raspy, like it's been a long time since he's used it.

"Caleb?" I ask and turn toward Sam.

"I don't think he was talking to us," Sam replies.

The ball's owner peeks out from under the bed. He can't be older than seven or eight, his wide eyes filled with fear. I back away from him but land on my bad foot, causing me to drop onto the braided rug. "Sam?"

"Yeah, momma, I see him. But how can *you*?"

"I don't know," I whisper as I jump back to my feet. "Maybe the leylines?" Dad was right; the rules blew out the window when the structure was in danger. And I think maybe we're all in a lot more trouble than just a madman with a gun upstairs.

"I don't follow," Sam tells me, mostly to remind me that he's still there as I find myself lost in my head.

"Dad said leylines affect the veil or whatever, which prevents us from seeing the dead. I don't have time to go into it, but if I can see them, it means the building is in danger."

"The water?"

"Water from the crack," a small voice says. Peter inches closer to me, his emaciated face pale and hollow.

"Was anyone feeding you?" My voice trembles with the question. He shrugs in response.

"What crack?" Sam asks.

"The crack in the long wall," Peter says, pointing out the door to where we came from. He leans in and whispers, "I think Lily wants back in."

"That's Caleb under the bed?" Sam asks him. "Who else is here?"

"Nathaniel," Peter's voice cracks as though it pains him to talk. "Fireplace." He scans the room. "Sarah, too. I don't know where."

"Caleb, Nathaniel, and Sarah?" Sam repeats, and Peter nods.

"We need to hustle, Sam."

Huffing through the pain, his gaze darts from Peter to me. "Okay, open the door, and we'll do our best to lure Momma down here to collect these guys." As I move out of his circle of candlelight, he grabs my wrist. "See if you can spy on anything happening in the foyer. It'll be a stretch from the sitting room peephole, but do what you can."

"Yeah, okay. After you deal with Alice, you and Peter should go to the kitchen and call Quinn. Then, I need you both out of the house. Get as far away as possible; don't let any Carmichaels find you unless it's Emily. Peter?" I focus on the little boy. "Can you help Sam?" His gaze darts between the two of us, and then he nods.

"Lydia?" He says in that gruff voice he gets right before he's about to kiss me. Yanking on my sweater, he pulls me down until his lips are devouring mine, his long fingers tangling in my hair, his tongue searching out my own. I don't like this; he's kissing me like he might not get to do it again. My palms find his jawline, and I pull him tighter against me. I kiss him, equally desperate, trying to reassure him that we'll be okay. I'm shaking when we part, his breath hot on my lips.

"Don't worry, we can blame it on the drugs again later if you want. Just be careful," he huffs out.

I blink. Did he just call me out? *Shit*. "I won't be long. Call Alice down here. Maybe we can save more than just Emily and Peter tonight."

His mouth forms a grim line. "I've never..."

"Never?"

"Never helped anyone 'cross over.' I don't know what to do."

"Oh, Sam," I whisper. "It's likely you just need to reunite them. You'll be fine. I've never met anyone like you. All of the others were frauds."

"I'm a fraud."

"You're not. I believe in you. Now I need you to believe in you, too. Charm her."

"*Charm* her?" His brow furrows in confusion.

"You're good at that," I tell him with a smirk, slipping up the stairs to open the hatch. Relief floods me as it opens easily this time.

The passage inside the wall insulates most of the noise in the foyer. I can't hear a damned thing. The full moon's glow shoots shafts of light through the peepholes, and dust flutters merrily in the beams.

Sam is muttering to himself down in the bunker, possibly trying to coerce Alice into the cellar, or he is talking to the kids. It's impossible to tell from here. They weren't nearly as spooky with Sam along.

Tiptoeing to the peephole at the passage's dead end, I peer through and spot Carmichael with the others in the sitting room. They're crammed on the long couch: Charlie at one end, Shirley and Evie in the middle, and Waller on the other, tilting his head back with a fresh black eye.

There's a weird contraption next to the peephole. Shaped like a curved funnel, it reminds me of the old-timey hearing aids they show in cartoons now.

I press my ear to the pointed end.

"Where did Lydia go? She should have been back with my daughter by now. One of you must have seen where she went. This is ridiculous. We're all learned men here," Carmichael sneers at the two women in the middle. "Well, most of us, anyway."

Waller sniffs around the blood attempting to escape his nose and shakes his head. "We told you, we didn't see which way she went. You were markedly talented at holding our rapt attention with your Smith & Wesson waving around."

Carmichael moves on Waller so fast it feels like he teleported. He cracks my godfather across the face with the aforementioned pistol and bends at the waist to study Waller in the eyes. "Yes, I see it. I see the pining for a girl twenty years younger than you. I see how you envy the esteem Court Fox once held. I see the greed in your eyes when you look at his daughter. You and I? We're not so different. We want power and more of it. And we'll do *anything* to get it. I am *protecting* my legacy. Surely you can understand that, James."

Waller clutches his jaw, a clear sign it's broken. He won't wait much longer before he kills someone in the living room. I have to find Emily and get everyone out before this whole building crumbles around us.

A light shines at the end of the hall, pale and slender as a moonbeam. A girl in a swimsuit, her long, blonde locks dripping onto the dusty wood beneath her feet. The light is coming from her. *Lily.*

I take a hesitant step forward, careful not to creak any worn floorboards. She doesn't run from me like she did in the basement. Silt from the pond sticks to her jawline, and her eyes, bruised and sunken, regard me dully.

"Can you help me?" I ask her in barely a whisper. She nods, slow and deliberate. My heart pounds. I've had nothing—no mushrooms, no acid—and she's here—she's really here. I want to run down to tell Sam so badly, but I'm terrified that if I let her out of my sight, I'll lose her.

"Can you tell me where Emily is?" She shakes her head. "Can anyone?"

Lily stares into me, no, *through* me, and I twist around to figure out what she's looking at. She lifts a waterlogged arm and points. It's Alice. She wrings her hands and glances between Lily and me.

"Tell her I will help her find her kids if she tells us where Emily is," I tell Lily. Alice shakes her head and points to Carmichael in frantic, panicked motions.

The man, the gun, the demands—this has all happened to Alice before.

"Lily, tell her she'll never be reunited with her kids again if I don't find Emily."

"Lydia?" Sam whispers from the stairway. He scooted himself up to the top of the stairs. "Tell me you're not threatening the ghost of a mother who lost her kids."

My gaze drops to his disappointed one. "She needs to tell us where Emily is, or she'll end up like her own kids."

"You can't threaten her. And you can't use her kids against her. What is *wrong* with you?"

"Tell her. Tell her, Sam. Lily says Alice can tell us where Emily is. She'll listen to you. They like you."

His brow furrows. "No. We're not doing it this way."

"Sam!" I whisper too harsh and loud, causing us to turn in the direction of the voices to check if they heard. "I am in charge, and you'll do as I say."

His eyebrows lift into his hairline. He turns to Alice. "Follow me," he tells her as he inches his way back down into the dark. Alice nods, her hands still wrestling against each other in her heightened anxiety. "You and I are going to have a conversation," Sam says sternly.

I want to hit him. I want to scream, cry, kick. I want to find that dumb little girl who never listens to me. He doesn't understand.

But then the smoke reaches us, and all of my ire sinks into the floor. The old candle we lit in the bunker has started a fire, sending flames and light spewing out of the basement.

"Alice," he whispers, harsh and demanding. "If you want to find your kids, we have to go. Now."

No. "No! You can't!" I tell him.

"Shut up, Lydia. You've done enough. We have to hurry now. We're out of time. For us, for Emily, for Peter, but we have to do this for Alice."

Anger flares up in me, and I shove him to the side. "Get up here. I'll take her. And fuck you for thinking I don't care." Reaching into the stairwell, I grasp Peter beneath his arms and lift him out of the smoky bunker.

Alice is confused. I hold my hand out to beckon her below, but she hesitates at the top of the stairs. "Move your pale ass now, or you'll never see them again." We hustle down the stairs. Alice follows me this time, and that's when it happens.

Carmichael's gun goes off with a thunderous boom.

CHAPTER
twenty eight

Adrenaline slams into me so hard it makes me woozy. Lily stands with Alice and me, a few steps above us. "Lily!" I hiss. "Can you help her?"

But her attention is on the gunshot that echoed and shook the dusty passage. "Lily!" I repeat. "I have to go! I have to get to them! Please, help Alice. Help Sam. Do you understand me? Nod if you understand me."

Her frightened expression slowly tilts down to my own. With the barest of nods, I sweep past her, the chill of her form icing my veins. Before running toward the sound of Carmichael's gun, my gaze sweeps the bunker one last time. Frozen in place on the stairs, I need to witness it. I need to be able to tell Sam that Alice found her kids.

The fire has caught hold of the bunk beds, blocking the way out into the cellar. Flames lick at the wood, making it glow hot and red before it crumbles under the weight of the fury, bed frames so old they're reduced to kindling in seconds.

And from underneath one of them, a little girl, Sarah, I assume, scurries out, unaware of the firestorm all around her. I choke on the smoke and cover my mouth with my sleeve while I point the girl out to Alice. Incredulity and despair overwhelm her face, fighting for dominance. Alice's sadness made her beautiful, elegant, and even terrifying, but in this moment of hope? Alice is resplendent. A mother reunited, and I hate Sam right now because I'm the one down here, and he's not, and he's the one who deserves to witness this. This moment is because of him.

Alice pulls the girl from the collapsing bed and turns to a cupboard beneath the pantry shelves swinging open. A boy, no older than three or four, peeks out. His head is full of bushy curls and wide eyes, and Alice pulls him into her embrace as well. There's a third child down here, and he's the oldest. I know this because he died trying to climb his way out through the chimney—the oldest child tried to save the other two.

A pale hand grips the fireplace frame from the darkness within the flume. Even over the crackling burning below me, the dust and debris spilling from inside the chimney can be heard clearly over the growing inferno. His gray hand, stripped of fingernails left behind in the brick mortar, clenches the wood framing, and finally, a bare foot touches the grate. A wisp of hair, and he's bent over at the waist, peeking out from his place in the chimney, the place he never reemerged from in life. He's so little that my heart lurches in my chest.

He's so *young*. The smoke is overwhelming, and Alice pulls her eldest out of the chimney and gazes at me expectantly. It occurs to me that I have no idea what to do at this point. I'm not the medium. I'm not even sure how I see them right now, leylines and crumbling foundations notwithstanding.

"Come on," I tell her and the kids and point to the stairs. "To Sam." Jars of moldering staples on the pantry shelves catch my eye, and I grab one that might be salt. Racing up the stairs, Sam is dragging himself further along the corridor toward the kitchen.

He turns to find me with the five ghosts in tow—Alice, her kids, and a curious Lily. How this appears in his current state of pain and LSD, I can only guess.

"You found them."

"I brought salt. I don't know what to do."

"I told you I've never done this before, Lydia. What makes you think I know what to do?"

"Because you *care*," I hiss at him. "I don't *care* about Alice Shippington and her kids, Sam. They're *dead*. I care about Emily Carmichael."

His face screws up into a frown. "I'm going to give you the benefit of the doubt because of this stressful situation we're in, but you and I are still going to have a conversation about this when we get out of here."

"*If* we get out of here." It's sharp and acidic, and he doesn't deserve my vitriol right now, but it's all I have left to keep me going.

"Lydia!" comes a shriek from the sitting room. It's Evie, and the horror caught in her throat makes my gut plummet into an oily slick of fear. I can't lose anyone else, not again.

Sam's long fingers wrap around my wrists, pulling me down to the dusty floor beside him. He grips my face and makes me look at him. "You need to calm down. We're going to leave this place. Do you understand me? You need to go, though. I'll make sure Peter is out; you need to find out what's happening with the rest of the team. I'll make the phone call, and we'll make our way to the topiary garden. Lydia, are you listening to me?"

I've barely understood a word he's said—topiary garden. Meet him in the topiary garden. Shaking the smoke and terror off my skin, I turn to look down at Peter and then Sam. "The topiary garden," I reply.

"You can do this, you're Lydia fucking Fox."

"I'm Lydia fucking Fox," I mumble back. He's right. I nod. A panel is in front of us, and a rope is next to it. Reaching out with shaking fingers, I grab the rope and pull it. The panel slides open, and we're in the kitchen pantry.

"Peter?" I say, turning to the boy. "Can you fetch Sam whatever he needs?" Peter nods, and I turn to Sam, my eyebrows raising expectantly.

"I think a bowl of water?" Sam takes the salt from me.

Peter runs into the kitchen to fill a bowl and hands it to Sam. Steeling myself for the worst, I move toward the sitting room, but I can't stop watching, and I'm still close enough that Sam can reach out to me for support if he needs it. Sam gestures for Alice to come forward. He pulls a toy out of his pocket—a miniature wooden horse and carriage, beautifully carved. It must have been very expensive once. When did he pick that up?

"What's the bowl of water for?" I ask.

"Nothing, I just wanted to get rid of the kid in case something goes bad." He waves the toy in front of the kids and digs into the old clay jar of salt I brought up from the cellar. Sprinkling the salt onto the carriage, he lights it afire with his Zippo filched from my pocket.

"I don't think the answer is 'more fire,' Sam."

"Shh," he scolds me. Curling his hand, he gestures for Alice and the kids to come forward. "You need to get gone, little momma. There's nothing left for you here. You've got yours, and they've got you. There's nothing left keeping you here. Go in peace, find the light, and follow it out. Ain't nothing but a thing now."

I'm uncertain whether she understands him, but then it clicks, and she blinks rapidly at something beyond or behind us or somewhere not for our eyes. She urges the children forward, then leans down, her hand slipping through the smoke wafting off the toy. Whispering something into Sam's ear, she places one cool palm on his cheek and the other on mine and smiles. I close my eyes to the sensation, and when I open them again, she's gone.

Sam lets out a breath. "There she goes. I hope she can rest now." Clearing his throat, he turns his gaze on me. "Emily is in Cecilia's room. Alice says she isn't moving. You have to hurry. Find the others. Find Emily." My team is yelling at each other in the other room. It sounds like chaos.

My heart is still banging around loudly in my chest, and I place my hand over it, trying to soothe the chaos within. Shaking, I wipe my hands on my skirt and pull myself up. And there's a *phone* in the pantry. Finally, something goes right tonight.

"Holy shit," I manage to breathe out. Pulling Sam the rest of the way into the pantry, I pull the rope next to the panel, which slides shut. Grabbing some dish towels, I shove them around the bottom of the door to keep some of the smoke in the passage. "You call Quinn. I'm going with Lily to find Emily, and then we'll figure out how to stop Carmichael."

"Do you think they're okay?"

I shake my head. "I don't know. I *do* know that if we don't save Emily in the next few minutes, we might not have another chance."

"Be careful," he tells me.

"Sam? I'm sorry. I'm sorry I'm screwed up, and I'm sorry I dragged you into it, and I'm sorry I can't figure out how to get us all out of this mess."

"Fucking shut up," he whispers and pulls me into another kiss. "You can't be nobody but you, Lydia. Stop talking like we'll never see each other again and find Emily."

Resting my head against his forehead for a second longer than I can spare, I push away and head through the archway into the sitting room. Evie and Charlie are crowded around Shirley, who is lying on the ground. I can't find Carmichael. Or Waller.

Evie's tear-stained face is red and petrified. Her gaze catches on me, standing in the doorway, unsure of what to do. My brain insists that nothing terrible will happen to Shirley if I don't go into the room.

"Where the fuck have you been?" Evie screams her fury at me. "Where the *fuck* have you been?"

The desperation in her voice propels my feet forward. I'm with her in an instant. Shirley is shuddering and gasping as her blood soaks into the Persian rug beneath her. "Hey, hey, Shirl, what's all this?" I ask as I drop to a knee and turn her to face me. Brushing away tears and sweat from her face, my attention turns to Charlie. The gun lies abandoned on the rug a few feet away. "Tell me what happened."

"I don't know," he tells me as he rips the silk pillow into a bandage and wraps it around where Shirley's shoulder is blossoming with blood. "Waller and Carmichael were arguing, and then all of a sudden, Shirley makes a grab for his gun. They wrestled with it for a few seconds, then it went off. And then Carmichael ran up the stairs, and Waller ran after him. I think they went into the west wing."

Convenient. That's where I'm heading. "Sam is calling Quinn right now. We found Peter."

Evie stops her sobbing and grabs me. "The cellar? He was in the cellar? This whole time?" She's squeezing the life out of Shirley's poor hand.

"Shirley? Can you hear me?" I ask her.

"I'm shot, not deaf. Fuck you and your department, Fox," she sputters out.

I can't help the laugh that escapes me. I lean down and kiss her forehead. "Welcome to the team, Henderson. Don't fucking die." I turn to Charlie now. "You need to get the girls out. The cellar is on fire, and I think the retaining wall down there is about to go. I don't know how long this house will stand. Meet Sam in the topiary garden. He has a dislocated knee, so I need you and Evie to help Shirley and Sam."

"What?" Charlie asks me. "Where are you going?"

"Emily is in Cecilia's room. Alice said she wasn't moving. I have to help her. Be careful. I don't know where the Burning Man is; they're visible now. The foundation is ruined, so everything has gone ass over tit."

Evie's eyes widen at my pronouncement. "Shit," she mumbles. "The Shippingtons. Can they be released now?"

"Already done. Now I just need to find Emily, and we'll be out of this cesspit."

"And C-Cecilia," Shirley stutters out. Her shivering is shaking the couch next to her.

"Cecilia? I'm pretty sure she busted Sam's knee," I tell her.

"She's still a victim, Lydia. Don't forget that. Whatever monster she's become, her father made her that way." She yanks on my wrist, crushing the bone in her bid to force me to listen to her. "Listen to me. Cecilia is as much of a victim as Emily or Lily."

I pull her off me and rub my tender skin. "I'll do what I can. But if she doesn't come willingly, I might have to choose. And I'm not choosing that bitch over Emily."

"Lydia," Charlie looks at me. "Carmichael is crazed. Watch out for him. I have no idea what's happened to Waller."

"I should come with you," Evie tells me when Charlie scoops Shirley up. "You need backup."

"I need you to help Sam, Evie. He's really messed up." I limp toward the stairs.

"*You're* really messed up, too. You have a hole in your foot. And what the hell happened to your face?"

"My team, my call," I tell her. "Besides, I'm not on my own. James is up there."

Evie's dark brows pull together. "He could be dead, Lydia."

"Well, if he's dead, it still doesn't mean he's out of the game, does it?" With a tilt of my chin, Evie follows my gaze to Lily standing at the top of the stairs, pointing toward Cecilia's part of the manor.

"Holy shit," Charlie huffs out from behind us. He couldn't see them when we were all on mushrooms.

I kiss Evie's cheek. "You're my friend. In case I haven't said it."

"I hate you so much," Evie blurts out with a fresh bout of tears.

"Find Sam. That's your only job right now. Oh, and try to meet Quinn by the gate in 45 minutes to an hour to catch him up. Can you do that for me?"

"Yeah, boss."

Charlie is hauling Shirley out the door, and I need to go before he dumps Shirley and tries to come back to stop me from running off on my own.

"I'll find Emily," I tell them. "I won't leave her. I promise."

Time is no longer my friend. At the top of the stairs, I make a decision. To avoid Carmichael, I turn left instead of right and tear down the carpeted halls as fast as my injured foot will let me to Emily's room. I have let time run its course, and it is now chasing me down these long, dark corridors. The fire will make the Carmichaels desperate. Slipping into the passage of Emily's closet, I attempt to navigate my way to the beauty queen's room.

I reach the back of Emily's closet and feel along the wall until my fingers brush against the latch. It's still firmly shut from the other side, just as I feared. Desperation surges through me, and I glance around the closet for something to use. My eyes land on the small desk chair Sam used to block the closet door earlier. Grabbing it, I slam the chair leg against the latch repeatedly. The wood splinters and cracks, but finally, with one last hit, the latch gives way. I push the panel open and slip into the hidden passage beyond.

I'm a few steps into the upstairs servant's passage when I realize I'm lost. I've never traversed this maze from one wing to the other through the hidden walkway, and minutes are slipping through my hands. Minutes Emily and my crew don't have. I can only hope Waller has Carmichael in hand. But from the beating he's taken, he likely underestimated the man.

I shine the light down one end, and it gets swallowed up before the hall turns. It's all the same when I turn and do the same the other way. I have to stop and think. Where am I? Making a decision, I bat away a web and slink forward with determination, wishing I had a weapon.

The creaks of the underused floorboards are sure to give me away. Worse yet, smoke is beginning to curl up through the cracks. Finally, I reach a peephole and find it's Carmichael's study, so at the very least, I found my way to the right wing.

A bright sliver of light slices through the clouds of dust motes, and I hesitate before peering into the room. The burning man, Ambrose Carmichael, sits in the wing chair by the fireplace. He studies the fire crackling and holds a glass of a dark, viscous liquid.

I hold my breath until my lungs begin to fight back. His head turns slowly toward where I'm hidden in the walls. His smile cracks and runs messily under the flames, licking across his skin. It reeks of barbecue and the morgue and something metallic. It coats the inside of my mouth, and I swallow down my lunch threatening to come back up. His eye pops and gurgles as it slides down his cheek, only to round back up and repeat it.

This man has been burning to death for years, and he lifts his glass to me. That greasy, wet smile flickers with knowing. He knows I'm going to burn it all down. His fucking legacy. His stolen house on the hill. All of it.

When that melting eye meets mine, I stumble back and hit the wall behind me. Muffled voices leak through the plaster and wood: Carmichael and Waller. They are out of my line of sight, but clearly, neither of them can see Ambrose Carmichael sitting in the same room as them—or they do and have chosen not to care. Waller's crisp, clipped tones come through the strongest, and I'm hoping he's gotten the upper hand.

Moving forward, I come to the turn that will take me to Cecilia. Cecilia is an unknowable in all of this. The light in her room dully illuminates the passage. I have no idea what I'll do if she's inside. Peering into the peephole, I see Emily lying prone on the bed. Alice said she wouldn't stir, but she still breathed as far as I could tell from her chest's slight rise and fall. Taking in the rest of the room, I can't find any sign of Cecilia, but I can't see the other side of the bed or the closet and en suite.

My gaze swings to my med pack. The contents are spilled out all around it, and one of the hypodermics and a bottle of sedative sit on top of her long dresser. Cecilia must have drugged her. I'm going to have to carry Emily out.

I step back to steel my nerves and glance at the latch. It's secured tightly shut, like in Emily's room. Someone sealed the rooms to prevent the girls from escaping through the secret passages. Lifting a shaking hand to the latch above my head, I slide it unlocked and creak the panel open as quietly as I can manage.

I chew my top lip and stick my head hesitantly into the room, ready to pull the panel back shut if someone catches me. The only person in the bedroom is Emily. She's tied to the bed by her ankles and wrists, like a sacrifice on an altar.

With an immeasurable amount of nerve, I slip into the room and feel for the girl's pulse. It's steady but so slow that I gasp. *Please, Sam, please reach Quinn.*

Small padlocks secure her limbs in the cuffs. The marks on the wood of the bedposts indicate that they have been on Cecilia's bed for a very long time. The key has to be somewhere close. I yank open the side table drawer and dig around; there's nothing. The same goes for the other table and the jewelry boxes on her dresser.

Maybe I can cut through the leather. I head into the bathroom for a razor, scissors, or anything. As I flick on the light, I freeze. There's Cecilia, tied up and gagged in the bathtub. Her eyes bulge when I enter the room, blinking rapidly in the sudden brightness.

I stumble back into the sink. Around Cecilia's neck is a tiny key. She wrestles and struggles with her bindings, and hysterical keening noises groan out from around her gag. "Calm down," I tell her, holding my hands up like I would to a spooked horse. Cecilia shakes her head frantically. Taking a couple of steps forward, I reach out with trembling fingers to wrap around the key and give it a good yank. Cecilia screams around the gag.

Rushing into the other room, I unlock the padlocks and rub some feeling back into Emily's cold hands and feet. Tonguing the inside of my cheek, I hesitate. I can't leave Cecilia tied up in the tub when the house is on fire. *Shirley and her nonsense.*

One step at a time, I make my way back to the bathroom. With a quick flick, I remove the gag from her mouth.

"Untie me!" she pleads.

My eyes narrow. "Did you kill Lily?"

"What? Why would I kill Lily? I was trying to protect her!" Cecilia thrashes around, struggling to sit up.

My brows draw together so hard it nearly hurts. "You're their mother, aren't you?"

Cecilia's eyes go wide with the accusation. "Wh-what?"

"You heard me. You're their mother. All of this blood purity shit. Your father is their father, am I right?"

"Lydia, please!"

"Answer the question, Cecilia! Or I'll leave you in this house to burn like Ambrose Carmichael! And you know as well as I that you'll never escape. You'll burn here until the end of time."

To her credit, Miss Massachusetts pales. "Yes. They're... they're mine. Daddy made me. And he would use Emily and Lily next because our girls were *purer* than me because of my mother. Please, Lydia, you have to believe me!"

A small part of me worries that her father tied her up to prevent her from hurting Emily. "You killed her so your father wouldn't touch her, didn't you? You killed Lily because your father set his sights on her next."

"Fuck you."

"Did he always make you wear the key to your freedom when he tied you to the bed?"

Defeated, Cecilia slumps back into the tub. "My idiot mother. My idiot mother killed herself, didn't she?"

"Why didn't she get you out?"

Cecilia laughs then. It's high and horrible. "Out? And do what? Tell the whole world what a monster the good Judge William Carmichael is? The man who would be senator? The man who would be president?" Her voice is cracking, reaching, and needling into something bordering on hysteria. "THE

MAN WHO WOULD BE PHARAOH? Oh, you haven't any idea the depths of depravity this man would bow to for power."

"Does he know about Peter? Does he know you didn't take Peter to the airport? Does he know you kept your brother, I'm sorry, *son*, locked in the basement?"

"You understand nothing," she seethes at me. "Daddy would never understand. Peter would tell. Daddy believes in family loyalty. He doesn't understand how a child's mind works. Peter saw me kill the old man. He was there, he saw the whole thing!"

"Why did you kill Pickering, Cecelia? Your dad already paid him off. Help me understand."

Cecilia makes a face. "Paid him off. Paid him off because he thought Pickering knew about us. But he was there that day. He saw what happened at the pond. That old man was going to take Daddy's money and go to the police anyway. Daddy thinks money buys anything," she scoffs. "I had a surer bet."

"But you couldn't kill Peter."

"Didn't I, though?" Cecilia is nearly hysterical at this point. "After Lily... I couldn't... not again. Not another one. Let me out of this, Lydia, and we'll take out Daddy together. We can end this. We can do it."

She's insane. "There's no group. It's just him, isn't it? It's all within the family? Ambrose? Your dad? They're not even real Thelemites."

"Crowley's vision was too small for my grandfather. Too narrow. Daddy said Crowley didn't understand the power we could wield. That he never understood how far we could go. That he never understood his own fucking tenet."

Shirley's reminder that Cecilia is also a victim echoes sickeningly in my brain. I can't squirm free from it. Squatting down next to her, I take in her restraints. It's the satin binding to her dressing gown wrapped about her wrists and ankles, but it doesn't appear to be... knotted.

Out of the corner of my eye, I spot the ax I had in the basement leaning against the bathroom counter.

"Oh shit," I manage before I'm tackled to the floor. My head smacks the tile so soundly that stars dance in my vision. When I open my eyes again, she's leaning over me, leering with a mad grin.

"Thanks for opening the door," she breathes into my face. "*Idiot.*"

CHAPTER
twenty nine

Madness slides over Cecilia's usual haughty expression, and I realize I've made a terrible mistake coming back here. She shoves her knee into my sternum and grabs the hairdryer on the counter. I can't breathe; my lungs burn with the effort to take a full inhale. Suddenly, the weight is lifted, and the heavy-duty hairdryer slams into the side of my temple.

I reach up, digging my nails into her arm holding the dryer. Cecilia roars at my audacity and brings the dryer down on my wrists, breaking my hold. I use the moment to twist beneath her and roll onto my hands and knees. My fingers desperately grab at anything on the tub's edge, finally closing in on a golden bottle of Breck shampoo.

Ripping the top off, I squirt the soap as hard as I can into Cecilia's face. The shampoo ends up all over my lap, the floor, her eyes, and her blouse—everywhere. The overwhelming floral scent gags me until Cecilia, blinded, lashes out and clocks me in the face again with the hairdryer. Her knees slip in the shampoo, and she slams into me, causing my head to bounce off the edge of the porcelain tub.

The whole room spins, and Cecilia screeches. I try to crawl out of her warpath toward the toilet. Everything hurts, and I can't clear the white spots cluttering my vision. "You absolute bitch," she wails. "You've ruined everything. I would've drowned your sister that day you came here if I had known that was the way she was going to go anyway. Both of you whining about going swimming while I'm sixteen and fucking pregnant!"

Spitting a wad of blood on the floor, I try to keep her talking. "Tavi knew something was off about this place! She said as much," I tell her while reaching for the towel bar. Pulling it down with all my might, I wrench it loose and crack it across her face.

"Lydia, stop!" Cecilia screams. "Stop fighting, it's useless. We always win. Carmichaels always win."

"Not today, you don't." I bring down the towel bar, but she grabs my wrists. *How can she see?* We both slip in the soap and crash onto the tile, rolling and trying to snatch the towel bar. She wrenches it from my hands but can't hold onto it herself, and it goes flying into her bedroom. Her hands are covered with that shitty gold shampoo, and she rubs it all over my face, blurring my vision, filling my nose and mouth with it. It's foul.

I will never erase the stench of Breck shampoo from my head for the rest of my life. She roars and slaps me back, trying to wrap her slippery hand around my throat. "Mommy's gone," she coos menacingly in my ear. "Mommy's here. I'm right here."

"We have to get out of here, you loony bitch. We have to save Peter from the cellar." It's a gamble, but she stops for a heartbeat, her hand stilling on my throat.

"Peter?"

"The basement's on fire, Cecilia. We have to find your brother."

"My *son*. How did you know about Peter?"

"Why did you lock him in the basement?" Maybe I can steer her back to our conversation when she was in the tub.

"Because he saw," she sits back on my stomach. "He saw me kill Gene." I can't make her out from the soap burning my eyes, but her blurry outline shifts to reach for the hairdryer again. "It was supposed to seem like an accident, but you said there's a fire, so it doesn't matter anymore." She brings the dryer down once, smashing my orbital socket, and lifts it above her head again. I'll be lucky if I don't end up with 'Clairol' imprinted on my skull when this is over.

Cecilia Carmichael means to beat me to death with a hairdryer in her bathroom.

Pulling every last bit of energy I have left, I suck in my breath and scream, "WALLER!"

This causes her to pause for a beat, enough time for me to buck her off and turn to crawl back to the toilet. Yanking the tank lid off with both hands, I swing it in her direction, breaking it in two when it meets her head. She slumps over. Blood pools slowly into the golden syrup covering the floor beneath her.

I have no idea if I killed her or not, and I don't care. Crawling through the mess, I pull myself up to stand with the help of the counter. I twist the tap and scrub the soap out of my eyes. A weird rage bubbles over into pained gasps and growls emitting from my throat. My face is soaked with blood and shampoo, and I can't see from one eye.

Snatching her hairbrush off the counter, I slam the end of it into the mirror again and again until I can't look at Octavia's judgmental fucking face in the glass anymore. "I HATE YOU!" I roar. "I HATE YOU!" My rage spent, it swirls down the drain with the bloody, soapy water, and I snatch a towel off the ring and dry my face. It aches so much. My foot, my face, something deep in my chest—everything hurts.

I kick Cecilia in the gut as I walk past her.

BANG.

Carmichael's gun goes off for a second time tonight. *James.* I run to Cecilia's bedroom door and pull the handle. It doesn't budge. Slapping my hand on the wood, I shout, "Waller! Professor! Are you okay? Talk to me!" As soon as I'm done grasping for his attention, I realize my mistake. If Carmichael shot Waller, I just told him where I was.

"Lydia?" Waller asks from the other side of the door.

"James?" I slump limply against the wood, the exhaustion from the fight threatening to pull me under.

"Hold on," he says. "I'll be right back." It takes him a couple of minutes, but he's back, and he's unlocking the padlock on the other side. The door swings open, and I fall into his arms. "I've got you, Lydia." He rubs circles into my back. "What the hell happened to you?"

"Carmichael?"

"Shot. I had to. He didn't give me any other choice," he mumbles. "Lydia, I saw him. I saw Ambrose Carmichael."

"Oh, James, I haven't caught you up." I glance up at him as he takes in Emily, the binds, and my medical supplies spilled out all over the dresser. "You'll have to carry Cecilia out. I'll take Emily."

"Where is she?"

"In the bathroom."

"I've got her. You grab Emily and make your way out. Is that smoke?" His brow furrows in concern.

"The basement is on fire."

"Well, that cocks things up a bit, doesn't it? That explains why I could see the old boy burning up in the study."

"Dad was right—"

"Court was right—" We say at the same time. He kisses my forehead. "You, my darling, look like hell. Are you sure you can manage Emily?"

"Be careful. Cecilia is an accomplice. She killed Lily and Pickering."

"And apparently you were next," Waller says. Scooping Emily into my arms, she's much heavier than I anticipated, and my knees buckle for a second. "You've got her?" he asks me.

"I've got it, go. We have to move," I tell him, and he disappears into the bathroom.

"My God, Lydia, what happened in here?"

"She started it!"

I move to sweep Emily out the door, but the Burning Man stands in my path. The house creaks and shudders beneath us. The foundation is giving way, which means...

He smiles a greasy, crisping smile at me, his skin crackling with fatty juices running down his chin as his cheeks slough open. With a step toward me, he leans in and touches the curtains on the four-poster bed. They ignite in flames.

The veil is too thin in the house now. He can hurt us, including Emily. "Waller?"

The professor steps out of the bathroom, and his eyes widen as he finds Ambrose Carmichael stalking Emily and me. "Go through the passage," he tells me. "I'm right behind you."

"But..."

"I'm right behind you, Lydia. Get Emily to safety."

Clutching her tight to my chest, I slip into the passage and run along the trembling floorboards. The smoke is so thick now that I can hardly make out a few feet ahead. Then, there's light.

When I turn to peek over my shoulder, the Burning Man has followed me into the corridor. His snarl of hate hastens my feet, and I'm moving as quickly as I can.

Until the floor cracks, and then I stop. Turning wide-eyed back to my pursuer, my attention darts from Ambrose Carmichael to the boards beneath my feet and back again. A snap and a crunch, and I'm falling through the floor.

Pulling Emily tight to my chest, I twist in the air, trying to ensure she lands on me and not the other way around.

We land with a dull thud on the floor below us. The wind is knocked out of my lungs, and I struggle to gasp for air. My good eye tears up, and I slap the floor beneath me, trying to find some oxygen to stuff back into my chest. Emily hasn't moved a muscle.

Finally, I heave in some smoky air and immediately hack it back out. Emily is heavy on my middle, and the passage is so narrow that it takes some finagling to get back up into a sitting position, never mind standing.

"LYDIA!" James calls out from above me.

"Don't use the secret passages. The wood is crumbling! I hate this house! And be careful of Ambrose. He can hurt us now."

"Too late," he says wryly, holding out his burnt palms. "Hang on. I'm coming down to you."

"Just get Cecilia out," I yell back up at him. "I'll find a way and meet you in the topiary with everyone else."

"James?"

"Yeah?"

"You should've brought Quinn."

"I know." He chuckles. I can't find him through the smoke. "You're so much like your dad."

"I know." Another crack shudders beneath me. I shake my head desperately, trying to pull Emily back into my hold so I can get out of the corridor. "James?" My voice sounds so small and pathetic like I'm five and too afraid to go into the haunted house at the carnival again.

"Lydia?"

Whoosh. The floor gives out below me, and I'm sent plummeting into the darkened abyss of the cellar. With a splash, I'm submerged under the flooding, Emily's weight holding me down. I twist and grapple with her, trying not to panic as I'm under at least three feet of water. Shoving her aside, I stand up and pull her with me.

My bones groan with the effort. She's so much heavier, soaking wet. Breathing heavily, I take in our surroundings. The flames have crawled up the walls into the first floor, so there's light, but the fire is blocking the exits. I'm stuck in this one room. The bunker and maze of halls are blocked. It's just me and this cavernous room with the staircase on fire and the pond groaning against the failing mortar of the stone retaining wall.

And the water is rising faster than it should be. I glance down at Emily in my arms. "Shit," I mutter. "Emily, wake up. Emily, come on, you have to wake up." She doesn't stir. I bend into her face to feel her breath on my cheek. The stinking pond water is nearly up to my waist now.

By the light of the fire, I spin around, searching for options. On one side are shelves and workbenches, now mostly underwater, but on the top of one of the shelves is a sledgehammer. A fucking sledgehammer.

Slogging through the flooding, I make my way to the shelf. Settling Emily on the top of the dresser stored next to it, I climb the metal supply shelf and pull the sledgehammer down, nearly bashing myself in the face in the process.

The retaining wall is leaking all along the mortar. Water sprays through heavily in one spot, and I turn to Emily, still unconscious on the dresser. It's too far. I'll lose her in the flooding if I break the wall from this distance.

Glancing around, I snatch the sheet off a standing mirror and jump back when it's not myself in the reflection but Octavia, dripping with lake water. No swollen eye or broken nose, just gray skin and blue lips, cloudy eyes and silt-ridden hair.

Leaping away, I shake it off. No. It's me. It's not her. I'm the one wet. It's me.

With my teeth, I tear the sheet into a strip and push the dresser with all my strength closer to the wall. I tie one end of the sheet around my waist and the other around Emily's waist, then double-check the knots that Charlie will definitely give me grief about later.

My gaze darts from Emily to the wall and back again, and I make a decision. Cold dread coils in my stomach, a visceral reaction to the deep water I know lies beyond that wall. Before I can change my mind, I pick up the sledgehammer and slam it into the crack.

Nothing happens. "No," I tell it like I can convince it to cave in on itself merely with my own disappointment. "No, no, no." My breaths come fast and shallow, my heart pounding in my chest like a drum. Swallowing my fear, knowing I'm going to be under so much water, I push my exhales out hard through my lips, hop up and down in the water for a few ticks and then pull that sledgehammer back and, with a scream of outrage, I slam that weighty tool into the wall so hard it jostles every bone in my body.

Again, nothing.

And then everything. *Everything* happens. The whole cellar groans in indignation, and I take a few hesitant steps back, grabbing Emily off the dresser and pulling her to the other side of the room. *I've made a terrible mistake.* "Oh fu—"

The wall bursts open like an overripe melon, and the water overwhelms both of us. The cold shock of it steals my breath, and panic claws at my chest. I have to swim up and wait for the room to fill before I can fight the current. The ceiling comes down closer and closer as we rise with the pond. I still have hold of her, but I've wrapped the sheet between us around my wrist twice now to keep us tighter together. It's almost unexpected when my nose grazes the wood beams over my head, and I take a final gulp of air before swimming down and toward the broken wall.

There's nothing but the sludgy, dark water, but I know I'm heading in the right direction. My legs are burning, and my lungs feel like they'll burst. Heavy, she's so heavy, tethering me to the black. Kicking with an all-consuming madness, I keep one hand outstretched until I hit the stone wall. Grabbing it to push me down to the hole, my foot hooks on the ragged edge of the hole I made, and I pull Emily through it and into the freezing pond outside.

My lungs tighten, and I cough a bit of my last breath and follow the bubbles up. The cold cramps me, and I only have one hand to hold Emily. I don't know if she's drowned or what, but I keep swimming until I can't. I just can't. It's too much. The falls, the fight, the fire, the flood, I'm so tired. It would be so easy just to let go and sink. I failed her. I failed Emily. I failed Lily. I failed Octavia. I am my sister, floating in a black sea of stars made of silt and slime. This is who I've always been. I've always belonged to the dark, to the cold, both alive and dead.

The darkness closes in on my vision, and I imagine lips on mine—soft, cold lips—and a breath being pushed into me. My eyes snap open, and she's right there. *Lily.* Bright and beautiful, she points in the direction we need to go, and I nod. Taking my hand, she swims up, up, and I break the surface with a huge gasp.

"Help!" I scream when I finally can. "Someone help!"

And there's splashing and yelling, and Charlie and Evie swim out to us to pull us to shore. I collapse on my back, gasping for breath, staring up at the indifferent stars. Charlie performs CPR on Emily next to me. She's so still. This can't have all been for nothing—it just can't.

I close my eyes when I hear her choking up pond water and curl into my side to scream out my anguish. It's out of control and eats me alive. Evie tries to comfort me, but I shove her away. Sam pulls me into his arms and won't let me go no matter how much I fight and flail against him.

"You're out, baby," Sam huffs in my ear. "Lydia, you're out. It's okay, you're okay." I wear myself out, and when the red and blue lights flood the night with their eerie color, I'm reduced to sniveling and shaking. Soaking up the warmth from him, I let him hold me through it all.

Quinn is there and the house is on fire. They're pulling Sam away from me to inspect his knee. "Where's Waller?" I finally say.

"We thought he was with you," Charlie tells me.

I shake my head. With a creaky voice I tell him how sorry I am about Cecelia, how I don't know if she's alive or not.

Charlie puts his hand on my shoulder. "Lydia, it's not your fault."

Someone drapes a blanket over my shoulders and I take it gratefully while Emily, Peter, Shirley, and Sam are loaded onto stretchers. Charlie and Evie help me to my feet. I see him, Waller, my godfather. He's off in the distance leaning against a cop car, arms folded, giving what looks to be a very clipped statement. We catch up to him and I catch the tail end of the conversation.

"Cecelia Carmichael woke up in my arms, there was a struggle, she pushed me down the stairs, and she ran into her father's burning study." Waller isn't facing the cop when he says this, however, he's staring directly at me.

I don't know how to respond. Part of me is relieved that I wasn't the one who killed her and the other part wishes she had gotten her due in court.

Charlie, Evie, and I turn and face the burning house, the flames reflected in the water. Charlie takes both of our hands and squeezes them gently, and I can't speak for Evie, but I squeeze back.

That was a terrible idea, Lydia.

Shut up, Octavia.

EPILOGUE

Five months later.

A tuxedoed band plays on the small stage set up in the school's botanical gardens. They're playing "Polka Dots and Moonbeams," a particular favorite of my mother's. In her honor, I'm nursing a lime gin rickey here in some dark corner, the little red straw chewed mercilessly in my anxiety.

"This isn't how you get people to empty their pockets, my dear. You need to show your gorgeous face—the Heroine Triumphant and all that," Waller says from behind me.

I snort. "Sure. Triumphant. I don't particularly feel triumphant." The dress, heavily sequined and borrowed from my mother, shifts on my hips as I sway from one foot to the other.

"You look beautiful, so stop being self-conscious."

My hair is teased into a partial beehive within an inch of its life—Waller's idea since many of society's matrons are the actual strings on the checkbooks.

Everyone wants to talk to me about the sordid details of the Carmichaels' dirty little secret.

But it burns and gags the back of my throat. I redirect the questions to the real reason we're all here: for the funding to continue to explore the abnormal in this normal little spot in New England. Waller insisted we needed a fundraiser since, apparently, shooting your primary donor to death in their own home isn't a professional look for a prestigious department of science at a school as reputable as Shelley College.

Evie steps onto the dance floor with her father, and he spins her around beneath the starlight. She's not wearing her glasses, which you'd think would make her eyes stand out, but she's squinting around until she finds what she's looking for. I follow her gaze.

Oh, of course. Shirley leans against the bar, wearing a gorgeous suit. The suit must piss Waller off. He gave us precise instructions to appeal to tonight's old money floating around. "You're kidding me," he grumbles next to me. "Can't your team act normal for one night?"

However, he's not looking at Shirley when I catch what he's glaring at—no, not Shirley at all, but Sam in a plum velvet suit. A singer steps up to the microphone, and the band strikes up a spirited rendition of "The Trolley Song." I smirk at him when his eyes catch mine.

Charlie is next to him, starched into his tailcoat. He keeps pulling at the collar and fidgets next to Sam's quiet, brilliant confidence. Leaning slightly to mumble something into Sam's ear, Charlie ditches him and heads toward Shirley at the bar. Sam moves toward Waller and me, picking his way through dancers rather than edging the dance floor.

"Professor," he says by way of greeting when he catches up with us. "Miss Fox." His fingers gently wrap around my own as he pulls my hand up to brush his lips across my knuckles. "You both look lovely tonight."

Waller scowls at this, and I grin at him. "He's right. You do look lovely tonight, Professor." His cheeks flush pink at my pronouncement, and he mutters an excuse to find the punchbowl, leaving Sam and me standing under some huge plant that must be sulking in the New England climate.

Sam's eyes sparkle under the twinkling lights.

"You look incredible—"

"That dress is amazing—"

We say simultaneously and then break off to laugh at ourselves.

"Will you dance with me?"

I nod and let him lead me onto the dance floor, where the singer steps back and lets the band play "Moonlight Serenade." Taking my hand in one of his and letting his other drop onto my waist, he peers down at me, a lock of his dark, curling hair falling over his eye.

"Seriously, Foxy, I knew you were beautiful, but this is…," he's stunned into silence for a moment. "You steal my breath away."

"Why, Wellesley, I didn't know you had it in you," I tease him. My voice is rough from the drink and the smoke in the air. We don't say anything, and then he leads me around in a more accomplished manner than I would have guessed. Finally, I glance up at him. "I guess I should thank you for helping Evie with this."

Evie and Charlie sidle up next to us on the dance floor, with Charlie towering a foot taller than Evie yet still managing to lead adequately. "Yeah, you should definitely thank him. It turns out party planning is not something I'm good at."

"I don't know, you knew where Lydia's mother's Rolodex was," Sam offers.

"Wait," my gaze darts between them while we dance. "You did this? All of this?"

"Turns out party planning is something I'm really good at," Sam shrugs.

This was a gala my mother would be proud of. The band, the music, the food, the venue—it was all perfect. "How? How did you know how to do this?"

He leans in and whispers, "I have untold multitudes of layers, pretty momma."

There he was—our Sam. Not this high-society Sam, though seeing him cleaned up and eloquent was mind-bending, but the Sam who stayed in a burning basement to reunite Alice Shippington with the children she had locked in there two hundred years ago. I'm at a loss for words.

"Don't gawp at me," he chuckles. "You make me nervous."

"You just surprise me at every turn," I admit.

"And that's a good thing, right? Keeping you guessing?" He spins me gently away from Charlie and Evie.

"What are we going to do about this thing between us?"

"What thing between us, Foxy?" he teases. "The one where you kiss me and run away? That thing between us?"

"I don't kiss you and—" He's joking. Sometimes I miss it. "Oh." I chew on my bottom lip.

"I hate your hair like this."

My eyes lock onto his. "Okay. A little rude."

"I can't run my fingers through it," he completes his thought.

Swallowing, I feel the heat burning my cheeks. "Waller doesn't want us fraternizing," I whisper.

"I know. That's why you keep pushing me away," he says. I clear my throat, but he leans in, his lips brushing against the shell of my ear. "So I'll be patient."

"Why?" My brow furrows as I remember the night we drank the tea. He is a field of stars, and I realize with dismay that he's *my* field of stars.

His thumb runs across my bottom lip as the weight of his stare pins me in place. The bouquet of him does something to my insides—the heavy spice of cloves, cherries, and something warm and masculine. The light in his eyes burns with something I can't name as he groans out an exhale. "You keep looking at me like that, and my patience will wear thin, Miss Fox." A delicious shiver runs down my spine at the timbre of his voice. He spins us back towards our friends.

Waller talks to Quinn at the arched entrance, and Sam and I regard each other. Then, the rest of our team catches our attention. At the end of our dance, Sam kisses the back of my hand, and we hurry over to Charlie, Evie, and Shirley.

"Quinn's here," I tell them. "Maybe he has news on Cecilia." Approaching the pair as they move toward the bar, I catch Quinn staring at me. "Detective Quinn? Any news? How are the kids?"

"Jack," he replies. "Call me Jack. And, well, yes and no. The kids could be better, honestly. We haven't been able to get through to Peter in the facility he's in and Emily isn't exactly thriving in the home the church set her up with. Maybe one of you girls could check in with her. Even though she keeps asking for Sam."

"I can check in on her with Evie," Sam replies and Evie nods.

Quinn continues. "Also, I have a couple of questions for you, as well as the check for services rendered."

"'Services rendered?' Oh my," Evie says. "That sounds positively dramatic." He shows Evie the check. "Oh, dramatic indeed," she replies. "But you left it blank."

"That's what I needed to talk to you kids about," Quinn informs us. "Who do I make this out to? If they close your department due to lack of funding, it'll get absorbed into the school."

Waller glances at the five of us, waiting for a response. Charlie places a hand on the small of my back. "He has a point. Maybe you should make an announcement," he says.

"Me?" I sputter. "You're the mouthpiece!"

Charlie grins at me. "Just this one time. Unfortunately, *my* name isn't outside of our science building. Everybody here wants to hear from you, Lydia Fox, daughter of Courtland Fox. Go, make an announcement, and get those checks. We believe in you."

Waller hops up on the band's small stage and whispers to the conductor. The music halts, and everyone looks up at him expectantly while he stands at the microphone. "Good evening, everyone. Alumni, fellows, and lovely wives, thank you so much for coming out to support our small department. I know many of you are here out of sheer curiosity. Gossip. The drama of one of our own falling so far from grace." A murmur ripples through the crowd. "But the real reason we're here is standing by the bar, wearing a rose gold dress I last saw on her mother. Her mother, who is much better at this than I, God rest her social soul." This causes small, nervous laughter from the ladies. "Lydia Fox has a big heart, bigger than she'll let on. She was given a case to follow up on some ghost sightings and saved Emily and Peter Carmichael from a terrible fate. You're all here to see her, am I right?"

A smattering of applause breaks out, and a spotlight falls on my face. "You have this, Foxy," Sam whispers into my ear and squeezes my hand. "Just be yourself."

Myself? Nobody liked me. Not even me.

"Come on up here, Lydia, and let everyone know who to make their generous checks out to."

My eyes flicker shut for a moment, and I swallow. Finishing the rest of my rickey in a single gulp, I make my way up to the stage to the clapping encouragement of my team at first and then the rest of the room. They're still clapping when I find my way to my godfather. "Lydia Fox, ladies and gentlemen." He relinquishes the microphone to me, and everyone quiets down.

I can't see anyone from the lights. So I pretend I'm talking to her. Octavia. "Hello, everyone," I greet. "I'm so glad you could all make it out here. It would mean so much to my mother. As most of you know, my sister Octavia was taken from us in 1969." The room is silent, only the crickets letting me know they're listening. "And then Court and Antonia later that same year. Many people refer to 1969 as 'The Summer of Love.' But for me, it was a year of loss. So much loss."

I search the audience for support but can't find anybody I recognize. My hand is suddenly swallowed up, and Sam, Charlie, Evie, and Shirley are standing next to me. They've all made their way to the stage, and this is it—my support. I can either take it or push it away. And truth be told, I'm so tired of pushing.

"My father, Courtland Fox, dedicated his life to that loss—that grief that binds a soul here, that much love or fury that can anchor a person to a time and place and make them never let go. He dedicated his life to helping the ones left behind, the ones who can't move on. And then… he moved on, along with my mother and my sister. And then I was the one left here, waiting, listening, trying to make sense of it all, like everyone else."

There's movement in the shadows below me, and some are nodding.

"We're here because we want answers. We want to know what else is out there. We want to know that when we lose the person we're holding right now, it's not the end. That we might still be able to have them in our lives. Or help them move on. To let go. There is so much out there that we don't know. Lily Carmichael helped me find her sister that night. Weeks, months after, she was drowned in her own pond by her sister and mother, Cecilia. Lily Carmichael showed me where to find Emily before Emily could join her. I'm not the hero. Lily Carmichael is. Let's give credit where credit is due.

"William Carmichael was our top donor, and his loss will be felt keenly in this department, whether he was a politician or a villain. You are all here because you want to hear the dirt. You want to hear how he had an incestuous relationship with his eldest daughter to keep their bloodline pure. To lift their status. I'm not here to talk about that.

"I'm here to talk about Lily Carmichael's bravery in staying in a place that caused her so much pain to take care of her sister and brother. I'm here to talk about Alice Shippington, the spirit of a woman who stood up to terrible men who did terrible things to her at the cost of her children, and how my friend here, Sam, reunited them and let them move on. Two hundred years later, Alice Shippington searched for the children she had forgotten she had locked in the basement. Two hundred years without the loves of your life. Think about that. Think about going that long without knowing how to move on, the loss still so keen it feels like the very day you lost them. That's what I want you to think about when you make your checks out to The Shelley Paranormal Society.

"And if you want to know the whole story, make sure you pick up a copy of James Waller and Shirley Henderson's book, Hemlock Hall, which will be out next fall. Enjoy the drinking and dancing, but don't forget to take in the person you came here with and what you're going to do when you lose them. Because the only constant is Death, and it's coming for us all."

There's a collective silence that clobbers me in the face. Charlie steps up to the microphone. "Let's find out more about what happens next. Yeah? Let Shelley Paranormal help. Help us figure it out. Thank you all so much for being here."

Applause.

We take a bow, and Sam guides me off the stage with the rest of our team. "Intense as always, Foxy. But damned beautiful while doing it."

Evie nods. "Yeah, we could have done without your portents of doom."

"Sorry," I whine.

"No problem. Thanks for the book plug, though. Waller is being a pain about keeping my name on the cover," Shirley tells me.

"Waller's all bark and no bite."

"I'll have you know, I have *some* bite. I took a hell of a beating from Bill Carmichael for you five," Waller reminds us.

"You did. It made you look quite rugged, too," Evie reassures him.

Quinn approaches us. "I had a couple of other questions, gang." He hands Charlie the check with *Shelley Paranormal Society* written across the front. "Waller said Cecilia Carmichael got away from him and locked herself in her father's study that night."

We all glance at each other. "And?"

"We only found the bodies of William, Esme, and the domestic in the house. Pickering in the bottom of the pond."

Charlie's brow knits together tight across his forehead. "You didn't find Cecilia?"

Quinn merely shakes his head. "You're sure she didn't get out?"

Waller clears his throat. "You need to keep looking. I was the last out of Hemlock Hall, and Cecilia was certainly dragged into the study by the ghost of her father. I saw it with my own eyes. He was screaming something about Ambrose Carmichael and had Cecilia by the hair. This was a few hours after we found Esme Carmichael hanging in the attic."

"I know you left the ghost thing out of your official statement, and, fine, I get it. But here's the thing," Quinn interrupts. "The only body in the study was William Carmichael."

"That's impossible," Waller tells him.

"I'm going out for a smoke," Sam announces. "This is giving me a headache."

"Sounds good," I say and grab my purse. An envelope is sticking out of the top. "Did any of you see who put this in my purse?" I pull the manila envelope free.

Nobody answers.

"I'm sure it's just a check, darling," Waller tells me. "Some of these folks like to donate anonymously."

I frown and open the envelope. Two Polaroids spill out into my hand when I upturn it. "It's not a donation."

A cold sweat breaks across my brow, and my heart hammers in my throat. I peer around the room, taking in all of the guests.

The first Polaroid is one I had taken and forgotten about. It was from the day I was first attacked in the cellar when Peter thought I was Cecilia. It was a near-perfect image of the ghost I had been following. A shimmering, beautifully transparent Lily Carmichael. It was evidence.

The second Polaroid isn't nearly as exciting. My legs almost give out beneath me as I stare down at an image of Cecilia Carmichael. Her wrists are tied to a bed, and a gag is in her mouth. She looks terrible—waxy, beaten, drugged. Sam hustles me onto the veranda outside the greenhouse. The rest of the group follows. In the white space below the photo, written in stark, neat handwriting, are the words, "I'll always protect you."

"What the hell does that mean, Lydia?" Charlie says, snatching the photo from my hands.

"It means," I say with a shaky voice, "that Octavia's killer has been following us. He's still out there."

Sam pulls me into his arms, and Evie rubs my back.

It's happening again, isn't it?

Shut up, Octavia.

The Shelley Paranormal Society *will* be back.
Book 2: *As The Crow Flies* coming soon!

ACKNOWLEDGEMENTS

First of all, thank you so much to the few of you who have purchased and read this book! You guys are amazing. I hope you stick with Lydia and her journey to finding out what happened to Octavia. I hope you love my little Scooby gang and watch as they navigate life through college and beyond. There's so much more to tell you.

This book wouldn't have been written without the many people in my life who have endlessly put up with me telling story after story after story to you, and you always *listened*.

To my Beta readers, some of who have been listening to me prattle on for more than twenty years now, I see, love, and appreciate you. Some standouts this time around have been Dayna, Janelle, Merry, Celeste, Kelsi, Praditya, Jen, and Nabeela. If you see any typos in this acknowledgment, it's because I was keeping you guys from editing it. Thank you for your hard work helping me edit this beast into a story worth telling. While Lydia's story is far from done, you guys made her 100% more likable.

To my two besties, Shoshana and Jessica, who have always been there for my mid-book freakouts or my breakdowns about self-publishing, and while you never pushed your advice on me, I know it's because you wanted me to work it out on my own. Which annoyed the crap out of me, but it worked, didn't it?

To my kids who have to listen to me tell them all about where I'm at in whatever I'm writing on our rides to and from school, I swear, I'm doing this for you even when it seems I'm on the computer all damned day. I love you guys so much, and I hope your book does better than mine, Yorick. And yes, Phineas, you can have the options for a dollar, my little filmmaker.

And, lastly, but certainly not least, to my long-suffering husband. You make my life everything I could have wished for. You put up with so much more than you deserve, and I have no idea how I got so lucky. You can keep asking me that, love, but I don't think I'll ever have an answer.

I love you so much.

About The Author

Daphne Winchester lives in Santa Clarita, CA (yes, *that* Santa Clarita, you zombie-lovers) with her long-suffering husband, two teenage sons, and three of the cutest but stupidest cats who have ever graced this world.

Her top two movies are Alien and Jaws, and she avoids space and the ocean as one should. Other people should follow her lead in this.